DISCARD

R0700063001

W9-ABT-915
... Boulevard
West Palm Beach, FL 33406-4198

Praise for The Saga ...

"A complex world based on a plausible system of magic and peopled with engaging and realistic characters."

—*Publishers Weekly* on *The Magic of Recluce*

"This is a very special fantasy, original . . . in its slow and thoughtful use of familiar fantastic elements and its skillful development of character."

—*Asimov's SF Magazine* on *The Magic of Recluce*

"The universe he's built is fascinating. I hope he visits Recluce, Candar, and their neighbors again in the future."

—*Amazing* on *The Magic of Recluce*

"Entwining issues of magic with maturation, Modesitt's thoughtful coming-of-age tale is adorned with a finely drawn, down-to-earth yet dangerous world, and an intriguingly ambiguous view of how good and evil interact."   —Carole Nelson Douglas on *The Magic of Recluce*

"Not just your typical fantasy novel . . . touching and intriguing."

—Lawrence Watt-Evans on *The Magic of Recluce*

"A splendid fantasy that grips from the first sentence . . . For once this is a book that really does cry out to be turned into a trilogy."

—*Interzone* on *The Magic of Recluce*

"The highly rationalized, scientific approach to magic is refreshing in a field full of mysticism. Modesitt also avoids the simple equation of order with good and chaos with evil—in Lerris's world, as in ours, a good balance is the best formula—and this more mature insight distinguishes his novel from run-of-the-mill fantasies."

—*Kirkus Reviews* on *The Magic of Recluce*

"Well written, the imagery arresting, the cultures complex and interesting, the characters drawing you in so that you care what happens to them . . . The aspect that pleased me most, though, was the theme threaded through the tale: that power blinds, shown with compelling force in the physical blindness of Creslin the Storm Wizard and the mental and spiritual blindness of others." —Jo Clayton on *The Magic of Recluce*

"L. E. Modesitt, Jr. builds both his characters and his world with authority and innumerable subtle touches, until they both convince. This is the sort of fantasy that takes on a life of its own, with real-seeming people in an unreal but very believable and self-consistent universe."
—David Duncan on *The Death of Chaos*

"A writer of exceptional fantasy, Mr. Modesitt leaves the reader in no doubt about the price of power and the bittersweet triumph of the human spirit." —*RT Book Reviews* on *The Chaos Balance*

"L. E. Modesitt, Jr. has been building a world that seems fantastic, with magic and feudalism rampant, but is riveted pretty thoroughly to the rigors of science fiction. That is to say, wizards can't do just anything they can imagine, and what they do needs discipline and energy. There's a consistency across this universe that makes the magic, the science, the politics, and the economy seem plausibly well integrated."
—*The San Diego Union-Tribune* on *Colors of Chaos*

"True to form, the author delivers a complex plot wrapped around finely textured settings and intriguing characters. Fans of previous Recluce novels will find this new series darker in tone . . . but they won't be disappointed." —*Publishers Weekly* on *Magi'i of Cyador*

"This is a writer who cares about his characters and his world. This is disciplined fantasy, not fluff. L. E. Modesitt, Jr. is uncompromising when it comes to the effects of magic, both on the natural world and on the human heart. There are no cheap solutions to the problems of Recluce. Because of that, it is a world worth returning to."
—Robin Hobb on *The Magic Engineer*

"Modesitt is as clever as his blacksmith heroes, finding ways to discuss today's environmental concerns and technological hubris in ways that can reach a public that prefers wish-fulfillment fantasy to more hard-nosed SF. . . . If people pay attention to what he is really saying—not just to the exciting, adventurous, gland-tweaking yarn he is spinning on the surface—there may be hope for our grandchildren."

—*Analog* on *The Order War*

"My favorite thing about L. E. Modesitt's books is that they don't go stale. I enjoy rereading them as much as I enjoy them the first time. On occasion, I enjoy them even more."

—*SFRevu* on *Natural Ordermage*

THE
MAGIC
OF
RECLUCE

Tor Books by L. E. Modesitt, Jr.

L. E. Modesitt, Jr.

THE
MAGIC
OF
RECLUCE

TOR® fantasy

A Tom Doherty Associates Book | New York

This is a work of fiction. All of the characters, organizations, and events portrayed in this novel are either products of the author's imagination or are used fictitiously.

THE MAGIC OF RECLUCE

Copyright © 1991 by L. E. Modesitt, Jr.

All rights reserved.

A Tor Book
Published by Tom Doherty Associates, LLC
175 Fifth Avenue
New York, NY 10010

www.tor-forge.com

Tor® is a registered trademark of Tom Doherty Associates, LLC.

The Library of Congress has cataloged the hardcover edition as follows:

Modesitt, L. E., Jr.
The Magic of Recluce / L. E. Modesitt, Jr.
p.   cm.
"A Tom Doherty Associates book."
ISBN 0-312-85116-2
I. Title.
PS3563.O264M34 1991
813'.54—dc20   90-29263
                                        CIP

ISBN 978-0-7653-3112-0 (trade paperback)

First Edition: May 1991
First Trade Paperback Edition: June 2011

Printed in the United States of America

P1

For
  Bob Muir,
    Clay Hunt,
      and Walter Rosenberry.

Too belated an appreciation,
but real for all the delay.

Foreword

The Magic of Recluce: A Twenty-Year Balancing Act

ROBIN HOBB

The quintessentially cliché fantasy novel will feature a young protagonist gifted with magic, a quest that involves travel and meeting strange folk, and a battle of good against evil in which said protagonist will save the world. The map to the book is easy to follow: the hero will discover his magic, master it, and defeat the villain. And when *The Magic of Recluce* was published twenty years ago, it might have seemed to some like yet another fat fantasy book, to be quickly devoured as it followed that rote path and then as quickly forgotten.

It wasn't. Twenty years later, here we are with over a dozen Recluce books added to the saga in the intervening years, and *The Magic of Recluce* just as readable and relevant to the genre as it was the year it came out. How many other twenty-year-old fantasy epics can claim that?

What sets Recluce and its characters apart? For me and for many other readers, it is Modesitt's rigorous world-building. Unlike many fantasy worlds, Recluce has not only an economy and geography that make sense, but a long history that involves far more than the present conflict. This is a world that offers a variety of philosophies, politics, technologies, and manufacturing and a variety of solutions to ethical dilemmas . . . and all of it makes sense in light of the conflicting magics that influence the world. The magic of Recluce is not arbitrary or limitless, but governed by rules that are as inflexible as those of physics, and just as impartial to "good" and "evil."

I'll admit to a certain amount of frustration the first time I encountered Lerris and his world. I stepped off the brink and into the page, plunging into a world where I was just as ignorant as the main character. Why, I wanted to demand, wouldn't anyone explain it all to me, right now? Why did I have to stumble forward alongside Lerris, uncovering each bit of knowledge with him? In retrospect, it was the best way to learn about the world and the working of the magic that governed it.

The solidity of the world-building made Recluce, for me, a place I'd lived for a time rather than a book I read. Here were characters I could relate to; magic, even genetically inherited magic, didn't solve all their problems. They still had to work for a living, and learning the skills to be good enough to make a decent living took time and effort. Rather than the solo hero emerging from nowhere to save the world, Modesitt's protagonists had families and backgrounds, connections that tied them to the world in intimate ways and made the problems of that world personal rather than theoretical. Rather than a simple battle of evil against good, or even a battle of chaos and order, L. E. Modesitt introduced us to a conflict that asked questions about "At what price do order and prosperity come, and who pays that price?" In the world of Recluce, good intentions can have disastrous results, and being gifted with magic may be more of a burden than a solution to all one's problems.

While *The Magic of Recluce* was our first introduction to Lerris and his world, readers would discover as the years passed and book after book about Recluce appeared that this was by no means the beginning or the end of the tale. This is a body of work that allows the reader to enter the world and then explore, sometimes stepping back into the past of Recluce and sometimes leaping forward into the future. To those who have never experienced Recluce, you come to it at a wonderful time, with over a dozen volumes (sixteen to date) to explore. Don't be surprised if you are left hoping for more!

THE
MAGIC
OF
RECLUCE

I

Growing up, I always wondered why everything in Wandernaught seemed so dull. Not that I minded the perfectly baked bread routinely produced by my father or by Aunt Elisabet, and I certainly enjoyed the intricately carved toys and other gifts that Uncle Sardit miraculously presented on my birthday or on the High Holidays.

Perfection, especially for a youngster learning about it from cheerfully sober adults, has a price. Mine was boredom, scarcely novel for a young man in the middle of his second decade. But boredom leads to trouble, even when things are designed to be as perfect as possible. Of course, the perfection and striving for perfection that marked the island, though some would term Recluce a smallish continent, had a reason. A good reason, but one hardly acceptable to a restless young man.

"Perfection, Lerris," my father repeated time after time, "is the price we pay for the good life. Perfection keeps destruction away and provides a safe harbor for the good."

"But why? And how?" Those were always my questions.

Finally, shortly after I finished the minimum formal schooling, in my case at fifteen, my mother entered the discussion.

"Lerris, there are two fundamental forces in life, and in nature. Creation and destruction. Creation is order. We attempt to maintain it—".

"You sound just like Magister Kerwin . . . 'Order is all that keeps chaos at bay . . . because evil and chaos are so closely linked, one should avoid all but the most necessary acts of destruction . . .' I know perfection is important. I know it. I know it! And I *know* it! But why does it have to be so flaming *boring?*"

She shrugged. "Order is not boring. You are bored with order." She looked at my father. "Since you are bored with us, and since you are not quite ready for the possibility of undertaking the dangergeld, how would you like to spend a year or so learning about woodworking with your Uncle Sardit?"

"Donara?" asked my father, obviously questioning my mother's volunteering of his sister's husband.

"Sardit and I have talked it over, Gunnar. He's willing to take on the challenge."

"Challenge?" I blurted. "What challenge? I can learn anything . . ."

"For about the first three weeks," my father commented.

"It's not as though you will ever be a master woodworker, Lerris," added mother. "But the general skills and discipline will come in useful when you undertake your dangergeld."

"Me? Why would I ever go tramping off through the wild lands?"

"You will."

"Most assuredly."

But the only thing that was assured then was that I would have the chance to learn how to craft some of the screens, tables, chairs, and cabinets that Uncle Sardit produced. Every once in a while, I knew, someone traveled from Candar or even from one of the trading cities of Austra to purchase one of his screens or inlaid tables.

Until I had a better idea of what I really wanted to do in life, woodworking was better than helping my father keep all the stone-work spotless or mixing clays or tending the kiln fire for mother. Although the same traders who visited Sardit also visited my mother's shop, I did not have the touch for pottery. Besides, pots and vases bored me. So did the intricacies of glazes and finishes.

So, within days I had left the neat and rambling timbered and stone house where I had grown up, where I had looked out through the blue-tinted casement window in my bedroom on the herb garden for the last time. Then, I had walked nearly empty-handed the half-day to my uncle's where I was installed in the apprentice's quarters over the carpentry. Uncle Sardit's other apprentice, Koldar, had almost completed his term and was building his own house, with the help of an apprentice stonemason, a woman named Corso. She was bigger than either of us, but she smiled a lot, and she and Koldar made a good pair. He was living in the unfinished house alone, but probably not for long. That meant that until another apprentice came along I had the privacy and the responsibility of the shop in evenings.

Still, it had been a small shock to realize that I would not be living in the guest room at Uncle Sardit's, but in the much smaller and sparsely-furnished apprentice's space. The only furniture was the bed, an old woven rug, and a single hanging lamp. The plain red-oak walls scarcely showed even hair-line cracks where the boards joined. The polished floors, also red oak, displayed the same care and crafting.

"That's what you're here for, Lerris. When you learn how, you can make your own tables, benches, chairs, in the evenings. Have to fell your own wood and make arrangements with Halprin at the sawmill for the rough stock to replace what's been seasoned unless you want to try to cut and rough-cure the logs yourself. Don't recommend that."

Sardit as a craft-master was a bit different than as an uncle.

I was going to learn about carpentry, and tools, and how to make screens and cabinets and tables, right? Not exactly. To begin with, it was just like the pottery shop, but worse. I'd heard about clays and consistencies and glazes and firing temperatures for years. I hadn't realized that woodworking was similar—not until Uncle Sardit reminded me forcefully.

"How are you going to use tools properly, boy, if you don't know anything about the woods you're working with?"

With that, he sat me down with his old apprentice notes on woods. Each day, either after work or before we opened the shop in the morning, I had to show him my own hand-copied notes on at least two kinds of trees, the recommended uses, curing times, and general observations on the best uses of the wood. Not only that, but each card went into a file box, the one thing he had let me make, with some advice from him, and I was expected to update the cards if I learned something of value in a day's work on a wood.

"What did you write down on the black oak? Here, let me see." He scratched his head. "You spent all day helping me smooth that piece, and the wood told you nothing?"

Once in a while, I saw Koldar grinning sympathetically from whatever project he was handling. But we didn't talk much because Uncle Sardit kept me busy, and because Koldar mostly worked alone, just checking with Uncle Sardit from time to time.

After a while, Uncle Sardit even nodded once or twice when reviewing my cards. But the frowns and questions were always more frequent. And as soon as I thought I understood something well enough to avoid his questions, he would task me with learning some other obscure discipline of woodworking. If it weren't the trees, it was their bark. If it weren't their bark, it was the recommended cutting times and sawmill techniques. If it weren't one type of wood, it was what types you could match in inlays, what differences in grain widths meant. Some of it made sense, but a lot seemed designed to make woodworking as complicated as possible.

3

"Complicated? Of course it's complicated. Perfection is always complicated. Do you want your work to last? Or do you want it to fall apart at the first touch of chaos?"

"But we don't even have any white magicians in Recluce."

"We don't? Are you sure about that?"

There wasn't much I could say to that. Practicing magicians, at least the white ones who used chaos, were strongly discouraged by the masters. And what the masters discouraged generally stayed discouraged, although there seemed to be only a few masters for·all the towns in Recluce.

I guess my old teacher, Magister Kerwin, actually was a master, although we didn't usually think of magisters as masters. They were both part of the same order. Magisters were those who actually taught.

So . . . I kept studying woods, trees, and tools, and after nearly a year began to make a few simple items.

"Breadboards?"

"Someone has to make them. And they should be made right. You can do it well enough to keep chaos at bay, and you can select from any of my designs or try one of your own. If you do your own, let's go over it together before you begin cutting."

I did one of my own—simple, but with an octagonal shape.

"Simple, but nice, Lerris. You may actually have a future as a wood crafter."

From breadboards, I went to other simple items—outdoor benches for a café, a set of plain bookcases for the school. Nothing with carving, although I had begun to do carving for my own furniture, and Uncle Sardit had even admitted that the wooden armchair I had built for my quarters would not have been out of place in most homes.

"Most homes. Not quite clean enough, and a few rough spots with the spoke-joining angles, but, on the whole, a credible effort."

That was about the most I ever got in praise from Uncle Sardit.

But I was still bored, even as I continued to learn.

II

"Lerris!"

The tone in Uncle Sardit's voice told me enough. Whatever I had done—I did not wish to know.

I finished washing the sawdust from my face. As usual, I got water all over the stone, but the sun had already warmed the slate facing, and the water would dry soon enough, even if my aunt would be down with a frayed towel to polish the stone within moments of my return to the shop.

"Lerris!"

Aunt Elisabet always kept the washstones polished, the kettles sparkling, and the graystone floors spotless. Why it should have surprised me I do not know, since my father and, indeed, every other holder in my home town of Wandernaught, exhibited the same fastidiousness. My father and his sister were both the householders, while mother and Uncle Sardit were the artisans. That was common enough, or so I thought.

"*Lerris!* Young . . . man, . . . get . . . yourself . . . back . . . here . . . *now!*"

I definitely did not want to return to the carpentry, but there was no escape.

"Coming, Uncle Sardit."

He stood at the doorway, a frown on his face. The frown was common, but the yelling had not been. My guts twisted. What could I have done?

"Come here."

He thrust a wide-fingered hand at the inlaid tabletop on the workbench.

"Look at that. Closely." His voice was so low it rumbled.

I looked, but obviously did not see what he wanted me to see.

"Do you see that?"

I shook my head. "See what?"

"Look at the clamps."

Bending over, I followed his finger. The clamps were as I had placed them earlier, the smooth side, as he had taught me, matching the grain of the dark lorken wood.

"With the grain of the wood . . ."

"Lerris . . . can't you see? This end is biting into the wood. And here . . . the pressure has moved the border out of position . . ."

Perhaps the tiniest fraction of a span, if at all, but all I had to do to correct that would be to sand the other end a bit more, and no one, except Uncle Sardit, and perhaps the furniture buyer for the Emperor of Hamor, would have ever noticed the discrepancy.

"First, you don't force wood, Lerris. You know that. You just aren't paying attention any more. Woodworking means working with the wood, not forcing it, not working against it."

I stood there. What could I say?

Uncle Sardit sighed.

"Let's go into the house, Lerris. We have some talking to do."

I liked the sound of that even less, but I followed his example and unstrapped my leather apron and racked my tools.

We walked out the door and across the smooth pavement of the courtyard and into the room Aunt Elisabet called the parlor. I never knew why she called it the parlor. I'd asked once, but she had just smiled and said it had been a name she had picked up along the way.

A tray sat on the table. On it were two icy glasses, some slabs of fresh-baked bread, cheese, and several sliced apples. The bread was still steaming, and the aroma filled the small room.

Uncle Sardit eased himself into the chair nearest the kitchen. I took the other one. Something about the tray being ready bothered me. It bothered me a whole lot.

The soft sound of steps caused me to look up from the tabletop. Uncle Sardit put down his glass—iced fruit punch—and nodded at Aunt Elisabet. She, like father, was fair-skinned, sandy-haired, slender, and tall. Uncle Sardit was smaller and wiry, with salt-and-pepper hair and a short-cropped beard. Both of them looked guilty.

"You're right, Lerris. We do feel guilty, perhaps because you're Gunnar's son." That was Aunt Elisabet.

"But that doesn't change anything," added Uncle Sardit. "You still have to face the same decisions whether you're our nephew or not."

I took a gulp of the fruit punch to avoid answering, though I knew Aunt Elisabet would know that. She always knew. So did my father.

"Have something to eat. I'll do some of the talking. Elisabet will fill in anything I miss." He took a wedge of cheese and a slab of bread and chewed several bits slowly, swallowed, and finished up with another gulp of fruit punch.

"Magister Kerwin should have taught you, as he taught me, that a master or journeyman who instructs an apprentice is also responsible for determining the apprentice's fitness for practicing the craft."

I took some bread and cheese. Obviously, the master was responsible for the apprentice.

"What he did not tell you, or me, is that the craft-master must also determine whether the apprentice will *ever* be ready for practicing a craft, or whether the apprentice should be considered for dangergeld or exile."

"Exile . . ."

"You see, Lerris, there is no place in Recluce for unfocused dissatisfaction," added Aunt Elisabet. "Boredom, inability to concentrate, unwillingness to apply yourself to the fullest of your ability—these can all allow chaos a foothold in Recluce."

"So the real question facing you, Lerris, is whether you want to take the dangergeld training, or whether you would rather just leave Recluce. Forever."

"Just because I'm bored? Just because I put a little too much pressure on a wood clamp? For that I have to choose between exile and dangergeld?"

"No. Because your boredom reflects a deeper lack of commitment. Sloppy work on the part of someone who is doing his best is not a danger. Nor is sloppy work when the honest intent is perfection, provided, of course, that no one has to rely on the sloppy work for anything that could threaten their life if it failed." Aunt Elisabet looked somehow taller, and there was a fire behind her eyes.

I looked away.

"Are you saying that you have honestly been happy trying to achieve perfection in woodwork?" asked Uncle Sardit.

"No." I couldn't very well lie. Aunt Elisabet would catch it.

"Do you think that it would become easier if you continued to work with me?"

"No."

I took another slice of bread and a second wedge of cheese. I didn't remember eating the first, but I must have. I sipped the fruit punch only enough to moisten my mouth, since I was cold enough inside already.

"Now what?" I asked before taking another bite.

"If you decide to take the dangergeld training, the masters will work with you for as long as necessary, in their judgment, to prepare you for your dangergeld. After training, you cannot return until you have completed the charge laid upon you.

"If you choose exile, you will leave. You cannot return except with the permission of the masters. While not unheard-of, such permission is rarely given."

"Just because I'm bored? Just because I'm young and haven't settled down? Just because my woodwork isn't perfect?"

"No. It has nothing to do with youth." Aunt Elisabet sighed. "Last year, the masters exiled five crafters twice your age, and close to a dozen people in their third and fourth decade undertook the dangergeld."

"You're serious, aren't you?"

"Yes."

I could tell she was. Uncle Sardit, for all his statements about doing the talking, hadn't said a word in explanation. I was getting a very strange feeling about Aunt Elisabet, that she was a great deal more than a holder.

"So where do I go?"

"You're sure?" asked Uncle Sardit, his mouth full.

"What choice is there? I either get plunked down on a boat to somewhere as an exile, knowing nothing, or I try to learn as much as I can before doing something that at least gives me some chance of making a decision."

"I think that's the right choice for you," said Aunt Elisabet, "but it's not quite that simple."

After finishing my bread and cheese in the strained atmosphere of the house, I went back to my quarters over the shop and began to pack. Uncle Sardit said he would keep the chair and the few other pieces until I returned.

He didn't mention the fact that few dangergelders returned. Neither did I.

III

Like a lot of things in Recluce, my transition from apprentice to student dangergelder just happened. Or that's the way it seemed.

For the next few days after my rather ponderous and serious conversation with Aunt Elisabet and Uncle Sardit, I continued to help out around the carpentry shop. Uncle Sardit now asked me to rough-shape cornices, or rough-cut panels, rather than telling me to. And Koldar just shook his head, as if I were truly crazy.

He shook it so convincingly that I began to wonder myself.

Then I'd hear Uncle Sardit muttering about the inexact fit of two mitered corners, or the failure of two grains to match perfectly. Or I'd watch him redo a small decoration that no one would see on the underside of a table because of a minute imperfection.

Those brought back the real reason why I couldn't stay as his apprentice—the boring requirement for absolute perfection. I had better things to do with my life than worry about whether the grain patterns on two sides of a table or panel matched perfectly. Or whether a corner miter was a precise forty-five degrees.

Perhaps it suited Koldar, and perhaps it kept the incursions of chaos at bay, but it was boring.

Woodworking might have been better than pottery, but when you came right down to it, both were pretty dull.

So I didn't mind at all when, several days later, Aunt Elisabet announced that I had better get my things together.

"For what?"

"Your training as a dangergelder, of course. Do you think that the masters just hand you a staff, a map, and some provisions, and hustle you aboard a ship to nowhere?"

That thought had crossed my mind, but I quickly dismissed it in the face of my aunt's insistence.

"What about saying good-bye to my family?"

"Of course, of course. We're not exactly barbarians, Lerris. They've been expecting you for some time, but you're not an apprentice any longer. So what you do is strictly up to you. The masters at Nylan are expecting you, and several others, the day after tomorrow."

"That's a good distance . . ." I hinted, hoping that Aunt Elisabet would indicate that the masters would provide a carriage, or a wagon. While I had a few silver pence, I certainly had no desire to spend them on riding the High Road. Nylan was a full day's walk, and then some.

"That it is, Lerris. But did you expect the masters to come to you?"

I hadn't thought about that one way or another.

Aunt Elisabet cocked her head, smiling, as if to indicate that the sunny morning was passing quickly. It was, and, if I had to be in Nylan by the following evening . . .

Another thought crossed my mind. "When on the day after tomorrow?"

"No later than noon, although I suppose no one would mind if you were a trifle later than that." Her smile was kindly, as it usually was, and the sun behind her still-sandy hair gave her the look of . . . well, I wasn't sure, but Aunt Elisabet seemed to be more than I had thought. Why, I couldn't say, just as I couldn't explain why woodworking seemed so incredibly boring.

I swallowed. "I'd better get going. That's an early rising tomorrow, and time to make on the road."

She nodded. "I have some flake rolls for your parents, if you're going that way. And you'll find a set of boots, with the right trousers and cloak, laid out on your bed."

I swallowed again. I hadn't thought about the boots, although my heavy apprentice clothes would have been adequate for most hard travel.

"Thank you . . ." I looked down. "Need to say good-bye to Uncle Sardit."

"He's in the shop."

After going back to my room, I found my clothes had been wrapped in one bundle, and that someone had laid out not only boots and clothes, but a walking staff of the heaviest, smoothest, and blackest lorken. The staff was almost unadorned, not at all flashy, but it was obviously Uncle Sardit's work, probably months in preparation as he had cut, seasoned, and shaped the wood, and soaked it in ironbath. The ends were bound in black steel, with the bands recessed so precisely they were scarcely visible against the darkness of the wood.

I held it and it seemed to fit my hand. It was exactly my own height.

Finally I shrugged, and looked around for the old canvas bag in which I had brought my old clothes. Not that there were many left after nearly two years of growing and discovering muscles in the process of woodworking. Don't let anyone tell you that precision woodwork isn't as hard as heavy carpentry. It isn't. It's harder, and since you can't make mistakes, not for someone like Uncle Sardit, it requires more thinking.

The last thing laid out was a pack. Not flashy, not even tooled leather, but made out of the tightest-woven and heaviest cloth I'd ever seen. Dull brown, but dipped in something that had to be waterproof. I wondered if Aunt Elisabet and Uncle Sardit felt guilty for deciding that I didn't fit in. Certainly the staff and the pack alone were magnificent gifts, and the clothes, although a dark brown, were of equal quality and durability.

That wasn't all. Inside the pack was a small purse. Attached was a note.

"Here are your apprentice wages. Try not to spend them until you leave Recluce." I counted twenty copper pennies, twenty silver pence, and ten gold pence. Again, a near-incredible amount. But I wasn't about to turn it down, not when I couldn't tell what might lie ahead.

I picked up the staff again, running my fingers over the grain, examining it once more, trying to see how the ends were mated so closely to the wood that the caps were scarcely obvious.

At least they, or my parents, whoever had supplied me, wanted to send me off as well-prepared as they could. I remembered from Magister Kerwin's dry lectures that dangergelders were only allowed whatever coins they could carry comfortably, two sets of clothes, boots, a staff, a pack, and a few days' provisions.

If you decided to return, of course, after your year or more away, and the masters approved, you could bring back an entire ship, provided it wasn't stolen or unfairly acquired. But then, the masters weren't too likely to let you return if you'd turned to thievery.

I shook my head, put down the staff, and examined the pack, realizing my time was short. Inside were another set of clothes and a pair of light shoes, almost court slippers.

Stripping to the waist, I headed down to the wash trough to clean up before putting on the new clothes. Uncle Sardit was humming as he buffed the desk he was finishing, but did not look up. Koldar was down at the sawmill, trying to find enough matched red oak to repair the fire-damaged tables at Polank's Inn.

I'd overheard my aunt and uncle discussing the fire, acting as if it had been totally expected, ever since young Nir Polank had taken over from his ailing father.

"Some have to learn the hard way."

"Some don't . . ." my aunt had answered, but she hadn't said anything more once I had entered the house for dinner.

On the washstones was a fresh towel, which, after the chill of the water, I gratefully used. At least I hadn't needed to take a shower. Standing under even partly-warmed water in the outside stone stall wasn't exactly warm. Cleaning that stall was even less enjoyable, but Aunt Elisabet, like my father, insisted on absolute cleanliness. We didn't eat unless we were washed up, and more than once as a child I'd gone without dinner for refusing to wash.

They both took a shower every day, even in winter. So did my mother and Uncle Sardit, although my uncle occasionally skipped the shower on the days that Aunt Elisabet was out visiting friends.

I folded the towel, and put it back on the rack.

"Getting ready to go?"

Uncle Sardit stood in the shop door, finishing cloth in his left hand.

"Yes, sir." I swallowed. "Appreciate everything . . . sorry I just don't seem to have the concentration to be a master woodworker . . ."

"Lerris . . . you stayed longer than most . . . and you could be a journeyman for some. But it wouldn't be right . . . would it?"

Since he was standing three steps above me, I looked up. He didn't seem happy about my leaving.

"No . . . probably get more bored with each day. And I don't know why."

"Because you're like your dad . . . or your aunt. In the blood . . ."

"But . . . they seem so happy here . . ."

"Now . . ."

I couldn't seem to find anything to say.

"Be on your way, boy. Just remember, you can always come back, once you discover who you are." He turned back into the shop and returned to buffing the already shining wood of the desk, without humming.

All of a sudden, there seemed to be so many things unsaid, so many things that had been hidden. But no one was saying anything.

It seemed so unfair. As if I couldn't possibly understand anything until I'd gone off and risked my life in the Dark Marches of Candar or the Empire of Hamor. Then everything would be fine . . . just fine.

And my parents—they never came by to see me. Only if I went to see them, or on High Holidays, or if they came to visit my aunt and uncle.

Up in the apprentice quarters, no longer mine really, I pulled on the clothes, ignoring their comfort and fit, and the boots. Then I picked up the cloak and folded it into the pack, and strapped the old clothes to the outside. Those I could leave at home, if it were truly home. Besides the new clothes and the pack, the staff was the only thing that felt right.

As I looked around the quarters, I wondered about my armchair . . . and my tools. What about my tools? Uncle Sardit had said something about taking care of them, but hadn't said how.

I found Uncle Sardit in the shop. He was looking at a chest, one I hadn't seen before.

"I thought I'd store your tools in this, Lerris, until . . . whatever . . ."

"That would be fine, Uncle Sardit . . . and could you find some place for the armchair?"

"I was going to keep it here, but I could take it back to your parents."

For some reason, I'd never considered the chair as belonging where I'd grown up.

"Whatever you think best." One way or another, I wouldn't be needing it for a while.

"We'll take good care of it . . . just take care of yourself so you can come back for it."

We stood there for a moment, with everything and nothing to say.

Finally, I coughed. "I'm not a woodworker, Uncle, but I learned a lot."

"Hope so, boy. Hope it helps you."

I left him standing there, turning to rack my tools in the chest he had made for them.

Aunt Elisabet was waiting at the kitchen doorway with a wrapped package. Two of them.

"The bigger one has the flake rolls. The other one has some travel food for you."

I took off the pack and put the travel food inside, but just strapped the rolls to the top. They weren't heavy, and while it was cloudy, the clouds were the high hazy kind that kept the temperature down but

13

almost never led to rain. That early in the summer the farmers would have liked more moisture, but I was just as glad I wouldn't have to trudge to Nylan through a downpour. I had a feeling I'd be traveling in enough wet weather.

"And here are some for you."

On a plate she had produced from nowhere were two enormous rolls, one filled with chicken and the other with berries that dripped from one end.

"If you want to get home by dinner, you'll need to start now."

"Dinner?"

"I'm sure your father will have something special."

I did not answer, nor ask how she would know that my father would have a special dinner, because, first, she would know, and, second, I was wolfing down the chicken-filled flake roll. In all the hurry to get ready for Nylan, I hadn't realized how hungry I was. When you chose dangergeld, you obeyed the rules of the masters, including their schedule.

After washing down the last of the first roll with a tumbler of ice-cold water, I took the second.

"You have enough time not to eat them whole, Lerris."

I slowed down and finished the dessert roll in four distinct bites. Then I took another deep swallow from the tumbler.

"Do you have your staff? Your uncle wanted you to have the best . . ."

I lifted the staff. "Seems to belong to me already."

My aunt only smiled. "You should find it helpful, especially if you listen to the masters and follow your feelings . . . your true feelings."

"Well . . . time for me to go . . ."

"Take care, Lerris."

She didn't give me any special advice, and since I wasn't exactly in the mood for it, that was probably for the best.

As I walked down the lane with its precisely placed and leveled gray paving-stones, I felt both my aunt and uncle were watching every step, but when I turned around to look I could see nothing, no one in the windows or at the doors. I didn't look around the rest of Mattra, not at the inn where Koldar was laying out the timbers from the sawmill, not at the market square where I had sold my breadboards—one had actually fetched four copper pennies.

And the road—the perfect stone-paved highway—was still as hard on my booted feet as it had been on my sandaled feet when I had first walked to Mattra.

I made it home, if Wandernaught could still be called home, well before dinner. But Aunt Elisabet had been right. I could smell the roast duck even before my feet touched the stone lane that was nearly identical to the lane that led from the street to Uncle Sardit's. Mattra and Wandernaught were not all that different. Some of the crafts were different, and Wandernaught had two inns and the Institute where my father occasionally discussed his philosophies with other holders or—very occasionally—masters from elsewhere in Recluce. But nothing very interesting ever happened in Wandernaught. At least, not that I remembered.

My parents were seated on the wide and open porch on the east side of the house, always cool in the summer afternoons. The stones of the steps were as gently rounded as I recalled, without either the crisp edges of new-cut granite nor the depressions of ancient buildings like the temple.

"Thought you'd be here about now, Lerris." My father's voice carried, although it had no great or booming tone.

"It's good to see you." My mother smiled, and this time she meant it.

"Good to be here, if only for a night." I was surprised to find I meant what I was saying.

"Let me take the pack and the staff—Sardit's work, it looks like—and have a seat. You still like the redberry?"

I nodded as I slipped out of the pack straps. My father laid the pack carefully next to the low table.

"Oh, I forgot. The top package is for you—Aunt Elisabet's flake rolls, I think."

They both laughed.

"Good thing we don't live closer, not the way she bakes . . ."

My mother just shook her head, still smiling.

For some reason, they both looked older. My father's hair was no thinner, and it still looked sandy-blond, but I could see the lines running from the corners of his eyes. His face was still smooth, with a slight cut on his chin from shaving. Unlike most of the men in Recluce, he had neither beard nor mustache. I could sympathize. Although I could have worn a beard, I followed his example, not blindly, but because whenever I worked hard I sweated buckets, and

I found even a short and scraggly beard more of a bother than shaving—cuts and all.

He was wearing a short-sleeved open-necked shirt, and the muscles in his arms looked as strong as ever. The woodpile behind the house was probably three times the size it needed to be. Dad always claimed that handling an axe was not only necessary, but good exercise.

My mother's angular face seemed even more angular, and her hair was too short. But she had always worn it too short, and I doubted that she would ever change that. Short was convenient and took less time. She also wore a short-sleeved faded blue blouse and winter-blue trousers, both more feminine, but essentially mirroring what my father wore—not because she cared, but because she didn't. Clothes were a convenience. That's why Dad did all the tailoring—except for holiday clothes—for Mother and me.

He was funny about that. He refused to let anyone see him work. He'd take measurements, fit partially-sewn garments, and adjust until they fit perfectly, but not with anyone around. When I was little, I thought he must have had someone come in. But as time went by, I realized that he understood clothes, understood too much not to have done the work. Besides, it's pretty difficult not to believe, when your father disappears into his workrooms with cut leathers and fabrics and returns with the products—especially when there's only one door and when you're an exceedingly curious boy trying to find a nonexistent secret passage. There wasn't one, of course.

While I was remembering, my mother had poured a large tumbler full of redberry, and Dad, after setting the pack down and recovering the flake rolls, had disappeared. To the kitchen, presumably.

"It's too bad you have to be in Nylan tomorrow," offered my mother, as I eased into one of the strap chairs across from her. My feet hurt, as I knew they would with the new boots, but I'd wanted feet and boots worked together as soon as possible.

"I didn't realize it would happen so quickly."

"Sometimes it does. Other times it takes weeks," added my father. As usual, I had not heard him return. He was always so silent when he moved, like a shadow.

"How many . . . will there be?"

"It depends. There could be as few as four dangergeld candidates. Never more than a dozen. And you'll lose two before the masters are through."

"Lose?" I didn't like the sound of that.

16

He shrugged. "Some people decide they'd rather accept exile than listen to the masters. Others decide they'd like to go home."

"Can they?"

"If they can convince the masters . . . it happens every so often."

Not very often, I could tell from his tone. "If they can't?"

"They can continue with their training or go into exile."

I got the feeling that you didn't just go wandering out of Recluce on any old quest without the approval of the masters.

Before I asked another question, I took several healthy swigs from the tumbler, then ate some of the plain flake rolls Dad had cut into bite-sized pieces. Mother had one or two, which was more than she usually had before dinner.

"What are the masters?" I finally asked, not that I hadn't asked the question several dozen times before of several dozen people. Usually the answer amounted to: "The masters are the masters, entrusted with the guardianship of the Isle of Recluce and the Domain of Order."

This time, though, my father looked at my mother. She looked back at him. Then they both looked at me.

"The answer isn't likely to mean what it should . . ."

"In other words, you aren't going to tell me?"

"No. I will tell you, as far as I am able. But I'm not sure that you will either like or appreciate the answer." He pulled at his chin, as he did when he was trying to find the best words to express something unpleasant.

"Try anyway."

He ignored my comment, and, for a moment, his eyes almost misted over, as if he were looking a world away.

I took the opportunity to drain the rest of the redberry.

My mother refilled my tumbler, and Dad still hadn't said a word.

Finally, he cleared his throat. ". . . Uuuhhmmm . . . you recall . . . Magister Kerwin . . . when he told you that the masters stood between Recluce and chaos because they were the defenders of order?"

I found my fingers tapping on the edge of my refilled tumbler.

"Bear with me . . . this is difficult . . ."

How difficult could it be? Everybody had a role in life, including the masters. Either they controlled Recluce or they didn't.

"Perhaps I should go back to the beginning. It might be simpler . . ."

I managed to keep from grinding my teeth, only because I some-

17

how could tell that he was not trying to put me off. But I still couldn't see why an explanation of who controlled what had to be so difficult.

". . . fundamental conflict between order and chaos, or, simplistically speaking, between good and evil. Though that's not exactly correct, because chaos and order do not by themselves have a moral component. More important, while certain components of order may be used for evil, and certain components of chaos for good, almost never can anyone devoted to chaos remain committed to good. Someone committed to good finds anything other than the most minor uses of chaos repulsive. That distinction is important, because someone committed to order itself, rather than good, can be corrupted, while seeming orderly in all he or she does . . ."

Curiosity was fighting boredom in my case, and rapidly losing.

"No . . . I can see you're bored already, Lerris . . . that explanation is too long. Try and remember the beginning, though."

My mother was slowly shaking her head. Finally, she interrupted. "Think of it this way, Lerris. It takes skill to be a potter. A potter may use his skill for producing containers. Those containers may be used for good or evil purposes. Most are used for purposes without much real good or evil. And most people find a truly beautiful and orderly vase hard to use for evil things. In the same way, it is much easier to use a chaotic or disorderly creation for evil."

That made sense, so far. "What does that have to do with the masters?"

"That's the hard part," said my father slowly. "And we may have to continue the discussion over dinner, because the duck is almost ready.

"The masters are responsible for ensuring that things in Recluce are what they seem to be, for rooting out self-deception, and for maintaining our physical defenses against the Outer Kingdoms."

"Physical defenses? Magister Kerwin said that Recluce had no armies and no fleets, only the Brotherhood of the Masters."

"As you will learn, Lerris, words can conceal as much as they reveal." He stood. "Wash up, and we'll try and answer the rest of this question over dinner. A good dinner shouldn't be kept waiting."

Since I didn't know when I'd get that good a duck feast again, I went down to the washstones to rinse the dust from my face and the grime from my hands, and tried to figure out a better set of questions.

The duck smelled as good as I remembered, and I put the questions aside until I had finished my first helping, which included another flake roll warmed in the oven, sliced and spiced sourpears, and some tart greens. The duck was tangy, moist, and not at all oily. Dad was one of the few cooks I knew who could manage the moistness without an oily taste—though I'd tasted few enough foods from other cooks.

I decided to slow my headlong pursuit of various foods and took a sip of water, cold from the deep well.

"About the masters . . . was Magister Kerwin misleading us? Do the masters act like the armies of the Outer Kingdoms? Isn't that a form of chaos?"

My father chuckled. "Yes, and no, to the first. No to the second, and, if true, yes to the third, although it probably wasn't intentional, which would mitigate the impact."

"But—"

"Kerwin let you think what you wished, which is a form of deception, particularly to an agile mind such as yours." He held up his left hand and took a brief sip of his wine.

I'd never liked the wine and still preferred cold water.

Mother continued to pick at her meal.

19

"Some of the masters deal extensively with the Outer Kingdoms, and counter chaos on a daily basis. We seldom see them, but they're properly called the Brotherhood. They wear scarlet and black. Then there are the masters, who wear black when undertaking their official duties, and whatever they please at other times. There are others as well, whom you will come to recognize in the days ahead.

"While each group has specific duties, all their duties revolve about maximizing reasonable order in Recluce. You remember the baker—Oldham?"

I nodded wearily.

"Who took him away?"

"The masters."

"What did they do with him?"

"Dumped him somewhere in the Outer Marches, I suppose. Or killed him."

"Do you know what he did?"

I drained the rest of the water from the tumbler before answering. "What difference does it make? The masters are powerful, especially the hidden ones."

"Hidden ones?" asked my mother.

"The ones no one knows about. How else would they know about people like the baker?"

"I take it you do not believe in magic, then, Lerris?" asked my father.

"How can I believe or disbelieve? The practice of chaos-magic is prohibited, and I've never seen anything that would be called good magic that could not be explained by either chance or hard work."

My mother smiled, a rather strange smile, almost lopsided.

"What point were you trying to make? What about the baker? Why was that important? Or was it just to show that the masters control Recluce?" By now I was as impatient as I had been when I had left for my apprenticeship.

"I'm not sure, Lerris, except to show that the masters affect everything in Recluce. By the way, the baker is still living, and doing fairly well in Hamor. That might indicate the masters are neither cruel nor vindictive, but only protective of us."

"Then why are they so secretive?" I was beginning to regret even getting into the argument. My parents hadn't changed at all, still talking around things, hinting, but never saying anything outright.

My father sighed. "I'm not sure I can answer that."

He hadn't been able to answer that question before I had left, either.

"Dear," added my mother, "right now we can't tell you everything, and you want explanations that require experience you don't have."

"That means you aren't going to explain anything."

"Hold it. You asked about defenses. I can answer that." My father practically glared at me.

I ignored him and speared another slice of duck.

"The Brotherhood does act as our army, and as a navy, too. As part of the dangergeld choice, you could choose to serve as a border guard with the Brotherhood, assuming the masters agreed. The masters themselves maintain a sort of watch against chaos-magic, even in its subtler forms, such as shown in the case of the baker.

"The coasters belong to the Brotherhood, although they fish as well as watch the offshore waters, and each ship that flies the flag of Recluce carries a member of the Brotherhood as well as a junior master."

"How many are there?"

"Enough," answered my father. "Enough."

I could tell that was all I was going to get, just from his tone, and, on my last night, it seemed stupid to refight a battle that would only end up frustrating us all. So I had some more duck, and slathered another slab of the dark bread with the cherry conserve.

"Any new neighbors?"

"There's a young couple building a place on the empty lane, the one that overlooks Lerwin's orchards." My mother was more than glad to lapse into small talk.

My father shrugged and reached for the cherry conserve.

Maybe we were too dissimilar. Or too much alike.

I had a third helping of the duck, as good as my first slices. I also enjoyed the lime tarts.

And, for the most part, that was dinner before I went off to Nylan.

I V

Sunrise found me awake and washing up, not that early rising was ever a problem.

As I splashed the cold water over my face to wash away the soap and scattered whiskers not already carried away by the razor, I could sense someone watching—obviously my father. My mother generally rose later than he did, although neither one would have been considered a night dweller.

I said nothing as I toweled myself dry, and made sure the razor was also dry and packed into my wash bag. Neither did he.

Without looking, I could tell he was smiling, and I refused to acknowledge his presence.

"I hope you have a good journey, Lerris. So does your mother." His voice was calm, as usual, and that irritated me even more. Here he was, seeing me off to dangergeld and all the dangers it entailed, as if I were headed back to Uncle Sardit's on a trivial errand.

"So do I. But I'd settle for survival."

"Don't ever settle for just survival, son. Survival isn't life . . . but I didn't come down to preach. Do you want something to eat before you leave?"

"Rather not leave on an empty stomach," I admitted, following him to the kitchen where he had laid out an assortment of fruits, two heavy rolls, and some cheese and sausage. The square, perfectly-fitted red-oak table was bare except for the woven straw mats and the food.

He nodded toward the tiled counter under the open window, where a brown cloth bag rested. "The bag has some additional provisions for eating along the way."

The cloth sack was already bound, but looked as though it contained at least as much as had been set on the table.

He set down a full mug of freshly-drawn water, knowing I preferred that to tea or wine, especially in the morning.

I ate, and he sat on one of the kitchen stools, saying nothing, for which I was grateful. What was there to say? I was required to undertake the dangergeld, not him, on pain of exile.

Eating what I could didn't take that long.

"Thank you." I gathered the sack under my arm and headed down to pick up my pack and staff.

To make Nylan by midday meant moving out without wasting more time. And what else could I say?

As I stood there on the stones, ready to walk away from my parents, and my mother who hadn't even gotten up to say good-bye, I wondered if this would be a final farewell, or what.

"She's awake, Lerris. But she will not let you see her cry."

Flame! I hadn't asked that. Why not?

"Because she is your mother. You ask us to accept you as you are. Cannot she be what she is?"

There it was again—that gulf that we never seemed to cross.

"Whether we do cross it, Lerris . . . that depends on you. We both wish you well, son. And we hope . . ."

I ignored the break in his voice as I turned away. Why in hell was he upset? Why didn't he understand?

I didn't look back, nor did I wave. My first steps were fast as I marched down the lane, but my legs let me know quickly that I was pushing, and I eased up before my strides took me clear of Wandernaught. I ignored the low hill and the black-columned temple upon it. What had listening to all the talks on order done for me?

For some reason, the staff felt even heavier in my hands than the pack did upon my back. As my thoughts seethed, something occurred to me. My father had responded to my feelings, but had I actually spoken them? Or did he know me that well?

I forced a shrug. Where I was going that didn't exactly matter. Not at all.

The morning was warm, warmer than I would have liked, and I opened my shirt almost to my belt, but the pack weight on my back left my shirt damp. The cloak I would need in the months and years ahead, assuming I lasted that long, was folded and rolled inside.

As early as I had left, there was no one else on the High Road, although in the orchards to the south of Wandernaught the growers were already among their trees, going about their business.

The High Road is just that—a solid, stone road, wide enough for four wagons abreast. It provides the central thoroughfare for Recluce, the one to which all major local roads can link, and all communities are responsible for its upkeep. When I was with Uncle Sardit, I spent a few days helping to replace and reposition several of the granite blocks, but the stones are so solid and massive that they don't need to be replaced often. The biggest problem is keeping the drains clear so that the rains don't erode the roadway on which the capstones are placed. Even that would be hard, because the entire roadbed is solidly constructed and faced with heavy riprap.

The next town toward Nylan from Wandernaught is Enstronn, more of a crossroads than a town, where the East-West Highway, almost as grand as the High Road itself, crosses the High Road.

Outside Enstronn, on the west side, I caught up with a low wagon carrying a load of early melons. The driver was walking beside her horse, singing softly.

". . . as if I cared, as if I dared,
And the stars are ice, while the High Road's run,
and the winter reigns for the summer's sun."

The song was unfamiliar, and I dragged my feet a bit as I neared her. For some reason, I wished I could put away the staff, but it was too long to carry easily while bound to my pack.

Her voice was pleasant enough, although from behind she seemed older than me. But she heard me and stopped singing, looking back at me from under a broad-brimmed hat trimmed with a wide band of blue-and-white fabric.

23

I slowed my pace to match her steps.

Dark hair, narrow face, and she looked about the age of Corso, mid-twenties.

"Up early. Must be important." Her smile was nice, too.

"Dangergeld," I admitted.

"You're a bit young for that."

"Not totally my idea." I swallowed as I answered. What right did she have to judge me?

Her eyes widened as they focused on the staff I still held loosely in my left hand. "And the staff, that is yours?"

"Yes." I wondered why it mattered at all whether a black lorken staff was mine. A staff was a staff. Right now it was a bother, though I knew I would need it once I actually left Recluce.

Her smile turned sad, somehow. "You'd best be going, then . . . and . . . if I could ask a favor . . . ?"

That stopped me. Ask me, not much more than a youngster, for a favor?

"If it's something I can do . . ."

"So cautious . . . yes . . . it's not much . . . I'm sure you can. Should you ever run across a red-haired man from Enstronn—he went by the name of Leith—just tell him that Shrezsan wishes him well."

"Shrezsan . . . ?"

"That's all. Perhaps too much." Her voice was businesslike. "Now, best be on your way to Nylan."

"You sing nicely."

"Perhaps another time . . ." She turned to look at the horse, flicking the reins.

Clearly dismissed, I shrugged.

"Perhaps another time, Shrezsan . . ."

She avoided meeting my eyes. So I picked up my stride to a traveling pace and passed through Enstronn without saying a word. That was easy enough, because no buildings may be closer to the highways or the high roads than six hundred cubits.

I spoke to no one else on the High Road for some time, instead turning over thoughts in my mind and finding no answers. No one seemed to like the dangergeld. But everyone accepted it as necessary. And no one could or would explain why—just great windy platitudes about the necessity of order in the continuing fight against chaos. So who was against order? Who in his right mind wanted total chaos? And what did the dangergeld have to do with any of it?

I walked and asked questions that had no answers. Finally, I just walked.

V

Just before mid-morning, when it became clear that I was going to be arriving in Nylan at least close to on time, my stomach began to protest.

After passing through Enstronn, I had also passed by Clarion, and a place called Sigil. Despite the elegantly-lettered sign, I had never heard of Sigil, and that meant it couldn't amount to much. Though I strained my eyes to the north of the High Road, and while I could sense that a few houses lay in that direction, I had been able to see nothing.

Beyond Sigil the road grew less traveled, and slightly more dusty. The sun continued to beat down on the dust and on me.

Ahead a blur appeared on the right side of the High Road. Even before I could see it clearly, I recognized it for a wayfaring station. A wayfaring station on the way to one of the main ports of Recluce?

Few citizens of Recluce travel that much, and the masters allow even fewer outside traders upon the isle. They always seem to know when strangers land on the open south beaches or sneak through the fjords punctuating the mountainous north coast. The mountains form a shield against the worst of the winter storms, but they also trap the warm damp winds from the south, which is why the highlands are so damp—almost a jungle in places.

The traders who have leave to travel Recluce are seldom young, and they always say little. Usually they are buyers of art, of pottery or other crafts. Sometimes they sell the southern jewels, the yellow diamonds and the deep green emeralds, that occur only in the far reaches of Hamor.

I wondered once why everyone used the same coins, before I discovered that everyone didn't. Most countries, except for the Pantarrans, use coins similar to the Hamorians—just like we did—copper, silver, or gold pennies. They all have different writing, but the weights are the same—unless someone's clipped the coins. Why? Probably because almost everyone sells to Hamor. Even the Austrans, for all their pride, use coins of the same weight. They call them different names that no one uses—even in Austra.

With so few people traveling beyond a few towns, I used to ask about the High Road, and why it had to be so grand. My father just shook his head. Uncle Sardit never even answered.

As my sore feet brought me nearer to the wayfaring station, the thought of a short break became more and more welcome.

The stations are all alike—tiled roof over four windowless walls, a door that can be barred, and a wide covered porch with stone benches. No furnishings inside, not even a hearth or chimney for a cook fire. Strictly for a quick rest or a place to wait out bad weather.

After pulling off my boots, rubbing my feet, and taking a sip of warm water from the water bottle as I sat on the back stone bench closest to Nylan—the coolest one—I opened the provisions my father had provided. The leftover duck was still good, and there were the last two flake rolls, one plain and one stuffed with cherry preserves. I finished up by eating one of the two sourpears and saved the other.

As I took the last bite of the fruit, I could feel someone approaching. So I looked to the west. Sure enough, a man was leading a horse and covered cart. While he looked to be a trader, I took the precaution of pulling my boots back on, wincing at the blisters I was developing. After that I replaced the provisions bag in my pack and tossed the few scraps out for the birds, out beyond the road.

The staff leaned up against the bench, where I could reach it easily, and my pack was ready to go. I just wasn't.

"Hello there," he called from the wagon post. The man was young for a trader, younger than Uncle Sardit, but with black ragged hair, and a close-trimmed full beard. His short-sleeved tunic was of faded yellowish leather, as were his boots and his trousers. He had a wide brown belt on which he wore a brace of knives. Shoulders broader than Uncle Sardit, and muscles to match.

"Good day," I answered, politely, standing. "Heading inland from Nylan?"

"Couldn't be from anywhere else, now could I?" He laughed as he said it, while he tethered the horse, a dark brown gelding. "And you?"

"From the east . . ."

He finished with the animal and stepped up the two stone steps. "Young for a myskid to be traveling, aren't you?"

For some reason, his tone bothered me, and I stepped back, ready to pick up the staff. "Some might say that."

"Never seen a place like Recluce. Nobody travels."

"Not many."

"You're about as friendly as the rest, aren't you? Don't think much of the rest of the world, I guess."

"Really don't know much about it," I admitted.

"First one I've seen who's willing to admit that there is a world off this overgrown island."

I didn't say much to that. What was there to say?

"Strange place. The women won't look at you unless you take a bath at least three times a week, and they don't talk to you anyway, except to buy or sell. Those characters in black, they have everyone scared, I guess. Even the empire doesn't mess with them."

"Empire?"

"Haven't you heard of Hamor? The Empire of the East?" By now, the trader had put one foot up on the other end of the bench.

He was just like all the other traders. Boring. He'd seen something I had not, and that made him feel better.

"You don't like me, boy? Just like everyone else? If you want my jewels, or you want to sell something—Tira! You don't have anything worth selling, except maybe that staff. Good work, there."

He reached for it, as if I weren't standing there.

The staff was somehow in my hands, although I didn't remember grabbing it, and I had brought it down on the back of his extended wrist.

Crack. Hsssss.

"Another damned devil-spawn! . . ." He backed away, his unhurt hand on a knife.

I could tell he was deciding whether to throw it, and I could feel my guts tighten. I hadn't meant to hit him, or do whatever the staff had done.

"The masters wouldn't like it if you did." It was a struggle to keep my words even, but I managed it.

27

"Devils take your masters . . ." he gasped. But he didn't use the knife. He took another long look at me.

I brought the staff down. It felt warm to me, as though it had been in the sun or next to the fire.

"So you're another one of them . . ." He was slowly backing away from me, although I had not moved.

"I'm nothing . . . yet."

"Damned isle . . ." He was next to his horse.

I swung the pack onto my back and started toward the near steps, the ones closest to Nylan.

"You can stay. You need the rest."

He watched me, but said nothing else.

I could feel his eyes on me, and the hate, deep as the North River in flood, and almost as wild. But I put one sore foot in front of the other, wanting to get as far from the waystation and the trader as possible.

Were all traders like that, underneath, when they thought people were helpless? And why had the staff burned his wrist? I knew woods, and some about metal, and the staff was just that—lorken and steel . . . wood and forged metal. Almost a work of art, and that was why the trader had wanted it, but no more than wood and steel, certainly.

I knew some staff-play, just because my father had insisted on it as an exercise. That had been years ago, before I had been Uncle Sardit's apprentice. I guess you don't forget some things, but even remembered practice and fear wouldn't make a staff burn someone.

Could it be that the trader was a devil? I couldn't believe that, much as the old legends spoke of devils that burned at the touch of cold iron.

I shivered as I walked, despite the sunshine, the heat, and the dust. Did all the reaction of the woman on the road and the trader have something to do with me? Or with the staff? But there was no magic in Recluce, and I was certainly no magician.

I shivered again and kept walking.

VI

Nylan has always been the Black City, just like forgotten Frven was once the White City. It doesn't matter that Nylan has little more than a village's population, or that it is a seaport used only by the Brotherhood. Or that it is a fortress that has never been taken, and tested but once.

Nylan is the Black City, and it will always be that.

From the High Road, at first it looked like a low black cloud of road dust, then like a small hill. Only when I came within a kay or so did I recognize its size. The walls are not high, perhaps sixty cubits, but they stretch from one side of the peninsula to the other, with the one gate, the one that ends the High Road. I'd seen paintings of the walls and castles of Candar, Hamor, and Austra, but Nylan was different. The walls were featureless. No embrasures, no crenelations. And no ditch, no bridge, no moat. The High Road ran straight to the gate.

The other end of the High Road is at Land's End, nearly a thousand kays eastward. Land's End is just that—where Recluce ends. Once it was a seaport, before the currents and the winds changed the Gulf of Murr from a sheltered haven into the most storm-tossed section of the Eastern Ocean. Ships landed there occasionally, but not generally by choice. The only official port was Nylan, which seemed strange to me even when Magister Kerwin taught us that.

The walls are not the most impressive feature of Nylan. The cliffs are. Black as the stone walls, smooth as black ice, they drop two hundred cubits to the dark gray-blue of the waves that crash against them.

I saw both walls and cliffs at midday, with the sun full upon them. Even in full sunlight, they resembled shadows. I shivered, grasping my staff, which felt warm in my hands, as if it were trying to dispel that inner chill.

Just looking at the massive black metal gates, the black stone, and the cliffs, I could see why they called it the Black City. I could also see another reason to worry about what I was getting into. Except I didn't have much choice.

The gate was open, wide open, with no one in sight.

So I walked up the last cubits of the High Road and into the narrow band of shadow before the gate itself, looking up at the featureless walls.

"What's your reason for being here, traveler?"

The voice was pleasant enough, and I looked for the speaker, finally locating her seated on something in a walled ledge seven or eight cubits above the road and beside the archway. Where she sat would be covered by the gates when they closed.

She wore black—black trousers, black tunic, black boots. A staff, dark like mine, rested by her hand. Her hair looked to be brown in the shadow.

"Your reason for entering Nylan?"

"Dangergeld," I answered slowly.

"Your name?"

"Lerris."

"From where?"

"Raised in Wandernaught; apprenticed in Mattra."

"Just about on schedule." Her voice was polite, but bored. "Once you go through the gate, turn left and go straight to the small building with the green triangle beside the door. Don't go anywhere else."

"And if I do?"

"Nothing. Nothing at all. Except you'll waste your time, and someone else's, if they have to go find you. Anyone who sees you will direct you back to the orientation building." Her voice was so matter-of-fact that I felt chilled again.

"Thank you."

She did not speak, but nodded as I passed beneath, through the archway that was another fifteen cubits overhead. The walls were thicker than I'd thought, perhaps as thick as they were tall. Up close, each stone looked like granite, but I had never seen black granite. Inside the archway, the shade and the breeze from the water were both a welcome relief.

Once back into the sunlight, I stopped at the crossroads for a moment to take in Nylan. One road went right, toward a squarish and massive low building. Another went left, and the largest split in a circle around a black oak and headed due west.

The city itself was a disappointment in some ways, fascinating at first glance in others. Trees, welcome after the featureless plains and fields that had led up to the wall, were scattered throughout Nylan. Some of them were apparently ancient, like the huge black oak lying directly before me that stood taller than the wall itself. I stepped several paces to the left and kept looking. All the ways were paved in the same black stone as the walls, and the low buildings, none more than a single story, were also of the same stone. The roofs were shingled with black stone, and although the color matched the rest of the stone, the texture seemed more like slate.

No building was closer than fifty or sixty cubits from another, although several rambled quite extensively.

The grass was emerald-green, brilliant, in contrast to the sun-faded grasses I had observed from the High Road and throughout Eastern Recluce. Few people seemed out and about, and most of those that were wore black.

Nylan stretched further westward than I had thought, easily another five kays before reaching the tip of the peninsula where, I presumed, existed the Brotherhood's walled and protected seaport. From what I could see, the ground sloped gently downward toward the west, allowing me to see that the pattern I saw close by generally continued further westward. The trees and areas of park land made it hard to tell for certain.

Outside of all the black, it looked pleasant enough, almost like an oasis of sorts. But the black was hard to ignore. It wasn't depressing. It was just there.

Finally I flexed my shoulders, grasped the staff, and walked down the black stone road. Why the woman had even bothered to say that the building had a green triangle by the door was a wonder. The narrow road ended at right angles to a much wider road heading westward. The only building there was the one with the triangle. I supposed that the colored shapes were used as some sort of identification. How else would you give directions when all the buildings, homes, and shops were the same color and construction? It seemed rather dull, almost boring. If you were as powerful as the masters were, why build everything the same?

The black-oak door was open, and I walked in. The door itself was well made, almost as good as anything that Uncle Sardit had done. So was the rest of the woodwork, although I could see I would be bored stiff if all the masters used were black oak and black stone.

"Another one . . ."

I looked up from my study of moldings to realize that I stood in an upper foyer. At the bottom of three room-wide stone steps sat five people, three women and two men, on two long benches.

I nodded and stepped down, realizing as I drew closer that, with the possible exception of one of the women, a muscular blond, I was easily the youngest, and the only one with a staff. Everyone else had a pack by their feet.

"Lerris," I announced myself.

An older man, perhaps in his late thirties from his looks, stood. "Sammel." He was balding and brown-haired, with deep-set circled eyes.

"Krystal." She was black-haired, black-eyed, white-skinned, and thin, with fine hair that spun down to her waist.

"Wrynn." Blond, wide-eyed, with wide shoulders and callused hands, she dismissed me instantly.

"Dorthae." Flat-voiced, olive-skinned, with strawberry ringlets of hair, she flashed a gold ring from every finger.

"Myrten." Sharp-nosed, with the eyes of a ferret, and hair like a shaggy bison, he spoke with a voice both high and cutting.

I nodded to all five of them and came down the steps, unslinging my pack and laying it carefully in the corner next to the empty spot at the far left end of the left-hand bench. I stood my staff in the corner as well.

"There is one more on the way, or so we have been told," added Sammel in a quiet and deep voice. He reseated himself and sat down.

I did not sit down. My feet were sore but sitting down was boring, and besides, I hadn't had a chance to look around.

The foyer, waiting room, whatever it was, was maybe ten cubits wide and not quite that deep. There were three doors besides the entry, one in the center of each wall. The benches were backed up against the wall opposite the front doorway and the stairs, separated by a closed door. All the doors were hung to open away from the foyer. All were black-stained black oak, bound in black steel, and all were closed.

The walls looked to be timbered and covered with rectangular dark oak-veneered panels, each panel edged with a finger-width molding. The three interior walls were topped with a triangular crown molding. The gray-plastered ceiling seemed almost bluish against all the black.

A portrait hung above each bench—a woman on the right, a man on the left. Naturally, they both wore black. Black was getting boring.

Nobody wanted to say anything; that was clear. I looked at Krystal, with her dusty-blue smock and trousers. She looked through me. But she was too thin and distracted-looking anyway.

Wrynn wouldn't look at me at all, just kept looking at the floor. She had nice legs. Even the fringed leathers she wore couldn't hide that.

Dorthae kept looking at Myrten, the thin-faced man, who returned the look.

Sammel just sat there, sadly looking nowhere.

And I wandered around trying to figure out what kind of tools the woodworkers had used to carve the panels, because I still didn't know anything about the dangergeld except that I had to do it.

What a sorry bunch.

Click, click, click.

Everyone looked up at the newcomer.

She carried a staff, too. Black as mine, but somehow more . . . *used.* Her hair was flaming red, and I could tell that her eyes were ice-blue. Dust covered a freckled face that made her look younger than she was. She could have passed for my age but was much older, at least five or six years.

"What a sorry bunch." Her voice was cheerfully hard.

"Speak for yourself." I hadn't realized I'd spoken until I heard the words.

"I am speaking for myself."

"I'm Lerris. Who are you?"

"Tamra will do." Her hard eyes scanned the others and ended up back on me. "Aren't you a little young to be here?"

"Aren't you a little presumptuous?"

"Tamra . . . Lerris," interjected Sammel, standing up. "Whoever is here is here with the acceptance of the masters. Can we leave it at that for now?"

"Fine with me." I was ready to throttle the red-haired bitch in her hard-heeled black boots and dark-gray trousers and tunic. She was wearing as close to black as she could decently get away with in Recluce, and flaunting it.

"The masters *this*, the masters *that* . . . what difference does it make?" Her voice was disgusted, but she took off her pack just like the rest of us as she came down the stairs. Then I realized she only came to my shoulder but she had carried a pack fully as big as mine, and while she was fine-featured and slender, she was not thin like

Krystal nor muscular like Wrynn. She was about the same size as Dorthae, but she had a certain presence.

She didn't sit down either, but put her pack at the end of the right-hand bench, next to Sammel's stuff. Then she looked at the pictures, which outside of their somberness seemed unremarkable to me. She ignored the quality of the woodwork and kept comparing the pictures.

Since she was ignoring me, like the whole sorry bunch, I walked over and stood in front of the picture on the left, trying to figure out why Tamra felt it was so interesting.

The man in the picture was in black, but not in the official-type robes of a master, and his hair was silvered gold, much like my father's. Even though they didn't look much alike, the more I looked at the portrait, the more I could sense a certain likeness. I pushed that thought away and looked for the technical details.

A shadowed bar behind his right shoulder caught my attention next. The height and the positioning indicated that it had to be a staff of some sort, but unlike the detail shown in the man's face, none of the background was depicted clearly at all.

I looked around the room. Tamra was still studying the other portrait. Wrynn and Krystal were talking in little more than whispers. Sammel and Myrten looked at the stone flooring, and Dorthae sat on the bench with her eyes closed.

My eyes returned to the portrait. It was the only thing in the whole foyer, besides the other portrait, that had any detail. That had to mean something—but what? I shook my head. More riddles. The masters had more riddles than a world full of jesters, and no one wanted to ask them anything.

For a moment I thought the man in the picture had come alive and was looking at me, but when I concentrated on the picture, it was as lifeless as ever. Accurate, perhaps, but lifeless.

I glanced at Tamra. She was looking at me.

She wanted to look at the picture of the man. I could tell. I nodded and moved aside.

Not a word from her as she walked over and stood where I had been standing. So I walked back to where she had been and tried to concentrate on the picture of the woman in black. The portrait woman was not blond, but brown-haired, and the artist had caught a glint in her eyes though they were black. The only live black in that picture was that of her eyes.

I was no artist, but it seemed to me that the same person had painted both portraits. That would have been hard to do, painting a series of masters, if you knew that these were the people who controlled Recluce.

Enough was enough, and I looked away from the painting. Wrynn and Krystal had lapsed into silence. Tamra glanced away from me with a funny look on her face.

"Thoughts?" I asked, without thinking.

She grinned and shook her head. Her expression was so knowing that I immediately wanted to bash her with my staff—except it was sitting in the corner. And besides, I had no reason. I just knew I would have.

"Careful, Lerris," boomed a deep voice.

I jumped. So did everyone else in the room, even Tamra.

How he had entered unseen bothered me, but the man's voice was bigger than he was. He had silver hair and broad shoulders, but he did not even reach to my shoulder. For Recluce, I was only a half-head above average, if a shade broader in the chest and shoulders.

He wore a tunic and trousers of some sort of silvery-gray. Even his boots were silver-gray.

"No black?"

Tamra shook her head at my comment. No one else did anything but stare.

"As you will learn, Lerris, one way or another, black is a state of mind." He bowed to me, then to Tamra, and finally to the others in a sweeping gesture. "I am Talryn, and I will be your guide to Nylan and for the first few days of your stay here." He gestured toward the doorway between the two benches, then stepped forward and touched the wood. The doorway swung open, and I could see the light flooding from the room. "If you will gather your possessions and follow me, we will begin with a meal."

Talryn stepped through the doorway.

I picked up my staff and pack, then nodded to Tamra. She inclined her head to me. I inclined mine back, but she still waited.

Finally, I walked after Talryn, and Tamra's light steps clicked after mine. The others shuffled along after us.

The doorway led not into another room, but into a long corridor lit solely from a clear glass skylight. I studied the skylight as well as I could without losing my balance while trying to keep up with Talryn.

A series of curved glass panels had been fitted into bent dark-oak framing for the entire length of the building. Through the glass, I could see that the skylight was nothing more than a continuous window into a small garden above us that filled the center of the building.

On each side of the corridor where we walked were massive stone supports, clearly bearing the weight of the garden.

Somehow, again, it was disappointing. The design and engineering had been well-thought-out and the effect was quite pleasing. But that was all it showed: good solid design and good engineering.

Talryn tapped another door, dark oak, at the far end of the garden corridor walk, and stepped inside. We all followed into a small room.

He waited until everyone had gathered.

"Through the door on my right, there are facilities suitable for you gentlemen. On the left are facilities for you gentle ladies. Please leave your packs and traveling gear in the open lockers. They will be quite safe there, and you can reclaim everything after we eat."

"Why different facilities?" asked Tamra.

"Because, even in Recluce, there are some who hold to the Legend, who feel men and women are different, Tamra."

"That's just an excuse."

"Perhaps. You may use the facilities or not." Talryn's deep voice was noticeably cooler. He turned from her. "Once you are washed and ready, step through the center doorway here and we will eat. During the meal, I will attempt to provide a general introduction to the dangergeld and what it may entail."

The way he stood before that door, almost like a guard, made it clear that a certain amount of cleanliness was mandatory. I didn't bother to wait, but headed toward the facilities. I was ready for both the relief and the cleanup, in that order.

Myrten dragged in after Sammel and me, as if he didn't like soap and water. That confirmed my opinion of him.

The masters not only had good engineering and sanitary facilities, they had an ample supply of warm and cold running water, and heavy gray towels. It took a fair amount of soap and water to get the road dust off my face, hands and arms. I really could have taken a shower, except the building facilities weren't that elaborate, for all the gray tile on the walls and floor. But I felt better, a lot better, by the time I finished.

VII

The table was filled with platters, mostly of fruit and vegetables, with a variety of cheeses and some thin slices of meat. Two smaller platters bore a selection of breads. I concentrated on the fruits, noting apples, sourpears, and chrysnets, not to mention the heap of redberries. The plates were heavy gray stoneware, serviceable and banded with a thin green border, like something that might have been produced by one of my mother's better apprentices after a year.

Beside the plates were matching heavy mugs, small towels in place of napkins, and spoons and forks. No knives. The black-oak surface was polished but bare, without even rush mats under the plates.

Talryn stood by the head of the table set for eight, three on a side and one at each end. The space on his right was vacant. On his left stood Dorthae. On her left was Myrten. The foot of the table was vacant.

So was the other space on the left, as were all the spaces on the right.

"If you would take the other end, Lerris . . ."

Since he was a master of some sort, and since it wasn't exactly a request, I moved over and stood at the end, waiting for the others to arrive.

Sammel came next, his balding forehead shiny and his remaining thin brown hair damp. The loss of road dust and grime made him look younger. He gave Talryn an almost shy smile.

"If you would take the middle, Sammel . . ."

Sammel did just what I had done. He nodded and eased up to his indicated position.

As he stepped around the table, Wrynn and Krystal appeared together, still whispering like girls after school. They stopped as they saw Talryn looking at them.

"If you would take the place between Myrten and Lerris, Wrynn . . . and you, Krystal, the space across from her . . ."

That left Tamra, who seemed already to be the last one anywhere. She still hadn't appeared and would have to sit next to Talryn. I didn't think that was coincidence, somehow.

Talryn let us stand for a little while longer, then nodded. "Please be seated. I think we should begin."

Even before we could get the heavy wooden chairs pulled out, Tamra appeared. Her hair was lightly curled and brighter than when I had first seen her, as if she had washed and shaped it, but it was as dry as if she had been sitting in the sun. She had also pulled it back from her face with a pair of dark combs.

She still wore the gray tunic and trousers, but a blue scarf around her neck added a touch of color. All in all, she made a striking appearance.

Talryn nodded to the empty space at his right.

Tamra opened her mouth, then shut it quickly as Talryn pulled out her chair for her. Her ice-blue eyes flashed like sun from a glacier.

Talryn moved the chair so easily that I tried to edge mine back with one hand. It didn't move. I quickly reached down with both hands and lifted it by its curved arms, sliding it back. Black oak, shaped and bent into a flattened point without a crest at the height of the chair back. The curved back was supported by four spokes twice the width used for household chairs. A flat black cushion covered the seat.

"If you are done inspecting the chair, Lerris, would you join us?".

"Sorry. The design . . ." I sat down and edged the chair forward to the table. Again, it took two hands.

Everyone waited, looking at Talryn.

"Go ahead. There's no blessing, no incantations, no mysticism—just good food." He reached for the platter of breads. "After all of you have served yourselves, I will provide the explanation I promised."

I reached for the cheeses before me, spearing several with the long wooden-handled fork, just ahead of Krystal. She already had taken a sourpear and a chrysnet.

"Would you pass the cheeses?" Wrynn asked. Her voice was flat.

"You done?" I asked Krystal.

"Yes." When she wasn't giggling her voice almost sang when she talked, but it didn't sound affected.

At the other end of the table, Tamra had piled her plate with everything in sight—sourpears, apples, cheeses, breads, and meat.

Beside me, Krystal offered the meat platter.

"Thank you."

She nodded, and, after removing several slices, I took the serving plate from her and offered it to Wrynn. The blond woman took twice what I had heaped on my plate, without looking at me—leaving me still holding the platter.

"Wrynn . . . would you pass this to Myrten?"

The woman still didn't look at me, but took the platter with a sigh and thrust it in front of Myrten, almost hitting him in the nose as he bent forward.

"Thank you." Myrten's voice was pleasant enough, but it sounded as though he had polished each word.

Wrynn said nothing to him, either.

I lifted the mug, sipping gingerly, and found it was some sort of juice combination—light, with a touch of sparkle.

Krystal, to my right, had produced a small knife and dissected her sourpear into neat slices. Just as quickly, she had eaten nearly half of the fruit. I tried not to gape, instead smearing some redberry jam over a thick slice of bread and munching through that, interspersing it with some of the yellow cheese.

"Where are you from?" I finally asked Krystal.

"Oh, from Extina."

I'd never heard of Extina.

"A little village near Land's End. No one else has ever heard of it, either." The small knife flashed, and the chrysnet lay in quarters, the pit removed nearly effortlessly. "What about you?"

"Wandernaught."

"Oh . . . is it true what they say about it?" She giggled, spoiling the momentary impression of a calm and dark beauty.

"What they say about it?" I'd never heard anything said about it.

"You know," Krystal giggled again, "that *nothing* ever happens there because the Institute really runs the Brotherhood." She popped two orangish chrysnet quarters into her mouth, one right after the other.

"Oooofff . . ." I choked on the last part of her question. The Institute running the Brotherhood? That collection of four buildings where people just gathered to talk to each other?

"Are you all right, Lerris?" broke in Talryn from the other end of the table. All conversation died away for a moment.

I nodded, managed to swallow the suddenly very dry bread, and reached for the mug of fruit punch, ignoring the glint in Tamra's eyes as she watched my discomfort.

Krystal, her eyes on me, brought forth the little knife and, with deft cuts, not even looking, created four miniature sandwiches out of a slab of white cheese, some dark bread, and one thick slab of buffalo.

I swallowed again.

"Are you sure you're all right?" Krystal asked, her voice concerned for the first time.

"Yes . . . just surprised. I've been to the Institute many times, even heard my father speak there, but no one acted as though they were running anything at all—except their mouths. It was boring . . . very boring." I took another sip from the massive brown mug. "You are right about one thing. Nothing ever happens in Wandernaught." I stopped, realizing that tears were welling up in the corners of Krystal's eyes. "Are you—did I say something?"

She shook her head, pursing her lips together.

Wrynn had stopped shoveling in her food and was listening, as was Sammel on the other side of Krystal. Myrten pretended not to listen as he played with a sourpear. Tamra, Talryn, and Dorthae were discussing shipping, or ships.

Krystal swallowed.

I waited, suddenly not as hungry as I had thought.

"It's just . . ." Krystal began. ". . . your father, to even speak there . . . and you're younger than anyone here . . . and you have to do dangergeld . . ." She shook her head slowly, the sandwiches left neatly on her platter.

My head seemed ready to lift off my shoulders.

"Is your father a master?" blurted out Wrynn.

I shrugged. "He never said so. He never did anything that made me think so, and he never wore black. I never thought about it. My mother is a skilled potter. People come from as far as Austra to buy her vases and figurines. My father was always the holder . . ."

"You sound as though you are reconsidering," observed Myrten. His voice was even more polished, as if oil-coated.

"I don't know. He's always talked a lot about the importance of order. I found it boring. Still do."

Krystal sniffed. ". . . no mercy . . ."

I didn't really expect mercy from the Brotherhood, but what did she mean? "Mercy?" I finally asked.

"All of you," interrupted Talryn before Krystal could reply, "I promised you an introduction and an explanation. I will try to make both short and then answer questions. Some questions I may not answer until later, but I will try to provide as much information as I can."

Once again, even before they started, they were saying they were going to hide something. I stifled a snort.

At the other end of the table, Tamra had adopted a look of resignation. Only Sammel looked really interested in what Talryn might have to say.

"First, the dangergeld. What is it, and why is it necessary? And, from your point of view, why were you selected?" Talryn took a sip from his mug.

"Stripped of all the piety, rhetoric, and rationalization, the dangergeld is simply a quest, a series of duties, or an exile—or some combination of all three—to enable you to discover whether you belong in Recluce, and, if so, in what capacity. None of you have been happy in what you have been doing. Unfocused discontent is contagious and leads to disorder. Disorder leads to chaos, and chaos to evil.

"After this meal, you each have a choice. You may accept dangergeld training, which can last several months, sometimes longer, or you can accept immediate exile. If you choose training, then depending on the results of that training you may be offered one or several options on how to fulfill your dangergeld obligation. Again, if you like none of the options, at that point you may choose exile.

"All exiles are transported, with their available funds and traveling gear, to one of three outside ports, depending on the time of year. Those are Freetown in Candar, Brysta in Nordla, or Swartheld in Afrit, north of Hamor."

At the last two names, most of the eyebrows around the table went up. I'd heard of Brysta and certainly wouldn't have been pleased to land there. Nordla was cold, and Brysta was as far north as you could get for an all-year port. Above Brysta, the winter ice sheets closed the coast.

". . . may not bring more than you can comfortably carry on your person. If any of you choose exile, the next departure will be in about ten to twelve days. You will remain in Nylan, although you may participate in any or none of the dangergeld training, as you please.

"For those of you considering dangergeld, training begins tomorrow. There will be classes on the details of what the dangergeld obligation entails, on the geography and customs of most major countries outside Recluce, on their economies and trade, on how money is handled—customs surrounding funds do vary, by the way—and on weapons familiarization and self-defense.

"We will also provide some additional background on the Brotherhood, since some of you may choose, or be offered, the option of performing your dangergeld in some capacity with the Brotherhood, depending on your own inclinations and the progress of your training.

"As always, your participation is voluntary—with two stipulations. First, should you choose not to participate in any training, you will be regarded as choosing exile. Second, you may not leave Nylan. Any attempt to do so will result in confinement until you can be exiled."

"Voluntary?" snorted Wrynn. "You don't play the Brotherhood's game, and you're locked up until you can be shipped off to Nordla or Hamor."

"You have already made a choice that you cannot accept living in Recluce," Talryn observed mildly.

"No. You made that decision based on your rules," countered the blond.

Talryn shrugged his broad shoulders. "The rules, as you call them, are accepted and honored by virtually everyone in Recluce. Do you honestly believe otherwise? That a handful of masters and brothers who have never raised a violent hand in centuries could override the will of our people?"

42

I almost laughed at that. The masters controlled all the education. They didn't need swords. Besides, a bunch of boring sheep would agree to any rules that would send the wolves away. But no one raised that question, not Tamra nor Wrynn.

Krystal giggled again, and sliced her drying sandwiches into halves, which she quickly ate. How she could eat so much and stay so slender I couldn't imagine.

"Why do you teach us about so many countries, and not just the area where we will be sent?" The calm voice was Sammel's.

"You may end up seeing more of the world than you think, and we would like you to have some idea of where you may end up. Also, you will find Hamorians in Nordla and Candarians in Hamor. Knowing their differing customs has proven useful to others and should help you."

Myrten gave his head the smallest of shakes. Tamra stifled a grin, although I couldn't see what was funny. Wrynn, beside me, took a deep breath and exhaled slowly. Krystal cut a green apple into a series of intricate slices arranged around the edge of her plate.

But no one asked another question, and Talryn volunteered nothing more about the dangergeld itself.

"You will probably have more questions. Anyone who does not want to undertake the dangergeld training, please see me when we finish eating. After the meal you will be shown your rooms, and you may spend the afternoon any way you like, including visiting the market in the harbor, or anywhere else in Nylan.

"Breakfast will be at the first bell. At the second bell, the first class will begin. You will be shown the class area on your way to your rooms." Talryn stood up. "Please finish as you like. I will be in the next room. When you are done, gather your things and join me there."

He pushed back his chair and departed, leaving the door behind him ajar.

Tamra raised her eyebrows, saying nothing.

"High-handed . . ." murmured Wrynn.

Krystal began eating the apple slices she had laid out around her plate.

Myrten pocketed two hard rolls and an apple, and Sammel frowned, either at Talryn's departure or Myrten's theft . . . or for some reason of his own. I took a last swallow from the mug, deciding against another slice of cheese. Enough was enough, and I was ready to find out what lay in store for me.

Tamra and I were the first ones on our feet. She hadn't eaten everything on her plate, either. .

As I glanced at her plate, our eyes crossed, hers looking at my partially-eaten meal. I had to grin, and, this time, she grinned back momentarily, although her expression hardened into a bored look.

I held the door for her, but she nodded. "Go ahead, Lerris. I'll hold my own doors."

"As you wish, lady."

"And I'm certainly no lady, not in the way you meant."

"I didn't mean anything, other than courtesy. If you don't like simple manners . . ." I let go of the black wood of the door and stepped back into the hallway toward the washrooms where my staff and pack were stored.

"Touchy, too. You should have red hair."

I ignored her comments, although I could feel the flush in my face.

"Healthy circulation, if thin-skinned."

Did the bitch needle everyone, or just those she could bully? I wished my thoughts were as quick as hers, but trying to match her would just make the situation worse.

43

The staff was where I left it, the lorken wood a shade warmer to my touch. Was that because we were in Nylan? Did it have some response of its own to magic or danger? I shook my head.

"Why the frown?" Sammel's voice was concerned. He probably always sounded concerned. He looked like his vocation was trying to do good whether anyone wanted it or not.

"Just thinking . . . wondering about all the black, whether it meant magic."

"It probably does. The Brotherhood couldn't have shaped the harbor or the cliffs without some fantastic forces. But they mean well, I think."

"So did Heldry the Mad."

Sammel smiled. "The Brotherhood doesn't hold mass executions."

I shrugged on my pack. "They settle for dangergeld and exile. That way the deaths are on someone else's hands."

"You are rather bitter for someone so young."

"That's easy when you're forced on a dangergeld for a reason you don't know by a group that enforces unspoken rules in unsaid ways."

That stopped him long enough for me to step around him and past Myrten. Tamra's back was in front of me as she passed by the table. No one was left there. Even Krystal had left several of the delicately-cut apple slices on her plate, where they were now turning brown.

I followed Tamra into the waiting room beyond.

". . . That's no choice." The voice was Dorthae's, and she was facing Talryn.

Talryn smiled a smile that wasn't really a smile, since his black eyes were hard as the stone of the paved floor underfoot. "You can choose either. Your actions already made that choice necessary."

"What . . . because I wouldn't stay with a man who turned out to be an unfeeling and unthinking brute?"

"No. Because you crippled him before you left him."

I winced. While there was a hardness to Dorthae, I hadn't seen just how hard she was. Yet she looked vulnerable standing before Talryn, even though he was no taller than she was.

Dorthae turned away, her lips tight.

Myrten and Sammel had followed me. Only Wrynn and Krystal were missing.

Dorthae glanced at me, saw my black staff and stumbled back toward Tamra, also carrying her staff. Dorthae cringed away from the redhead.

Tamra and I exchanged glances. She shrugged. After a moment, so did I.

Clearly, as I had recognized from the encounter with Shrezsan and the trader, I had some power, associated with the staff. What it was . . . that was another question. Unfortunately, everyone else thought I had some power, too, and they were just as clearly very wary of it. Wonderful—heading into a dangergeld cursed with an ability I hadn't even known I'd had, with the whole world ready to pounce on me for it. Sent for reasons I still didn't understand and which no one would explain. Just wonderful.

As I had pondered, Krystal and Wrynn appeared.

"You are all here. Good," said Talryn. "Follow me."

45

VIII

Pretty much in silence we walked up a set of wide black stone stairs. The side walls were of the same black stone. All the stone was smooth but unpolished, and it seemed to absorb light with almost no reflection. Each stone was set so tightly in place that the mortar between each was less than half a fingertip in width. That thin line of mortar was black. So clean were the steps they bore no trace of dust, although the light from the overhead skylights did not fall on the steps directly.

Talryn and Sammel were at the front of the group. I was at the back, just behind Wrynn and Krystal. From Krystal's blue leather belt, darker than her faded blue blouse and trousers, hung two sheaths, both containing knives, one barely a span in length. She wore a small matching blue pack.

"All this black . . . depressing . . ." muttered Wrynn, shaking her head, her blond hair fluffing out for an instant. She wore a brown pack like mine, except hers was stuffed to the bursting point and had several small bags tied to the outside.

"It smells like power," answered Krystal, touching her hand to the long black hair she had wound up into a bun after our rather late lunch. Then she emitted the faintest giggle.

If only she didn't giggle . . . I shook my head. She was nearly a decade older than I was, at least, with the hint of lines around her eyes—almost scrawny, except for her nicely-formed breasts.

"Creepy, if you ask me," muttered Wrynn again. Her right hand rested awkwardly on the haft of a long sheathed knife.

At the top of the steps was a foyer of sorts, windowless, and, on the far end, a set of doors that Talryn held open.

The breeze blowing toward me held a hint of spring, or rain—that clean smell that follows a good rain when the dust is washed out of the air. Yet I could see that the sky was as blue and nearly cloudless as when I had walked under the gates and into Nylan at midday.

"Gather round . . ."

So we gathered. I gave Myrten a wide berth. Smooth voice or not, he looked like he'd steal anything available just to prove he could. Dorthae didn't have that problem. She practically cuddled up next to him. I stood a pace or so behind Wrynn and Krystal, facing Talryn.

"Right ahead of us are the transients' quarters where you will be staying. Each of you will have a separate room," explained Talryn. "You can sleep there, or with anyone else in your group, as you please—but only with that other person's consent. Forcing yourself on someone else is a good way to immediate exile."

"*Now* . . . it's that way . . ." complained Dorthae.

Myrten sniffed. Wrynn grinned as if no one were about to force *her*—a thought with which I certainly agreed, wondering absently if, with her, *I* might need that protection.

I glanced around to find Tamra looking at me. She nodded once, then transferred her attention back to Talryn, who had continued droning on.

Had she understood what I had been thinking? How?

". . . washrooms and showers are at the end of the hallway. The small building on the other side of the square garden with the fruit trees is the dining hall where your meals will be served. You may eat there, or you may pay for meals anywhere in Nylan. The choice, again, is yours." He grinned broadly. "But the Brotherhood's meals are good, and the price is right."

46

"Only your life," said Dorthae softly, but loudly enough to stop Talryn momentarily.

He frowned, then shook his head. "Believe it or not, our interest is in saving your lives, not spending them." He cleared his throat before continuing. "Your introduction to the elements of the danger-geld will start tomorrow after breakfast in the classroom building—that's the one with the red square by the doorway toward the harbor from the dining hall. Now I'll show you your rooms. If you wish to trade a room with someone else, you certainly can, provided you both agree."

Without another word, he turned and opened the black-oak door, not even looking to see if any of us followed him. Of course, we all did. What else could we do?

My room, like all the others, had a narrow bed, just wide enough for one comfortably. The wooden frame was, thankfully, of polished red oak. A single sheet covered the mattress, and a dark-blue blanket was folded across the bottom of the bed. No pillows, not that I had slept with one since I had apprenticed with Uncle Sardit, and only a single small oil lamp on the table. There was no closet, but a square red-oak wardrobe, half hanging space and half open shelves.

47

A braided and multicolored oval rag rug perhaps three cubits across covered most of the blue floor tiles between the door and the bed, which was nearly against the outside stone wall. The half-open single casement window was in the middle of the wall, just short of the foot of the bed.

I pulled my cloak from the pack and hung it up, as well as my single spare set of trousers and tunic. The order-locked purse was there, with my apprentice wages, as was another purse I did not remember. I opened it. Inside were ten more gold pennies, worn, nothing more. I swallowed.

For some reason, I had trouble seeing for a minute, perhaps because I recalled the gold penny with the small clip out of it. My mother had remarked on it as coming from the buyer from the Emperor of Hamor. She refused to let me see her tears, but left me what she could. I grasped back in the bag for something . . . anything.

There was also a short-sleeved summer shirt, but I left it folded and put it on the second shelf. My leather case with the razor and soap I put on the top shelf. The few other underclothes I had fit in with room to spare, as did the small book my father had clearly tucked into my pack.

The Basis of Order . . . of all things. Who knew? I figured reading it might be something to do. Especially if the training got boring. I didn't leave it out in the open, but tucked it under the shirt. The purses I put back in the pack, which I folded and put on the top shelf. They would be safe—that I knew. I took ten coppers and a silver penny.

None of the rooms had locks, just bolts that could only be closed from inside. Then again, who was going to try to steal anything with the Brotherhood around? Even Myrten would hesitate .. for now.

I shook my head. The hour was early, and even if it were kays down to the harbor, a good walk, and even if my feet were blistered, I intended to try it, just to see if I could get a better idea about what Nylan really represented. And I didn't want to sit around and think about either the book or the extra purse.

The staff stayed in the wardrobe along with the cloak.

With a last look at the small room, I closed the door. Outside, the central hallway was empty, although I could hear voices in the neighboring room—Wrynn and Krystal. Their words were low.

The pathway toward the harbor was easy enough to find, since there were stone pedestals every hundred rods or so along each of the paths, with names and arrows pointing out the way.

Harbor—3 kays

Northway Depot—2 kays

Administration—1 kay

I kept following the arrows until I reached a black stone wall that ran north and south from one side of the peninsula to the other. It was low, a little over two cubits. Nor was it really a barrier, since there were no gates at the openings where the paths went through it. On one side were the almost park-like grounds that had stretched for more than a kay, with scattered low buildings.

From where I stood at the top of a long set of wide steps, I could look over the central part of Nylan—or the commercial district, whatever it was called. Behind and over the building tops, I could see the blue of the harbor and the tops of several masts.

Right beyond the wall, the ground fell away, in a grassy slope that dropped a good fifteen cubits in less than a hundred. On the other side of the downslope, the buildings began—all black stone, roofed in black slate. Each stood separately, set back from the black stone-paved streets and the shinier black curbs. Unlike Enstronn or Mattra or even Wandernaught, there were no hitching posts. Despite the width of the streets, they did not seem to be designed for horses or wagons.

People walked the streets, some carrying packages, some carrying nothing, some in black, some in all colors of the rainbow.

No one even looked up the hill. So I headed down.

Halfway down, I looked back up. The wall that had looked so low from the uphill side appeared at least fifteen cubits high from the base of the hill. Even accounting for more stone exposed on the downhill side, I didn't think the wall was nearly that high. But speculating on optical illusions wouldn't tell me any more about Nylan.

Once on the streets of the harbor area, everything felt more normal. People talked, and I could hear the babble of the market square ahead. With all the black stone, the city should have felt warmer, especially on a summer afternoon, but the breeze from the west was cool enough, apparently, to keep the temperature comfortable.

A sailor, red-haired and red-bearded, gave me a long glance as I entered the square. Half the booths, those on the north side, seemed permanent, workmanlike and well-crafted. Those on the south side, some of which were no more than half-tents or canvas-covered tables, seemed shoddy by comparison. Several seemed untended.

I nodded. The outland traders and ships had their wares on the south side.

"Young fellow—come see the amber from Brysta!"

". . . fire-diamonds from Afrit! Here alone! . . ."

Still, the calls from the hucksters were muted. Perhaps thirty shoppers filled the entire square, split among nearly as many vendors. Most of the shoppers were young, not much older than me. Danger-gelders, those doing duty with the Brotherhood, I guessed as I looked first at the booths on the north side of the square.

The first displayed some ceramics. Good work, but nothing to compare to my mother's. The colors were too vivid. A man sat behind them, perched on a stool, who gave me a passing grin as if to acknowledge I would buy nothing.

In quick order, I passed some carved and gilded mirrors; a gold-smith's display of rings, necklaces, and pendants; a smith's array of assorted steel tools, which seemed of high quality; leather goods,

49

including purses, belts, packs, and sheaths for various sizes of knives;
a bootmaker's display with several gaudy, if well-tooled, sets of boots.

At the woodworking stall, I stopped, surveying the items on display. All were small—breadboards, book holders, and mostly carved
boxes. No furniture, except a tiny pedestal table and a two-shelf book-
case of gray oak.

"You know wood," observed the boy minding the display. His brown
eyes almost matched his brown hair, and he wore a tan shirt.

"Some. You do any of these?"

"Only the breadboards. My older brother did most of the rest,
except the table and the shelves."

"Your father?"

"Mother. She sells mostly on consignment to Hamor."

The breadboards were adequate, as were the boxes, but I had been
doing better when I had left Uncle Sardit. Only the pedestal table
was clearly better than I could do.

"You think you do better work?" asked the boy.

"It doesn't matter now," I answered absently. Whatever I did from
there on out, it wouldn't be woodwork.

I left without saying more and walked across the square. The first
cloth-draped table was the trader who had been screeching forth about
amber. A single look told me that the amber was fair at best, and the
silver settings in which most of it was encased were worse.

The trader glanced away from my scrutiny, not even speaking.

The adjoining table was filled with uncut fire diamonds. Even from
the spread stones, I could pick out three or four clearly superior to
the others. Not bigger, just better. Displaying what I might have
called more order. But I couldn't afford them, and there wasn't much
point in bargaining over a lesser stone, not when I would need funds
more than diamonds before very long.

Several tables were vacant, their canvas flapping in the breeze,
barely held down by stones.

Further toward the corner closest to the harbor was a tiny man
sitting behind a half-dozen small and elaborately-carved ivory figures.
Those alone matched the quality of crafts displayed on the north side
of the square.

For a long time, I studied the figures. One, that of a young man
carrying a dark staff, appealed to me. Once again, I passed on without
even trying to bargain. Nor did the trader or carver try to entreat me.

From the square I walked down toward the four long wharves. Each gray stone structure rose out of the dark blue water of the harbor more than five cubits, with a central paved roadway more than ten cubits wide. At the first wharf, the one closest to the harbor mouth and farthest from the center of the market area, was a huge twin-masted and steel-hulled steamer. A thin wisp of smoke rose from the forward funnel. The ensign I did not recognize, but, with the blue-green background and the golden crown, I would have guessed the ship was from somewhere in Nordla.

A half-dozen loading carts, stacked with square wooden packing cases of differing sizes, waited for the ship's crane to transfer each into an open forward hold. What was in the crates I couldn't see. I walked down toward the pier. Although there was a small stone booth for a guard, the booth, spotlessly clean, was empty. Nor was there a guard around.

Click . . . click . . . My boots nearly skidded on the smooth pavement underfoot.

Whhhsssss . . . Ahead, steam drifted from the small tractor linked to the loading carts, though they were long like farm carts, each nearly ten cubits in length. The sides were of smooth-milled red oak, held in place by steel brackets.

"Stand clear, fellow." A woman I had not seen, wearing a set of black coveralls, waved in my direction then gestured toward the ship.

Whhheeeepppp . . . The crane lifted two more crates, cradled in a heavy mesh net, up off the next-to-last cart. The end cart was already empty.

The woman walked briskly toward me. Dark-haired, she was nearly as tall as I was, and as broad in the shoulders. She smiled. "Must be new in Nylan. Dangergeld?"

I had to nod.

"We're loading furniture right now. The ship is the *Empress*—out of Brysta, Nordla Lines. I'm Caron."

"Is this your dangergeld?" I blurted.

She laughed. "Not exactly. I started as a purser on the Brotherhood ships, but traveling got old. I liked dealing with cargo and making up shipments, handling the cube and stowage calculations—"

Whhhheeee . . .

"—Excuse me . . ." She was back at the cart, deftly jockeying two more crates into the net, without seeming to work up a sweat.

Whheeeeppp . . .

As the net lifted away, Caron returned. "So that's how I ended up here. I have a small farm not too far from Sigil, in the low hills north of the High Road. I spend my free time there."

"But . . . don't you need help loading all these ships . . . ?"

"There are four of us. That's enough. We don't handle that much bulk anyway. The economics don't work, not against forced labor or slavery."

Whheeepppp . . .

As she turned back toward the loading, I frowned. For a glorified stevedore, Caron was unusually bright, and perfectly willing to talk to a total stranger. Was she just another Brotherhood type, with quick and incomplete answers? In the direct sunlight, even though it was a shade cooler than normal for a summer day's late afternoon, I was beginning to sweat.

After wiping my forehead with the back of my sleeve, I looked at the steam tractor. Magister Kerwin had taught us about steam-powered machinery, how it created too much chaos unless properly designed and handled, and how it generated too much concentrated heat. Steamships could handle the heat because of the conductivity of the ocean and their relative isolation from other chaos-sources.

Whheeeeppppp . . .

Another full net lifted away, and the gregarious loadmaster, or whatever else she was, stepped back toward me.

"What do you think of Nylan?"

"Don't know what to think. I just got here today." I pointed to the tractor. "That seems contrary to the magisters' teaching."

Caron grinned. She looked younger—say about Tamra's age—when she smiled. "It only seems that way. If you consider the alternatives in order theory, the number of bodies required to lift that cubage, it works out about even. Plus, the fact that we can operate them without the usual catastrophes scares the hell out of the outlanders."

Whhhhhheeeeeeppppp . . .

Scares the hell out of the outlanders? For all of her direct speech, the woman still didn't really explain things. I watched as she single-handedly lifted a bulky crate into the net. Up on the steamer, two long-haired, bearded crewmen gawked at the ease with which the woman handled the heavy cargo.

Whhheeeepppp . . .

"Anyway," she continued, not even breathing hard, and as if she had never left, "loading them like this gets the point across."

"What point?"

"That they'd better not mess with the Brotherhood, or Recluce. What else?"

I shook my head.

"Think about it, young fellow. Sorry I can't talk longer, but the crates coming up are going to take all my effort. Good luck!"

She was back at the third cart, the fourth and fifth carts since emptied of their crates.

Wheeepppp . . .

I was the one shaking my head as I walked back toward the harbor wall from which the piers protruded. The wall stood another three cubits above the pier surface, not really a defensive bulwark, but a physical barrier that declared to the sailors on the ships that Nylan was foreign territory.

At the end of the second pier a long schooner was tied, flying the ensign of Hamor from the rear staff. Two armed guards stood by the plank to the ship, half-turned to face each other. From their posture it was clear they were not guarding the ship against Recluce, but discouraging unplanned crew departures.

I strolled toward the third pier, slowing as I saw that the guard booth was manned. Tied to the pier were three long and low shapes that had to be ships, but ships like none I had ever seen.

They were totally of black steel, with no masts, and only a low black superstructure beginning a third of the way back from the bow. Their bows were raked and sharp, somehow sharklike. Each flew a single ensign from the jackstaff—a solid black flag.

How I had missed them earlier I didn't know, except I could see what looked to be heat waves surrounding each.

I shivered, even in the warm afternoon sunlight. Yes, the Brotherhood had ways to protect Recluce.

"Young fellow, this pier is closed." The guard in the booth wasn't that much older than I was, but he wore what was clearly a black uniform, and I could sense, rather than see, the sword and club.

I just shrugged and turned away, looking down the pier again at the three strange ships. The guard watched me with a puzzled look on his face.

Wasn't I supposed to see the ships? Had the heat waves been a shield of some sort?

I glanced around the grassy space on the other side of the harbor walk. A scattering of people sat on the few benches. Down opposite the fourth pier, a meat vendor was selling sandwiches or something to the crew of the square-rigger that was tied up.

No one even glanced at the closed third pier. Shaking my head again, I began to walk back toward the market and toward my quarters, with more questions and fewer answers than when I had started.

The bell was chiming as I crossed the grass toward the dining hall, and the blisters on my feet were burning.

IX

Magister Cassius was black. I don't mean he wore black. His skin was a blue-black that glistened in the sun or the shadow. His short curly hair was black, and his eyes were black. Squarish, he stood more than four cubits, like a heroic black-oak carving. The only things light about him were the whites of his eyes. He did have a sense of humor, of sorts.

"Do you favor suicide or murder, Lerris?" His deep voice rumbled.

"What . . . huh?" Once again, he had caught me with my thoughts elsewhere, wondering, this time, about how the cliffs I could see through the open window had ever been made so black and so sheer. After all, just like old Magister Kerwin, he was pounding on and on about the basis of order.

"I asked you whether you favored suicide or murder?"

Krystal, sitting cross-legged on her pillow, suppressed another giggle. She had on the blue smock-like tunic and trousers, with sandals. And she still looked dusty, but that was because her clothes, pressed and clean as they were, had been washed so often the blue had faded away in spots.

Tamra continued to look at Cassius as if he were an insect under study. Over the gray tunic she had draped a vivid green scarf. Each day the scarf changed, but not the clothes. Either that, or she had a bunch of gray tunics and trousers.

Sammel looked from the Magister to me and back, then sighed.

I wondered how I would escape this time. "Neither . . ." I finally answered. "Both are very disorderly."

From the corner of my eye, I could see how Tamra shook her head.

Cassius almost sighed—almost, perhaps, the most fallible gesture I had seen from the Brotherhood. Then he continued. "We were speaking about order, a topic all of you have been exposed to since your birth. Unfortunately, for various reasons, such as Lerris's boredom, Tamra's equation of order with male dominance, Sammel's compassion for those unable to accept order, Krystal's unwillingness to concentrate, and Wrynn's contempt for weakness . . . none of you can accept order as the basis for a society."

I grinned, not really caring if I had been a target with the others, as I watched his gentle barbs bring the group alert. But I wondered why he had not said anything about Myrten.

Cassius turned and jabbed the short black wand he carried at me. "Lerris, you find order boring. Tell us why. Stand up. You can walk around and take as long as you want."

I eased off the brown leather pillow and stretched, conscious that even Tamra was looking toward me. I ignored her, or tried to. I didn't like being studied like a bug under a magnifying glass.

"Order is boring. Everything is the same. Every day in Recluce people get up and do the same things. They do them as perfectly as possible for as long as possible. Then they die. If that's not meaningless and boring, I don't know what is."

Wrynn nodded, as did Myrten, but Tamra's ice-blue eyes were hooded. Krystal suppressed a musical giggle and wound her long black hair around her fingers, letting the tips brush her feet as she watched from her cross-legged position.

I didn't know what else to say. After all, what I'd said was obvious. So I stood there. No one else added anything.

"Lerris, suppose, for the sake of discussion, there is a kingdom somewhere in this universe—"

"Universe?"

"Sorry. Just imagine another world. One where people have all the

55

children they want, without order, without rule. One where every generation, for no apparent reason, all the kingdoms go to war. The young men wear their armor and carry their weapons, and one-fifth of them die. Some kingdoms win, and some lose, but the only real result of the wars is that the weapons become more terrible and more effective.

"More children are born; more go hungry; and more of those who reach maturity die in the wars." Cassius paused and looked over the group of us. "All of you think about this imaginary world, not just Lerris."

I didn't think long. So what. So people died. People always die.

"Lerris, did you know that five thousand people died in Southern Hamor last year?"

I shook my head. What did five thousand deaths in Hamor have to do with an imaginary world? What did the imaginary world have to do with boredom? Or order?

"Do you know how they died?" Cassius' voice rumbled.

"No." How was I supposed to know?

"They starved to death. They died because there was no food."

Wrynn, sitting back against the black oak that paneled the lower half of each wall, pursed her lips.

Anyone could die without food. I nodded.

"Do you know why there was no food?"

"No."

"Does anyone here know?"

"Was that the rebellion?" asked Tamra. She seemed amused, as if she knew where Cassius was leading us.

I wondered how she knew about a rebellion in Southern Hamor. And who cared?

"There was food in Western Hamor," Cassius added slowly. "Enough food that the price of grain was lower than in years."

Myrten looked puzzled.

"Yes, Myrten?" Cassius acknowledged the ferret-faced man with the unruly hair as thick as a buffalo's coat.

"Couldn't they have at least smuggled some grain?"

"The Imperial Army blocked the roads. Some grain was smuggled, a great deal, in fact, but not enough to compensate for the fields burned by the emperor's troops."

There was a moment of silence.

"Lerris, has one person ever starved to death in Recluce?"

"I don't know." Damned if I would admit the point, although I wasn't sure which point I wasn't about to admit.

"So . . . you are saying that avoiding starvation is boring? That having happy and well-fed people is boring? Would you prefer to live in Hamor, where the lack of order leads to rebellions, oppression, and starvation? Is death preferable to boredom?"

"Of course not." My voice was louder than it should have been. "But you're saying that boredom is necessary to avoid death or some kinds of evil. That's what I don't accept."

"I never said that, Lerris. You did."

I started to open my mouth, except Tamra snorted. "Lerris, try thinking for once."

Krystal giggled.

I glared at her. She didn't look at me. Wrynn did, but she was shaking her head, even as she stretched out those long shapely legs.

No one said anything.

Magister Cassius finally sighed—a real sigh.

"All right," I demanded, "would someone explain to dumb Lerris?"

"You're not dumb," snapped Tamra. "You just refuse to see."

"See what?"

"Lerris . . ." rumbled Cassius, "order is necessary to prevent evils such as starvation and murder. Will you grant that point?"

I nodded. "Yes."

"You find excessive order boring, you said."

I had to nod again.

"Do you see the difference between the first point and the second?"

I must have looked blank. Everyone was shaking their heads.

Cassius took a deep breath. "Honest order prevents evil. That is a truth of life, and also of magic. On this . . . on our earth that truth approaches a fact." He paused.

"All right," I admitted, still wondering why he insisted on a difference between truth and fact.

"You call excessive order boring. That is a personal value judgment. When you apply that boredom to order, you are the one who says that boredom is necessary to avoid evil. Boredom is not a component of order. It is only your reaction. Boredom is not necessary to prevent starvation; order is. You just find that order boring."

Magister Cassius was just twisting words. Too much order was still boring.

"You all have a problem similar to Lerris's," continued the black man in black. "Tamra—you find order a tool of men. Therefore, you refuse to accept our way of life totally because order accepts the *valid* differences between men and women. You feel that women can do anything, if not more, than men can."

"We can," murmured the redhead, so low that no one seemed to hear it except me, although she was across the room from me. My hearing seemed to be getting better, or perhaps I was more alert. Tamra smoldered, but kept it hidden.

I slipped back down onto the brown leather pillow.

The Magister smiled faintly and turned. "Wrynn," continued the black man implacably, with his eyes turning toward his next victim, "you feel that strength is the answer to all problems, and that, given enough effort, anyone can be strong. Your philosophy would leave infants and the sick to grow—or die—as they could."

"That's not true . . ." Wrynn straightened on the pillow. Her brown-flecked green eyes turned cold.

"Then," Magister Cassius smiled, "would you explain it for us? Feel free to stand or walk around."

I watched Tamra, as graceful as a dancer, yet wound with a steel inside that would have dulled the sharpest blade. Her flame-red hair framed a freckled face that almost—almost—looked friendly when she was not speaking. She turned toward me, caught my eyes. I felt like a cold dash of water had been thrown across the room at me, and I looked toward Wrynn.

"Everyone has an obligation to be as strong as they can be. It isn't right for the strong to have to take care of those who refuse to be strong." Wrynn hadn't stood from her cushion, and her hands were clenched into fists. She looked down at the knife sheath at her belt.

"What do you mean by 'strong'?" asked Cassius in that low rumbling voice.

Wrynn looked at the polished black-oak floor planks, then at Krystal, and finally in the general direction of Myrten, who seemed to shrink further into the corner. Myrten always seemed to put himself in a corner when he could, a corner from where he could watch everything.

The room grew silent.

"You know what I mean. You just play with words." Wrynn's voice was harsh.

I agreed with her assessment of Cassius, of all the magisters and masters. All of them played with words, twisting their meanings, hiding more than they revealed.

"Come, now," Cassius's voice soothed. "You feel that strength is important. What kind of strength? Is a bully to be admired? Would you despise a small woman who required aid to stop a thief?"

"I don't admire bullies. I don't think much of people who invite theft or attacks. And I don't like thieves." Each word came forth filled with grit. Wrynn glared at Myrten, who for some reason looked away.

"So you feel order should rest solely upon strength and self-discipline?"

"I know what I feel." Wrynn glared this time at the magister.

"Fair enough." Cassius actually chuckled before wiping the smile from his face and turning toward Krystal. "And you, laughing lady? Why do you fail to pay much attention to order? Or to anything?"

Krystal didn't even look up at Cassius. She giggled and played with her long black hair.

"Krystal . . ." The booming voice turned cold.

Even I shivered.

Krystal looked at the floor planks. "It . . . doesn't *help* to pay attention. Things happen anyway. Thinking doesn't stop them." Her voice was barely above a whisper.

Wrynn sniffed loudly.

"Then you agree with Wrynn? That violence is the only way in which evil can be stopped?"

"Sometimes." She shifted her weight and looked at me.

"What do you think, Lerris?"

I wished she hadn't made that unspoken request, and especially that Cassius hadn't caught it. I coughed, trying to figure out what Krystal had really meant. ". . . ummm . . . at least sometimes it seems like perfectly good people can't do anything against evil or against accidents . . . and sometimes"—I recalled the baker—"people seem to be punished or exiled from Recluce just because they don't meet some unseen or unspoken standard. I guess I see that as unfair, that because they can't understand or aren't strong enough, they get punished."

"Do you think life is basically fair? Or that the Brotherhood has the obligation to be fair to an individual, when that fairness could threaten the safety of all Recluce?"

"I haven't seen that happen. I haven't seen any threat of that nature, but I have seen people who were not bad people exiled or punished."

Cassius smiled sadly, glancing from Krystal, who refused to look up, to Wrynn, who glared at him, and back to me. In the corner, Myrten licked his lips.

"Is living in Recluce a right or a privilege?" Cassius's question hung in the air like a spell.

"You're saying it's a privilege, that we have to meet certain conditions," I snapped. "That's fine, except no one ever explains the reasons behind the conditions. Just mind the rules; maintain order and banish chaos; and don't ask questions that we don't want to answer."

"I take it that you don't find the explanations satisfactory."

"You're right. I don't, and I don't think most of the people in this room do, either."

"So . . . the emperor has no clothes." Cassius' voice was lower and softer.

No clothes? What emperor? What clothes?

"This . . . philosophy . . . is all very inspiring. But how does this prepare us for dangergeld?" Tamra's voice was cutting, and she had stood up.

"Sit down, and I'll tell you. None of you are likely to believe me. But I'll tell you."

I shrugged. So did Wrynn. Tamra glared, but she sat back down. Cassius waited until the murmurs died away.

"It's really quite simple. Against perfect order, it is almost impossible for chaos-magic to prevail. Recluce is based on maintaining that order. Some people are order-sources; some people are chaos-generators; and some people can be either.

"Most people selected for dangergeld are either uncontrolled order-sources, or could generate either order or chaos without knowing it. The first step in dangergeld is to recognize that all of you have the ability to either allow chaos a foothold in Recluce or to help keep it from Recluce. You have to choose which, and the Brotherhood is not about to let you make that decision unless you're being watched and checked or unless you're outside Recluce.

"Since Recluce is not a police state, the best option is to let you see the rest of the world, or some of it, while you learn and decide."

Police state? That was an odd way of putting it. Only Hamor had police. For a moment, the room was still.

"So . . . you just throw us out for Hamor or Candar to murder, and everything stays fine with the sheep who remain?" Wrynn's voice was tight.

"Hardly. The current Emperor of Hamor is the grandson of a dangergelder who preferred the Southern Reaches and who was quite successful in taking over the Province of Merowey. The head assassin for one major power came from Sigil, not all that far from here." Cassius shook his head. "Believe me, the rest of the world will reward many talents. You're in the greatest danger if you believe in order and reject the Brotherhood." His eyes flashed toward me. "That's because you become a walking order-source in the realms of chaos and a threat to the chaos-masters."

"You're saying that because we have talent we have to leave Recluce until we master that talent?" asked Sammel.

"Not until you master it. That could take years. Until you decide within yourself your own course of action."

I almost bit my tongue. It was even worse than I thought. If I didn't accept the Brotherhood's stiff-necked order and rules, then I'd be thrown to the wolves, and, somehow, I didn't exactly see myself as a chaos-master. Why couldn't an ethical person use both order and chaos? Life consists of both.

"What about . . ."

The questions went on, but I didn't pay much attention. Everyone was just asking the same things with different words. So I was an uncontrolled order-source? Or worse. And no one still was describing what that meant, except that it was dangerous to Recluce.

My stomach growled, but no one heard as they argued with Cassius.

Krystal and I sat there in a quiet island. She looked at the floor, and I looked at everything and saw nothing.

X

The sun hung like a golden platter over the black stone wall that separated the Brotherhood's enclave from the seaport—that wall that seemed so low from the Brotherhood side, and so imposing from the market square below.

Even though it was but a few days past midsummer, the grass

remained crisp and green, the air clean, and the nights cool—the result of the Eastern Current, according to Sammel.

I hadn't thought much about it, not until Magistra Trehonna started in with her maps and lectures on geography, and how the placement of mountains and currents affected weather. Then she got into how geography determined where cities and towns were, and why places like Fenard, the capital of Gallos, sat on the edge of the hills leading to Westhorns because the higher elevation made the city more defensible and the two small rivers provided power for the mills. The only interesting bit was how the imposition of order and chaos at what she called critical nodes could change whole weather patterns.

That partly explained why some of the Brotherhood ships patrolled certain segments of the northern waters. But her lectures were like everything else—a piece of knowledge here, another one there, and a whole lot of boring repetition in the middle.

So I sat with my back against a small red oak and watched the puffy clouds in the eastern skies begin to darken from white into a pinkish-gray. Just because, I tried to see if I could discover the patterns behind the clouds, trying to look beyond their surfaces.

Again, I could see the faint heat-shadow–like images I had seen around the strange Brotherhood ships, but the ones in the clouds were natural. How I could tell the difference, I didn't know. But I did. After a while, my eyes began to ache. So I closed them and began to listen.

There were other dangergeld groups around. We met in the quarters and sometimes talked over dinner. They weren't much different, except they looked to be in better shape, and they all seemed distant. Friendly, understanding, but distant.

Two of them were seated on a bench on the other side of the hedge. Their voices carried.

". . . Brysta, that's what they say . . ."

"At least it's not Hamor . . ."

"Take Hamor over Candar . . . home of the chaos-masters . . . Emperor of Hamor likes *some* order . . ."

Cassius had mentioned that Candar was the most chaotic of the major continents. Tamra said that was because it was closest to Recluce, and there had to be balance. Cassius frowned, but hadn't corrected her. That meant she'd been right.

So what else was new. From Frven in Candar, the chaos-wizards had ruled most of the world—until they'd created a new sun in the sky and melted most of the capital's buildings and people like wax. Although that had been generations ago, the people probably hadn't changed that much.

"Could I join you?"

I almost jumped, opening my eyes with a start.

The musical voice belonged to Krystal.

"Sure . . . I'm not certain I'm much company."

"That makes two of us." She tucked her feet under her and settled down with a cubit of grass between us, shrugging her shoulders as if to loosen her faded blue tunic. The long hair was bound up with silvered cords. When she wasn't giggling or fiddling with her hair I enjoyed watching her. She was as graceful as Tamra, but without the arrogance, and behind the giggles I suspected there was more strength than either of us knew.

Thimmmmm . . . The chime from the temple echoed once, calling those of the Brotherhood who wished to join the evening meditation. I wasn't about to, and I'd noticed that Magister Cassius never did either.

Krystal did not move, but the two men on the bench on the far side of the hedge left.

"They're probably going to give thanks for being sent to Brysta, instead of Candar." The words popped out of my mouth.

"Where do you think we'll be sent?"

"Candar," I opined.

"You're usually right . . . I mean, about facts . . ." She looked down at the grass.

I straightened into a sitting position and stopped leaning against the oak. Both tree and ground were hard. The clouds above the eastern horizon showed gray, and the breeze from the west picked up, ruffling my hair. A hint of trilia tickled my nose, bittersweet-orange.

"What will happen to us?"

I shrugged. "I don't know. It seems like we're a strange lot, but I suppose all dangergelders are. Myrten's a thief, but how he lasted so long . . . Wrynn's really a soldier, probably belongs in the border guard. Sammel's a missionary in a land that already has a faith that doesn't place compassion above order. Tamra hates men, and half the world is male. Dorthae . . . I just don't know . . ."

"And you?"

63

"Me?" I shrugged again. I didn't want to talk about me. "Like Cassius says, I'm easily bored. What about you?"

"I think you're bored because you want to know everything and you don't want to admit it."

Thimmmmm . . . The second chime from the temple rang, indicating the evening meditation had begun.

"What about you?" I asked again.

"Me?" Krystal giggled just slightly.

I frowned.

"You don't like it when I giggle."

"No." I looked over her shoulder and down the grassy stretch toward the small garden just before the wall. Dorthae and Myrten were seated on opposite ends of the bench, playing some sort of card game. That figured. Myrten would find something with odds in it anywhere.

"I was contracted, you know. He didn't mind the giggling too much."

"I'm sorry." I hadn't thought about that. I was young. What if Koldar or Corso had been picked for dangergeld? Krystal was announcing that the Brothers had pulled her away from her husband/lover, just like that. "I'm sorry."

"Don't be. It was a good excuse to leave. He'll be happier. I already am."

"Just leaving?" I couldn't imagine my mother walking away from my father.

"You look at my hair. You see my breasts. So do all the men. Your looks are honest, at least." Her voice was low, almost whispery, yet still musical.

"True," I admitted.

She readjusted her position on the grass. Somehow the readjustment got her almost next to me. "Do you think about what I feel?"

Actually, I was wondering how she would feel to hold and touch, but that wasn't what she meant. "Not at first."

"Oh, Lerris . . ." her voice died off.

We sat there as the darkness drifted down upon Nylan.

"Would you just hold me?" Her voice was like a child's.

I did, and that was all I did. Not that I didn't think about more, especially later that night, alone in my bed.

XI

After we were well into the lectures from Talryn, Magister Cassius, and Magistra Trehonna—the lady with the glare that even quieted me—one morning Talryn marched us down another long but well-lit tunnel and out into a wide room, sunken partly into the ground.

Underground or not, the overhead and upper side windows admitted more than enough light. Unlike the teaching rooms, the stone walls were plastered over with an almond-shaded white finish. The flooring was the strange part, neither wood nor stone, but a greenish and springy substance that gave slightly under foot.

The same substance was used for flooring in the exercise rooms where Dilton tried to force us all into a better physical condition. I had tried, but hadn't been able to break even the slightest fragment from it, even though I could squeeze it enough to press a thumb's width of it up between my fingers, and the woodworking with Uncle Sardit had left them strong. The muscles in my legs were what suffered under Dilton, especially from the running and stretching.

The best part of the conditioning was watching Tamra and Krystal. I didn't really dare to do more than watch with either one. Sometimes, as with the time on the lawn, Krystal would sit next to me or ask for a hug, but she clearly wanted it as a brotherly gesture, or even as a fatherly one. And that was the way it stayed, no matter what my body said.

Why? Because deep inside the lady, I could feel, not knowing how, something that I wasn't about to tamper with. What? Like a lot of things, I couldn't say what, only recognize its danger. Like Tamra, like Candar. When I even saw maps of Candar, I wanted to shiver.

My musings stopped when I saw Tamra was smiling. She still wore the dark gray, this time with a blue scarf. No one had said a word about her clothing. Then, Talryn hadn't said a word about my dark-brown garments either.

Against the wall opposite the door we had entered were racks of objects, some clearly swords or knives. Half a dozen of each were racked next to each other, and there were five large racks.

"Candidates . . ." Talryn cleared his throat. He always cleared his throat after he got our attention. "This is Gilberto."

65

Gilberto wasn't tall. I'm taller than average, almost four cubits, but not that much taller than average. Gilberto stood nearly a head below me—more like Tamra's size. Wearing black trousers and black leathers over a black shirt and black boots, with his black hair and pale white skin, he looked like an executioner.

"This is Gilberto," repeated Talryn. "The world outside Recluce boasts an array of weapons. Gilberto will attempt to give you some familiarity with the most common and some minimal ability with one or two, assuming you are willing to learn."

Gilberto smiled crookedly, as if offering an apology. The expression turned him from a colorless executioner into a sad-faced clown.

Tamra studied him from one side. I just smiled back at the man. He looked funny. Boring or strange as some of the Brotherhood could be, I never doubted their abilities. Krystal pursed her too-red lips, trying not to giggle. Wrynn scowled. Myrten licked his lips. Dortháe looked at Talryn, then at Gilberto, without saying a word.

Gilberto acknowledged us, bending forward at the waist. The gesture was formal. "There are weapons on the racks. Please look them over. Pick them up. Handle them—touch at least one of each kind. Whichever one of them feels most comfortable to you, please take that one and sit down on one of the pillows at the end of the room."

The weapons-master's eyes turned cold. "Do not pick a weapon with your head. Do not pick whatever seems the easiest, or the most destructive. The weapons you use must reflect you." He paused. "Later, I will teach you about other weapons." He bowed again and gestured toward the racks.

Gilberto was serious. I knew that. So I edged toward the nearest rack, on which I could see swords—long ones, short ones, and some no bigger than long daggers. I looked at a narrow-bladed sword with a business-like handle, finally nerved myself to pick it up—and damned near dropped it. The chill and almost forbidding feel of the weapon nauseated me. As quickly as possible I set it down, wiping my forehead.

"Heee . . ."

Krystal and her damned giggles. "Go ahead. You pick one up."

She twisted her hair back over her shoulder and reached past me for the sword, easily holding it, turning it in her hands. "It feels fine, but not quite right." She set it down and reached for a slighter, shorter sword, although it had the same narrow blade.

I reached for the sword she had tried, the one I had let go of so quickly. The jolt and chill weren't quite as strong, but my stomach still twisted.

Looking for Talryn, I wondered what trickery he and Gilberto were up to. But Talryn had disappeared so silently no one noticed his departure, and Gilberto stood at the end of one of the racks, a thoroughly impassive, even bored, look on his face.

Tamra came up beside me, grinning, and reached for the sword that I had tried twice. Her mouth opened as her hand grasped the hilt. Then she tightened her lips, finally setting the sword down. "Not for me." A faint sheen of perspiration had popped out on her forehead.

I repressed a smile and walked down the first rack, looking at the daggers, many of which were finely crafted, even while displaying workmanlike effectiveness. Even running my hands over their hilts told me that the daggers were equally repugnant. I had handled knives before, and I had never felt so repelled. Clearly a spell had been placed on the weapons. But why?

From the corner of my eye, I could see that Tamra was as vexed as I, and her grin had long since disappeared.

The spears were only mildly uncomfortable. Next to them were a row of halberds, their axe-blades polished, glittering. But when I lowered my hand to one of the heavy brass halberds, I thought my stomach would empty on the spot.

Clunk. I pulled away so suddenly that one of the lower and shorter halberds rolled out of its resting place and struck the floor.

Even Gilberto turned toward me, his eyebrows raised.

Despite the look, I left the halberd on the floor. Damned if I was about to risk disgracing myself on the spot by losing what remained of my breakfast.

I waved him off, moving from the edged weapons toward the pistols. I'd never seen one up close, but Magister Kerwin had mentioned them in history, noting their limited effectiveness in warfare because of their unreliability at any distance and the problems created by their complexity, especially their susceptibility to chaos-magic.

I didn't even have to touch them. They were just as unfriendly, although I watched Myrten fondling one almost lovingly. So I admired their carved handles and blued steel and barely let my fingers pass over them, walking down that weapons rack toward the next.

On the next were various clubs. I tried several, relieved that I could at least pick them up. Not one felt comfortable, but my stomach didn't do flip-flops, either. The metal ones, like the mace, and 'the morningstar, screamed at me to leave well enough alone. After the experience with the halberd, Gilberto's instructions or not, I left them alone.

Next to the clubs were some coiled ropes. They felt all right, only faintly repugnant—but what could you do with a rope? How was it even a weapon? Then there were some sort of polished handles connected by heavy cords. Same thing there—I could handle them, but couldn't imagine how they worked.

Finally, I came to the staves. Surprisingly, there were two dark ones, of a polished dark brown wood—darkened white oak, rather than black oak or black lorken, like my staff. Also unlike my own staff, which Talryn had suggested most strongly that I leave in my room during instruction periods, none of the staves were bound in metal, although their finish was almost as fine as that which Uncle Sardit had imparted to my staff. One staff, which I took, nearly matched my own in length. The other was somewhat shorter. Both were the first weapons, if a staff were a weapon, that hadn't made me uncomfortable.

With the longer staff in hand, I looked at the remaining section of the last rack, which contained truncheons. One, more like a short staff, although it was pitch-black, beckoned almost as much as the full-length staff. I held it for a while, then returned it.

Tamra walked toward the staves. Her feet dragged, as if she wanted no part of them. Her lips were pressed tightly together, and she carried no weapon.

Beyond her, I could see Krystal standing by a brown leather sitting pillow, almost fondling the deadly sword. Myrten sat, examining the pistol which he had taken from the racks.

Sammel carried a pair of matched truncheons, and Wrynn was still poking around the blades.

My eyes shifted back to Tamra. Her forehead glistened with a layer of perspiration as she picked up a steel mace with iron spikes. The mace head was nearly the size of hers. Her lips tightened until I could see the whiteness in them even from five cubits away. Slowly, she set the mace back in the rack.

I had to admire her strength, even if she were far more stubborn than I. But why did she put herself through that kind of torture? It was torture; that was certain. Her hands were almost shaking by the time she finally reached the staves.

"Think it's amusing, do you?" Tamra's voice was like molten lead.

I shook my head. She didn't have to prove anything to me, and she certainly didn't owe any sort of proof to the Brotherhood.

She looked right through me as she picked up the other dark staff. The tension in her body eased, but the frown remained, like a line chiseled above the ice-blue eyes. Unlike some redheads, or Dorthae, Tamra didn't darken her eyebrows, and she seemed to scorn any kind of adornment except the colored scarves she wore.

"Tamra . . . Lerris . . . are you finished admiring your weapons?" Gilberto's voice was dry.

"Admiring is not the word I would have chosen," observed Tamra, her voice cold enough now to chill warm fruit juice—instantly.

Gilberto ignored her comments, stood there waiting, holding a short black baton in his hand, the length of a truncheon, as I scrambled to a pillow next to Krystal.

Tamra sauntered toward a pillow at the other side of the group, each step slow and deliberate. Gilberto waited. I would have clobbered her . . . with something. He just gave a slow and lazy smile, and I shivered.

Tamra smiled back sweetly.

Krystal giggled.

Gilberto turned to the group even before Tamra seated herself. "The weapons you have in your hands are the weapons most suited to your temperament." Gilberto's voice was dry. "That does not mean they are the best weapons for your defense—right now. If you choose to learn them, they will become the best weapons for your defense." The weapons-master surveyed the group, as if asking for questions.

"You keep talking about defense," asked Tamra. "Is your purpose only to teach us self-defense?"

Gilberto hesitated, glancing toward the open doorway to the tunnel through which we had entered, as if looking for Talryn. Finally, he answered. "Anything used as a defense can be a weapon. Violence is not the way of Recluce, or of the Brotherhood. You may use what we are able to teach you in any way you wish." He smiled faintly. "Those who find more joy in using weapons than in avoiding their use will appreciate Hamor or Candar."

Once again, one of the Brothers really hadn't answered the question. I was finding the lack of direct answers tiresome. I might conceivably be a child, but certainly none of the others were. Yet Gilberto treated all of us as if we couldn't be trusted to understand a complete answer.

"What do you mean by that?" snapped Dorthae. "You're not talking to children."

Gilberto shrugged, lifting his shoulders with an exaggerated care. "Very few people in Recluce enjoy weapons. The opposite is true in Hamor and Candar. If you enjoy using weapons for more than exercise, you probably belong in Candar or Hamor."

Krystal giggled . . . again. Her hair was up, this time in golden cords, and instead of playing with it, her fingers ran along the sword blade. For some reason, I remembered how surgically she used a knife at meals.

Wrynn frowned. She carried a brace of throwing knives.

Gilberto paused while he looked us over again. "Here . . . you will get exercise, and you will learn weapons, beginning with the ones you have picked out. Not those exact ones, but the same type."

"Why not these?" asked Myrten, grasping his pistol tightly.

"They're enchanted to seek affinities . . . which reduces their effectiveness. Now, please put them back where you found them, and I'll take you to the student armory, where you will be issued a set of weapons based around the one you chose."

The whole business seemed odd. Why have us choose weapons at all? Certainly the Brotherhood could have told who was suited for what weapons. Why did they bother? And what was the basis for deciding who was "suited" for what?

"What is the basis for these 'affinities'?" I asked, as Gilberto started to turn toward the other doorway—the one across from where we had entered.

"Your underlying character is the most important thing. If you have training with a weapon that is not suited to your character, that can confuse the issue, but Talryn indicated that was not the case for any of you."

"How would he know?" asked Wrynn.

Gilberto shrugged. "I just teach weapons. The masters know what they know."

He wasn't telling all he knew, but what else was new? That didn't exactly surprise me. Gilberto walked toward the doorway, then turned to wait for us to put back the charmed weapons.

I got up to return the staff. I liked mine better.

Tamra didn't look at anyone as she walked across the springy greenish floor toward the racks. Krystal took a long time to let go of the sword.

Staying more than a respectful distance behind Tamra, I followed.

The practice weapons were scarred, but sound. The cutting weapons had rounded edges, from what I could see, since I received a club, a truncheon, and a staff. As far as I could tell, only Tamra, Sammel and I received no edged weapons at all.

XII

Gilberto had been right about one thing. Training with the weapons was hard, and not just physically. Who ever would have thought about the proper ways to hold a truncheon? The staff . . . I guess I saw that as more like a sword or an unpointed spear . . . anything that long clearly required technique.

Almost all of what I learned was new, and with all the repetition in the lectures, the weapons classes were usually the most interesting.

"Lerris, used properly, that truncheon is a far more effective weapon than a knife. *Used properly* . . . you're holding it like . . ." Gilberto broke off and shrugged. "I cannot even make a comparison."

Most training sessions were like that. Initially, nothing I did was right. The same was true of almost everyone—except Tamra and Krystal. Gilberto said almost nothing to Tamra, except occasional suggestions. Krystal he paid more attention to, but not much. As far as any kind of blade went, she picked up what he had in mind immediately.

Me . . . it was like I had two left thumbs.

"Lerris, stop fighting yourself . . . just *relax.*"

How many times I heard those words, I don't recall; but hear them I did, time after time.

Once we had some basic idea of what we were doing, Gilberto began pairing us off—first against him, or one of his apprentices; then, occasionally, against each other.

Eventually I found myself facing Tamra, not exactly in the field I had wanted.

We stood on opposite sides of a white practice circle on the spongy green flooring. Outside, the late summer sky was overcast, which was the exception rather than the rule, and the light filtering through the long and high wall windows was grayish.

Tamra smiled. Her face lit up when she smiled, but it was not a pleasant light at all. "Rules, Magister Gilberto?" The fingers of her heavy padded gloves tightened on the hard wood of the practice staff—the center part that was unpadded. Not that the padding on the ends was all that heavy. Her eyes were on me, as if she were studying some insect or a painting on a wall.

A wisp of her flame-red hair peeked from under the leather and wood of the padded practice helmet.

"Tamra . . ." began Gilberto. Then he shook his head. "No blows to face, knees, elbows or groin."

"I can live with that," announced the redhead.

I thought I could, also, but I didn't like the look in Tamra's eyes, or the instinctive ease with which she took her balanced stance. Then, again, I overtopped her by nearly a head and probably had twice her physical strength. And I hadn't done that badly against Demorsal, one of Gilberto's apprentices, over the past days.

Besides, Tamra deserved anything I could land on her, the arrogant bitch. Always so damned superior, as if she didn't really belong with mere dangergeld trainees.

"Two to one she takes him . . ." Myrten's raspy whisper annoyed me more than the bet. He laid odds on everything.

I couldn't see as well as I would have liked. The helmet restricted my peripheral vision, but I felt as though Myrten had rasped his bet at Sammel. Sammel shook his head.

"Start when I tell you. And stop at the bell. Do you understand? Ready?" Gilberto stepped out of the circle, then glanced at Tamra. "Tamra?"

She nodded.

"Lerris?"

"Yes." I nodded without taking my eyes off Tamra. I didn't see why everyone thought a match between Tamra and me was such a big deal. She clearly had more experience, but I was stronger, and almost as quick.

Myrten probably bet on her because I'd trounced him in the last round. At least I was halfway decent at *something*.

"Go!"

Tamra circled to my right. I pivoted.

Thwack. I barely managed to throw my staff up to block her first thrust.

Thwack . . . thwack . . . thwack . . .

I danced back, still on the defensive.

Thwack . . . thwack . . . thwunk

". . . oooofff . . ." Her last blow crashed into my lower-right ribs. Her staff moved like lightning bolts, flashing this way, forking back, always probing.

Thwack . . . thwunk . . .

Another blow . . . to my ribs on the left.

Thwack . . .

Fwooopp . . . My staff slipped past hers and bounced off her upper leg.

THWUNK . . .

I could feel the floor rising at me, but there wasn't anything I could do about the momentary blackness and the stars that greeted me.

". . . poor bastard . . ."

". . . sufficient, I trust, Magister Gilberto?"

I squinted and sat up, trying to still the swirling inside my brain.

"Sufficient, Tamra." Gilberto's voice was dry. "Are you all right, Lerris?"

My head felt like a log flayed out of its bark. My ribs were an unbroken ache, and Tamra was almost openly smirking. "Fine. Just fine." Standing up required most of my remaining strength.

"Why don't you take a hot shower?" suggested the weapons-master.

I didn't even argue. Most of the time, whether the water was luke-warm or warm didn't seem to matter. The idea of hot water, another luxury enjoyed by the Brotherhood in Nylan, never seemed more welcome.

"Krystal . . . Wrynn . . . long knives . . . use the wooden ones."

73

My feet found their way, somehow, to the lockers where I stripped off the padding and the loose exercise clothing that I'd been supplied.

"She was a little hard on you." Demorsal was leaning against the wall.

". . . Ummmmm . . ." The tunic was halfway over my head.

"But that's because you're fighting yourself, and you don't even want to admit it."

"Not you, too?" I pulled off the tunic. "Just what the hell do you mean? Everyone keeps telling me not to fight myself."

"I shouldn't tell you . . . Talryn says that we all have to discover ourselves."

"Talryn be damned," I muttered, sitting on the bench and pulling off the soft exercise pants. I was going to be sore—really sore, shower or no shower. "At least, tell me how to keep from getting killed the next time."

Demorsal grinned. His black eyes twinkled. "I just did." He wasn't much taller than Tamra, but she never seemed to lay a staff on him. Neither did I, but he didn't hit me except lightly.

"I'm stupid. Tell me in another way."

"You got decked when you tried to attack. Every time. Why?"

I shook my head. I wished I hadn't, and put it between my hands to keep it from coming off.

"I'll ask it another way. Why did Tamra hit you the hardest when you attacked? Why don't I hit you hard when we spar? You leave openings, you know, especially when you try to attack."

"I don't know," I groaned. Questions I didn't need, not when my head was pounding.

"Because I have the same problem. I can't attack."

About that time I finally realized what he was saying. Finally. "Is that why I wasn't allowed edged weapons?"

Demorsal looked around the lockers. "You believe in order. You have to. Use of weapons conflicts with order. For you to make an attack, you have to fight yourself first, then your opponent. You can't help getting clobbered that way."

I looked at him. "Tamra uses a staff, and she clobbered me."

"She's a little crazy, but think about it . . . she hit you hardest when you attacked . . . and I've probably said too much. Hope you feel better." The senior apprentice turned as I stood up to head for the showers.

The pieces fit, but I didn't like it. Then again, I didn't have to like it. If I wanted to survive, I just had to adapt to my own limitations. But I didn't have to like it. I certainly didn't.

XIII

When I had free time, usually in the afternoon of our rest days—every eighth day of the Temple calendar—I still walked down to the harbor area in Nylan, checking the scattered ships from across the oceans, seeing how many countries traded with Recluce and how.

Were they using steel-hulled steamers, or wooden-framed square-riggers? I never saw anything resembling a galley, although Magister Cassius indicated some coastal states to the far southwest of Candar, the ones around the smaller Western Ocean, operated slave galleys for coastal defense forces.

I always looked for the telltale sign of concealing screens and for the black ships of the Brotherhood that no one ever talked about. I didn't talk about them either, since I wasn't about to admit I had seen them unless someone else already said something. None of our dangergeld instructors did.

It was the same old story. If I asked about something and they didn't want to talk about it, the answers were always platitudes or so vague that I already knew most of what they said.

Still, I kept visiting the harbor—usually alone—with some of my dangergeld funds, just in case I found something useful. I hadn't, but that didn't mean I wouldn't.

Once Krystal and I went together, on a sunny and cloudless afternoon. A brisk wind was blowing in from the west, so stiff it tugged at our tunics and hair. Krystal had bound her hair up, with the silver cords this time.

Crackkk . . . *thrappp* . . . *crackk* . . . The canvas on the outside trading tables cracked almost like trees breaking in a storm as we walked through the center of the market square. Less than half the

75

booths on the Recluce side of the square were occupied, and but a handful on the outland side. A man in pale green browsed at the woodworker's stall, and the same youngster sat on the stool. I grinned, but he continued to watch the customer.

Just a handful of people, mostly dangergelders or members of the Brotherhood, wandered around the square.

"There's a weapons table."

"You want to see what's there?" I asked. "It won't be as good as what you have."

Without stopping, Krystal looked sideways at me, raising a dark eyebrow on a face more tanned than when she had arrived in Nylan. Her natural pace nearly matched mine, despite the difference in our height. "What I have? I have nothing except a belt knife and a small cutting knife. You expect me to step out in Hamor or Candar with those alone?"

"Sorry."

Krystal stopped in front of the table.

On light-blue felt were laid out a number of blades. A thin man with a waxed mustache, ropy arms, and a gray leather vest sat on a stool opposite us. His expressionless black eyes met mine.

I looked through him. After all, I wasn't shopping for blades.

Crackkk . . . The canvas of an empty table snapped in the wind, and the sting of salt air brushed my face.

The proprietor transferred his unspoken demand to Krystal, who had lifted one of the thinner blades, the plainest one on the table. Even to me, it was the best. Not that I really wanted to even touch it.

"You like that one?" His deep voice was flat, almost expressionless, like his eyes.

She set the blade back on the felt. "I prefer this style . . . to . . ." she gestured at a scimitar with a swirled and gilded hilt and guard. "Do you have any others like it?"

In the hands of the dark-skinned trader appeared two other blades. Around one glimmered scabrous blood-red force-swirls. Just looking at that unpatterned display turned my guts.

Krystal reached for it.

"No! Not that one." I spoke before realizing it. But I didn't want her even to touch the blade, not with the real hint of evil embodied in the chaos. For the first time I saw, really *saw*, a clear distinction between honest chaos and true evil.

76

Crackkk . . . The flapping canvas punctuated the moment.

Krystal frowned, but her hand stopped short of the hilt.

"It is said to be cursed," admitted the trader. His voice was still flat.

My eyes focused on him, as they had on the blade, but discerned nothing, not that I would have known what to look for.

"Try the other one . . ." I suggested.

"You're telling me about swords?" Krystal's voice was anything but musical, almost waspish.

I shrugged. "The pattern's . . ." How could I tell her what I saw? How can you say that a pattern of force-swirls that no one else sees says that the sword will lead its wielder from chaos into depravity . . . or worse? How can you describe a set of unseen forces that are so chaotic that their only coherence is opposition to order? I had to shrug again. "Please . . . Krystal . . . just trust me."

An odd look, one I couldn't identify, passed across her face and was gone.

The trader looked at me. "You are an apprentice master, then?"

His flat voice bothered me. Something was missing, although I couldn't say what. "I am what I am," was my answer—conceding nothing, admitting nothing.

He inclined his head slightly, but waited for Krystal.

"Lerris . . . what about the other blade?" This time she made no movement toward the sword.

The second blade, slightly smaller, showed no force-swirls, only the honesty of forged metal.

"It's an honest blade, not turned to any use."

Krystal took it gingerly, then examined it in more detail, studying the metal in the sunlight. She did all the things with blades that people who like them do to discover whether they might be right for them, like flexing them and waving them around, and balancing them to determine whether they are hilt-heavy or blade-heavy.

She liked it, that I could tell.

So I studied the trader. Assuming most people had a soul, or that inner spark that passes for it, he didn't. There was no life beyond the physical, and I tried not to shiver.

That didn't make his wares either good or bad, but it meant looking them over most carefully, and I wasn't sure I was the one to do that. But the blade seemed all right.

Krystal set the sword on the felt, slowly.

"How much?" I asked.

"Ten gold pennies."

Krystal looked at the blade. "It's good, but you could buy a Recluce ordered blade and a scabbard for that."

"It's not ordered."

I understood immediately. "That's an advantage in Candar, but not for us." I shrugged, and started to turn.

"Eight . . ."

"It doesn't matter," Krystal said quietly.

"Six . . ."

The west wind picked up, swirling my short hair.

Cracckkk . . . crackkkk . . .

"Five and a silver," suggested the trader.

"Four and two silvers," I countered.

"Done, apprentice." His voice was still flat.

"Lerris . . ."

I ignored Krystal, knowing she could not pay for the blade; but she had not had anyone to help her, and I did not think my mother would have minded.

"But . . ."

The trader placed the sword in a cheap scabbard.

I dug out the price in coins, marveling that I had even thought to bring enough.

Crackkk . . .

The trader's eyes kept darting toward me. He took the coins as if he wanted us to leave, without a nod, and I gave the sword and scabbard to Krystal.

"Lerris . . ." She tried to push it back at me.

I pulled my hands away, gambling that she wouldn't want to drop the blade. "Let's go. We can talk on the way."

As we started toward the harbor wall, the trader began to pack his wares, hurriedly, but I ignored him, looking at Krystal. I wondered how he had gotten the devil-blade into the square, but that wasn't my real concern at the moment.

"It's yours."

"I can't take it."

"It's yours," I repeated. "You need a blade, and you need it before you end up in Candar or Hamor."

"I can't . . ."

"Krystal . . . you need it. I know you need it, and you know that. Call it a favor. Call it a loan. Call it anything you want."

She stopped. We were opposite the fourth pier, the one closest to the market square, and only a small sloop without an ensign was tied up. "We need to talk."

"How about here?" I pulled myself up on the black stone wall. As I scrambled around, I scanned the harbor. Besides the sloop and an old sailing ship with a combination of masts I couldn't identify, the harbor was empty. Not even a sign of a Brotherhood ship.

She set the scabbard and blade on the flat stones and vaulted up next to me. We sat with our backs to the water, facing a two-story building of black oak and black stone. The sign over the locked double doors read, in three languages it seemed, "Supplies." The first line, in black, was Temple Script. The second was in green, which suggested Nordla, and the third was in purple, edged with gold.

It was funny, when you thought about it, that Candar and Recluce shared the old Temple Tongue, although there were people in all cities who did, since it was the main trade language, while Nordla and Hamor had totally separate languages. I would have expected Candar to have its own language.

I suppose that was why Magistra Trehonna insisted we learn a little of Nordlan and Hamorian.

"Lerris." Krystal's voice was insistent, breaking my reverie, overriding the *lap, lap, lap* of the waves against the stone sea wall.

I shifted on the hard stone, turning toward her, but letting my feet dangle. She was already cross-legged.

"You didn't have to do that. It's not as though . . . I mean, I see how you look at Tamra . . ."

"Tamra . . . what does she have to do with anything? She's an arrogant bitch."

Krystal smiled faintly, but she didn't giggle. She just waited, and the water lapped against the stones, and the wind gusted through my hair and pulled strands of hers from the silver-cords, softening her straight strong features in the afternoon light.

The sun felt warm on my back, not unpleasantly so, and I waited to see if she had anything else to say. It was simple. She needed a sword, and I could help. I couldn't help the world, and I wouldn't help people who didn't make an effort. I guess I agreed at least partly with Wrynn.

"Lerris?"

"Yes."

"Why?"

I shrugged. "Because you don't ask. Because I like you. Because you take me for what I am. Because you don't hide behind half-truths and platitudes. Lots of reasons, I guess."

She shook her head. "What do you think will happen to me?"

"I don't know."

Krystal looked down at the rectangular stones, black granite, that paved the road to the piers. The seawall where we sat was made of the same stone. "I don't think I'm meant to stay in Recluce . . ."

I felt the same way about Krystal, but couldn't say why. So I didn't. I'd seen her lose herself in fencing with Gilberto. Already, he was hard-pressed by Krystal—and he had the experience. "What will you do?"

She didn't answer me. Instead, we sat there quietly.

"It's mine! Mine!"

From around the corner where the supply store faced the pier dashed two youngsters—a boy and a girl. The girl was running lightly ahead of an older or bigger boy, waving something in her hand.

"You give that back . . ."

The girl stopped at the dark wooden bench before the closed exchange. I wondered how you obtained currency or drafts or whatever traders needed that way on rest days.

"All right. Here's your stinky model. Let's go out on the pier."

"You go. I'm going home." The dark-haired boy tucked the model into his near-empty pack.

"Oh, come on." The redhead smiled at him.

"I'm going home."

"Just for a moment?"

"Oh . . . all right. But there's nothing there but that little ship."

"So?"

The two walked past where we sat with only a passing glance, the girl almost skipping above the stones, the stocky boy plodding after her.

"There we go . . ." I didn't know why I said those words, but that was the way I felt.

Krystal glanced over at me. She shook her head slowly.

I shrugged. That was the way I felt. "We ought to be going."

And we did, but neither of us exactly danced back to the dining hall and the chimes that announced the evening meal.

XIV

As the summer drew to a close, some things improved.

As far as weapons practice went, Demorsal had been right. So long as I concentrated just on defense with the staff, nothing happened and I got better—so much better that even Gilberto couldn't break through. Then he taught me how to use the staff against blades, and that was interesting. Why a swordsman would ever want to take on someone trained with a long staff was beyond me, but Gilberto assured me that some would. So I listened. Even there, I could barely make one move toward him.

I was almost disappointed that he didn't pair me against Tamra, but he just grunted and said, "You're as good as you'll ever need to be with the staff and truncheons. Now you need to learn about blades."

That was worse than the staff had been. Every inch of my body seemed to have welts from the wooden blades. I must have used more hot water in two eight-days than in my whole life.

This time I improved faster, though, because I decided my whole use of any blade was to weave an impenetrable defense. I'd never hold out against a really skilled blade-master, but the idea was to learn enough to defend against the common ruffian types.

Gilberto insisted I learn attacks.

I was terrible. "Why bother?"

He insisted. "There are times when an attack is a defense, and your body will recognize those times. You need to learn these automatically."

Occasionally, as a respite, he let me spar with the staff against Krystal and Myrten and Dorthae. That was more for their benefit, in case they were faced with a staff, but it was still interesting. Only

81

Krystal ever came close to touching me. Of course, I couldn't attack much, but occasionally I found I could tap them lightly in embarrassing places.

Krystal laughed.

Myrten looked more like an angry buffalo. "Think it's funny, do you . . . ?"

I couldn't help grinning, and, strangely, he grinned back. "Young-old magister, you're still a good kid . . ."

A good kid? Not sure I ever would have called myself that. Or a magister. Me? But . . .

Outside of the physical training, things got worse . . . or didn't improve.

Magistra Trehonna left, and was replaced by a smiling man named Lennett, who immediately launched into discussions on the theory of order. The theory of order? Who cared about the theory of order?

Magister Lennett did, it turned out. And he insisted that we did, especially Tamra and me. Tamra smiled sweetly and asked polite questions.

"Does that mean that a chaos magician must employ order?" Her voice was almost dipped in honey as she leaned toward him. She eased forward on the gray pillow where she sat.

How she had found a gray pillow, I didn't know. The rest of us used brown.

"Exactly!" bubbled Lennett. His eyes danced.

My stomach turned at the sickly-sweet tone.

"Even to manipulate chaos requires the use of order. In essence, a chaos magician sets up a fundamental conflict by his veryexistence—"

"They are at war within themselves?" asked Tamra.

That was obvious, but why did Tamra keep playing up to him?

". . . why chaos magicians have short life-spans unless they use other methods to artificially prolong their existence; and few have the talent. Fewer still can master the order-chaos conflict on that plane."

I thought about reading the book my father had tucked away, but I never got around to it. Besides, in traveling, I suspected, I would have more than enough time to read.

". . . and—Lerris!"

"Yes?"

"Can you explain the magic-reality strength theorem?"

I repressed a sigh. "That's the idea that the greater the magical composition of a construct, the less strength it has compared to something made out of natural materials by hand, rather than by magic."

"And what does that mean?" Lennett smiled and looked around the room.

Myrten was running his hand through his unruly black hair, while Dorthae looked at Myrten, and Krystal looked toward the afternoon clouds. Sammel tried to stifle a yawn.

Tamra smiled brightly. "It means that magic can diffuse strength or material over a greater area, but cannot build things that last."

So . . . what else was new? Chaos-magic was great for destroying things, but you still had to hire stonecutters and masons to build anything.

"That is not precisely correct, as you"—he glanced from Tamra to me—"will discover."

Myrten snickered.

"Order magic can be used to enhance natural strength, both by providing a defense against chaos and by strengthening the internal order of substances." Magister Lennett shook his head. "But that is really a subject of advanced study. The important point, as Tamra has noted, is that an equivalently-armed individual can prevail against a number of magical constructs, provided . . . *provided* you are adequately trained and weaponed."

"Magister?" asked Sammel. "What about cases like the power of the ancient wizards of Frven? Or the White Knights?"

Lennett shook his head. "You are confusing two aspects of chaos. In pure destruction or chaos magic—that is, loosening the bonds of order which hold all materials together—chaos cannot be successfully opposed except by three factors. First is will. Your will to survive prevents any direct magical attack on your person except by the strongest of the chaos-magicians. You are still subject to temptation, and that is another issue entirely. Second is the natural strength of materials. A young person generally has greater resistance to magic, as does a building built of the strongest stone and best-braced timbers. Third is order magic itself, which can suffuse all things with a strengthening of internal bonds . . ."

What Lennet said was probably true enough, but it was also generally meaningless. Only a strong magician would ever try a personal attack. Anyone using magical constructs would not employ them unless they were equipped with superior weapons. The White Knights

83

had swords that would have made most great warriors damned near invincible. I remembered that from my lessons with Magister Kerwin.

". . . the greatest strength of chaos is its ability to thwart complexity . . ."

"Is that why most nations don't use much steam machinery?" Tamra smiled brightly once again.

Wrynn snorted audibly.

I tried to relax. Theory was fine, but I for one was getting very tired both of Tamra's phoniness, and of Magister Lennett's enthusiasm for explaining the obvious and avoiding the explanations behind the obvious. What was order magic? How did it strengthen internal bonds? Why did no one admit to practicing it? For that matter, how did chaos magic work?

Magister Lennett kept asking questions, and I began to think about Candar, about what I would have to do, and what I might face there.

84

XV

From the beginning—or at least it had seemed that way to me—we had been destined for Candar. But understanding that, and finding out that we would actually be leaving Recluce, were two entirely different things.

We all waited in the same room where we had first gathered after entering Nylan. This time, each of us went in to see Talryn separately.

The dark oak-paneled walls seemed even gloomier the second time around, and the pictures of the two masters on the wall seemed to have a more knowing look to them, almost as if they had a secret they weren't about to share.

I knew that was nonsense, but when I looked at the man in black I wanted to shiver. I didn't look at the woman. She reminded me of Tamra, for all that there was no physical resemblance.

Sammel went in, and he didn't come out. I presumed that he left through the other doorway. Then Talryn called for Dorthae, followed by Wrynn and Myrten. Krystal and Tamra each sat on a bench. Krystal sat on the edge, ready to stand up in an instant. I understood.

I wasn't about to sit anywhere. I still didn't know much more than when I had arrived early in the summer, although I was in better shape and knew enough about half-a-dozen weapons to get myself into real trouble.

What I didn't know was why I was being sent from Recluce. Oh, they'd all explained how I was a danger to the order of our wonderful island nation. But not one had explained exactly why.

"Krystal . . ." Talryn waited by the half-open black oak door.

Krystal stood up slowly.

"Good luck," I said softly.

She gave me a faint smile, then a shrug.

Talryn's face remained professionally cheerful, like that of a dedicated executioner.

Click.

Tamra glanced up at me from the bench. Unlike Krystal, she was almost casual, half-draped along the dark wood. The sharp blue of her scarf and the brightness of her hair made her seem somehow out of place in the somber setting of the anteroom. "Fond of older women?"

"No. Just like women." I was so damned tired of her edges. She didn't want to understand anything, just to use it. "Particularly women who don't mind admitting that they're women."

"Oh . . . the submissive kind."

I shook my head, not bothering to look at her. "Good as you are, Tamra, Krystal could cut you into little pieces. That's not submissive, not by chaos or by order. Krystal is my friend. That was the way she wanted it."

"So you're the submissive one, then." She half-smiled, stretching out on the bench, cat-like.

I didn't bother answering. Tamra would twist . . . use . . . anything I said. Instead I studied the stone underfoot, trying to touch the patterns of its existence, trying to trace out the hidden breaks in the stone. According to Magister Lennett, all materials had patterns. The wood I understood, and, were I ever to work it again, that understanding would allow me to craft more finely than most journeymen. The heavier materials—like slate, marble, granite, iron—were tougher.

85

The stone floors in Nylan were different. All the stone used by the Brotherhood was different. The hidden breaks weren't there, and each paving stone seemed complete by itself, yet fitted into a larger pattern. Worked metal felt that way, but not most stone.

"Tamra." Talryn merely announced her name.

As she sat up, rather abruptly, I thought about looking up to see her leave, but kept my head down. She'd just turn my concern against me.

Click.

Alone in the anteroom, I finally sat down under the picture of the woman master. Why did I even care about Tamra? Krystal needed me more than Tamra, didn't she? Tamra didn't need anyone, except to insult them in order to feel superior. She was good at that, because she was better than anyone else, both in brains and physical skills. So why did she have to keep proving it?

"Lerris." Talryn's voice was calm, and this time he wasn't smiling.

I took a deep breath and rose, wishing I had my staff with me. Everything was packed, but waiting, in the room that had been home for the late spring and long summer.

He held the door open for me, then closed it. I stood by the table where we had eaten so many eight-days earlier.

"Sit down, Lerris." Talryn took the same chair, the one at the head of the long table.

I pulled out the heavy black-oak chair. This time it moved easily. I said nothing, waiting for Talryn to say whatever he had to say, since whatever I thought clearly didn't matter.

"You could be a problem, Lerris. You keep expecting someone to hand you the answers. Life isn't like that. Neither is the dangergeld. Because you demand answers and reasons, no one wants to give them to you."

I tried not to sigh. Another lecture I didn't need.

"So I will. We've discussed it. You may not believe me now, but try at least to remember what I'm about to say. It *might* save your life."

I almost smiled at the melodramatic touch, but decided to listen. It couldn't hurt.

Talryn waited.

Finally, I nodded.

"First, you are a potential order-master. You have the talents to be a chaos-master, but not the disposition. You aren't contemptuous enough, and you never will be. Trying the chaos path will leave you dying young in Candar, if it doesn't kill you outright.

"Second, you're strong enough to tempt most chaos-masters into trying to corrupt you. Third, you refuse to understand that each master must find his or her own meaning in life." Talryn sighed. The master in silver actually sighed. "Finally, what we're doing is unfair to you."

"You admit that?" I couldn't help asking.

"We admit it."

"Then why are you doing it? I don't understand."

"Because your doubts and your open skepticism are enough to disrupt anyone who spends much time with you. Normally, two masters work with each dangergeld group. Sometimes only one."

Talryn, Trehonna, Gilberto, Cassius, and Lennett—not to mention the occasional appearances by others—that totaled five, plus apprentices like Demorsal.

"Four . . . five perhaps. It took that many to keep your efforts damped, and we'll all have to work that much harder for another year to catch up."

"Why?"

Talryn sighed again. "You have great potential, Lerris—for order or chaos. How you use it is your choice. That choice is not simple. Not at all."

I opened my mouth.

Talryn raised his hand. "Let me explain. The reason *why* you call upon order or chaos is meaningless. If you destroy a tree for firewood to warm a freezing child, you have still given yourself to chaos. Likewise, if you heal a murderer, you give yourself to order."

"What?" I couldn't believe what Talryn was saying.

"That's why handling order is so difficult. You have to have good intent, and using chaos for a good purpose leads to greater disorder."

I still couldn't believe him. "I couldn't even fell a tree to save a child?"

Talryn smiled sadly. "I didn't say that. I said you could not use chaos forces. You could use an ax or a sword to cut branches. Where physical force doesn't affect human life, it doesn't affect order or chaos either."

I shook my head.

"Oh . . . it's worse than that, Lerris. Far worse." His tone was almost mocking. "What I said is not *quite* true. You can occasionally use chaos in service of order—but only when balanced by higher-order considerations. Indeed . . . if you choose to serve order, you may have to. If you wish to be an order-master, every use of order must be calculated. You may be lucky. You may intuitively understand those balances, but without being able to check such intuition logically, how will you be able to tell the differences between what is intuitively correct and your underlying desires—and we all have them—to take the easier path?"

"You're asking for . . . a man . . . a woman . . . someone who is perfect . . ."

"Didn't I tell you we were being unfair?" asked Talryn softly. His tone was not mocking now, just soft.

I looked down at the polished surface of the table. "Are you done?"

"Not yet. I have to lay our charge upon you. It seems simple. It is not. You must travel Candar beyond the Easthorns to the Westhorns, and you must not return until you feel you are ready. You must also travel alone; that is, not in company of anyone else from Recluce."

"What the hell does that mean?" I think I glared at Talryn.

He met my glare. "You will know what it means. Do you have any more questions?"

I had lots of them, but they were the kind I couldn't ask. Why me? What did I ever do? Why didn't anyone ever try to explain things? Why was everything either on faith or through experience I didn't have? Why did they train us together and then say not to travel together? "No. None that make any difference."

"All right." He stood up, tired-looking, the first time I had seen him show any really human feelings. "I will not see you until you return. We wish you well, Lerris. The rest of your group is waiting. Your ship leaves shortly."

"Now what?"

"You pick up your things and walk to the pier where the *Eidolon* waits." He gestured toward the other door, also of black oak, but did not move.

I nodded. "Thank you for your frankness. I hope I can use it."

The gray man said nothing, just watched me. So I took the hint, inclined my head, and walked away from Talryn.

Would we be traveling in the strange black Brotherhood ships that everyone ignored? Or in the hull of some Candarian duchy's freighter? From what Talryn had said, I still didn't know.

There was so much I didn't know. Even Talryn had behaved as though he were bending some great rule or tradition to say what he had said. He believed it—that was for sure, and that made it a little scary. Never to use a destructive power . . . even in the service of good?

I shivered. My feet carried me down the long underground hallway, well enough lit by the late afternoon sun, and the green of the gardens beckoned through the overhead glass. But I still shivered.

XVI

Talryn was right. Sammel, Myrten, Dorthae, Wrynn, and Krystal all stood outside, waiting. The late-afternoon westerly swished the leaves of the red oak under which they had gathered. Behind us, the dangergelders' quarters loomed black even in the sunlight.

Sammel wore his pack and a pair of shortswords—short staves, a closer look revealed. Myrten wore no obvious weapons, nor did Dorthae. Wrynn had on her belt both a short sword and a throwing knife. A second knife was concealed in the hidden thigh-pocket of her trousers.

Krystal wore her faded blues and the blade I had bought her, although she had replaced the cheap scabbard with an older but sturdier one of hardened gray leather. She nodded at me.

I wiped my forehead and nodded back, then walked over to her.

"Talryn was hard on you," she observed.

"I'm fine." I really didn't want to talk about it.

"Tamra came out looking the same way."

"What about you?" I asked.

She didn't giggle, just smiled gravely. "He told me I might be happier in Candar, and to weigh what I really wanted carefully."

A cold weight settled in my guts.

"Are you all right?" As she spoke, her hand was warm on my shoulder.

"I'm fine."

"What did Talryn tell you?" Her voice was gentle, again musical.

I shrugged. "What he told everyone, I guess. That I had to find myself for myself. Except it's going to take a long time."

Krystal nodded. Her fingers squeezed my shoulder, then relaxed. "You'd better get your pack."

"Thank you." I didn't look at the others as I headed past Wrynn and Myrten and through the open doorway. One door was ajar—Tamra's. I didn't look inside.

In my former room, my things were where I had left them. The pack lay on the bed, the staff beside it, along with the knife—not that I expected to use the knife for anything besides cutting brush, meat, and other non-intelligent objects. My heavy cloak was rolled into the top of the pack. With the knife on my belt, I slung the pack half over my shoulder and picked up the staff. The door I left open as I left—a minor protest against the order of the Brotherhood.

90 Tamra had left her door open as well.

By the time I stepped outside—my feet moving from the smooth stones of the interior hall to the heavier, weathered, paving-stones of the walkway that would eventually lead to the harbor—everyone was waiting.

Waiting with Tamra and the rest was a woman I had not seen.

"My name is Isolde," she announced. "I will be your guide from here to Freetown." Her hair was silver-blond, cut squarely across the back of her neck, and her eyes were dark gray. She wore a faded green one-piece coverall and black boots. At her belt were a pair of knives, one on each hip. The belt was wide, of black leather with a triangular silver buckle. "The *Eidolon* is a Nordlan half-steamer registered out of Brysta. We have two cabins, which shouldn't be that much of a problem since Freetown isn't much more than a day and a half under normal conditions . . ."

Problem? Why would two cabins be a problem? I glanced over at Tamra, but the redhead was staring at the ground, ignoring Isolde and me. Even from nearly ten cubits away, I could see Tamra's fingers were white from how tightly they gripped her staff.

". . . make the transition easier, we have an inn in Freetown where you will all stay, assuming you wish to, tomorrow night. Once we reach the inn—it's only a short walk from the harbor—you'll receive a last briefing on the current conditions in Candar. Things like which provinces or duchies to avoid, and why.

"Two days from now, you'll be on your own. Any questions?"

". . . *Uhhhhmmmm?*" coughed Myrten. "Who pays the passage costs?"

"Those have been taken care of by the Brotherhood. So have your meals and lodging at the Travelers' Rest. After that, all expenses are yours." Isolde glanced around the group, looking for other questions.

"Why are we going on a Nordlan ship?" Wrynn's voice seemed to silence even the breeze.

"Why not?" Isolde's tone was amused. "The *Eidolon* is headed where you are going, and it's a lot cheaper than sending a Brotherhood ship on a special run."

"It also tells the world that Recluce is harsh enough to throw out its own." As she spoke, Tamra barely glanced toward Isolde.

The brittleness of Tamra's voice surprised me, as did its ragged sound. Was this the confident woman who had thrashed me so soundly with the staff in our initial sparring? The woman who understood order theory better than Magister Lennett?

"That is also partly true. By your actions or beliefs, you have chosen not to accept Recluce. Until you do, you are from Recluce, but not of Recluce."

I almost shivered. Isolde's matter-of-fact tone was more chilling than any of old Kerwin's lectures had been. No threats, no scare tactics—just a statement. Unless you believe, you don't belong.

Tamra glanced up from the grass, and I tried to catch her eyes. No wonder she was upset. All the excellence in the world didn't matter, only what she couldn't bring herself to accept. The redhead looked away, back toward the harbor.

"If there are no other questions, let's be on our way."

Slinging my pack onto both shoulders, I straightened, ready to leave. Sammel and Dorthae stood on each side of Isolde. Myrten picked up his pack.

Without another word, Isolde left, leading us straight down the main walkway, straight through a market square largely deserted, except for a pie vendor who was closing up and a sailor from somewhere stretched out on a table, sleeping.

The *Eidolon*, moored at pier number one, the one closest to the sea, carried one square-rigged mast and whatever they called a sloop's mast. A mizzenmast, I thought. Amidships, between the masts, were two paddle wheels, one on each side. A black stack, slashed with a diagonal green stripe, ran up between the masts as well. The sails were furled on the masts.

"Hello, the *Eidolon*!" called Isolde.

"Hallo . . . the pier . . ." A tall blond man waved vaguely.

Isolde didn't bother to call again, but walked up the steeply-inclined gangplank, leaving us to follow.

I followed right after her. Waiting wouldn't solve anything.

"Stand right over there," ordered our guide, pointing to a clear space of deck to the right of where the ship's officer waited.

I followed her directions and positioned myself by the railing. A quick glance toward Nylan reassured me that I could still see the market square, though most of the tables and booths had been deserted even before we had passed by on our way to the harbor.

". . . eight passengers, as agreed with Captain Heroulk . . ." Isolde started right in with the mate on duty, a man with a short blond beard and a sleeveless shirt that revealed heavily-muscled and bronzed arms.

At first, as I stood by the rail, I could smell nothing except a lingering scent of something—salt, soap, varnish. The deck was clean, aside from several coils of heavy rope by the foot of the masts. The railing, as my fingers brushed it, felt faintly tacky, and glistened as though recently varnished.

Two sailors stopped their work on a windlass, or something like it, to survey the group that had trooped on board.

"Witches, the whole lot . . ." observed the older, a wiry man with salt-and-pepper hair.

Clank. His hammer knocked the handle loose from the assembly.

". . . see if you can pry loose that broken edge . . ."

"The ship seems clean enough, if small," noted Myrten, stepping up next to me.

"Small?"

"Haven't you seen the Hamorian freighters? Some of them are nearly three hundred cubits long."

I shrugged, not really having thought about it.

"Good thing it's only a day and a half. I'd hate to go to Hamor on his. That would take nearly two eight-days."

Tamra stood by herself further down the rail toward the bow. I walked away from Myrten and stood next to her. She said nothing, just looked up at the black wall overlooking the harbor area, much as I had first looked at that same wall, wondering how it could look so insignificant from behind and so imposing from the waterfront.

"Are you all right?" I tried to keep my voice low.

"Does it matter?" She sounded tired.

"Yes."

"Why?"

I didn't know what to say. ". . . Because."

She didn't say anything. She just kept looking from the harbor wall to the hill wall and back again.

After a while, I eased away, thinking she wanted to be alone.

"Oh . . . sorry . . ." In backing up, I backed into Wrynn.

"Since it's only you, Lerris . . ."

I *thought* she was joking, but held up my free right hand, since I was still holding on to my staff with my left. "I apologize."

"We'll accept," added Krystal with a soft smile. She didn't giggle.

"All right!" interrupted Isolde. "Let's get your gear stowed. Follow us."

Wrynn shrugged. Krystal and I both shrugged back. All three of us followed Isolde and another officer—the officers were all taller than the crew, and had yellow collars on their sleeveless shirts—aft and down a narrow wooden staircase. The sailors all called it a ladder.

"I'll bunk with Sammel, Lerris, and Myrten," announced Isolde. "We'll take the first cabin."

Myrten's face went blank, as did Dorthae's. I thought Wrynn and Krystal nodded, but couldn't see for sure in the dimly-lit passageway.

The cabin was the size of a large pantry with four built-in bunks, two on each side, one above the other. Each bunk had a thin pallet covered with a faded linen sheet and a folded brown blanket—no other covers. The floor space between the bunks was less than three cubits. A single porthole graced the outboard side, opposite the door.

Two lockers fitted side-by-side under each lower bunk.

Isolde threw her pack on the top outboard bunk. "Lerris, you're the most agile. Why don't you take the other top bunk?"

Since it wasn't really a question, I put my pack up on the other top bunk.

"You can use the lockers. No one on the ship will steal anything." She glanced at me. "Please leave the staff on your bunk until we land."

Always the staff. I tucked it next to the pallet, then squeezed my pack into one of the lockers. Sammel eased his smaller pack into the other one.

Myrten was shaking his head as he knelt to get into the other locker.

"Is it all right if we go back on deck?" I asked.

"Of course. Just stay out of the crew's way."

So I went back up the ladder.

Whufff . . . whufff . . . Through the timbers I could feel the steam engine, as if the ship had come alive. A helmsman stood at the wheel on the bridge, flanked by a silvered and weathered man I took to be the captain, since his entire shirt was yellow.

"Lines aboard!"

"Lines aboard, sir!"

Clang!

"Pressure on the boilers! Stand by for paddles."

Thwap . . . splat . . . thwap . . . Slowly, ever so slowly, the paddles began to turn as the *Eidolon* eased off the pier.

I nearly tiptoed to the rail to watch the *Eidolon*'s departure.

Tamra stood by the same point on the rail as when I had left her. She must have gone below because both her staff and pack were absent, but her posture was the same.

With its black slate roofs, black streets, and black walls lit by the low western sun, and with the grass hidden behind walls, Nylan looked more than ever like a brooding fortress rising from the sea. Nothing reflected the reddish near-setting sun, except the water itself. In a way, the scene reminded me of one I'd seen in one of my father's history books—the White City of Frven, under the chaos-masters. But Frven had been all white, and it had perished. Nylan endured, its black order stolidly guarding Recluce.

A shimmer of distorted air caught the corner of my eye, and I turned my head to see one of the long and mastless black boats of the Brotherhood trailing the *Eidolon*. A single narrow turret gun bore on the Nordlan ship, shifting slightly as the Brotherhood ship easily drew up and took station on the *Eidolon*'s stern.

"You do that so easily." Tamra's voice was pitched to me, barely carrying the three cubits between us.

"Do what?"

"See the unseen."

94

I shrugged. "I never thought whether it was easy or hard. I just looked. It *is* a strange-looking ship, though."

"It's not really fair, you know." The redhead's voice was expressionless, so expressionless that I felt colder than the sea breeze whipping through my tunic should have made me feel. "They don't care how hard you try. They don't care how much you learn. They don't care."

I edged closer. "The Brotherhood, you mean?"

"They don't love. You're the child of one of the high temple masters. You don't swallow their beliefs, and they throw you out younger than anyone else."

High temple master—my *father?*

The Brotherhood ship increased its speed and veered toward the right, pulling up beside the *Eidolon*. The impression of order and power pounded at me from more than a hundred cubits away.

"You don't even know, do you? Is that fair?"

"No. But they don't go by what's fair, Tamra. It's already pretty clear to me that they go by what works. If we get in the way . . . then we go."

She turned to me, and her face was white. "You agree with that?" Each word was evenly spaced, dropping like a hammer on a forge.

I wanted to step back, but the ship lurched, and, instead, I grabbed the railing. The *Eidolon* had passed the breakwater, and the waves were higher.

Thwup, thwup, thwup . . . thwup, thwup, thwup . . . The paddles churned, dipping into the water with increasing speed, and a heavier and thicker plume of whitish smoke billowed from the stack.

". . . foresail . . ." Sailors were scurrying over the masts as well, releasing and adjusting the canvas of the sails.

"Do you agree with them?" asked Tamra, thrusting her face closer to me.

"I don't know."

"Oh . . . shit . . . uhhh . . . arrghhh . . ."

"Can I do anything?"

"Yes. Just . . . leave . . . me . . . alone . . ."

As I stood there, she emptied the contents of her guts over the side. I danced away, since I was downwind and didn't have that much in the way of spare clothes. But Tamra was too busy turning her stomach inside out to demand answers to any more philosophical questions.

So I walked toward the bow and watched the black ship heading north, moving at a speed that seemed unbelievable. No paddles, no sails—just a wake, and a thin trail of black smoke. No one even saw it, except the two of us; and Tamra was too sick to care, from waves that were scarcely two cubits high.

Off the bow, the sun dropped toward the now-black waters of the gulf.

Thwap . . . splat . . . thwap . . . The paddles dipped, and the *Eidolon* rolled, and we all were carried cubit by cubit, rod by rod, kay by kay, toward Candar.

Isolde stood at the rear of the bridge, tacitly ignored, while Myrten shuffled the cards under a swinging lantern and Tamra clutched a rail still tacky from varnish.

I just watched the white foam spill from the wave crests.

96

XVII

The waves remained moderate across the entire gulf, giving the *Eidolon* a near-constant rocking, pitching motion the entire trip. The half-steamer maintained a west-northwest heading.

I hadn't slept well, waking time and time again, but I *had* slept— unlike Sammel, who had eventually shared Tamra's discomfort with the ship's motion, and spent much of the night at the rail.

Isolde slept like a log. She even snored. Myrten arrived back late, and his purses were far fuller than when he had left, proof that knowing the odds was profitable anywhere. He also rose first. Even his quiet movements were enough to keep me awake.

I followed him up the ladder and onto the sun-splashed deck, where various members of the crew were already working—varnishing the other railing, disassembling another winch. Ignoring the industrious types, I trailed Myrten into the ship's mess.

Wrynn, Dorthae, and Krystal were already there.

I eased onto one the oak benches across from Myrten—the table was empty except for us.

Scufff . . .

Sammel stood there, swaying, but not in rhythm to the pitching of the ship. I motioned to the table. He finally staggered to a spot at the end of our table closest to the wall and away from anyone.

Breakfast was dried fruit—apples, red currents, peaches—hard biscuits, and a tea so strong even I winced. The tea was excellent for softening the biscuits.

I ate slowly, not looking up. Clearly, the crew had eaten earlier, much earlier. The mess room, under the bridge, took a space not much bigger than our two cabins together. The two tables were bolted to the floor, as were the backless benches. The grooves in the table would hold something, perhaps trays for dining in heavy weather.

Sammel tried the biscuits, and a touch of tea. After no more than half a biscuit, he got up and left, still greenish around his ears.

Wrynn, Krystal, and Myrten wolfed down everything in sight.

Despite his late night, Myrten looked fresh and rested, although his black hair was more unruly than ever. Myrten was the first to leave, without even a grunt. Dorthae followed him out, a glint in her eye. Wrynn fingered the hilt of her throwing knife, then followed the pair.

Krystal smiled, shaking her head.

"Something funny?" I asked.

"Not exactly," she answered, except that it wasn't an answer. She continued to sip from her mug, but took nothing else from either of the polished wooden serving platters.

"That's not an answer."

"Men . . ." She shook her head. Her hair was bound up, not in silver or gold cords, but in dark blue, as if she didn't want to call any attention to herself. "Men . . ." she repeated, as she stood up, leaving the mug on the table. Her steps were quick and sure, not that the deck rolled or pitched much, and she was gone before I could figure out what I could have said to keep her.

Just as I was finishing up a second biscuit and some dried peaches by myself and getting ready to leave, Isolde arrived with Tamra in tow.

For an instant, like the palest of china fired by my mother, precious and breakable, the redhead paused. "Urrrppp . . ." The burp destroyed the fragility. "Excuse me." She slumped onto the bench where Myrten had been sitting.

Isolde poured the dark tea into two brown hard-glazed earthenware mugs.

"Honey?"

Tamra nodded, swaying slightly to the roll of the *Eidolon*.

I downed the last of my mug and looked around for a place to leave it.

"Don't leave just yet, Lerris."

"Where would I go?"

Tamra sighed. Isolde glared, and I raised the empty mug to my lips so I didn't have to look at either for a moment. Then I took the heavy teapot and poured another mug, dumping in a large glob of honey from the server, an iron-gray squat pitcher that matched neither the mugs nor the teapot.

"You're quite a pair," began Isolde, her voice matter-of-fact. "One of you believes that success lies in accomplishment, and the other believes that having answers will explain everything. One of you hates privilege but covets it desperately; the other has it and has rejected it unthinkingly."

Tamra and I exchanged glances.

"You're both in for some real surprises." Isolde took a deep swallow of the tea and pulled a pile of mixed fruit off one platter—mostly dried apples. Next came some of the squarish and crumbly biscuits. The guide in the faded green jumpsuit alternated fruit, biscuits, and tea.

I drank more of my own tea, bitter even with the large glob of honey I had dropped into it.

Tamra nibbled at a biscuit, sipping from her mug enough to be able to swallow the crumbs she had placed in her mouth. Without a colored scarf, dressed just in dark gray, she looked washed-out, like a limp china doll.

Finally, as the silence dragged out, I put my half-empty cup in one of the holder slots in the center of the table and stood up, glancing from Isolde to Tamra and back. Neither looked at me, and neither said anything. Isolde just kept eating, slowly and methodically. Tamra stared at the smooth brown wood of the table beside her mug.

I almost paused to see if either would say anything, but kept moving.

Outside on the main deck, the wind had picked up and whipped through my short hair. My steps took me toward the bow, where I stood with the sun on my back watching the wind carry spray from the crests of the dark-blue waves. The *Eidolon* didn't exactly cut through the sea, nor did she lumber. Just like Isolde, the ship was efficiently matter-of-fact.

That solidity was helpful, because my thoughts were anything but solid. Me—a potential order-master? Born to privilege? Convinced that answers would solve everything? How could I even decide what I wanted to do without knowing? Talryn, Kerwin, my parents, even Isolde—they were all saying that everything was obvious, that I was blinding myself, and that I just had to choose. Choose what? What did it mean? Eternal boredom if I chose order? Early death if I chose chaos? From what I already saw, the alternatives weren't exactly wonderful.

Whhstttt . . . The *Eidolon* plowed into a bigger-than-normal wave, the spray from the impact almost reaching the railing where I leaned. The ship seemed quieter.

Of course! The paddles were silent, and the steam engine was cold. While the wind held, the captain didn't need to burn the coal.

I wondered if my belated recognitions were typical, that I didn't see things obvious to others until later.

"May I join you?"

I jumped. Tamra stood almost next to me, not quite so pale as at breakfast.

"Fine."

"You looked worried . . ." Her voice was softer, but still carried an edge.

Did I really want to talk to her? Ever since I'd started the danger-geld she'd been a bitch. I sighed. What would it cost me? We weren't exactly going anywhere, and she certainly wasn't boring.

"Yes . . . I guess I was . . ."

"You didn't know your father was a high temple master?"

"No."

"I . . . I'm sorry . . ."

Her words didn't sound sorry.

"You don't sound sorry."

"Do we have to fight?" she asked.

"No. But do you have to doubt everything I say or do?"

"It's . . . hard . . . I look at you. You had everything. And . . ."

"And what?"

She didn't answer. Instead, she just leaned on the rail next to me and looked at the waves.

Silence and the swishing of the sea were preferable to a dubious discussion. So I watched the water too.

"Lerris?"

"Yes?"

"I'm sorry."

"For what?"

"For . . . why do you make it so hard for me?" Her voice was tight again.

I thought for a moment, biting back what I really wanted to say—that she was a conceited bitch who wanted to run the entire world. But what good would that have done?

Whhhhssstttt . . . The spray almost touched the edge of the deck.

I watched the waves for a while, and she watched beside me.

Finally, I tried again. "Do you remember when we met . . . the first thing you said was something like I was a sorry sight . . . when I was learning staff work, you took the first opportunity to beat the crap out of me . . ." I looked back at the water, wondering if I'd said too much, wondering why I even bothered.

"Oh . . ." She actually sounded taken aback, and it felt like she was surprised.

I shook my head.

"You don't make it easy, either, you know." Her voice was quiet.

I could barely hear her above the waves, the whisper of the wind, and the creaking of the ship. "What did I ever say?" I asked.

"That's it. You never let anyone see you. You're bored, or very polite, and we all know what you feel. That's why no one can get very close, not even Krystal, and she wanted you a lot."

Krystal? She was older . . . only said she needed a friend . . .

"You're upset again."

I glared at the waves instead of Tamra.

"And angry."

"Why do you push at me?" I asked.

"Because . . . I'm scared . . . and you're scared . . ."

Scared? Me?

"Yes, you, Lerris. You're scared, scared shitless, no matter what you tell yourself or anyone else."

100

Whhssstttt . . . The *Eidolon* lurched, and a sheet of water sprayed past me, leaving me with wet hands and a tighter grip on the railing.

Scared? Maybe? But who wouldn't be?

When I looked up again, a lot later, Tamra was gone. I wished she hadn't left, somehow. But she was still a bitch.

The rest of the day held the same pattern. The *Eidolon* plowed west-northwest. The wind held. The crew kept working on repairs. Sammel stayed seasick, and Isolde and Tamra avoided me. The crew avoided us all, except to ask brief questions of Isolde. We ate bread, cheese, fruit, and tea after the crew did at midday.

I walked the deck, studying how the ship was put together, trying to sense the underlying patterns, the forces, the stresses. In a way, it was like Uncle Sardit's work—simple on the surface, very solid, and a lot more involved than I had thought.

Tracing the flow of the woods, the way the masts were stepped, the flow of the hull and the timbers and braces—that were easy. The metals were harder, especially the mechanical stuff.

Whuffff . . . *whufff* . . .

The belch of the engine and the acrid scent of burning coal broke me away from trying to feel how the stem and the bowsprit were joined.

Flappppp . . . *thwipp* . . .

Aloft, some of the crew were furling sails. Not all of them, but the mainsails.

A line of green hills had stretched southward off the bow—on the side opposite where I had been sitting propped against the forward hatch cover. When I scrambled up, I could also see a fainter line to the north, covered with a haze that had seemed more like low-lying clouds.

Freetown couldn't be that far away, not if we were at the edge of the Great North Bay.

Splattt . . . *thwap* . . . *thwap* . . . *splatt, thwap, thwap* . . .

The paddles began to bite into the calmer waters of the bay. Then the sun dimmed as the *Eidolon* moved under the high hazy clouds and into suddenly damper air.

Back behind the ship's bridge, a crewman hoisted a huge Nordlan flag to the top of the aft mast. I wondered who the Candarians didn't like. Except that wasn't the way to look at it. Who didn't the Duke of Freetown like? That was the question.

"Are you ready to go?" Isolde stood by my elbow.

"All I have to do is gather my pack and staff."

"Leave them there for now. It will be a while, but we need to get ashore as soon as the *Eidolon* ties up."

"Safer for us or them?"

Isolde didn't answer, perhaps because she had left.

The *Eidolon*, with the grizzled captain on the bridge, continued to make surprising speed, the engine substituting for the sails, which now hung nearly limp. Once we had neared the hills and entered the bay, the wind had died, as had the waves.

Sammel appeared at the rail, followed by all of the dangergelders but Dorthae—and Isolde. Myrten wore a white bandage on his forearm, which showed only when he reached to steady himself on the railing.

The sun had disappeared totally behind the shapeless clouds by the time the ship rounded Cape Frentala. Freetown, at first glance, was not prepossessing. Only a single spire graced the gray sky, and the harborfront was mostly of low wooden buildings. The piers were of heavy weathered and unpainted gray timbers, except where a brown line showed the replacement of an older plank by a newer one.

102

"Get your gear . . ." Isolde, now wearing solid black and looking grim, was talking to Sammel, but I didn't need a personal reminder. At her belt was a sword, also black-hilted, and a long knife.

In the short time it took me to go down the ladder and claim cloak, pack, and staff, the *Eidolon* was jockeying up to the pier, where a handful of figures waited.

"Tax guards . . ." muttered Myrten. For whatever reason, he stood nearly next to me at the railing.

"Tax guards?"

"The duke wants his cut first."

"Of everything?"

"Everything. Isolde will have to shell out a gold penny for each of us."

"We have to pay to come here?"

"Hell, isn't it?" Myrten smirked.

I hadn't thought about that. Would we have to pay entry taxes in other provinces? My stock of coins was looking less and less adequate.

"Dangergelders!" called Isolde.

I turned to see her motioning and followed her gestures. Someone wanted us off the *Eidolon* as soon as possible. The gangplank was barely in place as we lined up and walked down. A pair of seamen were still tying lines to the bollards on the pier.

A round-faced official with gold braid on both shoulders and a silver breastplate waited at the bottom of the plank. Behind him stood ten soldiers, each wearing a sword but carrying a club ready to use. Their breastplates were cold iron. Behind them lurked a shadowy presence, a woman in white, with the same sense of disorder I had felt once before, in the blade the trader had tried to sell Krystal.

In the dampness I wanted to shiver, but tightened my grip on my staff. Strangely, it felt even warmer now than on a sunlit day.

"Dangergelders?" rasped the round-faced man. His eyes looked beyond Isolde, avoided looking at any of us.

"Seven," noted the woman in black.

"That will be seven golds."

"You have a receipt?"

The round-faced man looked to his right, where a thin youngster scribbled on a tablet, then handed the single sheet to the tax agent.

Isolde offered the coins and took the receipt.

"Weapons?"

"Nothing except the normal—staves, swords, knives, and a few pistols. All for personal use."

"Magicians?"

Isolde hesitated briefly, so briefly I doubt the official caught it, before answering. "No magicians. Two blackstaffs."

"That's another four golds."

"Since when?" Isolde fixed full concentration on the official.

The round-faced man said nothing, but his forehead was damp.

"Since . . . since . . ."

"This afternoon, perhaps?"

"Magistra . . . it has not been a good year . . ."

"Additional duties are not in the Agreement."

The round-faced man swallowed. His forehead was clearly wet now, and not from the dampness of the afternoon. He swallowed again.

A soldier, his iron breastplate bearing a four-pointed star on the upper left, eased forward from the armed group.

Isolde shifted her weight ever so slightly, and I imagined she was smiling, although I could not see her face, wedged as I was into the narrow space just at the foot of the plank. Myrten was in front of me, breathing noisily. Krystal's hand was on the hilt of her blade.

"The duke has insisted, has he?" prompted Isolde. "With your head on the line?"

A few drops of rain splattered on my face, and the wind from the hills overlooking the city seemed ever cooler. I glanced back toward the *Eidolon*. The weathered captain and two officers stood at the top of the plank, watching. All three carried halberds I hadn't even seen during our passage.

Clearly, we weren't expected back aboard.

"No .. Magistra . . . but the needs of the duchy . . ."

"Then I demand the right of instant trial." Isolde took a step forward, and the tax official squirmed backward.

Myrten looked at me. I looked back. Right of instant trial? Our lectures hadn't covered that.

"But . . ." protested the official.

"You wish to repudiate your own laws?" asked Isolde softly.

The man shook his head mutely.

I jabbed Myrten in the ribs. "Move. We're too crowded." I tried to whisper, but Tamra looked around Wrynn and Myrten and glared at me.

I shrugged and rolled my eyes.

She shook her head, but edged outward.

"Who represents the duke?" demanded Isolde, ignoring the shuffling our movements created. Her voice cut like a knife.

"I do." The soldier who stepped forward was the one who had moved earlier. He topped any of us, even me, by half a head, and Isolde by more than half a cubit. His face was lean, clean-shaven and unscarred, but his short black hair bore traces of silver, and his eyes were flat and lifeless.

"Blood or death?" asked Isolde.

"It has to be your death, Magistra. You are an outlander, and death is prescribed if you fail."

"I was talking about you." Isolde's voice was cold enough to make the tax official scuttle back further.

The soldier inclined his head. "That is your choice, Magistra, but I will fight until I cannot. That is also prescribed." His voice was polite, but rough, as if unused.

One of the soldiers unrolled a reddish cord that had presumably once been scarlet. A cord-defined square about ten cubits on a side appeared on the gray pier planks. The square was about two-thirds the width of the pier.

Two soldiers took positions, with unsheathed swords, at opposite corners.

"Your corners, Magistra?"

Isolde did not take her eyes off the Duke's champion. "Krystal . . . Lerris . . . take the other two corners."

The tax collector's eyes widened as Krystal stepped forward. He paled, I thought, as she unsheathed her blade, and took the corner farthest from the *Eidolon*. That left me the corner only cubits from where I had been standing.

The wood of my staff was almost uncomfortably warm.

". . . blackstaff," murmured one of the soldiers in the guard group, which had retreated to the shore side of the pier as if to block our way to Freetown.

"Are you ready, Magistra?"

"I'm sorry for you, Duke's Man." Isolde sounded sorry, yet I wondered why she was so confident. The whole thing was a setup. The man had to be the best in the duke's forces.

"Are you ready?"

"Yes."

They both stood for an instant, blades out. Isolde's back was to me.

The man's blade flashed, impossibly quickly. Yet, in scarcely moving her own blade, Isolde somehow deflected the attack.

Flttt . . .

. . . hsssttt . . .

. . . hsssttt . . .

Blades caressed, never meeting directly, edges sliding against each other.

Clank . . .

Thud . . .

The Duke's champion lay face-down on the pier, separated from sword and life. Just as suddenly as it had started, it was over.

The tax collector's mouth hung open. So did those of the other soldiers.

I held my staff ready, wondering what would happen next.

"I trust you will record that the duke's proposed tariff on blackstaffs has been nullified." Isolde's voice had reverted to a merely matter-of-fact tone at least as chilling as the coldness she had conveyed moments earlier.

". . . uh . . . yes, Magistra . . ."

One of the two soldiers who had served as corners began to reel the faded reddish cord back onto the spool. I stepped aside, but continued to watch the remainder of the squad. So did Krystal.

Two others hoisted the body and began to carry it toward the horse-drawn wagon that waited at the causeway at the end of the pier. Another retrieved the sword.

The thin youth scribbled some more onto his tablet, and the tax collector wiped his sweating forehead with a darkish cloth.

"You understand, Magistra . . . Duke Holloric . . . we only serve his requirements . . ."

Isolde nodded briskly. "Convey our best wishes to the duke. We trust he will wish to continue maintaining the Agreement without further attempts at one-sided changes."

"Yes, Magistra . . ." He backed away, then turned.

The soldiers followed him back down the pier. Not one looked in our direction.

I looked at Tamra. She raised her eyebrows. I nodded. We both knew. For whatever reason, it *had* been an attempted setup by the duke. And the Brotherhood had known. I suspected Isolde was one of the best the Brotherhood had, and that was scary. Giving away nearly a cubit and a half an arm's length, she had dispatched the duke's best in instants.

No wonder the soldiers wanted off the pier.

I glanced back at the *Eidolon*. Only one guard remained by the railing, just a regular crewman. He grinned at me, then let his face turn impassive as the captain walked past him to the top of the gangplank.

Isolde turned to face the man.

"Our appreciation, Magistra. Our appreciation."

Isolde nodded, and he nodded back, then turned back to his command.

"Let's go." Isolde looked unruffled and was five paces gone toward the shore end of the pier before we started after her.

By the time we reached the causeway, the tax collector, the wagon, and the troops were gone, carried into the mist that clung even more heavily around the wooden buildings of Freetown.

Given all of the bollards on all the three long piers, Freetown seemed deserted. Only the *Eidolon* and a smaller fishing boat rested at the piers, and there were no traders, no cargos obvious for unloading or loading.

I caught up to Isolde. Her steps were still quick, and she didn't even look at me as we stepped off the pier and onto the stone pavement of the causeway. "Will your success teach the duke anything, or will this . . . embargo . . . whatever it is . . . go on?"

"Who knows?" For the first time, her voice sounded tired.

"You didn't want to do that?"

"Lerris . . ." The exasperated sound of her voice was more effective than an explanation.

"Oh . . ."

"That's right. Now, we need to get to the Travelers' Rest before the duke gets any more ideas. We'll turn at the next street, if you can call it that."

The buildings looked almost ghostly in the dim light and heavy fog and mist. Every so often, an oil lamp peered through the gloom, or a single person scurried away from us.

Tamra had caught up and walked beside me as we followed Isolde up the street away from the harbor proper. Every step seemed to echo, and no one said a word. We just kept walking.

XVIII

The fog thinned by the time we had stumbled and generally trudged uphill for several long blocks. In the middle of an open space where two narrow streets crossed, I paused for a moment. Over my shoulder, I could see the mast tips of the *Eidolon*.

"Oooofff . . ." Sammel, head down, ran into my shoulder.

"Sorry . . ." I turned and took several quick steps to catch up to Tamra and Isolde.

Overhead, higher clouds had turned dark gray, and a touch of a damp breeze brushed my cheek then was gone. The mist still dropped a faint gauze curtain over the buildings we passed. Many were deserted, or at least dark. From a handful of windows oozed the golden light of lamps. The acrid tang of wood smoke mixed with the dampness of mist.

"Ghost town," muttered Myrten from somewhere behind me.

"We're the ghosts," responded Isolde. Her voice was so low I doubted that Myrten had heard her.

I supposed we were, outsiders haunting the streets while, inside, the Freetowners huddled around the lamps and fires that held an unseasonably early fall at bay.

"Here we are," announced Isolde.

I glanced ahead over her shoulder.

The building's weathered timber walls looked gray, spirit gray in the thinning mist and growing dark. But a golden glow poured from every first-floor window, and the blue shutters were folded back to let the light escape, almost as if making a statement that the structure would not draw into itself against the forces of chaos.

"Travelers' Rest" proclaimed the sign hanging over the wide double doorway. The doors themselves, their thick brass handles glinting in the light of the two oil lamps that flanked the doorway, were still folded back against the wide timbers of the front wall, almost as if daring the dark to enter.

108   I took a deep breath, feeling some of the tension begin to leave me as I followed Isolde through the doorway.

A second set of doors, red oak like the first, although half the thickness, swung open at her touch.

Within moments we all stood on an open polished wood floor separating a parlor-like area from a wooden counter. Like the doors, the counter was finished and smooth-planed red oak, without ornamentation except for matching oak coping covering the corner joins. The wood was protected by a dull varnish that radiated the gold of the lamps on the wall. Right before us was a wide wooden stairway with a brownish-carpeted runner covering most of the stairs themselves.

To our left opened another archway, through which I could see a series of tables covered in red checked cloths, with individual chairs drawn up to each table.

Behind the counter stood a gray-haired woman with a cheerful smile. She said nothing as Isolde turned and looked us over.

"Each of you has a single room. It has been paid for. You may make other arrangements if you wish. We will have dinner together in the small dining room which is behind the one you see on the left. Meet there as soon as you are settled. You can leave your weapons in your rooms. They will be safe there. Now . . . please check in at the counter."

Her words reflected long practice, and while I was wondering how many groups she had escorted to Freetown, she had already stepped up to the counter.

"We didn't think to see you again, Magistra."

"The unexpected can change everyone's plans." Isolde laughed an off-tone laugh. "Here's the normal."

Clink . . .

The momentarily-widened eyes of the woman in the faded green blouse indicated that the payment was scarcely normal.

"Did you meet the new tax collector?" asked the counter lady.

"Ah, yes. We also met the duke's new and late champion."

"Oh, dear . . ."

"I doubt the duke's enforcers will be here immediately, but I won't be staying after this group leaves tomorrow, not this time."

"The new duties are unpopular, and rumor has it that the Hamorian legate left Freetown rather suddenly. No ships are likely to enter the harbor until some certainty is established." The innkeeper raised her eyebrows slightly as she eyed Isolde.

"If Hamor is thinking of acting, that's certainly true. No ships are likely to be seen."

I didn't frown, but I knew how Isolde was leaving. The only question in my mind was what else she might be doing before she left.

"Come on, Lerris. Don't gape. Step up." Isolde had stepped aside without my noticing it.

"Ah . . . a young blackstaff . . . I'll bet the harbor guard didn't like that. Especially now."

"No . . ." I looked at the open ledger, which had a space only for each traveler's name—no country. Scrawling down my single name beneath Isolde's, I started to step away.

"Here's your key, young man. Room fifteen, second floor at the back." The key hung from a brass square nearly the size of my fist. I took it and headed up the stairs, not looking at anyone, just trying to keep my staff from banging on the staircase railing posts.

I followed the upstairs carpeted hallway, also lit by a set of oil lamps, to the back and number fifteen. Two doors stood side by side—fourteen and fifteen. The key opened my door easily, without so much as a squeak, then swung quietly closed at my touch.

Click.

The room held a double bed, a low three-drawer red-oak dresser topped with an oak-framed mirror, a washbasin table with towels, and a wardrobe. A braided rag rug covered the wide and polished gold-oak planks from next to the bed to just before the dresser. The single window was closed, flanked by cheerful red-checked curtains tied back with thick white cords. A lamp over the low headboard lighted the room. The bed was covered with a handmade red quilt showing a pattern of geometric red-and-white snowflakes.

After hanging my cloak in the wardrobe, I stripped off my tunic and rummaged through my pack.

The water in the basin was warm, and with the small bar of soap, the razor from my pack, the water, and the heavy towel, I did my best to make myself presentable.

The mirror showed me as clean-shaven, tanned, reasonably decent-looking—but young, still too young to be doing what I was going to have to do beginning in the morning.

Picking up the tunic and looking it over, I decided it was still adequate. Slightly grimy, but wearable, and there wasn't either the time or the place to wash it. So I put it back on, and used a dampened corner of the towel to remove a few of the more obvious smudges.

As I placed the pack in the wardrobe, I had to shake my head. The "Travelers' Rest" was definitely more than it seemed—the sort of inn that probably only the very well-off could afford. The staff just barely fit inside the wardrobe and only at an angle, but, Isolde's words to the contrary, I didn't really want to leave it in plain view. The lorken was cool to my fingers, reassuring me that at least I wasn't in the presence of overt chaos, although that was scarcely likely with someone such as Isolde leading us.

With a last look around the room, I picked up the key, opened the doorway, and stepped out onto the hall carpeting and almost into Krystal, who was backing out of her room.

"Oh . . . sorry," I apologized.

Clank. My key jangled against hers.

We both smiled, more from nervous relief than from humor.

"Rather lovely quarters for us outcasts," I observed.

"Lovely? I suppose."

"You don't think so?" For some reason, I didn't want to walk away from her.

"Are you going to change what you are because of lovely quarters?" Her voice was both soft and musical, more relaxed than I had heard it.

She had me on that one, and I wondered why I would listen to Krystal, and think about what she said, when if Tamra questioned me I was ready to fight.

"What are you thinking, Lerris?"

"Oh . . ." I didn't really want to tell her. "Just . . . that I can listen to you, even when you raise questions."

"I'll take the flattery." She bestowed a soft smile on me.

Clink. Wrynn stepped from her room into the hallway and looked at us.

"Are you two going to talk forever, or can we get the sermon and have some dinner?" The blond looked at us, then bent over and inserted her key into the room lock.

I decided not to follow Wrynn's example, since I really doubted that locking the door made any difference in this particular inn.

"Shall we go?" I asked Krystal.

"I suppose we should." She turned and made her way down the hallway toward the stairs, the sword I had given her still at her belt.

Sammel, Myrten, Dorthae, and Wrynn were already seated at the rectangular table in the small dining room when we arrived. The place at the head of the table had been left for Isolde.

I sat in the vacant chair at the foot of the table. Krystal sat on my left and Myrten on my right. My other choice would have been to the right of Isolde's chair. I left that for Tamra.

As I pulled out my chair, Isolde, face washed and hair brushed, stepped through the archway from the main dining area. Looking up, I nodded at her, receiving the barest inclination of her head in return. She glanced up one side of the table and down the other side, pausing as she stopped at the empty space left for Tamra.

Almost as if she had been waiting for the notice, the redhead stepped through the archway.

Isolde's eyes flicked back to the rest of us, without really looking at any of us. "This is the last place where you can freely mention your origin," began Isolde, her hands resting on the back of the red-oak chair at the end of the table. As when we had left the *Eidolon*, she wore black, all black. Tunic, trousers, boots, belt, and neck scarf. With the pale skin, she looked like a soldier—or worse. "Once you step outside the walls of this inn, you are subject to local customs, thieves, bandits, and soldiers—to mention the most obvious dangers.

"As a practical matter, the road outside the main gates is generally safe for at least several kays into Candar, except for petty theft and assault, which can happen just about anywhere."

"Except Recluce . . ." muttered someone behind me.

"Except Recluce," affirmed Isolde. "But for various reasons, you have all found Recluce too confining, or Recluce has found you in need of the outside world. It is for that reason that you will travel alone. You made your decisions alone, and you must face the consequences alone, at least until you are ready to make your final decisions. But you all know that.

"First . . . I promised an update on local conditions. As you discovered earlier, the duke has decided to use his control of the port to attempt to raise more revenue. Most of the trading nations are avoiding the port, and there will be more unrest in Freetown, enough that you should probably consider leaving the area quickly. Spidlar and Hydlen have taken over much of the trade, and the routes south of the Westhorns to Sarronnyn . . .

"Sligo, north of here, has suffered unseasonable weather, including early snowfalls, and food is getting scarce . . .

I couldn't help yawning, but I managed to stifle it without it being too obvious. Krystal frowned, though.

". . . safe to travel in either Gallos or Kyphros, but not from one to the other because of the increasing skirmishes along their borders . . .

Finally, she looked around the room. "You have had enough lectures—"

I agreed with that wholeheartedly and hoped she wouldn't be using that as a lever for yet another one. I was hungry.

"—And I won't be adding to them—much."

I almost groaned.

"But there is one last thing to consider. Those outside Recluce refer to their world, the rest of the world, as the 'real world'. Candar will become your real world. If you die here, and some of you may die, you will die, permanently. But Recluce is also a real world, in many ways more solid than Candar. You have to decide which world is real for you. Which reality, with all its rules—whether they are the rules of order, or the mixed and changing rules of order competing with chaos—will be yours."

She gestured toward the archway through which a serving boy brought a tray heaped with dishes. "Here is supper. Afterwards, you may sleep in the rooms upstairs, or not, as you please. There will be fruit and pastries here in the morning. You may leave when you please, but you will all be out of the inn before sunset tomorrow. Those of you leaving Freetown should not wait until the last minute. Someone is always robbed that way. Given the current mood of the duke, I would not recommend staying in Freetown, but that is indeed your choice, the first of many."

Abruptly, she stopped, then pulled out her chair, and sat. The plates came down upon the checked cloth, and the innkeeper, appearing from nowhere, briskly set a glass before each of us.

"Wine or redberry?"

"Wine," answered Tamra.

"Redberry . . ."

"Redberry . . .

"Wine . . .

"Redberry," I answered, in turn, watching as the liquid nearly filled the heavy tumbler, then smiling as Myrten speared three chunks of steaming meat with a knife and deftly transferred them to his plate.

We were all hungry, even Isolde, and little enough was said until later, when Tamra sipped from her tumbler, then asked brightly, "What will happen to the Duke of Freetown?"

Isolde looked up from her plate at Tamra. Her face was expressionless even as she smiled. "Why . . . whatever will be, will be."

"That's not exactly an answer," pressed Tamra.

"No. It is true and polite, and I will be happy to discuss the matter with you in much greater depth once you return from your danger-geld—assuming you choose to return and do not find Recluce too confining." Isolde returned to cutting a sliver of buffalo from the slice upon her plate.

Tamra glared, while the black magistra ignored the redhead's impatience. I couldn't help smiling.

"You're amused?" mouthed Krystal.

After wiping the grin from my face, I answered, trying to keep my voice low enough that it would not be heard over the pleasantries being exchanged by Sammel and Dorthae. "Tamra has trouble when people don't manipulate easily."

"Don't we all?"

I shrugged. Krystal was probably right, but Tamra's whole attitude was to insist she was right and that the world should recognize it.

"Good luck to you all." Isolde's quiet tone stilled the small room. "From this point on, you are all on your own. I hope to see you again, but that is your choice." She nodded, turned, and walked out, the heels of her boots echoing faintly on the hardwood floor as she crossed the empty main dining room.

". . . abrupt . . ."

". . . typical of the masters . . ."

Rather than say anything, I gulped a mouthful of redberry juice, then waited, looking to see who stayed and who left, except that the table quieted, and we all ended up looking at each other.

"For all of the pleasant surroundings, they still don't really care." Tamra's voice broke the silence.

I pulled back my chair. "I need some sleep." I would have liked to talk to Krystal, but the thought of saying anything with Tamra hanging on every word bothered me.

"It's early yet," complained Myrten.

Nodding at the innkeeper, back behind the counter, I took the stairs two at a time. I wasn't up to another argument, and staying downstairs would have led to that. Besides, after the next morning, I might never see any of them again, and I was getting tired of Tamra's attitude. Then, it was clear she was tired of mine.

The door opened easily, and I stepped inside. The room was just as I had left it, except darker, because the blackness outside was absolute, with not even a single light showing anywhere when I stepped to the window. The fog and clouds seemed thicker, but how could I really tell?

. . . *click* . . .

As I sat on the edge of the soft bed and pulled off my boots, I heard Krystal's door open and close, but no sound of voices. Off came the tunic and trousers, and I reached up and turned off the lamp.

With the quilt around me, I was asleep in instants, although I thought I heard a faint knock on my door once, just as I was dropping off; but I was too sleepy to get up and check, especially since it was probably my imagination.

Still . . . I wondered, but I dreamed of neither red-headed girls nor of dark-haired women.

XIX

Once I stepped outside the inn the next morning, I could sense more strongly what I had felt the night before and what Isolde had alluded to in saying we would be safe there without weapons. For all the faded blue paint on the shutters, the weathered timbers and gray-painted plank walls, the building radiated order. No barred windows, no heavy doors, no guards—just order. Enough order that it just would not appeal to anyone bent on disorder.

The clouds and fog of the previous day had vanished, except for higher puffy gray-and-white clouds that scudded quickly across a bright-blue fall sky.

I looked at the inn again. The thick shutters were supported by heavy iron hinges, with iron hasps for the sliding locks that would be on the inside when the shutters were closed against weather or other forms of attack. The iron was clean and black, the hinges clearly functional. The red oak of the door had faded under the varnish to a grayed gold that almost matched the big bronze door handles on the double doors that were now folded back against the planks for the day.

From a timber projecting above the open doors and perhaps two cubits below the second-floor window hung the neatly painted sign—"Travelers' Rest." The gray paving-stones were laid edge-to-edge from the front wall to the curb, a distance of five cubits or less, and stretched from one side of the building to the other. Already, the stones had been swept.

Glancing up to the room where I thought Tamra had slept, I could see a glimpse of red through the half-open window. But the sea breeze gusting up from the harbor fluttered the fabric enough to tell me it was only one of the bright red curtains. Then I looked toward the back of the building, but Krystal's room window was around the corner. She had either left earlier, or was still asleep.

I shrugged and shouldered my pack, which didn't seem nearly so heavy as when I had left Wandernaught, and, after a last look at the Travelers' Rest, turned my steps toward the livery stable that had been listed on the wall behind the front desk of the inn. If I had to reach the Westhorns, it wasn't going to be on foot, not unless I wanted to take years. A thousand kays or more—I still resented Talryn's flat pronouncement. Someone definitely wanted me out of Recluce for a while.

"Watch it, outlander!"

I dodged a thin man wearing a short cloak, a ragged tunic not concealing a mail shirt underneath, and a short sword in a battered scabbard. Then I smiled politely, and stepped aside. He stopped and studied me.

I waited, shifting my hands on the staff ever so slightly.

"Told you to watch it . . ." His speech had a twang to it. Above his short gray and ginger beard, his face bore large pockmarks. The odor of stale beer, dirt, and other assorted filth almost forced me back another pace. "But you look like the peaceable type . . . so just hand over that pack."

I stood there for a moment, frozen, not having expected an attack within a block of the inn.

"I said, hand it over!"

I smiled, moving the staff up into a defensive posture. "I think you have the wrong person." I hoped my voice didn't shake the way my knees threatened to.

"Ha!" His blade whistled out. "Now! Let's have that pack!"

All I dared to do was wait. The sword edge glittered even in the cloudy light of the morning.

"Be a shame to carve you up, outlander . . ."

I would have liked to shrug, but I didn't, instead watching his eyes.

Clunk. I blocked the short blade, knocking it away.

"You do know how to use that staff a little, but not enough . . ."

. . . clunk . . . clink . . . clunk . . .

The responses were nearly automatic as I concentrated on anticipating his moves.

. . . clunk . . . clink . . . clunk . . .

He wasn't nearly so good as Krystal or even Demorsal. So I waited, parrying, turning the blade rather than meeting it edge-on.

. . . clink . . . clink . . . clunk . . .

Sweat was pouring from his face, and he was breathing hard.

. . . clink . . . clunk . . .

Crack! . . . Whsssttt . . .

"Aiiieee . . . !"

116

Clank . . .

Suddenly, it was over. The small man, not much above my shoulder, I realized, backed away from me, leaving the sword on the dusty stones, clutching the back of his wrist where I had struck to disarm him.

"Black bastard . . . witch spawn . . ." He did not move, but stayed well beyond the reach of the staff.

I didn't really know what to do. I didn't want the sword. I really didn't want to hurt the man. He was more hungry than evil, but I couldn't exactly turn my back on him.

"So . . . up to trouble already, Lerris?"

I recognized the voice, took a quick glance over my shoulder to see Myrten strolling toward me. Even as I glanced back, the man who attacked me was darting away down the street and twisting into an alleyway on the right.

"That was stupid, youngster."

"What?" Still holding my staff with one hand, I reached down and picked up the fallen sword. Just a plain blade.

"Looking away from him. Good thing he didn't have a throwing knife." Myrten wore a bright green tunic and dark green trousers. His cloak was heavy dark-gray leather. Like me he carried a pack, but his was half-slung over his left shoulder. He looked more like a clean-shaven minstrel or a bard than the thief I felt he innately was. Two large knives hung from his belt, but I could sense the small pistol under the left-hand false knife.

I looked up the street. No one else had followed us out of the inn. Myrten was right. I shrugged. "I didn't expect something quite so soon."

"What you expect isn't what happens, particularly when you get close to chaos." He half-laughed.

I shrugged. "Want the blade?"

"You could sell it," he suggested.

"Me?"

Myrten laughed again, a short bark. "You're right. That would be more than a little out of character. I'll sell it and split the profit."

That seemed more than fair. "Fine. But where?"

"Let's just keep walking. There's bound to be something." Myrten seemed much more at ease on the streets of Freetown than in Nylan.

"What about—"

117

"We're not traveling together, and we'll certainly leave Freetown separately."

At the next cross-street, Myrten stopped. With dirt and clay packed over the paving stones and squarish mud-holes where some stones were missing entirely, the street looked more like an alley frequented by thieves or worse. Myrten nodded toward the left.

I frowned.

"It's early. Too early for the real professionals." Myrten stretched his legs out, moving quickly, especially for a man so short.

"What about our friend?"

"Him? He was just hoping for an easy mark."

Most of the doors we passed were shut and barred with cold iron. Iron doesn't have any magical power, despite the rumors. It's effective because it takes so damned much chaos to break through it that doing it isn't worth the effort. That was what Magistra Trehonna had said. It made sense, I suppose, which was why swords still carried the day and firearms were a novelty.

After we had traveled nearly fifty rods down the narrow street, crossing yet another, wider street like the one on which the Travelers' Rest was situated, Myrten slowed.

We stopped before a narrow storefront. The planks were carefully painted in rust, and the shutters were black, trimmed in the same rust color. A square iron hook the size of my fist held open the iron-banded red-oak door.

"Norn's—Weapons" read the square sign above the iron grate that covered the single narrow window.

"Shall we?" asked Myrten.

I tried to sense what sort of place Norn's might be . . . and failed. At least the shop did not radiate chaos. Neither did I feel any underlying sense of order. "It feels all right."

Myrten hadn't waited for my assessment. So I followed him inside, suspecting a neat and dark shop with rows of weapons racked on dusty walls. I was wrong. The bright space inside, no more than ten cubits wide, stretched back nearly twenty cubits, light coming from a high roof that seemed more glass than timber. Ranged along the left wall were four large cabinets, each standing open to display its contents.

First I checked the nearest cabinet—lightly oiled, polished, with dovetailed and mitered corners, made of solid grayed oak, originally probably red oak, with a tracery of fine lines bespeaking age. It contained knives, even more varieties than I had seen in Gilberto's armory.

"May I help you?" The tanned and white-haired man who waited by the second cabinet stood a half-head taller than me. Spare, wide-shouldered, but his eyes seemed to twinkle.

I studied him for a moment—deciding that he was indeed what he seemed.

Myrten, for some reason, looked at me. I nodded.

"We were . . . *bequeathed*, as it were . . . this blade."

The white haired man smiled faintly. "You're clearly from Recluce, and someone wanted to take advantage of you early."

Myrten frowned.

"Why do you say 'clearly'?" I asked.

"Your friend"—he gestured at Myrten—"*could* be from Dirienza or even Spidlar. You, on the other hand, would never seek out Freetown. A ship from Recluce ported yesterday, with passengers staying at the Travelers' Rest."

I nodded. "It's that well-known?"

"Not quite *that* well-known, but known among those who make their living that way."

Something about his speech tickled my recall, but I couldn't place exactly why.

"About the blade . . ." prompted Myrten.

"Oh, that? May I see it? You could set it here." As he spoke, he pulled out a sliding shelf from the cabinet. "By the way, my name is Dietre."

The cabinet's workmanship was first-rate, since the polished flat wood scarcely whispered into place. Myrten set the plain sword on it.

Dietre studied it carefully, then reached toward the base of the cabinet and pulled a small pendulum from a narrow drawer, adjusting it before letting it swing over the steel of the blade. "Hmmmm . . . neutral, at least." He looked up. "Would you mind if I pick it up?"

Myrten looked at me.

"No."

"You're either trusting or very confident, young man." Dietre smiled.

"Myrten is good with his knives," I observed.

"I suspect you're better with that staff, and I, for one, unlike the past owner of this blade, would not care to test you." He held the blade lightly, moved it around, balanced it, and then set it back on the wood. All his motions were deft.

I felt my earlier suspicions were confirmed, but wondered how Myrten had known about the shop.

"Interested?" asked Myrten.

"It's a serviceable weapon. Nothing more. Relatively untainted, but unordered." Dietre shrugged. "The going rate for one of these is around a gold pence. My markup would normally be two silvers. On the other hand, you probably saved Freetown some trouble by handling this quietly, and I *am* the West Side councilor. Say, a gold penny."

"Fair enough." Myrten didn't hesitate on that, but he glanced at the third case, the one with the pistols.

"You have some interest in the pistols? Firearms aren't much good except for hunting, and pistols are scarcely the best for that." Dietre's tone was bemused as he lifted the blade and slid the shelf back into the cabinet. "Take a look. I'd like to put this up."

I raised my eyebrows. Most dealers would scarcely have mentioned leaving customers with a set of weapons. Dietre had some protection I hadn't detected.

The white-haired dealer walked toward the back of the shop, where he laid the blade on a narrow work bench under a rack of tools. Then he walked back to the third case where Myrten was studying the weapons.

I ignored both of them, trying to figure out the patterns of the shop itself, an island of concealed order in an almost random section of Freetown. Behind the front door was a second archway, as thick as the outer wall. A single plank covered the bricks or stones. The framing pieces didn't overlap the plank edges, though.

How it worked, I wasn't sure, but it was mechanical, and no one was about to leave the shop without Dietre's permission, open and unprotected as the place looked. The cabinets fit the same pattern— good solid workmanship that would have taken forever to break into once they were closed. Impenetrable to casual chaos-use.

". . . three golds?" asked Myrten.

"That's low."

I really didn't care about their bargaining, but I did want my five silvers. Buying Krystal her blade had been too impulsive, probably, and I realized that I could have used those golds. But she needed a good blade. Tamra hadn't approved. I shook my head, wondering if anything I ever did would meet with her approval.

"Three and half it is," agreed Myrten.

I turned back to the two, waiting for the settlement.

Myrten struggled to bring out some coins from the guarded pockets in his belt. "Two and half to you, and I give the five silvers to Lerris."

Dietre nodded, neither smiling nor agreeing. "Whatever's easiest." He did not remove the pistol from the cabinet.

Myrten gave me the five silver pennies first, and I put them into the front pouch, the obvious one. Then he handed five more to Dietre, followed by two golds. Dietre checked all the coins with the pendulum.

"Chaos-counterfeiting?" I asked.

"You can never tell." Apparently satisfied, he replaced the balance and walked toward the workbench. The coins vanished into an iron box bolted to the bench. Then he walked back toward us. "Is there anything else you need?"

"Not here," I answered.

Myrten just shrugged.

"Then . . . good luck, especially to you, youngster. A lot of people don't like the blackstaffers, even young ones, and there aren't ever enough of you to dispel the myths. Good day." He turned back toward the work bench.

I looked at Myrten. He looked at me. Then we left.

Outside, I stopped. "Is Cinch Street the next one ahead?"

"Yes. If you can trust the map in the inn. Good luck, Lerris." He turned back the way we had come, and I started toward Cinch Street. The alleyway got narrower with each step, and the eaves of the second floors seemed to lean down on me. A shadow fell across the stones and refuse alike.

I started, then relaxed. A puffy white cloud had scudded across the morning sun, and the shadow lifted almost as quickly as it had fallen.

Outside of a beggar boy who scuttled behind a refuse heap as I passed, I saw no one until I reached the next street—Cinch Street. Myrten had been right.

Turning left, I started uphill. The slope was gentle, but I had to watch my steps. Many of the reddish sandstone paving-blocks had split or shifted out of place. Cinch Street had been added later, and more cheaply. The paving-blocks in the unnamed alley-street had been of granite and better-placed, even though the way had been narrow and neglected.

I marched perhaps a hundred rods, almost to the top of the hill, before I reached the stable. "Felshar's Livery," proclaimed the weather-beaten sign carrying simple line drawings of a horse, a saddle and bridle, and a squarish object that I gathered was a bale of hay. The gray wood of the sliding plank door was pushed back.

After taking a deep breath, I stepped into the building, a wood-planked passageway into an unroofed space. Under foot was hard-packed composite of clay, horse droppings, and who knew what else. In the central court, a single swaybacked horse was hitched, without a saddle, on the right side. At the far end was a smaller horse, a large and shaggy pony, really.

Crraccckkk! A whip cracked toward the pony, which lashed both rear feet toward the bearded man in faded gray.

The man ducked back from the hooves. "Hamor take you!"

Wheee . . . eeeeiii!

An aura of hatred poured from the liveryman, so strong that I could sense it without trying. I swallowed, then called, "You there! Are you Felshar?"

". . . get yours later, beast . . ." muttered the man, as he coiled the whip and turned toward me. His expression shifted to professed pleasure, but the hatred boiled underneath.

"Felshar will be back in a short time. I'm Cerclas. How may I help you?" His voice was as slippery as the bottle of leather-oil set beside the racked saddles by the tethered horse.

I shrugged. "I don't know that you can. Thinking about a horse."

Cerclas smiled faintly, his eyes running over my dark brown traveling clothes and cloak, noting the staff with a frown.

"Horses are dear this year."

I lifted my eyebrows. "Oh?"

"The drought in Kyphros, and the heavy winter in Spidlar—they were hard on the stock, and few travelers returned with mounts."

I nodded toward the swaybacked horse—a nondescript grayish color. It looked gentle, unlike the small shaggy beast. "That one?"

"Five golds." Cerclas shrugged. "That's a steal. But feed is dear, too."

I really didn't want to deal with Cerclas. The man smelled worse than the horses, and his eyes were bloodshot and kept drifting to my pack. Like a lot of the traders who visited Nylan, he lied. But, even with my growing awareness of order and chaos, I couldn't tell how much.

"There aren't that many travelers, and there may not be any for a while. Your stable is nearly full." I was guessing, but it seemed right.

"There are always travelers in Freetown," observed Cerclas.

"What other mounts might you have?" I walked toward the shaggy horse.

"A war-horse, a traveler, and some others . . ."

For some reason I wanted to look at the small horse. A welt the length of my hand lay across his flank, clearly raised by the recent whipping. For the moment I merely noted it, trying to understand why Cerclas had been so angry at the horse.

The animal was well-fed and untouched by anything resembling chaos, unless it was far more subtle than I could detect.

Wheee. . . . eeeee . . .

I barely kept from jumping.

"Mean little bastard, isn't he?" Cerclas stood by me. "If you don't know horses, stay away from ponies. They're smart, and that makes them dangerous and mean. I can show you some better mounts. In the stalls over on the right."

"All right." I let the liveryman lead me toward the nearest stall, where a chestnut munched on hay from the manger.

"This one is a battle-trained gelding. He'll stand up to anything."

I nodded. The chestnut seemed healthy, well-treated, although there was something about him that bothered me . . . his size, I wondered, looking up at his ears? Or something else? "How much?"

"Fifteen golds."

That was a more honest price than the one he had quoted for the swayback.

"What else?"

"Here we have a mare . . . good traveler, but not nearly so good in a fight. Eight golds."

The mare was a blotchy-colored horse, black-and-white patches across her body, with a short cropped mane. I liked her less than the chestnut, and just nodded to Cerclas. "What else?"

He walked to the next stall, where a hulking brown beast of a horse munched placidly on hay so dry it crackled. "Plowhorse broken to

123

ride. He's not much good in battle, gets nasty when mares are around, but could carry two of you and your gear. He could also pull a wagon if you needed it. Six golds for him. He's worth more, but there aren't many caravans around this time of year, and he eats a lot."

We looked at three others, all broken-down mares. I didn't like any of them and found my feet carrying me back toward the central yard. As I stepped past the shaggy little horse, I could feel a sense of rightness about him, but kept moving toward the overpriced sway-back.

Wheuuunnnn . . . The nag's whinny was half-whine, half-groan.

I shook my head. I'd be lucky if the old gelding made it much past the gates of Freetown.

"At five golds, he's a bargain," commented Cerclas.

"Is that what the glue works would pay?"

Cerclas coughed into his tangled beard, then straightened and fixed his glance on my staff. His eyes widened. "He's a long way from the glue works, and you need transportation, I'd venture."

"I do, or I wouldn't be looking at horses. But even at two golds, this old fellow wouldn't get me halfway to anywhere."

Cerclas shrugged, scratching the unkempt gray-and-black thatch at the back of his head, then spat noisily on the clay.

"What about that undersized horse over there?" I asked.

"That's not a horse. He's a mountain pony, tough as they come. Felshar hasn't priced him."

I repressed a smile. That failure might be enough. Walking over to the pony, but avoiding those effective hooves, I stepped up toward his shoulder. While I was no judge of horses or ponies, he seemed broader in the shoulders than some of the larger horses, and his legs, while shorter, seemed sturdier.

"He might be able to carry me," I let my voice ooze doubt.

"He'll carry you and another," admitted the liveryman, standing well behind me.

I touched a streak on the pony's flank.

Wheeee . . . The animal twitched, but did not move away from me.

"These welts . . ." I shook my head. "Still . . . two golds?"

"Felshar hasn't priced him . . ."

I shrugged. "What good would it be to price him? Most buyers wouldn't take him until these heal. Felshar would certainly know that."

This time I could sense the uneasiness in the liveryman.

"Three golds, if you throw in a saddle, bridle and blanket."

"I don't know . . ."

I shrugged again. "Well . . . I need to check elsewhere, then . . ."

Cerclas scratched his head and spat again. "Felshar wouldn't complain too much if I got four . . . I don't suppose . . ." He stepped closer to the pony.

Wheeeee . . . eeee . . .

The liveryman stepped back.

"Let's see the saddle and bridle first . . ."

In the end, I paid more than I had to, three golds and seven silvers, but I got a decent saddle and blanket. The bridle wasn't a bit-type, but a choker, sort of a hackamore. But I had the feeling that the force of the bridle wasn't going to matter much anyway. If I couldn't persuade that pony to do something gently, he wasn't about to be forced.

The only other sticky point was the chit.

"I never learned my figures. Felshar does that."

"Fine. I'll write it up and you put the chop on it." I'd seen the chop hanging next to the boxes where the chits were lying.

"How do I know . . ."

125

I held up the staff. "Everyone knows if you carry this, you don't lie. I couldn't afford to. The price is too high."

At the sight of the staff, he stepped back. "I don't know . . ."

"Felshar knows you don't cheat a blackstaffer, and that they don't cheat you. Maybe you didn't get an outrageous profit, but you got a fair price, and you're getting rid of some trouble." I looked pointedly at the pony's flank.

". . . suppose . . . wouldn't hurt . . ."

That was how I ended up riding down Cinch Street toward the gates of Freetown. The old lance cup, with the addition of a strip of leather, was adequate enough to hold my staff, although I had a tendency to lurch in the saddle perilously close to the dark wood when I wasn't paying attention.

The pony's name was Gairloch. I knew that when I touched him to saddle him. He did try and puff out his belly, but, following Cerclas's instructions, I kneed him, not very hard, and not nearly so hard as Cerclas recommended, to get him to let out his breath.

Don't ask me how I knew his name, but I did. That bothered me, but there wasn't much I could do about it.

Surprisingly, Gairloch didn't rock all that much, and the old saddle was broken in enough that it wasn't too stiff. The straps and girths had been replaced recently, and I had checked the stitching and rivets to make sure they were solid, but the seat looked like it had weathered more than a few caravans.

If Gairloch were as adept on the trail as he was in avoiding city potholes, I would be better off than I had hoped—although, as I looked overhead, we might be getting wet sooner than I had hoped.

The early morning gray-and-white puffs of cloud were darkening and thickening as Gairloch bore me onto the worn but even gray stones leading to the city gate. The walls were scarcely impressive, rising only about twenty cubits. Two squarish towers, each with crenelated parapets too small to be very useful, framed the gate. Graying and iron-bound timbers comprised the city gate itself, a gate that waited in a recess in the walls behind the towers. A stone bridge spanned the space between the towers. When closed, the gate sat in a stone groove and was backed with stone on all sides, making it difficult, if not impossible, to batter down. But any attacker would have gone for a less defended point on the low walls in any case.

Set toward the city from the walls was a stone hut, and outside the hut waited a pair of guards. As I watched, a small cart, pulled by a swaybacked horse that could have been a mate to the one I had seen at Felshar's, rocked over the stone gate groove and onto the pavement by the guard hut.

The rear guard waved the cart, driven by a woman with straggly hair and a hooked nose, toward the other side of the roadway. "Over there. Don't take the whole road!"

Whstt-chuck. The long reins clacked, and the cart lurched slightly away from us.

"Halt!"

The other guard stopped looking bored as he took in my dark cloak and the pony.

"Where'd you get that horse, boy?"

"Felshar's, officer." There was no sense in being nasty to the man. Besides, he was bigger than me, and, if paunchy, probably could use the sword that one hand rested upon.

"Any way to prove that?"

I shrugged. "I have a bill of sale with Felshar's chop." Then I touched the staff, which was faintly warm to my ungloved fingertips. "And, besides, would I lie about it?"

His eyes moved to the staff, widened like Cerclas's eyes had widened, then moved to my face.

"You're young for that . . ."

"I know. They've been telling me that since the spring." I unfolded the thin parchment from my belt. "If you'd care to look . . ."

The look on his face—that, and the fury behind his eyes—warned me.

Clang . . . thwackt . . .

. . . whssssttt . . .

". . . Aiiiee . . . thief!"

Somehow, I had managed to stuff the parchment into my belt and grab the staff from the holder quickly enough to knock aside his sword even before he positioned himself. The second tap—and it was scarcely more than that—was to his cheek, but the brand was instantaneous.

Gairloch didn't wait for my heels in his flank, but began to trot, then gallop, through the still-open gate. The gate couldn't be closed, not in the instants Gairloch took me past the second guard and through the gate gap in the wall.

Cloppedy, cloppedy, cloppedy . . . Gairloch's hooves rang on the stones, and I dropped the reins and grabbed his mane with my right hand, trying to keep from hitting anyone with the staff, hanging on as we careened down the causeway.

"Look out!"

"Runaway horse!"

"Thief! Traitor!"

A set of peddlers scrambled off the causeway into the mud-filled trench on the right, and Gairloch angled around a slow-moving wagon pulled by a single plodding horse which barely lifted its head. I could have reached out and touched the dusty harness, so close did we pass.

The traffic on the causeway probably saved us from an arrow in the back, but by the time we cleared the causeway where the day's incoming produce and shoppers all funneled toward Freetown, we were out of range of all but the strongest of crossbows, assuming any were ready and in place on the guard-tower parapets.

The clippedy-clop of Gairloch's hooves changed to a muted drumming as he carried me along the packed clay of the highway. No stone roads or highways in Freetown, it seemed. We galloped past a crossroads, which carried more traffic than the road we traveled, and kept heading into Candar.

Before too long, I reined in Gairloch, keeping in the middle of the road, which was surprisingly firm considering the continuing rain and dampness of the night before. Gairloch dropped to a trot, then a walk.

"Good horse." I thwacked him on the shoulder, careful not to touch the welt raised by the liveryman.

Whnuffff . . .

"I didn't like them much either."

I glanced at the causeway and the dark spot that marked the gate. Nothing seemed to have happened. No other horses had followed us. The intermittent stream of people, horses, and wagons still headed up the stone pavement toward the city.

Then I realized I was still holding the staff in my hand. The wood had cooled until it was no longer warm to my touch. Half of the leather thong I had used to tie the staff in place was missing, ripped in two when I had grabbed for the staff to defend against the guard. I replaced the staff in the lance cup, tying it in place with the remaining leather.

Looking from the staff to the road, my eyes fixed on the rectangular stone post by the road. "Hrisbarg—40 K" proclaimed the weathered stone.

I let go of Gairloch's mane and straightened up in the saddle, chucking the reins lightly as we headed down the rise on the road to Hrisbarg.

Already it had been more of a day than I had planned. Assaulted by a thief, attacked by the duke's gate guard and probably declared a criminal in Freetown—all in the first day. I didn't know where I was going, except I knew that Hrisbarg was where I had to go first before I could get to the roads leading to the Easthorns and eventually the Westhorns.

Would the Freetown guards spread the word? Or would they take it out on the other dangergelders? Or had the others left while I had been haggling with Cerclas to get Gairloch?

My guts wrenched a little, wondering if I could have left Freetown without causing so much of an uproar. I shrugged, knowing I couldn't undo what I had done, but also knowing I might end up paying for it somehow, some way, when I really didn't want to. So Gairloch and I started the long walk toward Hrisbarg.

Thrummmm . . . thrummm . . .

Above us, the clouds thickened and rumbled, promising more rain.

XX

The man in white smiles, a warm and reassuring smile that spreads through the coldness of the public room, which the dying embers in the dark hearth barely warm. "Innkeeper! Could we have some warmth?"

As the woman in gray leathers watches from the dark corner table, a heavy-set man lumbers forward. He wears shapeless leather trousers, a worn brown tunic, and a soiled linen apron over which protrudes a sagging gut. "Your lordship, there's no wood and no coal, naught but the little we got on the grate. The black bastards cut us off, and there's none to be had for us working folk."

A hissing whisper of agreement wafts across the scattering of men and the few women who huddle at the tables closer to the near-dead embers on the hearth.

"Bring me some stones, then."

"Stones?"

"Yes, stones. You wish to warm your inn, do you not?"

Confusion and hope war upon the innkeeper's face, but he retreats from the still-smiling man in white, who turns to the veiled woman beside him and says something in a voice low enough that not even the hovering serving-girl can catch the words.

At the kitchen door, the innkeeper motions, then speaks quickly to the pregnant girl who responds. He remains by the doorway, surveying the dim and chilly room.

In the shadows, the redhead in gray leans forward and the hood of her cloak slips back, revealing the clean lines of her face and the fire of her hair.

A thin-faced man grins through his straggly beard and eases from

129

his seat toward the table where his prey waits. His hand touches the hilt of the sharp knife at his belt.

Even before he has reached the shadows, the redhead has turned toward the thin-faced man.

"You look like you need a man." His voice is ingratiating.

"In that case, you aren't the one."

Only the dark-eyed and veiled woman who sits beside the man in white watches as the thin man edges toward the redhead.

"Uppity wench, aren't you?"

"No. Just pointing out the obvious." Her voice is cool, detached, and her eyes go right through him.

Oblivious to the confidence behind her words, he reaches for the empty chair.

"I didn't invite you to join me," she observes.

"Don't need no invitation." He leers and begins to sit.

Her staff and foot move simultaneously.

Cruump . . . Both chair and bearded man crash to the gritty plank floor.

130   "Bitch!" His hand reaches for the knife.

Before he can reach her, she is standing, dark staff in hand.

Thud . . . crack . . . thump . . .

He pitches forward onto the floor.

The innkeeper lurches from his post by the kitchen door. "There'll be no fighting . . ."

"You're right. There will be no fighting," declares the redhead. "When this idiot wakes up, tell him to be more careful." She stands while the innkeeper drags the unconscious man toward the doorway, then resumes her seat to finish the bread and cheese upon her table.

Across the room, the dark-eyed woman nods and leans toward the man in white. In turn, he nods and smiles.

Shortly, the pregnant kitchen-maid struggles to the hearth with a basket full of dripping stones, looking from the innkeeper to the man in white. "The stones you wanted, your lordship."

"Stack them on the grate, if you would."

The girl complies, her eyes darting from the slender lord in white to the hulking innkeeper.

"Thank you, girl. Here."

Her eyes widen as she takes the silver, but she inclines her head as she covers the silver and thrusts it into the hidden pocket in her wide belt. "My thanks, your lordship."

The man in white stands and turns to those at the tables. "All of you are cold. Would you like some warmth?" His fingers point at three figures at a table near the wall.

"I can tell you have come in from the winter rains. The warmth is on me." He turns and gestures toward the stones, cold and damp upon the grate.

HSSSSSSSSSSssssss! A flare of white sears from the grate.

Even the redhead in the shadows winces, and a hush drops over the tables.

When the brightness fades, steady coals glow from the heap of coal that has appeared on the grate, and the warmth begins to radiate across the public room.

The dark-eyed and veiled woman rises and walks toward the redhead's table.

"Lord Antonin and I would like to invite you to join us," she offers.

The redhead cocks her head, thinking. "Why?"

The dark-haired woman looks at the staff and smiles pleasantly. "Should we discuss it here?"

"I suppose not," answers the redhead with a wry smile as she stands and follows the dark-haired woman.

"I am Sephya, and this is Lord Antonin," offers the veiled woman as she resumes her seat.

"Be our guest," offers Antonin.

"Why?" asks the redhead.

"Why not?" he answers. "You doubtless have some questions, and we may be able to provide some of the answers."

As the redhead eases the battered chair toward the table, she studies Sephya. Despite a fine figure, the veiled woman is older than she had first looked, with fine lines radiating from the corners of her eyes and the color in her face supplied by rouge.

"Why don't you start by explaining why you flaunted your power? And why you invited me to join you?" Her tone is half-humorous, half-sharp.

"A deed is a deed. Do you believe that appearances can really deceive, young lady?"

"Go on," suggests the redhead.

"Actions speak louder than words. There are those here who shivered from cold. Did the righteousness of Recluce warm them? Will the innkeeper feed his fire for them from the goodness of his heart?"

"That is a well-used argument, Antonin. One good action does not make a man good. Nor does a single wrong action make a good man evil."

The outside door opens, and a gust of wet chill air momentarily disperses the warmth from the hearth—until the door closes with a *thud*.

"Actions do speak louder than words," Antonin insists, his voice melodious. "Tell me why it is wrong to warm those who are cold."

"I don't like answers that are questions. How about a straight answer?" The redhead looks toward the back wall and the door.

Antonin shrugs, as if to deplore such directness, then looks her in the eye. "What use is a good thought if it does not translate into good action? I'm sorry," he grins. "Let me rephrase that. The purists of the world of magic, such as the Masters of Recluce, believe that the form of magic determines whether it is good or evil. They insist that the use of chaos-magic to warm those who would die of cold or to feed those who would starve contributes to evil. I cannot accept that reasoning. Is not a human life worth more than a label?" He shrugs again. "I ask you to think about that. Think about the beggars you saw in the cold streets outside. In the meantime, share our meal."

"And?"

Antonin smiles warmly. "I have certain business with the duke. If you're interested in working with us, I will be in Hydolar in somewhat less than an eight-day from now. At the Grande Loge. Either meet us there, or leave a message."

He takes a slice of meat from the platter and nods toward the empty plate before her. "You need to see more of Candar, and to reflect upon what you would do with your abilities. Enough of talk. Enjoy the meal."

The redhead glances from Sephya to Antonin, but no glances have passed between the two, nor have any of the twisted energies that she has seen in Recluce. Shortly, she spears a slice from the platter, and the three eat.

XXI

Compared to the High Road of Recluce, or even to the lesser East-West Highway, the way from Freetown to Hrisbarg seemed little more than a narrow lane. Straight, but narrow. Right outside Freetown the road had split, going north, south, and west, and I had taken the one road that had not paralleled the coast.

Hard-packed clay comprised the center of the road, perhaps as wide as a farm wagon. The years of travel had created a surface that seemed to resist the light rain, at least in the center of the roadway. Heavy ruts and churned ground surrounded the hard-packed and level central section of the highway.

I had tried to unstrap my cloak from the top of my pack while riding and had almost fallen off Gairloch in the process, saving myself with a desperate grab at the front edge of the saddle.

Whheeee . . . uhhhh . . .

"All right . . . I'm sorry . . ." So I reined to a halt in the middle of the road, looking behind again. We had covered more than five kays without seeing any pursuit, and the rain was threatening to change from a fine drizzle into something heavier.

As I clambered off Gairloch, the insides of my legs twinged. After only a fraction of the distance we would have to travel, my body was protesting, not exactly a promising sign.

Thrummmm . . . Overhead the clouds continued to darken, threatening more than mere drizzle. Behind the tumbled stone walls beside the road, the meadow grasses bore only a tinge of green amid the tan of the end of the season. The washed-out brown of the long scraggly blades at the base of the wall testified to more than casual rain, as did the puddles in the middle of the unmowed field beyond. At the base of some of the grasses were blackened stalks, showing rot from the continual rain.

The stony outcroppings even in the middle of the fields, the shorter grasses on the other side of the wall, and occasional breaks in the walls and the trampled hoof prints leading across the road from one wall break to another, all pointed toward the fields as sheep or cattle pasture. I had seen neither, unless a few grayish blurs to the south were scattered sheep or goats.

Thrummmm . . . thrumm . . .

Splatt . . . splattt . . . The cold raindrops on my head prompted me to complete my recovery of the cloak and to replace the pack behind the saddle.

My legs twinged again as I climbed back onto Gairloch.

"Let's go."

Wheee . . . eeee . . .

Thrummm . . . thrumnmm . . .

Splattt . . . splatt . . .

Things were going just wonderfully. After being assaulted, threatened by a city guard and having to flee, we were now headed through a cold and miserable rain to a town I knew nothing about, on the way through more towns about which I also knew nothing, in order to reach and cross two mountain ranges I had no great desire to reach, let alone cross.

Wheeee . . . eeeee . . .

Ahead, a shapeless lump appeared on the road, resolving itself into a coach drawn by a pair of huge horses. From a short pole beside the driver, who was covered from head to foot with a hooded and shiny gray slicker, drooped a reddish flag.

I looked for the less muddy side of the road, and nudged Gairloch toward the right onto a patch of grass that rose above the churned road-edge mud.

"Geee—haaaa!"

Crack!

A chill accompanied the coach, almost like a cold wind, that blew softer, yet colder, as it approached.

Crack!

"Gee—haaa!"

The hoarseness and the mechanical nature of the coachman's call twisted every nerve in my spine as the coach rumbled along the level center of the road toward me.

The coach itself was of polished white oak, varnished heavily until it was nearly gold, supported not by iron springs, but by heavy leather straps. Even the axles and wheels were totally of wood. Yet the coach's workmanship could not be obscured by the mud streaks upon the wood or by the mist and water droplets which sprayed from it on its headlong journey toward Freetown.

"Gee-haaa!" The coachman never looked aside as he drove past.

134

Behind the coach rode two men, seated side-by-side on chargers that mirrored the chestnut gelding I had seen at Felshar's. All the horses moved at a quick trot, as fast as seemed possible for a longer trip.

Both soldiers wore the shiny gray slickers like the coachman, but shorter, more like jackets that allowed them to use either their white lances, secured in holders like the battered lance cup which held my shorter staff, or the white-scabbarded swords they bore.

The soldier closest to me glanced from under the hood, but his scrutiny was mechanical, as though he had not even really seen me, or as though he had seen a figure and passed on that information as he watched—although his mouth did not appear to open.

For the moment that the coach passed, midday seemed more like a stormy night. Then all that remained was a dissipating sense of disorder, the soft rumble of the wheels fading away, and a hoarse "gee-haaa!"

I shook myself and chucked the reins, hoping that Isolde had completed whatever she had to do and had found the black ship that doubtless waited unseen somewhere near the harbor.

Tamra—I hoped her procrastination hadn't left her open to the chaos-wizard that had ridden in the white-oak coach, but there wasn't much I could do. Not then. I swallowed, wiped the water off my forehead, and watched the road, noting absently that the coach's passage had left only the faintest of indentations on the road.

Splatt . . . splatt . . . The cold rain gusted in icy drops from an ever-darker sky, and I looked for some sort of shelter, but the road stretched straight ahead, level, for at least another five kays, bordered by the same tumbled stone fences, the same withered grasses, and the same distant and scattered sheep. Not one house nor homestead had I seen since crossing that first hill outside of Freetown. Yet the sheep indicated that someone lived somewhere—and that said that no one wanted to be close to the road I traveled. I shivered again.

Wheeee . . . eeeee . . . Gairloch tossed his head and droplets flew back onto my cloak and face.

"I know . . . it's cold and wet. But there's no place to stop."

Wheeeee . . .

"No place. Nowhere . . ."

So we kept plodding along the road.

No wagons, no more coaches, and a steady beating flow of water

135

from over head. Finally, when my cloak was nearly soaked through, its treated leather heavy on my shoulders, we reached the first low hill at the end of that near-deserted meadow valley. By then, the rain had eased to a mere chilling mist.

Some scattered pines bordered the road, and the stone walls lapsed into tumbled low piles of rock. On the hilltop, more of a hillock really, sat another pile of stones, the remnants of what had clearly once been an extensive farm or estate.

There was no immediate sense of chaos or disorder, only a feeling of age . . . and maybe under it all some sadness, although my father, Kerwin, and Talryn would all have assailed me for ascribing an emotion to a description of order or its lack thereof. At least Gairloch couldn't comment on sloppy logic.

From that second hill, the terrain became less ordered and more wild, with hills covered mainly with pines, although a few gray oaks, their leaves turning yellow-brown, were scattered along the lower reaches of the hills, especially near the few permanent streams. While there were countless brooks and streams flowing with rainwater, only one even approached looking like it had cut a permanent channel.

Again, I shivered. Whatever it was, as miserably normal as the rain and the surroundings seemed, the cause of the rain was not precisely natural. Why, I couldn't say; but that the extent of the rain was unnatural was clear, even while I could detect no sign of chaos.

The water was natural. Gairloch enjoyed lapping it up from several of the brooks, but when I stopped to let him graze, he did not seem particularly interested in the straggly grass. So I pulled myself back into the saddle and finished munching on the travel bread I had brought from the Travelers' Rest.

The other unnatural thing was the road itself, which ran straight where it could and curved gently when it could not and climbed gradually if neither straightness nor curves were possible. Once Gairloch and I had passed through the lower hills, in the higher hills the road narrowed not a jot. Nor did the grade steepen. The sides of the hills seemed planed away at a gentle angle, without the overhanging boulders or outcrops I had half-expected to see.

In time, I almost struck my forehead.

". . . wizard's road . . . of course!" Magistra Trehonna had mentioned that there were some in Candar, but I hadn't paid much attention to the details. She was even more boring than Talryn.

Wheee . . . eeee . . . added Gairloch.

While I wasn't that good at extending my senses, particularly in the rain, once I realized what might be there I could almost feel the hard white stone pavement under the packed clay.

I shook my head as the light dimmed, and Gairloch plodded downhill toward a few scattered lights that the intermittent stone posts had led me to believe might be Hrisbarg.

Three or four kays short of the town the road forked, and a large arrow roughly chiseled into a stone post twice the size of most distance stones pointed down the right-hand branch. Above the arrow were the letters HSBG.

The left-hand road continued straight, without lights or dwellings nearby, toward the next line of hills. Only a line of coach tracks indicated that the road was ever used.

After the turn, the remainder of the route to Hrisbarg was churned, muddy, and, in parts, required near-fording of the streamlets that meandered across the excuse for a road that we traveled. I almost wished we had stayed with the wizard's road, gloomy as it was, that had arrowed straight into the hills—especially after it began to rain again, the cold pelting flow that quickly resoaked my cloak.

Wheee . . . eeeee . . . eeuuhhh . . .

"I agree. But do we really have any options?"

Gairloch was silent on that point.

The first huts we came to were roofless, dark, and deserted. Then came huts with roofs, if apparently deserted. Finally Gairloch set his hooves on the thoroughly-churned mud of central Hrisbarg.

The main street in Hrisbarg seemed to consist of equal sections of puddles and mud. Instead of stone pavement, or even stone walks with storm drains, they used mud. The stores were fronted with raised plank walkways. Some had posts and steps for tying carriage horses or single horses, but most just had plain planks slapped down.

Even in the drizzle, I could see the woodwork of those walks was abysmal—green wood, rough spiking, not even a rudimentary effort to keep the walking surface level.

Whhffffff . . .

Gairloch shook his head and consequently his mane, spraying pony-scented water all over my cloak and face. The cloak was designed for it. My face wasn't. My obvious belt pouch had several silvers remaining, enough for a night at an inn and a stable for Gairloch—particularly

137

after the day we had completed and the kind of night it was turning out to be.

One or two stores had oil lamps in front, but Hrisbarg lacked street lamps as such. Even with my excellent night vision, I was having trouble, what with the drizzle and the strangeness of Candar.

Whhhhhffffff ..

Another sound of disgust from Gairloch and another, finer, spray of water flipped across me.

"All right . . . we'll try to find an inn . . . or something . . ."

I began to look in earnest, although I also kept my eyes open for signs of the road to Howlett. The Brotherhood had been singularly unhelpful with the directions that I needed to spend a full year in Candar and pass through Howlett to the cities beyond.

After all, I mean, was my dangergeld just to spend time in Candar and pass through Hrisbarg and Howlett and get to the Westhorns? Not bloody likely. If they hadn't been so deadly serious, it could have been a joke. And, once again, no one told me anything I couldn't figure out first—except why Talryn had been so insistent on my getting to the Westhorns.

138

Down a lane to my left I saw a faded sign with what looked like an "H" and some sort of howling creature. Outside of a few dark buildings on the corner and some small cottages huddled further down the road, I could see nothing. Nor did I feel anything. Certainly no inns, road houses. So I kept Gairloch headed toward the far end of Hrisbarg.

The sign read "The Silver Horse." Predictably, since apparently no one in Candar besides the merchants and the clergy could read, under the letters was a horse, badly painted, with flaking silver paint that looked gray in the rain.

With a chuck of the reins, I nudged Gairloch toward the slope-roofed and weathered building next to the inn.

"Uffff . . ." My legs almost collapsed under my full weight.

"Sir?" Standing there was a stableboy not much taller than my elbow.

"Do I pay you or the inn?" I asked.

"It's three pence a night, five with a separate stall, oats, and a full manger."

I handed him a penny even before I touched the rolled-up pack. "That's for you to take special care of my horse."

"Yes, sir." The youngster stepped back.

"Which stall?"

"You could have the one under the eaves there . . . ?"

I got the message. If I took the one with low headroom, none of the bully boys with the big horses would bother him. And Gairloch didn't need the extra space as much as being left to rest and feed.

"That's fine." I led Gairloch there myself, letting the dark-haired youngster open the half-door, as much to keep him away from the staff that could have been a lance in the dim light of the single covered tin lamp that hung from the beam by the doorway.

Before even starting to unsaddle Gairloch, I removed the staff and tucked it under the straw by the outside wall. No one but someone attuned to order/chaos forces would notice it, and it wouldn't be that much good to me against an accomplished chaos-master anyway.

"I can help you," offered the boy.

I didn't protest as he unstrapped the saddle, since Gairloch didn't seem to mind, merely *whuffing* and shaking his head. Besides, the youngster's hands were far defter than mine, and my legs were still shaking.

With Gairloch mainly settled, and the saddle and blanket racked to dry, I was ready to try The Silver Horse itself. My leg muscles spasmed as I limped across the muddy courtyard to the inn. Faint light glimmered through the small leaded windowpanes facing the stable.

The open outer door was of rough pine, covered with peeling white paint. The inner door, which I checked as I pushed it open, was of good red oak, but the varnish was worn and cracking and the hinges had been reset too many times. It took some time for me to wipe all the mud off my boots using the worn rush mats, but I managed, not that it mattered much. The floor was scarred and stained wood, with dirt-heaps in the corners.

Inside, only one of the lamps in the narrow hall was lit, and it smoked and flickered.

"Hello, the inn . . ." I called.

A muffled voice answered from somewhere. ". . . coming . . ."

". . . At this hour?" questioned another voice, sharper than the first, and nearer.

Waiting, I looked around the inn. On my right, through a square opening the size of a double door, was a dining area, and the faint

139

glow of coals glinted from the stone fireplace. On the left I noted a small sitting area with three wooden benches covered with oblong cushions. A second wall lamp, damped low, illuminated the sitting area. The bench backs were spooled and unpadded. In the center of the benches stood a battered low wooden table, used primarily as a bootrest, if the indentations on the table edge were any indication.

As in Freetown and on the road, travelers seemed few indeed. "Yes?"

The voice was the sharp one and belonged to a waspish lady dressed in a faded brown dress and stained yellow apron. Her face was clean, if angular, and her silver-streaked hair formed a neat bun at the back of her head.

"How much for a room, and some supper?" My voice was hoarse, rough from the wet and cold.

The eyes raked over me. "A silver a night." She paused, and the dark vulture eyes took in my soaked cloak. "Paid in advance. That includes bread and cheese in the morning. Dinner is extra—what's available on the bill of fare. Not much is left tonight."

After fumbling with the obvious front pouch, I produced a silver and five coppers. "For me and for my horse."

Part of the vulture look vanished as she took the coins. "You rode in this weather?"

"It seemed like a good idea when I started. Freetown wasn't a place I wanted to stay. Then there wasn't any place to stop, and . . ." I shrugged.

The woman glanced at the door, then back to me. "Hrisbarg is part of the duchy, and Majer Dervill likes to stop here."

I got the message. "Travelers don't always know the local weather, madam, and I was just hoping for a warm inn and some hot food."

"We can help there. Just go in and sit down. Annalise will see to you shortly. Unless you want to see a room first?"

"I think I'd like to see the room. At least to lay out the cloak and dry out."

"Clean towel and basin are another copper."

"Two towels, with fresh water in the morning," I countered.

She smiled. "In advance."

So I paid another penny, wondering if I should have asked for a chit, but deciding against it. The towels were thick and clean, both of them, if a shade gray, and the basin held clean lukewarm water.

The room itself was barely large enough to hold the sagging double bed and battered red-oak wardrobe. The bed had a single coarse sheet over an even lumpier-looking mattress, covered with a heavy brown blanket. A wall sconce held a single scrawny candle that the thin innkeeper had lit from her lamp.

The door had no lock, but with so few guests I decided to risk my cloak and pack for the moment.

When I returned to the dining area, another body sat at the table closest to the fire, a man in a dark blue uniform and a posture that was arrogant even while slouched at the table and cradling a mug of something.

I took a wall table for two on the other side, not quite so close to the fire.

After a casual look at me, the soldier took another deep swallow from the mug. "Annalise!"

"A moment, please," returned the pleasant voice I had heard but not seen earlier.

I stretched out, enjoying the warmth of the room and beginning to feel more human and less chilled.

"Thank you, Herlyt. I didn't know we had another customer." The blond girl, probably not even my age, nodded to the soldier.

"But . . ."

She ignored him and walked straight to my table, long blond braids swinging at her shoulders. "Good evening, sir. I'm afraid the larder is a little low tonight. We still have some bear stew, and a pair of chops, I think. Wheat or corn bread, and stewed spice apples. Also some white cheese." The open smile displayed strong if uneven white teeth. The open low collar of the peasant blouse showed some other strong features, especially as close as she stood.

"Which is better, the chops or stew?"

"The stew," called Herlyt. "Take the stew. Those chops have been heated every night for a week. Get me another mug, Annalise."

Annalise raised her eyebrows, then nodded faintly.

"I'll try the stew, cheese, apples, and a few slices of wheat bread. What is there to drink?"

"Mulled cider, hard beer, Largo wine, and redberry."

"Redberry."

"Real drinker you got there, Annalise. Real manly fellow."

141

Annalise shrugged as if to dismiss the soldier. Then she grinned. "Would you like anything else?"

"Not right now, thank you." I managed not to grin back at her, but she *had* asked.

Before turning from me, she wiped any expression from her face. Then she retrieved the mug from the soldier. "Another hard beer?"

"What else? That's all you'll ever provide, and I still have to pay for it." The bearded man stared at the fire as tentative flames hissed over a pair of green logs.

Annalise disappeared through an open door into what I took to be the kitchen, reappearing with two mugs almost without leaving my sight.

Thump. Herlyt's mug arrived without a word from the girl.

"Here you are, sir." My mug came with a plate that held cheese and wheat bread. "Are you from Howlett, Eagle's Nest, or Freetown?"

The stiffened position of the soldier alerted me.

"I guess I'd have to say not any of them. Came down the coast road and decided not to stay in Freetown with all the rain and gloom. They told me there were no ships anyway."

The soldier relaxed fractionally, and the girl nodded. "That's a long ride."

I grinned. "It's a cold ride." Then I sipped the redberry, breaking off some cheese to go with a chunk of the wheat bread.

As I ate, forcing myself to take each bite slowly, she withdrew to the kitchen, and the soldier retreated into his mug.

"Sir . . . ?"

An enormous steaming bowl appeared in front of me, accompanied by a smaller plate of spiced and sliced red apples. Both dishes were heavy earthenware, with the fine cracks of age radiating through the glaze.

Herlyt had been right about the stew, though; it was spicy, hot, and tasty. But I pushed back the bowl before I finished it, knowing that to eat any more would leave me ill, and then some.

"Will there be anything else?"

I glanced over at the soldier, slumped face down on the table.

"Later?" I asked, testing her earlier grin.

She shrugged, but did not smile.

"How much?"

"Five or a half-silver."

After draining the redberry, I gave her a silver and got back five coppers, one of which went to her, and into her belt before she went into the kitchen.

With a regretful look backward, I climbed the creaking stairs to my room, checking my pack immediately once I had closed the door. Nothing had been touched.

Even as I struggled out of my trousers, I wondered if Annalise had really meant anything by that nod.

She hadn't . . . or at least I collapsed into sleep with no gentle tapping on my door or other interruptions.

XXII

The morning dawned no less dreary than the day before, drizzle and intermittent rain dropping from formless gray clouds that churned but never seemed to move.

I woke once before I got up, when the angular innkeeper replaced the water basin with fresh water, both quietly and efficiently, and with barely a glance toward me or the wardrobe. After that my eyes closed but my mind spun, asking question after question. Like, why was the Duchy of Freetown getting so much rain? Or why had a chaos-master been in the strange coach barreling toward the port? And why had he used a coach?

With a groan, I eased my feet over the side of the sagging bed, wincing as I did. My thighs were as sore as I could ever recall, even after beginning Gilberto's conditioning exercises, and my shoulders were stiff. Sitting, even on the bed, was painful.

Washing helped, as did some stretching.

Then I checked my clothing. The cloak was dry, all the way through, as were my trousers. The dried mud on the legs mostly came off with a little scraping and the moistened edge of the towel I had used the night before. Still . . . I could see that washing my clothes was going to be another requirement before too long, unless I wanted to smell like the stable.

Outside the wind whistled, and the rain splatted against the inn.

After dressing and pulling on my boots, I checked my pack, smiling as my fingers touched the book. *The Basis of Order*—I still hadn't gotten around to looking at it, but I supposed I would, sooner or later. My father had a reason for everything.

I closed the pack and folded the cloak across it, debating whether to bring them downstairs with me. Finally I shrugged. Why not?

Without even a single light, the narrow hallway appeared gloomier than the night before. My boots scuffed on the bare wood of the floor.

". . . attack on Freetown . . ."

". . . any of them around here."

I paused at the top of the stairs, deciding to wait a moment to see what else the speaker said.

"The courier said there were two blackstaffs, and several others, including a black warrior, a damned woman."

"Majer, I wouldn't even know what a blackstaff looked like. All we have are two commercial travelers and some well-off young student. The commercial travelers I see three or four times a year. The student—he's barely old enough to let loose on his own."

"Did you see any weapons with him?"

"Weapons? Hardly. A short knife."

"Where is he?"

"You might check by the fire."

"Come with me, and point him out, Natasha . . . if you would be so kind."

"Certainly, Majer . . . assuming he is there."

Click . . . click . . .

As the heavy boots passed the stairs, I eased down the stairs further, casually, as if I had not heard a word, but trying not to step heavily.

Annalise stood by the desk counter, her eyebrows raised. Then she pointed toward the doorway and mouthed something.

I grinned, waved, and ducked through the main doorway, yanking on my cloak as I did so. While the majer and Natasha looked for me by the fire, I dashed through the rain to the stable, glad I had brought the pack with me.

Sploosh, sploosh . . . sploosh, sploosh, sploosh . . . My boots sloshed through the puddles in the courtyard clay.

The wide sliding door was ajar. The stableboy was nowhere to be seen as I scurried toward Gairloch.

Rain or no rain, storm or no storm, I needed to put some distance

between me and Freetown's finest. While they might be persuaded
that I was not a blackstaff, something told me that the majer was
under orders to round up anyone who might be from Recluce. The
questioning would not be gentle.

I would have liked to see whether Annalise had anything in mind
besides flirting . . . but that was out now. Besides, she only had played
up to me to avoid Herlyt, or because any man with a horse was bound
to have money.

Trying to saddle Gairloch in the dim inn stable was a joy, knowing
that I didn't have much time. First, I got the saddle blanket on sideways. Gairloch whinnied at that, but he didn't actually buck until I
threw on the saddle.

Thunk. The saddle slammed down on my feet and onto the planking.

"All right, you miserable beast." I rearranged the saddle blanket,
then eased the saddle into place, but could barely get the cinch closed.

Gairloch, gray looking in the gloom, skittered but did not make a
sound as I fumbled with the closures. Something . . .

Finally, I reclaimed my staff from the straw and placed the black
wood firmly, but gently against the pony's forehead.

"Whufffffff . . ." When he let out his breath I yanked the cinch tight.
I suppose I could have kicked him, the way the saddler in Freetown
had, but using violence unnecessarily bothered me . . . besides being
boring. The staff trick worked, although why the pony would pay
attention, I still didn't know. That bothered me, too, but not as much
as kicking him would have.

I had trouble with the hackamore, until I slowed down and forced
myself to be calm. All that left was tying my pack in place and putting
the staff in the lance cup. Then I untied Gairloch and walked him to
the sliding door of the stable.

"Hallo! Hallo, the inn!"

That voice was too hearty for my liking. Even behind the stained
beams and planks of the stable door, I could picture yet another duchy
cavalry officer, dripping rain from his shiny blue or gray waterproof,
looking for a warm brew and a solid stew, or for the majer with even
worse news or more punitive orders.

"Damnable innkeeper . . . no stableboy on a morning like this . . ."

Realizing he was coming in, stableboy or not, I tied Gairloch to
the beam fronting the first stall, then swung the door open.

"You . . . keeping an officer in the rain . . ." The officer, wearing a

145

gold leaf on his collar, had been reaching for the door. He stood at least a half-head taller than me, and his horse made Gairloch look like a toy.

"My apologies, officer. But the stableboy is ill . . ."

"Leave that pony, man, and take care of a real horse!"

"Yes, sir," I answered. "The end stall on the right is the only one free. It's dry and clean." While I wanted to clunk the arrogant bastard on the skull, I doubted that I could have reached the staff before ending up spitted on his saber.

"That's fine, but make sure he gets a rubdown and a brushing . . . and no cold water, or I'll drown you in it." He thrust the reins at me.

"Yes, sir." I took the damp leathers and chucked them. The horse was better-trained or less stubborn than the ones I'd seen at Felshar's. He actually followed me. The cavalryman watched to make sure I was headed where I said.

"Who has the pony?"

I did not turn, but gave a shrug. "Young fellow, not much older than me."

"I'll be back in a shake, man, and don't forget it."

Sploosh . . . sploosh . . . His steps toward the inn were quick.

I wrapped the reins around a post, tying them in a quick knot that I yanked tight. Then I dashed for Gairloch, untying his leathers, and scrambled into the saddle right inside the stable. I remembered to duck as we stepped into the downpour. I was still trying to get on my gloves as he stepped through the open doorway.

Whhnnnnn . . .

Clearly, the cold rain on his face did not please him, but when the latest cavalry officer and the majer got together, I definitely didn't want to be around.

I kicked Gairloch gently with my heels and he began to walk, then trot. I grabbed his mane to steady myself, but let him move. The rain, like icy needles, lashed at my unprotected face and head, since I hadn't bothered with the cloak's hood.

I was lucky I'd even remembered the cloak, the way things were going.

Guiding Gairloch around the small lake that covered half the road in front of the dry-goods store, I looked ahead, trying to make out the turn where the road to Howlett began. Supposedly Hrisbarg was one of the wool towns, the only one inside the duchy. Howlett was a wool town, too, but it was across the border in Montgren, another duchy, except it was ruled by a countess who didn't like the duke.

I chucked the reins again once we were back into the more solid mud.

"Halt! In the name of Candar! Rogue wizard! Rogue wizard!"

We were turning onto the lane that stretched ahead to the Howlett road. I kicked Gairloch in the flanks again, and he began to run, but only for perhaps a hundred cubits before he settled back to a quick walk.

Clang! Clang!

For all the shouts by the cavalry officer and the chimes on the alarm, no one followed us, at least not immediately and not that I could tell. It seemed pretty stupid. I mean, just because someone thought I was a blackstaff from Recluce, and just because I left in a storm, the idiot was trying to rouse the whole town of Hrisbarg.

Then again, I had been lucky, damned lucky that I looked so young. Why was everyone on the entire continent out against anyone from Recluce? Just what had happened in Freetown?

I kept looking over my shoulder, trying to feel whether anyone chased us, but could not see or feel anyone. All I felt was the rain, the ice, and the cold.

The road was empty, at least as far ahead as I could see through the mist and the rain. As Gairloch settled into a walk, I leaned next to the staff, nearly brushing it with my cheek before drawing back from the heat.

Trying to feel what might be around, I reached out with my feelings, my thoughts, trying to get a sense of chaos . . . anywhere. Other than a vague sense of unease connected with the road ahead, I could find nothing.

The staff cooled as we rode westward through the mud and rain. Traveling the road to Howlett was worse than the road from Freetown had been. Water slopped out of the sky and froze in chunks on the browned and dead grasses. The rain coated the oaks with ice sheaths, and turned the thorn bushes that twisted from the shardstone road walls into a tangled crystalline barrier.

The road itself—half ice, half black mud—*squuushed* with every step Gairloch took. Once again, I missed the desolate wizard's road that had covered most of the distance between Freetown and Hrisbarg.

Each step of the pony made my stomach churn, and with every

147

other step, the wind gusted and threw the icy rain under my cloak. I worried about his hoofs and fetlocks, or whatever they were called; but I worried more about me. So we kept going.

As I shivered in the saddle, I recalled fondly the heat of the day when I travelled to Nylan, at least in comparison to the chill that had already numbed my legs from boot-top to thigh. My buttocks remained painfully unnumbed.

My staff rested in the lance cup of the old cavalry saddle. That meant I swayed into it every so often, since it protruded well above the saddle. Flexing the reins every so often split the ice off them, but I had to keep brushing ice off the saddle and my cloak. The only thing the rain refused to freeze to was my staff.

The staff had saved me at least twice, and made me a target of everyone in Candar, or so it seemed. This last time, I had managed to escape without even using the staff, or letting anyone know I had it, but they were still after me.

We stopped twice, both times to let Gairloch drink and to let me stretch the kinks out of legs that felt like permanent cramps.

In time, close to midday, the rain stopped, the wind picked up, and ice began to form on the remaining puddles. Then I began to sense warmth in the staff again, as the road straightened and began to climb toward a low hilltop. Through the mist I could make out some sort of building.

"Oh . . . of course." Since the duke and the countess didn't like each other, the building was a border station . . . and another damned problem, since someone might well have warned the guards. I shrugged, pulled off my left glove carefully, and touched the lorken—hot enough to melt ice, and that meant some sort of danger.

"Well, Gairloch, they said you were a mountain pony . . . how *much* of a mountain pony?"

He didn't answer, didn't even flick his head, just kept walking.

I tried to think it through. Probably no one had warned the road guards. But even if they hadn't, word would get out that someone from Recluce had entered Montgren, and no one seemed to be very friendly to anyone from Recluce, especially blackstaffers.

In the end, the answer was simple—avoid the border checkpoint. Accomplishing such a simple answer was more difficult. Tangled low brush sprang from the roadside at every point, and most of it was ice-covered.

Reining Gairloch to a halt off to the side of the road by a higher patch of brush that would shield us from scrutiny, should any of the guards possess a spyglass, I tried first to study the slopes and the land around us, low rolling hills covered with sparse clumps of bushes and an occasional cedar, with white oaks along the watercourse lines between the hills.

Few people in the duchy lived alone, or away from the towns. On the hillside that sloped away to my right, a black line ran nearly perpendicular to the road—the uncovered remnant of a stone wall nearly buried by the meadow turf. But no trees. As I stared, I could sense the same wavy heat lines that concealed the black ships of Recluce, except these were older and fainter and tinged with unpleasantness.

In a way it was too bad the wall wasn't headed where I was, but the disorder bothered me.

I shrugged. We couldn't stand behind the bushes forever.

Whheeee . . . eeeeuhhh . . .

"I know . . . I know . . ."

So I turned around and let Gairloch pick his way downhill to where the road turned out of sight of the border post, nearly half a kay. As I recalled, there was another brook that looked like it meandered down in the same general direction as the border post, but with the hill between us and the post.

I chucked the reins and Gairloch stepped across the flowing water and out onto the meadow. Keeping the hill to my right, we began following the watercourse, roughly parallel to the road.

. . . ppeeeeepppp . . .

The sound of the insects or frogs or whatever it was reminded me that I had heard very little, certainly no birds at all, since I had arrived in Candar.

We crossed a low mound that stretched across the end of the meadow, and I knew that it had once been a homestead—but long, long before.

The brook narrowed as we continued and angled more to the left, southward, than I would have liked; but most of the space was open meadow, rather than brush or straggly cedars.

Another kay and the brook was barely a cubit wide, and angling back toward Hrisbarg.

"All right, we go over the hill."

Gairloch shook his head, spraying mist on me, and we started up the gentle slope, taking less time to reach the crest than it had to circle the second hill, even though Gairloch's steps grew edgier and edgier as we neared the crest.

I could sense nothing—neither heat nor cold, but an emptiness, a lack of even nothing.

Wheeeeee . . .

As we came through the mist to the hilltop, I shivered.

A pile of whitened and glazed stones graced the hilltop. Two of the pale white-granite monoliths remained standing, although their crowns were melted like candles left in the sun. Surrounding the chaos-circle was dead-white bleached gravel. Outside the gravel was a whitish clay that slowly darkened until it merged with the scraggly grass.

Wheeeeee . . . Gairloch shied from that whiteness.

Less than a handspan from my face, my own staff began to glow with a black light that urged me away from the stones.

Even with the age of the destruction, even after all the years that had passed, I didn't even look at the twisted patterns, but edged Gairloch around the dead-white stones.

Beyond the hilltop, north and west of us, I could see the hilltop where the border station lay, and the angle of the road descending toward Howlett—away from us, of course.

Not until we reached the bottom of the hill and turned back west did I remember taking a breath.

"Whuuuuuuhhh . . ."

My knees were shaking. For someone who had questioned magic and chaos, that ancient structure had been pretty convincing. The whole hill had radiated destruction. No wonder people didn't live nearby.

That was the worst. After that, the scattered brambles, and the wind that got steadily colder—all those seemed merely natural. The road itself was also a natural disaster, churned half-frozen mud, but somehow Gairloch mushed on.

Someone had to have seen us, but we saw no one, not until we were back on the road to Howlett, watching the scattered flocks of black-faced sheep, and their shepherds bundled against the cold. Then we passed a slow-moving wagon heading in the same direction, and an old coach headed toward Hrisbarg.

Neither driver gave me more than a passing glance.

150

XXIII

Dusk was falling by the time we struggled—with stops for water for Gairloch, and vain attempts to stretch out the permanent cramps in my legs—along the quagmire that was called the road to Howlett. Even from the outskirts I could tell that Howlett made Hrisbarg look like Imperial Hamor. Hrisbarg had rough wooden sidewalks; Howlett had none. Hrisbarg had defined streets; Howlett had a rough clump of structures. Hrisbarg's buildings had peeling paint; Howlett's had none.

But the rain had begun to fall as ice-needles, and the wind howled in from the north, freezing my cloak as solid as plate armor.

Almost at the edge of Howlett was a careless building, accompanied by another not much better than a large shack—the Snug Inn and its stable.

Wheeee . . . eeee, was Gairloch's only comment as I led him inside the stable.

"Three pence, and he'll share a stall with the other mountain pony," commanded the heavyset man by the sliding stable door.

I looked at the small stableboy racking a saddle while the big man collected. The stableboy shrugged.

In the open space to the right stood an unhitched wagon and a coach—that same golden coach that I had seen on the road to Freetown. I looked back at the heavy man to catch what he was saying.

"You stable him . . ." added the man. ". . . damned ponies, kill anyone not their master . . ."

I handed over the three pennies.

"At the end. There's another one like him there."

I led Gairloch along the narrow way toward the back, and eased open the stall door, holding it so that it didn't fall off the worn wooden hinge-pins, then glancing at the bleached and cracked support timbers of the stable itself, still wondering about the golden-finished white-oak coach.

Wheeee . . . eeee . . . The whinny of the other pony subsided as I let Gairloch take his own time.

Both sniffed the air, while I wanted to sneeze.

In time, I got him in and unsaddled. I quickly stowed the staff in the straw, along with my pack, and searched until I found an old brush. By then, the stableboy, not the collector, was watching.

"Any grain?"

He gave me a wary look, and I produced a copper penny. The boy produced a battered bucket, and I split it between the two, although I gave Gairloch the largest share.

Finally, I felt Gairloch was settled enough for me to chance the inn.

Once inside, the odor of unwashed herders, rancid oils, stale perfumes, and smoke left my eyes stinging. Squinting through the haze, I peered over the crowded tables. Those in the back, toward the narrow but drafty door through which I had entered, were long trestle tables with benches. Beyond them were square tables, of a darker and polished wood. Between the two types of tables ran a flimsy half-wall with three wide openings for the inn's servers.

Everyone on the road to or from Howlett seemed stranded in the same inn. On my side of the half-wall, men and women were shoulder to shoulder at the trestle tables. A few of the tables for the local gentry, or whoever the privileged ones might be, had vacant chairs around them, but none of the tables were unclaimed.

The Snug Inn, despite its name, was not snugly built.

Uncle Sardit would have listed in detail all the faults in the construction. While I scarcely had his experience, there were some poor design features evident even to me. The outside eaves were not long enough to keep the wind from blowing underneath and into the upstairs rooms. Likewise, the stone facing of the front wall had been built for style and was beginning to pull away from the heavy timbers that framed the side walls. The curves in the rough beams that framed both side and front walls showed that they had not been properly treated or cured.

Inside was worse. The hallway dividers separating the common and gentry sections had been carelessly sawed and nailed together with small spikes, needlessly splitting the wood. After my short tenure with Uncle Sardit, I could have done better and probably done it quicker than whoever had built them. The gentry's tables were square, sharp-edged, and probably gave the inn's servants bruises. Again, a few minutes with a plane or even a shaping saw would have produced a better and more serviceable table.

The common tables were green-oak trestles, sawed or split before the wood had cured. With the amount of red oak, black oak, and even maple available in Candar, I wondered why the tables were green oak.

I looked over the mass of people, wincing at the din. Though I had stood there for what seemed a long time, no one even looked at me.

Finally, I made out a space on the bench next to a man in a rough brown coat, halfway across the back of the commons area. I edged toward it.

"Watch it . . ."

"Young pup . . ."

"My apologies," I offered to the man whose elbow I had jostled, even as I ducked past him. He glared over the edge of the chipped ceramic mug he held to his beard-encircled mouth.

"Won't bring back the mead . . . worthless time for a storm . . . *Lass!* More mead!"

From the smell, whatever mead was, I didn't have any desire to taste it. Nor did I have much desire to stay in the Snug Inn, except that I was hungry. Since I hadn't learned how to eat hay or oats, that meant entering the inn.

I looked at the space beside the man in brown, then shrugged and eased myself into place, wishing somehow I had brought the staff, but knowing it was safer in the straw of Gairloch's stall. I still didn't like leaving it.

"You?" asked the brown man, bearded and hunched over his mug of steaming cider. From his muscles and his belt, I would have guessed a carpenter.

Of course he didn't know me. I hadn't told him. "Lerris, used to be a woodworker before I left home." All of which was true enough.

"Woodworker? Too damned fair for that." He glared at me.

I sighed. "All right, I was an apprentice woodcrafter—never got further than benches and breadboards."

"Hah! Least you're honest, boy. No one would admit that, weren't it true." Then he glared back at his cider, ignoring me.

Left to my own devices, I waved at the serving girl. A black-haired and skinny thing, she wore a sleeveless brown leather vest and wide skirts. She ignored me as well. So I began to study the people while I waited for her to get close enough for me to insist on something.

At the table closest the hearth sat four people—a woman veiled below her eyes, wearing a loose-fitting green tunic over a white blouse, and presumably trousers. She was the only veiled woman I had ever seen. But if her lower face were unknown, her clothes were tight enough to reveal that her figure, at least, was desirable.

Her forehead was darkish, as were her heavy eyebrows and her hair, bound with golden cord into a cone shape. Over the back of her chair was a heavy coat—of a white fur I had never seen.

Two of the other men were clearly fighters, wearing surcoats I could not identify and the bowl-cut of hair worn under a helmet. One fighter was older, white-haired and grizzled, but his body seemed younger. His back was to me and I could not see his face, though I would have guessed it was unlined, despite the white hair. The other fighter was thin, youngish, with a face like a weasel and dark black hair to match.

Between them, across from the woman, half-facing the fire, was a man in spotless white. Even from that distance, more than ten cubits, I could see his eyes were old, though he looked more like Koldar's age, perhaps a trace older, perhaps even into his third decade. But the eyes had seen more, and I shivered and dropped my glance as he turned in my direction.

The man in white smiled. His smile was friendly, reassuring, and everyone in the dining area of the saloon relaxed. I could feel the wave of relaxation, and I fought it off, just because no one was going to tell me what to feel. Was he the one who rode in the golden coach?

"You in the back. I see you are cold. Would you like some warmth?" I felt he was looking at me, but his fingers pointed at three figures huddled against the timbered wall behind me and to my left. The two men and the woman, all clad in the shapeless gray padded jackets that marked them as herders of some sort, ignored the question and looked down.

"Fine," said the man in white. "I can tell you have come in from the blizzard's chill. The warmth is on me." He gestured, and in our corner of the long room, I could feel the dampness and chill dissipate, though we were far from the fire.

The woman looked away from the wizard, for that was clearly what he had to be, and made a motion, as if to reject the heat. The two men looked down.

Me . . . for the first time since Gairloch and I had ridden out of

Hrisbarg, I felt comfortably warm, as if the long table where I sat were the one before the hearth, rather than the farthest from the fire. Yet the heat thrown by the wizard chilled me as well, inside, and it felt familiar, as if I too could have called it forth, though I did not know how. Nor did I want to try.

At a small table in the corner nearest the hearth sat another man, the only person in the crowded inn sitting alone. He wore a dark-gray long-sleeved tunic, belted over similar trousers by an even darker belt. A dark-gray leather cloak lay over the chair beside him.

His hair was a light brown that seemed gray, though from my distance he did not appear old.

"The man in gray . . ." I mumbled to the carpenter.

"Arlyn, call me Arlyn." His eyes were glazed, not with alcohol, but as if he had been looking somewhere else. "Lass! More cider." Arlyn waved the brown mug in the air. Several drops of cider splashed across my face.

After wiping off the cider with the back of my hand, I asked, "Arlyn, who's the man in gray?"

"Justen. Gray wizard. Almost as bad as the white one. Antonin. Antonin will take your soul and your body. So they say." He waved the mug again.

This time the serving-girl turned toward us.

"What's for a traveler?" I made my voice hard.

Her eyes turned to me from the mug she had lifted from Arlyn's hand, running over my dark cloak, sandy hair, and fair skin. "Perhaps you should join the dark one, young sir."

Arlyn looked at me again.

"I doubt I could afford such luxury."

The girl, for she could not have been much older than I, actually flashed a quick smile before her face turned cold and professionally false again. "Two pence for the fire, and five pence for the cider. Mead is ten pence a mug."

"Food?"

"Cheese and black bread is ten pence; cheese and bear and black bread is twenty."

"Cheese and black bread with cider."

"Twenty-two pence." She paused. "Now."

I shrugged. "Half now, and half when I get the food. Someone will take the cider."

Her face looked bored and tired already. "Fine. Twelve now. For fire and cider. Ten when you get the bread and cheese."

I fished twelve pence from my belt, glad in this surly lot that I had managed some change in Hrisbarg. "You'll break a traveler in this weather."

"You could stay outside." She slipped the coins through a narrow slot into a locked and hardened leather purse on an equally heavy leather belt, and handed me a wooden token. Then she was picking up mugs and coins all the way along the table, passing out tokens as she stacked the empty mugs on the heavy wooden tray.

The door behind me opened, and another rush of cold chilled the back side of the common room again.

A pair of road soldiers stood there, wearing heavy short riding jackets, swords, and carrying long-barreled rifles—used in peace-keeping, not in warfare, not when the smallest of chaos-spells destroyed their effectiveness.

A thin man, wearing a greasy brown apron and waving a truncheon, waved toward the pair. "Areillas, Storznoy!"

156 The bigger soldier—four cubits tall, with as much flab as muscle—jabbed the other, a man not much taller than the serving-girl. Then the two walked toward the innkeeper and the kitchen.

Conversations dropped off to whispers, or less, as the two made their way toward the innkeeper.

The heavier soldier said something to the thin innkeeper, who looked puzzled. The soldier raised his voice.

". . . said . . . demon horseman seen on the Duke of Freetown's deadlands . . ." repeated the smaller soldier.

The innkeeper shrugged. "Demon weather anyway."

"Roaches . . ." mumbled Arlyn the carpenter.

"Why?" I asked, wondering about the demon horseman.

"Paid by the Montgren Council to keep the road safe between the border and Howlett . . . paid by the Thieves' Guild for an exemption . . ." Arlyn looked for the serving-girl. "Where's the cider?"

The road soldiers went through the wide stone arch into the kitchen and the serving-girl came out, holding high a tray of mugs, somehow not spilling a one. Vapor whispered from the hot cider as she neared the chilly end of the common area where we sat.

Thunk.

Thunk. The dark-haired server avoided my eyes as she set the mug down before me and the next before Arlyn.

Thunk.

"Look!" I yelled in Arlyn's ear, pointing toward the wizard in white. The carpenter started, and I switched mugs with him.

"Look where . . . just Antonin . . ."

"He pointed this way," I tried to explain.

"Yell not at me . . . youth . . ." Arlyn growled.

"I am sorry . . ." And I was, but not because I had yelled.

Arlyn looked at the cider, but did not drink immediately.

I took a sip of mine. "Oooo . . ." The searing of my tongue and throat explained why the carpenter had waited.

A hush dropped over both the gentry and common areas of the Snug Inn. I saw that the man in white was standing, looking over at Justen, the gray wizard, whatever a gray wizard was.

"A deed more than a deed . . ." said Justen, so softly that I could not hear all of his words.

"A deed is a deed. Do appearances really deceive, Justen the Gray?" Antonin stood by his table.

The woman in the green tunic ignored Antonin, her veiled face turned toward Justen. The gray wizard said nothing, nor did he even stand.

"Actions speak louder than words. There are those here who hunger. Will righteousness feed them? Will the innkeeper feed them from the goodness of his heart and deprive his family and kin?"

Justen seemed to smile faintly. "That is an old argument, Antonin, one scarcely worth answering."

"Is it wrong to feed the hungry, Justen?"

The wizard in gray shook his head, almost sadly. I wondered how he would answer the white wizard's question.

"Is it wrong to feed the hungry, Justen?"

Even the herders in the corner turned toward Antonin.

"You among the herders—does one of you have an old goat, a tired ewe that will not survive the winter? Come . . . two silvers for such an animal. Certainly a fair price."

I found myself nodding. Even in early winter, a fair price for an animal that might easily die in the frigid eight-days ahead.

The wizard in gray shook his head once more, then sipped from his mug, watching as Antonin beamed from where he stood by the table.

"Innkeeper, for the use of your serving table, a silver also?"

The innkeeper, wiping his thin hands on the greasy apron he wore, smiled briefly, not with his eyes, as he looked at the crowd. "Enough, esteemed wizard, but I would hope in your charity that you would make good any damages . . ."

"There will be no damages." Antonin gestured toward the herders. "Who will take my two silvers?"

"Here, lord wizard." A bent man shuffled forward, his curly and dirty gray hair springing wildly from his head. His leathers were filthy, so battered their original color was lost beneath the dirt, and so tattered that the yarn laced through and around them barely seemed to hold either his vest or trousers together. Dirty raw wool poked from the holes in trousers and vest.

"Bring me the animal."

"Will he slaughter it here in the inn?" I asked.

Arlyn chuckled. "You'll see no knives here, youngster. The one's a great wizard."

"Too great," mumbled the traveler on my other side, who had said nothing since I had seated myself. He turned to his companion, an older man dressed in faded green with a heavy green cloak still wrapped around him.

A chill wind bit through my own trousers as the herder left, though the doorway was open only an instant or so. Outside the wind was beginning to moan, and the early dusk was nearly gone. I wondered how much more ice would fall before I could leave the inn. Or would it be snow by morning?

Arlyn's slurp reminded me of the mug I held between both hands. I sipped the cider carefully, but could taste nothing foreign. Still, I waited after my first sip.

Thunk.

"Ten pence." The serving girl laid down two heavy slabs of black bread and a thin wedge of yellow cheese. "And the token back."

I handed her the token and a silver.

Now I had the cheese and bread, and wondered if I could eat it— safely.

As I glanced toward the gentry section, I found the eyes of the gray wizard upon me. He nodded slightly, as if to say that I could.

I looked at the cider mug between Arlyn's hands. The wizard's face was unreadable, which was answer enough. But why would he even answer my unspoken question? And why did I trust the man in gray and not the one in white?

Taking a small bite from the tangy black bread, I tried to figure out the answers. Tamra would have called me a fool for even entering the inn. Sammel would have shared the stable with the animals, and who was to say who was right?

The outside door opened, wider, and the wind dispersed the lingering warmth that had grown from the body heat of the crowd. I swallowed another chunk of the dry bread, washing it down with the lukewarm cider.

Baaaaa . . .

The herder passed near the end of our table, nearly brushing the man in green, as he carried a scrawny sheep slung over his shoulder toward the wizards.

The inn door had shut, and the sudden odor of filthy sheep and unwashed herder nearly choked me. Had I not escaped from the ice and blizzard so recently, I might have been tempted to forsake the stench of the inn for the clean cold of the outside. Trouble was that the outside was too cold.

"Watch . . ." hissed the man in green to the traveler beside me.

Thump.

159

Arlyn's head dropped onto the table. The cider mug was still half-full. I looked, listened, but he was still breathing.

"Your sheep, ser." The herder set the animal in the space beside the wizard's table.

Splattttt . . .

The sheep repaid the warmth by defecating on the rush floor.

The innkeeper looked nervously at the wizard.

Antonin smiled, then gestured. Both soil and odor vanished, although the faintest odor of brimstone remained.

For a moment, everyone stopped talking, even the gentry.

Baaaa . . .

"You . . . promised . . . two . . . silvers . . ."

"You shall have them, my man." Antonin drew the coins from his purse and laid them on the edge of the table.

. . . *snaaaaath* . . . *snathh* . . . Arlyn the carpenter was snoring.

The herder pulled a small iron hammer from his pouch and touched each coin with it. They remained silver.

"Stupid . . ." muttered the man beside me.

The fellow in green nodded.

Stupid? To check the coins provided by a wizard? I would have, but with Arlyn asleep, snoring on the table, there was no one else I dared to ask why it was stupid.

Antonin stood, swinging his sleeves back to reveal bare arms. Not heavily muscled, as I would have expected, nor thin like a cleric's, but knobby like a merchant's.

"Before you go, friend herder . . ."

The herder turned back and looked down.

"You, my friend . . ." The white-robed wizard gestured toward the innkeeper. "The two largest trays you have."

"Long ones be all right?"

"Those would be best, friend."

If nothing else, the continued use of the word "friend" was not just annoying, but boring.

With a sour look as he sipped from his mug, the wizard in gray glanced from the sheep to the wall, then let his eyes pass over me and along the common crowd.

In the meantime, the innkeeper brought out two enormous wooden serving trays and set them upon the trestle table just beyond the gentry's area. The veiled woman had turned her chair to watch, but the older fighter at Antonin's table kept his back to me.

The tradespeople, including a woman tinker with a broad face and muscles that would have exceeded those of either Koldar or his stone-mason wife-to-be, reluctantly shuffled off the benches and stood at the end of the table away from the innkeeper.

Antonin stepped past two gentry tables, both filled with travelers wearing fur collars on their cloaks—no women—and approached the trestle. He motioned to the herder. "Pick up the animal and put it on the table, right over the trays.

The herder did so, nearly effortlessly.

The table shivered as the sheep wobbled there.

"Watch," hissed the man in green. I was watching, as was everyone in the inn.

The wizard advanced; the herder stepped back, his hand on the leather belt where he had placed the silver coins.

Antonin raised his hands.

I closed my eyes and looked down, not knowing why.

SSsssssssssss . . .

Light like a sunburst flared across the room with the sharp hissing sound.

Even with my eyes closed, the light had hurt. I squinted, blinking. The tears helped, and I could see long before anyone else could. Antonin had a nasty smile on his face, the look of a bully pleased at a beating administered to a small child.

Justen had an even more sour look upon his face, and the rest— from the commons to the gentry—were still blotting their eyes, trying to see. Except for the veiled woman, who was looking at Antonin from deep-set eyes whose expression was unreadable from where I sat.

". . . ooooooo . . ."

"Look at that . . ."

In my observation of the wizards, I had forgotten the sheep. I tried not to gape with everyone else. But I did. The two trays were heaped with succulent sliced and steaming mutton, with joints at the edges, and with sweetbreads piled at each end. A sheepskin rug lay on the floor beside Antonin, who was toweling off his forehead with the back of his wide right sleeve. Outside of the joints on the tray, there were no bones.

Sweat suddenly poured down my forehead. The common area felt like the kitchen when Aunt Elisabet baked bread for all the neighbors at winterdawn.

I watched as the wizard in white smiled at the innkeeper, then at Justen, the gray wizard.

"Meat. Honest meat for those who would go without." Antonin turned to Justen. "Actions do speak louder than words, brother wizard. Tell me that it is wrong to feed the hungry."

"It is not wrong to feed the hungry, but it is wrong to feed their hungers."

I never liked obscure answers, and I didn't like Justen's. If he thought that Antonin was a showman, he should have said so. Or that he served evil by tempting hungry people. But he didn't. Justen only smiled sadly again. Did the man ever do anything besides disapprove of the white wizard?

Antonin the white wizard faced all of us in the common area. "Come forward, those of you without a penny for food. There is enough for a small portion for all who are hungry." His voice was hearty and friendly, and the words sounded genuine, but the real invitation was the smell of roast mutton.

First came a boy in a patched jacket, the apprentice of some tradesman. After him came a thin girl in leggings too big and an old herd coat too small. Before the shuffle of their feet had reached the trestle table, half the commons were pressing after them. Only the whiteness of the wizard kept the crowd in a line.

Arlyn snored on the table, but the man next to me and his companion in green had joined the crowd. Tempting as the mutton smelled, the odor repelled me as much as attracted me. So I munched through the rest of the hard black bread and the thin cheese wedge while the others jostled for the mutton.

The innkeeper emerged from the crowd carrying the sheepskin, the one thing of lasting value, and disappeared briefly into the kitchen with the prize, emerging quickly with a large truncheon and another man with an even greasier apron and a larger club.

Antonin sat at his table and sipped from a real crystal glass—wine, not mead or cider, glancing once or twice in my direction. I tried to ignore him as I swallowed the last of the cider.

The gray magician—Justen—stood up and pulled his cloak around him. Then he walked toward me. I stood, wondering whether to meet him or flee. Then I shrugged.

162

"Let us check the animals, apprentice."

I nodded, realizing that, for whatever reason, he was offering some sort of protection, and followed him into the blizzard that separated the inn from the stable.

Whheeeeeeeeee . . . The howl of the wind was lower, only a half-wail compared to the shrieking that had forced me inside earlier. The needle-ice no longer fell, replaced with fine white powder so thick that it blurred like heavy sea fog.

"You near lost your soul there, young fellow."

I wanted to leave him right then. Another person knowing better than I did, ready to preach and not explain. But he hadn't asked anything. So I waited to see if he would explain.

He didn't, just walked toward the stable. I followed.

XXIV

The woman in gray watches the roadside from the bench seat of the wagon, holding her staff tightly in one hand. She tries not to think about the similarity between the rolling of the wagon and the motion of the cargo ship that had so recently carried her to Candar.

On either side of the road, the dull gray-brown of damp and rotting grass, interspersed with patches of black weeds, stretches to the hills on the north and to the horizon on the south. Beyond the southern horizon lies the Ohyde River, and the point where her journey will end—Hydolar, where the road and the river meet.

Ahead on the road, she sees three thin figures, their ragged and uneven walk like that of so many others that she and the wagon have passed.

Crack!

"Hyah . . . hyah . . ." rumbles the driver without looking at the whip he has cracked or the two draft horses pulling the now-empty wagon that had carried cabbages and potatoes. He wears a heavy belt filled with more than gold, and a cocked crossbow rests on a stand to his right. "See anything, Maga?"

On the road ahead, the two younger men ride a pair of rail-thin horses. The sandy-haired one bears a long rifle, good only against the desperate, but necessary on the road they travel.

Beyond them, beyond the three figures that the wagon lumbers around, she can sense only the emptiness of another set of minds, trudging away from Freetown and the soggy desperation of too much rain and too little sunlight.

"Nothing except some more hungry people . . ."

"Good for us, at least," rumbles the driver. "Never got so much for cabbages and potatoes."

She grips her staff and tries not to think about either ships or the gnawing pains in the minds and bellies of the vacant-eyed men and women and children stumbling along the road toward the sunlight of Hydlen.

XXV

"Sers! The doorway, please!" The pleading voice came from what I first took to be a pile of rags and blankets. The stableboy had heaped a worn saddle blanket over a pile of rags and burrowed his own tattered leathers underneath. He was huddled in a nook where he could watch the big sliding door. Beyond him loomed Antonin's coach, not quite lit by an internal flame.

"Of course," I found myself saying as I quickly slid the heavy slab back into place and plunged the stable back into gloom.

Whhhhh . . . . . . thip, thub, thip, thub . . . The doorway creaked and rattled in the wind.

The darkness didn't bother me, since I didn't seem to need much light to see by any more. Turning toward Justen, I found he had left and walked toward the stalls in the rear.

Gairloch was still double-stalled with the other mountain pony, dark gray with a creamy mane.

Wheeeee . . . nun . . .

"Good girl . . ."

I should have guessed. "Yours?"

Justen nodded.

"Gairloch's male."

"That won't matter for now. Rosefoot's pretty tolerant. She likes company. Where did you get him?"

"Freetown."

Justen nodded again. "I thought so. It would be odd for them to have a mountain pony, though."

"The liveryman led me to believe that was why I could afford him. Mean-tempered. I rescued him from the gluepots." I shrugged. "That was what they told me, anyway." I shivered. The stable was cold. Not so bad as outside, but not a whole lot warmer than an ice house.

Justen climbed onto the half-wall that separated the stalls. To our right was a tall mare who turned her head in our direction, skittishly. A white blaze covered her forehead.

The gray wizard crouched on the stall half-wall and eased toward the outside wall. Just above him was a squarish opening partly framed with hay wisps. He stood up in the opening, his head out of sight. With a sudden jump, he pulled himself up into the space above the stalls. "Come on, youngster, and bring that staff you hid next to your pony. They'll rest better, and so will you." He disappeared, and I could hear the rustle of straw or hay.

"How . . . ?"

"Can't you sense it?" His voice was muffled.

He was right, though. When I tried to reach out and feel for the staff, like farseeing, it almost burned into my brain. I grabbed the half-wall for support. After a moment, I reached down and reclaimed the dark staff. To my hand, the wood held only a faintly reassuring warmth.

Wheeeee . . . Gairloch tossed his head, more like a nod. It had to be coincidence.

"Are you coming, young man?"

With a second thought, I reached down and grabbed my pack as well, brushing off the straw and slinging it half over my right shoulder. I clambered up on the wall, then scrambled, far less gracefully than the gray wizard, up through the square opening.

"Ac . . . *chewWWW*!"

"The dust will settle shortly." Justen had pulled off his boots and his belt and was piling more of the loose hay into a bed.

"We're staying here?"

"You can stay where you want. I prefer not to stay under the same roof as Antonin. I sleep better."

I sighed. There it was again. More assumptions, more statements, and no explanations. "Could you explain a few things to me?"

Justen stretched out on a cloak that suddenly was more than twice it original size, and looked to be twice as thick. "A few. If it doesn't take too long. I'm tired, and I intend to leave early tomorrow. I'm headed toward a little hamlet called Weevett, and then to Jellico. Jellico's the town where the Viscount of Certis reigns. Once upon a time, Howlett belonged to Certis, but nobody remembers. Back then all it had was sheep, and no one really cared, even before the dead-lands. Now Howlett belongs to Montgren, and no one really cares except the countess."

I frowned, trying to sort out my questions. Finally, I gave up. "You said my soul was in danger from Antonin. Why? I mean, how could he have hurt me that way?"

Wooooooooo . . . *rat, tat, tip, tat* . . . Momentarily, the wind picked up and ice chunks rattled against the roof overhead.

Justen wrapped the overlarge cloak around himself. "Take off your boots. Your feet need the air." He shrugged, trying to make himself more comfortable on the straw. "Antonin is the strongest of the white magicians. A chaos-master, if you will. Wielding chaos is extraordinarily hard on both body and soul, and most white magicians die young. Powerful, but young. Antonin, and Gerlis, and by now I would suspect Sephya, have attained the power to somewhat postpone their early demise, by transferring their personality and ability to other and younger bodies, preferably to bodies already equipped with the talent and unaware of their own defenses. You fit the bill admirably. That's why I decided to move you away from Antonin. He was preoccupied with Sephya and her . . . situation. He didn't really sense you. Your innate defenses are good enough to conceal you from a quick look."

I shivered again. "Thank you." I struggled and eased off one boot, realizing that while the ice and rain hadn't gotten through the thick leather, my feet were indeed damp. The second boot came off easier, but my left foot was just a trace smaller than my right anyway.

"Oh, don't thank me. I did it for me, not you. None of us gray magicians could afford to have Antonin controlling a body with your latent powers. His knowledge is already too great."

"What do you intend, then?"

"Not much. You can devise your own hell once we're clear of Antonin. Tomorrow, assuming you're willing, on the way to Jellico I'll teach you enough to allow you to block anyone from taking over your body without your consent. Plus, if there's time, a few other tricks that are pure black and won't prejudice your decision."

"My decision?" The words were grunted as I levered off my right boot.

"Whether you intend to be a black, gray, or white magician." Justen yawned. "I am tired, and so are you. Get some straw together and go to sleep. Rosefoot will certainly let us know if anyone tries to climb up here. So will your pony and your staff. Good night."

He rolled over and left me sitting in a pile of straw, my pack and boots by my feet, my head twirling with unasked and unanswered questions, and my thighs aching still from too much riding.

For all the aches and questions, I was asleep before long, listening to the *wooooooooo . . . rat, tat, tip, tat . . .* of the wind, ice, and snow, even as I wondered who Justen really was and whether I should trust him. But I slept anyway.

XXVI

Waking up in the Snug Inn stable was nearly the reverse of falling asleep, except colder and noisier.

Whooooo . . . tip, tap, click, clack . . .

The wind continued to blow, and my breath was frost-steam in the chill air, so cold that even the dust seemed to have been frozen out of the air.

Rrrruuuurghh . . . My stomach contributed to the turmoil as well. With one eye open I glanced through the gloom toward the other side of the loft where Justen had spread his cloak. I sat up abruptly, nearly banging my head on the roof truss. The gray wizard was gone. The straw had been pushed back into place as if the man had never been there.

I stretched, jerking myself out of the warmth of my cloak, and brushed the straw off my trousers and tunic, bit by bit, stepping from foot to foot on the cold rough planks. After getting a few stray pieces out of my boots, I pulled warm feet into the cold leather, wincing as I did so.

Scrambling sideways onto the planks by the open bay to the stable below, I stood and stretched again. Then I glanced down at the ponies. Both Rosefoot and Gairloch were chewing something more substantial than hay.

Where had Justen gone?

To the inn? Or on some wizardly errand? Or a more mundane bodily need—one that I needed to take care of as well?

Rrrrrrrr . . . My stomach reminded me of its very unwizardly needs . . . that, and the fact that I had yet to think through my trip toward the Westhorns. I was still reacting. The last planned step I

167

had taken was to purchase Gairloch. After that, everything had been reaction. Not one thumb's worth of travel food lay in my pack or in the empty saddle bags.

"Stupid . . . really stupid, Lerris . . ."

Somehow, things kept getting in the way. I had forgotten to stop at the market square in Freetown because I had wanted to get clear of the town. That decision had been sound, but there was no place on the road to Hrisbarg, and I had been forced out of Hrisbarg and on to Howlett. Now I really didn't dare to go back into the inn . . . not after what I had seen of Antonin, and what Justen had said. Still, perhaps there was a general store or something, among the buildings standing in the sea of frozen mud around the inn, where I could buy some sort of provisions, including some blankets or the equivalent.

I shook my head, then followed Justen's example by shoving the straw back into place and by shaking out my cloak. My teeth felt fuzzy, my stomach empty, and my muscles sore. I checked my pack, then gathered both staff and pack for the descent to the stable.

Creeaaa . . . aaakkk . . . The stable door opened, then slid shut again. I ducked back out of sight.

"Good morning . . ." Justen's head popped through the opening from the stable. "Give me a hand, would you?"

I was glad to, since he had two steaming mugs, and a large platter, covered with a ragged cloth, which also steamed.

"I thought you might like something to eat before we left." He easily sat cross-legged on the hard floor and picked up one of the cups, easing the cloth off the platter and revealing four large bran biscuits and a battered apple.

I sipped the cider, warm but not burning, and overspiced with cloves. The warmth and the liquid helped ease the headache I hadn't realized I had.

"You know, young friend, it would help if I knew your name, or at least what you would like to be called." Justen took a large bite from the biscuit he held.

"Sorry . . . it's Lerris," I mumbled, trying not to lose any of the biscuit crumbs. While bran biscuits wouldn't have been my choice for breakfast, my stomach received them gratefully. "You're Justen?"

He nodded. "Otherwise known as the gray wizard, that damned fool, and other less flattering terms." A deep swallow from the battered earthenware cup followed. "The apple's yours."

I didn't protest, and ate it right down to the core, squishy spots and all.

"Antonin has been requested to assist the new Duke of Freetown . . ."

"Oh . . . he told you that? But he was already in Freetown."

"Does that matter? He serves whoever pays," snorted Justen. "He didn't tell me, though. He told one of his guards, who told Fedelia, who told someone else." The wizard finished his second biscuit and topped it off with the remaining cider from his mug.

Rather than answer immediately, I chewed the last of my second biscuit. "The old duke's actions seemed designed to anger many people."

"Particularly Recluce," observed Justen dryly. He stood up and brushed a few crumbs from his cloak and trousers.

"What would Recluce do?"

"Nothing major—besides flooding the duchy, ruining the fall hay, and ensuring that no major trade flowed through Freetown until the duke's death. Nothing besides destroying—publicly, and with a woman—his champion, and presumably using the same woman to assassinate him in his own castle."

169

I shook my head. "All of that scarcely seems possible."

"Not any more possible than an untrained blackstaffer escaping the duke's guards, riding the deadlands untouched, and avoiding the attention of the most powerful white wizard in Candar."

I tried not to shiver at his matter-of-fact words, instead following his example of standing and brushing away the crumbs. "What next? Is there anywhere I can get some trail food and some blankets and a waterproof travel cloth?"

Justen shrugged theatrically. "That's no problem at all. Expensive here in Howlett, but . . . necessary."

"Why . . . why are you helping me?"

"Who said I was? I'm more interested in not helping Antonin. Doubt is a powerful weapon. Once he learns you were right under his nose, that will create more than a little doubt, and he certainly needs some doubt in his life right now." Justen looked below. "Let's go. It's still early, and there's some snow falling, enough to make farseeing difficult." He vaulted down onto the half-wall below, then dropped into the stall next to Rosefoot.

Crack . . . thump . . . thud . . . I followed, not nearly so gracefully, banging the staff on the wall, dropping the pack, and nearly losing my balance off the half-wall of the stall.

Justen said nothing as he began to saddle Rosefoot.

I looked around.

"There," pointed Justen.

He was right. Beyond the small door was the outhouse. By the time I returned, Rosefoot was saddled, and Justen was checking rather full saddlebags. The gray wizard said nothing as I struggled with Gairloch, offering neither assistance nor criticism.

"All right," I mumbled, after what seemed like forever.

He nodded and opened the stall door. I led Gairloch out, and Rosefoot followed without Justen even touching her reins. Like Gairloch, Rosefoot wore a hackamore, not a bit.

"Sers . . . ?" pleaded the ragged stable boy as he eased back the sliding door.

I looked at Justen, who grinned, then tossed a copper at the smudged face protruding from the assemblage of leather and rags. The coach stood beyond, polished and waiting, but the horses were still in their stalls.

"Thank you, gray wizard. Good luck."

"Good luck, Gorling."

Creakkkkk . . . I eased onto the saddle, my thighs not protesting quite as much ás when I had left Hrisbarg.

Feather-light and chill, the wind brushed my stubbly cheeks, and like a gauze curtain, the light snow blurred the hills beyond Howlett. For all the howling and rushing of the night before, the storm had deposited only enough snow to provide a light blanket on the ground. Each hoofprint showed the frozen mud beneath.

A single plume of gray smoke spiraled from the main chimney of the Snug Inn, and flattened mud around the front doors of the inn showed that even though it was far from even early mid-morning, many had already left. Most of the tracks seemed to lead toward the road to Hrisbarg.

Now that there was a new duke, the merchants and traders were losing no time. I shook my head.

Justen eased Rosefoot closer to Gairloch. "Do you want to bargain, or to let me do it as if you were my apprentice? You're paying."

"What do I gain?"

"If I do it, everyone will link you with me . . ."

"But if I do it, they give me greater status and assume I'm the one who rode the deadlands."

"Perhaps not, but they will think of you in individual terms."

"It could cost more if you purchase things. You're a great wizard—although they won't cheat you on quality."

Justen smiled. "That covers it. It's your choice."

I shrugged. "I'm not up to being a hero this morning. I suspect I'll have plenty of opportunity in the days to come."

"The last building on the right," said Justen. His soft voice carried, yet I had the impression that I was the only one who could have heard it.

Built of the same wide gray planks as the stable of the Snug Inn, with the gaps between the warped edges chinked with dirty mortar, the one-story structure bore no sign, and only the planks that approximated a walkway from a hitching-rail to the battered and red-painted doorway indicated the possibility of a commercial enterprise. A single mule was tethered at the rail as Justen eased himself from the saddle, stepped across the frozen mud crests, and wrapped Rosefoot's reins to the post. I followed his example, far less gracefully.

Crrrreeeaaaakkk . . . The three men seated in wooden rocking chairs around the hearth on the left side of the room barely moved, even with the alarm from the hinges of the ancient door. The fire in the hearth, consisting mostly of red coals, barely flickered.

Heaped on four tables between the door and the hearth were all manner of saddle-carried gear—blankets, hand-shovels, hand-axes, canteens, saddlebags—and the majority were frayed and worn. To the left, on five shelves, were arrayed an assortment of small packages wrapped in oilcloth: trail food.

Justen stepped up to the first table.

"Another apprentice, wizard? Last time, you said you weren't up to one more."

Justen gave the heaviest man a rueful look. "And you said I wouldn't see you here another winter, Thurlow."

"What do you need?" Thurlow leaned forward but did not leave the chair, spindly-looking to hold his bulk.

"Canteen, basic travel food."

"What you see is what there is."

I let my fingers run across the assortment of bedrolls and blankets, stopping when my fingers recognized a certain tight weave and waterproofing that matched my pack.

Justen nodded minutely, and I set it aside for the moment, while he casually picked up a canteen and an assortment of small oilcloth-wrapped packages.

"Got everything?" grunted the heavy man as he levered himself from the chair and waddled toward the tables.

"Just a few things."

"How about a silver?"

Justen shook his head slowly. "I'm a poor traveling wizard reduced to taking apprentices, and you treat me like a rich merchant."

The other two men, much thinner than Thurlow, guffawed, but they had stopped rocking as they watched.

"Pretty young for an apprentice." Thurlow's deep-set black eyes raked over me.

"Times are rough all over."

"Seven pennies, but that's because you've always been kind to an old man."

"What about that bedroll—the brown one?"

"That? It's Recluce-made, worth at least five silvers. Something like that stays dry anywhere but the sea itself." Thurlow's voice was indifferent.

172

"Some folks don't like Recluce products," Justen answered.

"That's true, but they're good, you have to admit."

"How did it end up here?"

"One of their kids—dangergelders, they call them—sold it to someone I knew in Fenard. Prefect outlawed the sale of Recluce-made stuff. So he sent it to Jellico, and I got it there. The viscount doesn't care."

"One silver?"

"Not much good to me, but it is worth more."

In the end, Justen paid not quite three silvers for the bedroll, canteen, and five packages of food. I couldn't have done nearly so well.

"Well, wizard . . . you won't see me here another winter."

"And you won't see me with another apprentice," countered Justen.

They both laughed, and we left with me carrying everything.

Outside, the wind had picked up.

"Ah . . . hum?"

Justen raised his eyebrows as I laid the bedroll over the saddle in order to pack the food parcels.

I looked back at him.

"Two plus nine," he reminded me. His face was impassive, but I wondered if he were trying to hide a smile.

I dredged three silvers from my belt pouch, noting that my funds were disappearing all too rapidly, and remembering that the bedroll had belonged to a dangergelder who hadn't gotten very far before he'd had to sell it. I shivered, although I wasn't even cold.

A few fine swirls of snow whipped past my face as I packed the food into one saddle bag, and rolled the waterproof cloth of the one-piece bedroll into a tighter bundle that I tied behind the saddle.

"We'll fill the canteen along the way, in one of the cleaner streams."

I also agreed with that. Howlett didn't look as if it were the most sanitary of communities.

Without another word, Justen untied Rosefoot and chucked the reins. I was still struggling with Gairloch when he had reached the edge of Howlett and took the left-hand road. It took me almost three kays to catch up because Gairloch insisted on an even walk, barely faster than Rosefoot.

Even then Justen said little, though we rode side-by-side on the crooked road.

XXVII

Justen reined in his pony.

I did the same, but Gairloch decided he didn't want to stop, at least not there. First, I had to lean all the way back, using all my weight on the hackamore, wishing for the moment that mountain ponies used real bridles with bits, if only to get Gairloch's attention.

Then, he stopped—all four feet instantly frozen.

Only the stirrups kept me anywhere near the saddle—that, and the fact that the stubby saddle horn had somehow grabbed my belt and almost eliminated any future offspring.

"Uhhhmmmp," was all I could say, spitting out horsehair as I disengaged my face from the now-immobile pony's mane.

Justen managed not to laugh. In fact, he didn't even grin. Just sighed.

Once I was generally back in position on Gairloch, the gray magician inclined his head toward the left. At one time there had been a crossroads, but the post showing the town that lay down the narrow path to the left had been split by weather and the part with the name was missing. The arrow still pointed through the gap in the brush, with the notation "5 k." remaining on the bottom on the squarish pillar.

"To the left are the . . . is the old town of Fairhaven. I usually take my apprentices through there . . . but since you aren't an apprentice . . ."

"Why?"

"Because it gives most of them a unique perspective. Those few who totally failed to understand never became masters . . ."

No matter where I went, I couldn't get away from it. More veiled messages. Do what you want, but . . .

I shrugged. "Fairhaven, if you don't mind, then."

"It will add half a day or more to the trip."

"Doesn't matter to me, but if you feel we have to get somewhere quickly . . . you said Weevett is another day. There's two days and more hills before we get close to Jellico."

"It's worth the detour . . . in more ways than one." Justen didn't seem to make a gesture, but Rosefoot began walking the trail toward Fairhaven. Unlike most of the roads I had traveled in Candar (except for the wizard's road leaving Freetown), the path, though overgrown near the edges and far narrower than the twisting main thoroughfare, was straight.

I swished the reins, but Gairloch didn't budge. Flamed stubborn pony! Just as I was ready to jab both boots into his flanks, he ambled forward after Rosefoot and Justen, as if he had intended to do so all along.

The path seemed scarcely more than an overgrown trail, if that, straight though it was. Though I scarcely qualified as a tracker, I looked for traces of earlier travelers, without leaning too far over in the saddle.

In the dried mud, perhaps half a kay from the fork, I saw a series of widely-spaced deer-prints, but neither hoofprints, wheel-ruts, nor boot-prints.

At one time, the road had obviously been much wider, wide enough for four wagons abreast, if the regular line of trees behind the low bushes and undergrowth signified the old road boundaries. The trees were white oaks, their branches bare in the cold.

In places, leafless creepers now crossed the track, positioned to assault the road in the spring. In less than a handful of years, the brush would reclaim the trail entirely.

"Justen, does anybody still live in Fairhaven?"

"I'm not certain. The last time I was here, there were still a few . . . inhabitants."

"Wasn't it once an important place?"

"Very important. You can see how straight the road is."

As we approached the top of the gentle grade, the trees seemed taller, and the wind picked up, with a hint of another storm.

Looking back over my shoulder toward Howlett, and the not-so-snug Snug Inn where I had met Justen, I studied the overhanging gray clouds. But they looked no different than they had that morning—the almost featureless gray of winter, without the darkness that usually signified approaching snow.

I sniffed at the wind, sensing a bitter odor like ashes or slag, which blew from the direction of Fairhaven.

Had the once-prosperous town caught fire?

Straining in the saddle, I looked forward as the trail crested.

175

Nothing. The road continued straight ahead, straight down a gentle grade into a wide and shallow valley, dotted with small hills and scattered trees.

I looked again, then at Justen, whose eyes looked straight ahead, seeing nothing, or perhaps something I could not see myself. Without realizing it, I shivered—not from the cold, but from something else.

The taller trees seemed to form a pattern, although I could not discern exactly what it was. All of the taller ones seemed to be deciduous, and only a scattering of scrubby juniper brush showed green against the browns and blacks of winter.

Closer at hand, about a quarter-day ahead on each side of the trail, were two large hillocks, or heaps of white clay, or . . .

"Justen . . . was this whole valley Fairhaven?"

"As a matter of fact, it was."

Some recollection from somewhere tickled my thoughts, but as I strained to remember, whatever it was disappeared.

"Those were the north guard towers?" I pointed to the white heaps ahead.

"No . . . Fairhaven didn't need guard towers. Those were the gates. They were always open."

By now I could see the so-called gates. Under a light covering of dirt, the hillocks were a dead pure white. Nothing grew on them. Nothing. As we rode closer, I realized why. Something had melted the stone. Melted it like sugar candy at a carnival.

My eyes flickered from the melted gates to Justen, who was sitting on Rosefoot with his eyes closed, concentrating as his pony picked her way past the old towers.

The odor of old slag and ashes was stronger, almost overpowering, and a cloud of unseen darkness loomed ahead. Everything looked normal for a winter's day in Candar: gray and brown, cold and sere, with the northern wind at my back. Except for the dead whiteness of the melted gates . . .

For some reason, I put my hand on my staff, the one that marked me as different whether I willed it so or not. The black steel bands at the top were warm to the touch, even through my gloves.

"Lerris." Justen's voice was low. "There may be trouble ahead. Do exactly as I say."

"What?"

"Do what I say. Do not leave the road. Hold your staff, but do not unlash it. No matter what."

His eyes were still closed, his features expressionless.

OOOoooooooooo . . .

At first, the sound recalled the wind, but the breeze had disappeared once we passed the gates. Overhead the sky was darker somehow, although the clouds looked the same as before, and it was not even quite midday.

The odor of dead fires and slag was stronger now, but there was still no sign of anything that had burned, not any time recently.

The leafless bushes by the roadside seemed somehow twisted, and the few leaves left hanging from the autumn before were all white. So were the branches themselves—a near-shining white, although I had never seen a bush with slick white bark. Even the bark of the birches was off-white and rough.

OOOOOoooooooooooooo . . .

I clutched the staff with my left hand, gripping the reins even tighter in my right. Gairloch plodded on down the gentle grade.

Ahead the road flattened and widened. Under the dust and mud I could see traces of stone paving-blocks. Behind the bushes now were roofless buildings, only a story high.

"This was the old town center, made of solid stone. Granite, in some cases."

I glanced back from Justen, who still rode with his eyes closed, to the ruins beside the road. The roofless buildings were more intact than the gates. Except for the debris piled around and against them, several looked as though a new roof and some interior work would make them habitable.

OOOOOooooooooeeee . . .

"Ahead is the newer town center, where the council held court . . ."

How anything in ruins could be called new was beyond me, and I was getting nervous about the howling sound. Justen seemed to ignore it as he talked and rode, his eyes still closed.

Justen had to be looking at *something*. He was a wizard. Antonin had said he was, and he had a number of apprentices who had become masters, or so he had indicated.

OOOOOOOOOEEEeeeeeeeeeee . . .

The sound was closer, on the other side of the "newer" town center.

My left hand still on my staff, warmer to the touch even through the leather of my gloves, I tried to study the ruins, even as Gairloch and Rosefoot picked their way toward the howling.

The stone-melting that had destroyed the city gates had struck even more wildly around the "newer" square. The ruined buildings were twisted as if they had been hot white wax flung through a whirlwind and then stomped flat by a giant foot.

"This was built by the Magician's Council, the old square by the Stonecutters' Guild." Justen did not open his eyes, but, for the first time, his voice sounded strained.

I shook my head. Why bother with the descriptions? The place was clearly dangerous. By now the smell of ashes made every breath almost burn.

"Don't look at them. Just look straight ahead. Recognition leads to fear, and fear increases their power."

"Whose power?"

"The howlers' power."

I clutched the staff, ready to pull it free, if necessary.

"Don't!"

I tried to relax my grip on the dark wood, forcing myself to look straight ahead.

OOOOOOOOOOOOOOOEEEEEEEEEEEEEEEEeeeeeeeee . . .

From the corner of my left eye, I could see a shape flicker, trying to grab my attention.

177

I glanced down at Gairloch's mane, and the whitish shape disappeared.

"With each generation, they are weaker. And with each person who passes successfully their powers are diminished." Justen's voice was faint, but clear.

The road began to slope upward as we continued southward.

"OOOOOOOOEEEEEEEEE!"

I started, looked straight ahead at the suddenness of the sound.

On the trail, standing on a liquid-white paving stone, was a twisted and turned figure, white and streaked with red, but shining.

I blinked, trying to look down, but the figure seemed different . . . more human . . . almost as if wearing a red-and-white robe . . . and the twisted white was more like a reverse shadow cast behind him.

"Mine!"

The robed figure seemed to spring from the pavement, which spread to resemble a wide avenue, along which tall oaks rustled in the wind.

Mine!

178 As the second voice echoed in my thoughts, I found the staff in my hand, up before my face.

The figure hit the staff as if to rip it from my hands, which were bare against the wood. The impact rocked me in the stirrups, jolted me back in the saddle . . . and it was gone.

"*Accuuuuughhh . . .*" I was half-coughing, half-retching, surrounded by the foulest odor I had ever smelled, a cross between rotten fish, wet ashes, and brimstone. The mist burned my eyes, and I could see nothing except a tan blur that was Gairloch's mane.

Managing somehow to empty my stomach without losing the staff or my balance, I teetered in the saddle, finally straightening up.

Justen had said nothing. But I could tell both ponies were moving forward, still on the old trail. By the time I could see and breathe, I could also see why Justen had said nothing. He lay spread over Rosefoot's neck, somehow in the saddle, but very still.

At the same time, the feeling of the white oppression, more sullen than darkness itself, was gone, although the gray clouds seemed lower than before, and darker. The darkness was that of an approaching storm.

Swishing the reins, I tried to get Gairloch to move closer to Rosefoot. Grudgingly, the pony obliged.

As I drew abreast of the other pony, I could see that Justen was breathing. His arms were thrust into sheaths on each side of Rosefoot's neck.

Mind-throwing? Had the wizard sent his thoughts elsewhere? The sheaths indicated that he was prepared for his body to be carried without his consciousness. And he was still breathing.

Still, I rode next to him, hands still on the staff, feeling the warm wood against my hands.

Something about that bothered me, but I wasn't about to sort that out until we were out of the valley, *well* out.

The Council of Magicians, Fairhaven—something in my studies, something that Magister Kerwin had said, had to do with this place.

OOooooeeee . . .

The sound hadn't been a real sound at all, only a sound in my mind. The howler hadn't been able to make a real sound until I recognized him.

I let my thoughts seethe, took another look at Justen—who was still breathing—and wondered what I should do.

Rosefoot kept stepping forward, and so did Gairloch. So I waited, wondering where the magician's thoughts had gone.

Ooeee . . .

The cry had more of the feel of a mental whimper, as if whatever cried were about to die forever.

How something that was dead could die was beyond me, but that was the way it sounded.

Both ponies kept picking their way up the long gradual trail, still heading straight south, until we passed through another set of melted stone gates. The south set contained dark streaks embedded in that dead white, as though they had burned and then melted.

The odor died down, and I finally put the staff back in its straps. Justen still lay sprawled across Rosefoot—still breathing—and the ponies kept walking.

Then I realized something. The palms and the insides of the fingers of my gloves, except for just the fingertips, had burned away; but there were no burns anywhere on my hands. Nor were there any other burns on my clothes; just a line of charred leather, outlining the missing sections of the gloves. It was a wonder they had stayed on so long. I peeled them off, folded them, and tucked them into my belt.

179

The afternoon began to grow darker and I glanced overhead, but the clouds were still about the same. The wind was picking up, the way it often did in the late winter afternoons.

"Uhhhhh . . ." Justen started to shake his head, then stopped as if in pain, as he slowly righted himself.

"Lerris . . ." he looked back over his shoulder without finishing the sentence for a time. Then he spoke again. "That should be the end of Frven."

"Frven?"

"That's what they called it at the end."

This time I did shiver—shudder would be more like it.

Fairhaven . . . Frven. The second name should have been familiar from the first. City of the Chaos Council, brought down in a hail of fire more than two centuries earlier. I shuddered again.

"You saw Frven . . . Fairhaven . . . before it became the chaos-masters' city?"

Justen, still looking back, nodded absently. "I was younger then."

I tried not to shudder a third time. Justen looked about my father's age, and he had been alive two centuries earlier?

"You helped bring it down?" It was a wild shot, but everything seemed strange.

"Two ma—magicians created another sun, right above the city, so hot it melted everything like candle wax in a furnace." Justen straightened in the saddle, and I noticed that the arm sheaths had disappeared. "We need to keep moving, since it will be late when we reach the main road." He shook his head to clear it. "I should say that it already is late."

"How can it be late afternoon already?"

"That's a property of Frven. It used to be much worse."

Justen lifted his canteen and slowly swallowed nearly all the contents.

The brush and trees beside the narrow road were beginning to look more normal, with only traces of the shiny whiteness in their stalks and trunks, but the way still looked deserted.

"Lerris . . ."

"Yes."

"You have a problem . . . a real problem."

I sighed. Now all I needed was someone else to tell me that I had a problem—a real problem. But what was I to say to a magician?

"Yes."

"You did two things wrong and one thing right in Frven. You didn't listen closely enough and paid attention to that soul—I think it was Perditis—and almost let him become real again. That would have raised every magician in Candar against you both, because Perditis would have taken your body and soul. You used your staff for defense. That was right. But then you burned your gloves off to grasp the staff."

"Why was that wrong? The gloves, I mean."

"Because you used destruction to enable preservation. That very nearly cost you your soul again, and might have if I had not been able to shield you."

"Shield me?"

Justen did not answer immediately, but began chewing some travel bread, as if he were starving, while he rode. Finally, he swallowed and spoke again, his voice dimmed by the faint whistle of the wind and the *clop, clop* of hooves.

"I didn't intend staying in the second plane nearly that long, but, since I was there, I decided to seal off most of the rest of the lost souls. Should have done that earlier, I suppose, but it's such work."

Justen was sounding suspiciously like my relatives, not ever exactly answering anything while blaming me for my failures. On the other hand, I *had* felt that howler or demon grasping at me, screaming *Mine!* Besides, where had the day gone? We could not have lost five or six hours on a less than twelve-kay trip on a straight road, narrow though it was.

I sighed again, swaying in the saddle. Riding was still not natural to me, and my legs, though in shape, were still not used to the pony.

"All right. Once again, I seem to be missing something."

"Young Lerris," answered Justen dryly, "you also seem to have forgotten a few other things, such as letting me know that you are magister-born, that you carry the staff of a magister, and that you have not chosen your path."

My mouth must have dropped open. I could say nothing. Magister-born? Not having chosen a path? The staff didn't surprise me, for some reason.

Justen shook his head sadly. "Once again your origin burns through."

"But . . ."

"Nowhere else do they send out their best, untrained and untested, to find their way in a world that either ignores them or tries to destroy them."

"Destroy?"

"Yes, destroy. You are from Recluce the beautiful, the isolated, the powerful. The island nation that has humbled every fleet sent against her, destroyed every challenge contemptuously, and refused to take any real responsibility outside her own boundaries."

"But . . ."

"No : . . it's not your fault, not yet, and I suppose that is why I will help you, young Lerris. Then, at least, I will have someone to blame if Recluce continues to ignore the world. Not that poor Justen can do anything about it."

"Wait a moment," I protested. "You've been around two centuries, and you let Antonin do all his fancy tricks and you never raised your staff, never said a word. Why not? How can you blame Recluce? Or me?"

He just sighed. "So much potential, and so much ignorance . . . where, oh where shall I start?" He eased Rosefoot closer to Gairloch.

182   The road ahead seemed to merge into a much wider, but heavily-rutted highway.

"Is that the main road?"

"It is, but the next decent place to stop is about three kays farther along. So I'll try to answer your questions . . . while I can."

This time I took a swallow from the canteen attached to Gairloch's saddle, after looking in all directions. The main road was empty, as were most roads in Candar late on a winter afternoon. I tightened my cloak against the slowly rising wind. Most of the snow, small dry flakes, had blown clear even before we had left Howlett. In Eastern Candar, the snow is light and seldom sticks, unlike the high ranges of the Westhorns, where winter means snow upon snow until even the evergreens are buried to half their height.

"Even if you are from Recluce, you know that there is order and there is chaos. Magic is either, or some of both. White magicians follow chaos. Black magicians follow order. And gray magicians try to handle the best of both, and are regarded with great suspicions by both black and white."

"White is chaos, but why?"

"Lerris, do you practice being obtuse?" Justen sighed. "White is the combination of all colored light. Black is pure because it is absent all light."

That was something that, strangely, no one had ever mentioned— not that I remembered, anyway. I nodded for him to continue as we finally picked our way off the old road from Fairhaven, or Frven, and back onto the main road. I could once again see dusty hoofprints, a day old or more, in the chalky dirt.

"The problem with both white and black magic is their limitations. Most white magicians are just a little bit gray. No one can handle pure chaos, not anyone born since the Fall of Frven. There are a number of black magicians. I can tell that from their actions, but a truly good black magister cannot ever be discovered unless he or she wishes it."

I must have frowned.

"That's because of the limitations. Look . . . think of it this way. Too much chaos and even the internal order of your body becomes disorganized. That's what happens, in a way, when you become old. White magicians all die young, and the more powerful die younger, unless they switch bodies like Antonin."

"Switch bodies? But how?" I kept sounding stupid, and I hated sounding stupid. But Justen was answering some questions, more than old Kerwin had.

"He has worked an arrangement with . . . several local rulers. He provides certain services, and he can have the body of anyone condemned to die. He's in his fifth body now, but I doubt he can survive more than one more transfer." Justen stopped speaking and looked up the road, as if measuring the distance. He swayed a bit in the saddle, and I realized he was pale as fresh-bleached linen.

"You see, young Lerris, with each transfer it takes longer to rebuild his body image and energies because his soul ages, even though his body doesn't. Chaos disrupts the soul itself."

I could see the peaked roof of a wayfarers' hut and the cleared space surrounding it, as we plodded around a gentle curve—a refreshing change from the deadly straightness of the road into and out of Frven.

The hut looked empty, though well-kept. Neither surprised me, for Justen had indicated Weevett was but a few hours' ride ahead, and most travelers would prefer a warm inn to the best of huts.

"We should stop." Justen said nothing besides the three words, and I realized that it took all his energy merely to remain in the saddle.

Nothing more than four stone walls, two shuttered windows, a door, a thatched roof, and a small hearth—but it was swept clean and empty, for which I was grateful.

At the same time I wondered why some poor soul had not tried to appropriate the place, since it was far more hospitable than the ramshackle thatched wattle-and-daub dwellings outside Howlett and, presumably, Weevett.

Even though I half-dismounted, half-fell off Gairloch, the pony remained fast as I turned to look after Justen. The wizard in gray was gray all over. He said nothing as I helped him off Rosefoot and onto the stone bench outside the hut.

With short gusts, the wind was picking up, swirling scattered pieces of dried and colorless straw around my boots, puffing dust and scattered snowflakes at Justen's face.

I found a short axe in Justen's pack, poorly-sharpened but adequate, and carved out some shavings to start the fire. There looked to be a small creek downhill from the hut, but Justen needed the fire more than he needed the water.

The flint and axe-steel were sufficient; but then, I've never had trouble starting fires.

Justen watched as I unstrapped a small kettle from his saddle kit. "Going to the stream."

He might as well have been asleep, for all that he looked at me. For some reason, I stopped and took my staff from the makeshift sheath on Gairloch. The pony tossed his head once, and chuffed. His breath was like steam. I swung the kettle in my right hand and grasped the staff in my left, though the water was almost within sight of the hut.

As I scrambled down the path, worn down by years of usage, I felt watched. But then, one way or another I had been watched all day.

Crack.

Thunk!

A figure in rusted armor lay at my feet, between me and the stream bank.

The staff had moved in my hand, reacting before I had seen more than a flicker of movement.

This time I studied the overhanging trees, and the underbrush. But now there was a sense of emptiness.

Hsssssssss . . .

As I looked back down at the fallen figure, mist began to rise, slowly at first, then quickly, forming a small luminous whirlwind. The shaggy man who had been inside the armor was gone, and only the rusted metal links and few plates remained. Then they began to crumble in on themselves, and they too were gone.

For somebody who hadn't been sure about magic, I was seeing a lot. Or I was losing my mind. I preferred to think that magic was real.

Scooping up a kettle full of water, I hurried back to the hut. Justen had straightened himself up a little, but still sat in the chill outside, rather than by the small but bright fire.

I hung the kettle on the hook over the fire, then I took Gairloch's reins and stood there, wondering whether I should unsaddle him and let him browse or tie him near the hut. Finally I began to unsaddle him, lugging the tack and saddlebags into the hut. I unclipped the reins but left the halter part of the hackamore in place.

Rosefoot whinnied gently, as if to ask for the same treatment. I obliged her as well. By the time I finished, Justen had dragged himself into the hut and onto the single rude bench inside.

"Any tea?"

"Bring me the reddish pouch."

"This one?"

He nodded, and I handed the pouch, more like a small bag, to him.

"Here. Two pinches in the kettle."

Using the wadded corner of the horse blanket, I levered up the lid of the kettle and eased the black stuff inside. It didn't look like tea, but within minutes the hut began to smell like senthow tea.

I rummaged around until I found two tin cups, and poured from the kettle.

Then I looked outside again, but both horses were well within sight, grazing at a patch of grass sheltered by greaseberry bushes. By now it was almost dark.

"The horses?"

"They will be all right now."

"Now?"

Justen sipped the tea from his cup. His smile seemed lopsided. "That blow you landed on the warimage echoed enough to warn off all but the strongest of white creations."

"Warimage . . . ? White creations . . . ?" I shook my head. Again, I was sounding stupid.

"After you have something to eat, young Lerris. I could use some sustenance as well." The pallor was gone from his face now. He merely looked tired.

"What do you suggest?"

"Take one of the green packages and empty it into the pot. You'll need some water. It makes fair stew."

After another trip to the stream, some time heating the water, and some time waiting for the gooey mess to cool, I was surprised to find it tasted like stew, and not a bad one.

Then I had to clean up the pot, and repack all the packages. Justen watched with an amused look, almost relaxed in the firelight.

As I finished repacking, I remembered some of my earlier questions.

"You never did finish explaining that bit about why Antonin couldn't grab another body."

"There is nothing else to explain. Chaos corrupts the soul. The more corrupt the soul, the faster it ages a body. Each transfer exhausts both body and soul. At some point, the soul cannot recover enough from the last transfer before the next one must be made."

186

"Which body are you wearing?"

"My own. It's really much easier that way, although it does create a number of limitations—as you saw today."

"You could have been killed."

"Only if you had been captured. That was one reason why I had to keep shielding you and rending the revenants. You beckoned to all of them, and you have very few defenses against . . . deep temptations."

I sipped my cool tea. Justen had long since finished his.

After saying nothing, I finally stood up and added a small log to the fire.

"Did you mean what you said about choosing a path?" I finally asked.

"You are magister-born, a born magician if you will, like it or not, and all magicians must choose a path—black, white, or, for a few, gray."

"Me? A magician? Hardly. Not a good woodworker, and not a potter. But a magician? My mother's a potter, and my father . . . well, I always thought he was just a householder."

This time Justen shook his head. "Humor me, young Lerris, and you *are* young . . ."

—Humor him? Why should I? What did he expect, insisting I was some sort of magician in secret?—

". . . but you have to make a choice."

"Why? I could refuse to choose anything. Even assuming I'm what you think I am."

"Refusing to choose is a choice. In your case, your choice is more limited because of what you are."

"Huh?"

Justen squared himself on the bench, looking more and more like Magister Kerwin, though Kerwin was white-haired and frail-looking, and Justen was brown-haired and thin-faced, with smooth skin. "If you chose the white, you can never return to Recluce, for the masters bar anyone associated with the white from your island nation. Second, your soul screams for order and explanation, even though you want to reject it. And your desire for order would keep you from mastering more than the simplest of chaos-manipulations.

"While you are now in effect stumbling through the gray, in the end the conflict of balancing order and chaos would destroy you. So . . . you either choose the black, or risk destruction in white or gray . . . or you reject all three . . . and become a soul for a white master like Antonin to feed upon."

"Wait a moment! Just like that? Thank you very much, and I should become a black master on your say-so?"

Justen pulled his cloak around himself. "No. You can do whatever you please. You are not my apprentice, only my traveling companion. Doing the wrong thing will kill you; but then, doing the wrong thing will kill anyone, sooner or later. You just have to decide earlier. You can decide I am totally wrong. You can walk out of here tonight, and I will understand.

"If you wish to travel with me, you must decide on something. Because, undecided, you are a target for every free spirit, and every chaos-master, in Eastern Candar."

"Where were they before?"

"That was before you used the staff." Justen rolled over, and was asleep before I could find an answer.

If there was an answer. I looked at the fire for a long time. Then I checked the horses, then the fire again. Finally, I pulled my own cloak about me, determined that I could not sleep.

Once again, I was wrong.

187

XXVIII

The man in white sits back in the light-colored wooden rocker. His eyes flicker in concert with the flames from the fireplace, absently, as though he is unaware that his room is the sole one in the inn with its own source of heat. "What have you seen so far, lady, of the goodness of Recluce?"

She purses her lips, but says nothing.

He does not press her, instead remains waiting in the chair, as if content to let her consider his question fully.

Her eyes slowly move from his lightly-tanned face to the fire, and back again. "I have seen suffering, but that scarcely can be attributed to Recluce," responds the woman in gray leathers, the blue scarf setting off the brilliance of her hair and the fairness of her complexion. Standing as she does by the low table, she looks taller than she is. Her eyes turn momentarily toward the other woman, who sits quietly in the ladder-backed chair to the left of the hearth.

"Have you watched the rains turn and turn again, soaking the life out of the fields? Did you see any ships bringing foodstuffs into Freetown?" His voice remains level, mild.

She considers the import of his words. "You seem to indicate that the Masters of Recluce created the suffering."

'I would think it was obvious, lady. But perhaps you should take some more time to watch and reflect upon what you have seen."

"I don't think that we need to fence with words," adds the dark-haired woman. Her voice is throaty, but businesslike. "You would like to learn how to wield your powers for good. We believe that we can help you."

"What do you want?" asks the redhead, still looking at the man in white. "You're not exactly offering your help out of the mere goodness of your heart."

"I could say so, but either I would be lying or you wouldn't believe me." The corners of his mouth crinkle, and his eyes lighten for an instant. "You have noticed, I am certain, how reluctant the Masters of Recluce are in using their powers for good beyond the isle itself. And I am equally certain that you have asked yourself why they do not help alleviate the suffering that exists. Why do they blockade Freetown?" His arm moves languidly toward the darkness beyond the curtains. "Such blockages seldom trouble the powerful. Only the poor, and those who work, suffer the lost wages and the shortage of food."

The redhead shifts her weight from one foot to the other, so slightly that she does not move. "You talk nicely, Master Antonin, but what have you done to help the poor? Besides ride around in a golden coach?"

"You saw me warm those who were cold, and I have fed those who hungered."

The truth rings in each of his words like silver, and the redhead steps back. "I need to think about this."

"By all means, but you are welcome to travel with me to see first-hand what I do to lift the suffering imposed by Recluce."

The redhead frowns, but says nothing.

189

XXIX

With the dawn, Justen looked almost as young as he had when we had met at the Snug Inn, except for the dark circles under his eyes and the tiredness in his voice.

He supplied the packages; I got the water and cooked up some porridge that looked like mush but tasted more like a good corn pudding. We drank some more of the senthow tea.

Justen made no effort to hurry, and that alone told me the wizard was still exhausted.

As I rolled up my bedroll—much more comfortable, even on the hard-packed clay floor of the wayfarers' hut, than the scratchy straw of the Snug Inn's stable—I caught sight of the corner of a book, its black leather cover worn from obvious use, protruding from the edge of Justen's pack. While the volume bore no aura of either order or disorder, an impression of great age permeated the leather and its parchment pages. My eyebrows lifted, wondering what sort of book the gray wizard had carried for so long, whether it contained spells, or procedures, or what.

Justen caught my glance, reached down, and eased the book out. "Here. You can read it if you want."

"What is it?"

"*The Basis of Order* is what it's called. All of the black magicians use it."

I tried not to swallow. "Is it that important?"

Justen smiled. "Only if you intend to become an order-master."

"Is that an old book?" I was trying to recover.

"My father gave it to me when I left home."

"Where are you from, Justen?"

He waved me off. "No place I really want to discuss. Do you want to borrow the book?"

"No . . . not right at the moment . . . I don't think . . ."

"Any time . . ." He lay back, letting his eyes close, appearing, again, far older than the mid-thirties I had first supposed.

I looked at the ashes in the not-quite-ruined fireplace. The age of his book and the white hair after fighting off the demons of Frven showed Justen was more than he appeared, and far older.

The Basis of Order? Just what had my father given me? Was Justen from Recluce, or from a Candarian family of order-masters?

Still tossing the questions around in my mind, I re-rolled my bedroll and tied it tightly into its cover, setting it beside my pack before heading into the morning to check on Gairloch and Rosefoot.

Outside the air was chill, the dark featureless clouds high overhead, and the wind out of the north. The sparse fragments of brown grass crunched underfoot.

The two ponies had clipped the grass by the greaseberry bush, as well as chewed some of the less-dried leaves from the bush itself. Then they had moved toward some higher grass in a depression closer to the brook, where they continued to browse.

After watching the two munch, and Gairloch toss his head and amble to the brook for a drink before returning to eat more of the long brownish grass, I finally walked back into the hut.

Justen's eyes opened. "Are you ready?"

"To leave?"

"No. I'm not ready for that. I meant ready to learn how to protect yourself from wizards like Antonin or demons like Perditis."

"Fine with me." I just hoped it wasn't too boring. Even if it were deadly dull, the alternative was worse.

Justen sat up, leaning his back against the wall and ignoring the grime that touched his fine gray linen tunic. "All it takes is practice. What you have to do is concentrate on being yourself. Say something like, 'I am me; I am me,' over and over if necessary."

"Why?"

Justen sighed. "When someone wants to invade your mind, they want to take away your ego, your sense of being a unique individual. You have to fight that. And there are two steps to fighting. First is to recognize that you are being tempted, and second is to assert yourself."

"What do you mean?"

"I'll just have to show you." His voice tightened as he looked at me. "Don't you really want to know the real answers to things, Lerris? Why the masters forced you out without explaining? Aren't you more than a little bit tired of being put off and told to find things out for yourself?"

"Of course! Haven't I said so often enough?"

"Then look at me. Look for the answers." His voice shook, but he was offering what no one else wanted to offer.

So I looked at Justen, watching as the distance between us seemed somehow to decrease.

Now . . . just think about the answers you deserve . . .

The words were gentle, and I did, wondering why I had been thrown out before I even knew what I was.

Justen stood next to me. *What wouldn't you give to know the answers? Just reach out with your thoughts, not your hands, and I will show you the answers . . .*

My thoughts? Why not? Thoughts were just thoughts, and I might yet find out . . .

I tried to cast my thoughts, like my senses, toward the figure next to me.

White!

A white fog that curled around me so tightly that I couldn't see. I couldn't speak—trapped somewhere in nothingness; a nothingness bright enough to burn my thoughts.

Answers . . . answers . . . answers . . . The words echoed without sound through my head, but I could not speak, could not see.

191

Was I standing? I couldn't even see my arms, or move, or even feel whether my muscles *could* move.

Justen? What had he done? Why?

. . . answers . . . answers . . . answers . . .

In the white fog, that mind-blinding light, were shafts of yellow, red, blue, violet—all spearing me, slashing at one thought, then another.

. . . answers . . . answers . . . answers . . .

Finally, I remembered what he had said about insisting that I was myself. But had that been a trick also? Another way to gain my confidence? To catch me in a web of white?

. . . answers . . .

Was Justen really the one who needed the new body? Why had I trusted him?

I . . . am . . . me . . . me . . .

Had the white retreated a shade, become not so blinding?

. . . answers . . .

I . . . am . . . me . . . me . . . Lerris . . . Lerris . . .

I kept thinking the words, repeating them until I felt myself come together somehow. *I . . . am . . . Lerris . . . Lerris . . .*

". . . Lerris . . ." the words stumbled from my mouth as I crashed to the floor of the wayfarer's hut.

Thud . . .

This time, blackness reached out and grabbed me.

When I woke, I was still lying in a heap on the dusty clay, and it was well past midday.

My head felt as though each of the colored light-spears had ripped through it trailing barbed hooks, and my tongue was swollen, my mouth dry. Still, I slowly eased myself into a sitting position, wondering what had become of Justen.

I looked over to the bench.

"Oh . . ."

The gray wizard lay there, his hair thin and silver, wrinkles across his face; he was breathing unevenly. I glanced at my own hands, but they were still mine, if shaking.

My legs wobbled as I half-stumbled, half-crawled to Justen's pack and fumbled out the red pouch. When I grasped my staff to help me stand, the reassurance from the wood helped, and I tottered out and toward the brook.

Wheee . . . eeeee . . . Only Gairloch whinnied, but Rosefoot raised her head as well, and both watched me as I filled the kettle, trying not to feel like each chill northern gust would topple me into the water.

Justen was still breathing, but still old, and unconscious, as I rebuilt the fire and heated the water.

Whatever the potion was that smelled like senthow, it killed my shakes and returned me to the realm of the living—the tired living. Then I eased a drop or two onto Justen's dried lips.

"Oooo . . ." His eyelids fluttered.

Another few drops, and he was able to swallow.

In time he croaked, ". . . some stew . . . the blue pouch . . ."

So I made that. This time, hearing my steps to and from the brook, neither pony even lifted a head from grazing.

After a mouthful of stew, which despite its blue tinge tasted like a venison pie, I looked at Justen. "Did you have to show me so convincingly?"

He shook his head slowly. "Strength rises to strength. If I had really tried to take you over, not just isolate you, one of us would be dead." Some of the silver hairs had darkened and his hair seemed thicker. A few wrinkles had eased, and the gray wizard merely looked old, rather than ancient. "Did you learn?"

"Uhhh . . ." I thought for a moment. What had I learned? "I think so. That wanting something badly can let someone else enter your thoughts or body . . ."

"Just your thoughts. Once they control your thoughts, the body comes next."

I shivered. "Would I have stayed in that white forever?"

"For a long time. An isolated personality dies over time, or goes mad and then dies. The white wizards don't talk about it, but it takes several years, and I once did restore someone. He avoided me thereafter." Justen took another sip of the tea, followed by the stew.

"Does insisting on being yourself hold off that whiteness if you realize it soon enough?"

Justen frowned. "That depends on the wizard. With someone like Antonin, you have to reject his temptations from the first. Give him the slightest edge, and he'll manipulate your emotions like a minstrel uses a song. With a less determined master, or one less skilled, you can even break free from isolation if you were tricked into it. When that happens the energy recoils, and the spellcaster gets it back negatively. That's what happened to me. You were so interested in getting answers, so easily manipulated, that I didn't see how much strength you had underneath."

I didn't know whether to be pleased at his acknowledgement of my strength, or irritated at my gullibility.

"Will and understanding are the keys, Lerris. Not just to mastering order, but to mastering anything." Justen leaned back as he finished the cup of stew.

"I take it we're not going on to Weevett this afternoon?"

"You'll collapse in three kays, and I couldn't even get on Rosefoot. Does traveling seem like a good idea?"

Put that way, it didn't.

"Besides, you need to do some reading." He was holding out *The Basis of Order*. "Trying to teach you by showing you could end up making me permanently old, or killing you."

I reached for the book.

"After you clean up. At the least you owe me that."

Back to the brook I trudged, still wondering why I trusted the gray wizard. Every time I thought about that whiteness where he had almost entrapped me, I wanted to shudder. Yet I could tell that he hadn't particularly wanted to put me there. And he had paid a greater price than I had—twice.

That left his reasons untouched.

No answers came as I used a damp cloth to wipe the cups clean after having rinsed them in water so cold that it hurt my hands to the bone.

Justen was stroking Rosefoot's nose as I walked back to the wayfarer's hut, and providing the pony—both ponies—with something they ate from his open palm. I didn't want to talk to him right then and kept walking.

Inside the hut, I could see the book laid on my folded bedroll, but I set the damp cups on one end of the bench to dry. Then I put another log on the fire, picked up the book, and sat on the bench where Justen had been.

With not a little resentment, I opened to the first page.

Order is life; chaos is death. This is fact, not belief. Each living creature consists of ordered parts that must function together. When chaos intrudes . . .

Fine. That I knew, if not expressed precisely that way.

Order extends down to the smallest fragments of the world. By influencing the smallest ordered segments to create a new and ordered form, an order-master may change where land exists and where it does not, where the rain will fall and where it will not. . . .

In contrast, control of chaos is simply the ability to sever one ordered element of the world from another . . . focused destruction . . .

My head was aching after less than two pages, and I closed the book. How did the philosophy I had just read have anything to do with escaping the whiteness in which Justen had attempted to trap me?

Closing my eyes, I tried to reason it out.

First, when I wasn't thinking clearly, either in Frven or when Justen offered me answers, I could be tempted. And temptation meant letting my mind open to someone. Whoever controlled a body's thoughts, then, must control the body.

But . . . if that were so, anyone could take over anyone else, and that didn't happen.

So . . . it took talent . . . but that talent could be blocked or thrown out . . .

I opened my eyes and looked for Justen. He wasn't in the hut, but outside brushing Rosefoot. With a sigh, I closed the book and trudged back outside.

The wind had died down, and a hole in the clouds to the south let in a stream of sunlight on the hills to our left.

Justen had stopped brushing and was watching the light play on the gray and brown and white of the hills.

"Justen, is self-knowledge the same as stonework, good stonework, when it resists chaos?"

He nodded. "There are dangers."

I must have frowned.

"Not even Antonin can control a poor shepherd who fiercely resists, but his power is great enough to destroy him or her."

"But you said that Antonin could control me?"

"Through temptation." Justen kept brushing Rosefoot as he talked. The gray wizard's hair was now mostly dark, with only traces of silver, and only a few wrinkles remained. "He would take you as his apprentice, show you how order works, and how you could control chaos. He would intoxicate you with the power of destruction—always for good. Feeding the poor, clearing the roadways—until the internal conflict between order and chaos built and destroyed your self-image. By then, you'd not want to take responsibility, and Antonin would relieve you of that burden. Sephya and Gerlis are more direct."

I shivered, seeing for the first time, really, what he had meant. And all that because of not understanding?

For the first time, then, I got angry, really angry, so angry that my jaw clenched, and my eyes burned. So angry that I felt the chill air around me as a relief from my own heat.

To avoid some minor chaos in Recluce, to avoid a little unpleasantness, they shipped off me, and Tamra, and Krystal, and all the others, without even spelling out the temptation problem, knowing that all dangergelders were flawed, seeking answers or power or *something*. And that thirst would leave us all potential victims of the Antonins of the world.

Justen watched, an amused smile upon his face.

"What's so funny?"

"You. You've read a few pages, and you're ready to tear apart all of Recluce." He kept smiling.

"How do you know?"

"I felt that way once, too."

"You're from Recluce."

"I didn't say that. I said that I felt that way," he corrected me gently. *Wheeee . . . eeee . . .* Gairloch jabbed his nose into my shoulder.

I reached for Justen's brush—another item I really needed if I were going to take care of a horse. Then I thought about my dwindling funds and almost groaned. Everything seemed to cost something . . . and far more than I had thought possible.

XXX

Absently fingering the green scarf at her neck before letting her left hand drop, the redhead looks at the hearth where no fire burns.

Her thoughts turn, as they have so often, to the unanswered questions. Why has the white wizard been so willing to share his knowledge, to accept her as an equal, when the Masters of Recluce had so grudged every speck of knowledge?

The staff warms under her palm as she ponders, not really watching the white mage as he sits in the chair that is not quite drawn up to the inlaid table. He frowns with perhaps the first frown she has seen.

"Why frown?" she asks. "These are certainly better quarters than the inn at Hydolar. It appears that the viscount does provide for those who do good."

"You are still skeptical," comments Antonin, his mellow voice conversational. "What would it take to convince you? Perhaps another technique you can use to improve your understanding?"

Her lips quirk in an expression that is neither smile nor irritation, but some of each.

"This one is simple enough to show you, just as I showed you how to cloak yourself from the sight of those who do not need to see." His voice assumed the tone of a patient master. "I promised you that I would teach you how to reach your full abilities. Have I not kept my promise?"

The redhead nods grudgingly.

Antonin sighs softly. "Then, perhaps I should provide another lesson—one that will improve your understanding as well. I assume that you would like to know why the Masters of Recluce hide such simple techniques, and why the Brotherhood forced you out without even bothering to acknowledge your abilities?"

The woman in the green scarf nods again. "Haven't I said so?"

"You have. But you have also said that mere words are not enough, that words conceal as much as they reveal, and that you are more than a little bit tired of being put off." He sighs, again softly. "You will have to concentrate. Put both hands on your staff, and look down at the mirror here."

She frowns, for she had not seen the mirror appear on the table, but she looks into the misty swirls that resemble white clouds blocking the images that must exist behind the mists.

"Look deeply into the glass. Look for the answers." His voice resonates slightly. "The mirror represents the barriers in your thoughts, the barriers to full understanding. Think of nothing at all, of silence, of stillness . . .

Now . . . just think about the answers you deserve . . .

The words hang in her mind, not in her ears.

What would you not give to understand? Reach toward the glass with your thoughts, just your thoughts, not your hands, and I will show you understanding . . .

The redhead topples forward before the dark-haired woman catches her shoulders.

"It took you long enough . . ."

"Sephya."

The coldness of her name stops the woman's mouth.

"Now . . . before she can assert her identity. Now . . ." His forehead is beaded in sweat, and fine lines seem to have instantly aged his face.

The dark-haired woman grasps the hands of the immobile and wide-eyed redhead and begins to turn the redhead's face so that their eyes meet—lined dark eyes and clear blank eyes.

On the table the white mists swirl in the mirror that reflects the struggle.

Shortly, only a pile of dust remains where the dark-haired woman had been seated. As the redhead stands, the fire in her hair flickers, then begins to darken.

"I never did like red hair . . ."

Antonin passes his hand across the mirror, and the glass reflects the dark-beamed ceiling above. "The viscount will be expecting us shortly. Wake me when the time is right." He totters toward the expansive bed.

The dark-haired woman gestures at the dust on the chair, which swirls, flares, and vanishes. "And she thought she could trust you . . ?"

The white wizard glares, but says nothing as he stretches out upon the white coverlet.

XXXI

The next morning, which was ushered in by bright sunshine and cold gusty winds, Justen again appeared to be the not-quite-youthful gray wizard, up and saddling Rosefoot while I was still rolling my bedroll and trying to wash and shave in the icy brook water. The fallen leaves from the brush around the brook no longer crunched underfoot, but neither was it warm enough for there to be the moldering smell of spring.

Cleaner was definitely colder than having a dirty face and hands, but I swore that Justen hadn't winced when he washed. Did gray wizards use their powers to heat cold water? Probably, but if it were a chaos-power, I'd forego hot water through magic. The feeling of chaos-isolation was too recent.

I wiped off my trousers and cloak as well as I could, wondering how Justen's light-gray clothes always looked so good, when my own darker garb was beginning to look ratty. Then again, I wasn't certain I really wanted to know.

Wheee . . . eeee . . . Gairloch pawed at the ground, as if to indicate his readiness to take to the road and that he'd had enough of old grass and greaseberry leaves.

So I strapped on my bedroll and pack and climbed into the old saddle. "How far is it to Weevel, or whatever it is?"

"Weevett. We should be there before midday . . . depending on the road." Justen rode easily, not really using the reins, nor lurching in the saddle the way I still did.

With the wind coming at us out of the west, I could already smell the faintest hint of wood smoke, and over the low hills before us rose only a single thin plume of twisted white or grayish smoke. The valleys were either cleared for pasture or were natural meadows, with no sign of crop fields or orchards.

Before we had gone much more than a kay, we passed a rude hut set back from the road on the right and surrounded with a split rail fence, behind which milled a few hogs. Someone in shapeless leathers was pouring water into a long trough. Beyond the fence grazed several dozen sheep.

"When did we leave Montgren?"

"Actually, we haven't. The countess holds Frven, but that really doesn't count. Nobody wants that land. The border between Montgren and Certis is on the other side of Weevett."

"More guards, I suppose?"

"No guard posts, just two stone pillars. The countess is a realist. She just hangs or shoots those who displease her, the ones her few soldiers catch. They don't catch too many, since most of her modest guard is at Vergren."

Vergren was somewhere generally northwest of us, according to the maps I had studied.

I hadn't traveled all that far, and here I was about to enter the third kingdom or duchy or whatever. "Are they all as small as Montgren?"

Justen shook his head. "Some are, like Freetown. Hydlen and Gallos stretch over three hundred kays north and south. Kyphros is even bigger, and it's the only duchy that actually would qualify as a true kingdom. That has bothered the Prefect of Gallos ever since the previous autarch carved out the realm from the surrounding kingdoms."

200

The names of Gallos and Kyphros were familiar, but that was about all. There was something else about Kyphros, but I didn't recall what at the moment.

We rode past a second rough hut, this time on the south side of the road, again with a split-log fence enclosing another wooden trough, and black-faced sheep indistinguishable from those behind the fence on the north side of the road.

The tops of the gentle hills contained ample trees to supply the rails for the fences, as well as logs in numbers far greater than necessary for the few buildings likely to be found in Weevett or those in Howlett. Even Vergren—the smallest capital in Candar, famed only for the diversity of its wool products—would not have made a dent in the lumber that could have been taken from the heights of the hills, especially since a fair number of the trees were red or black oak.

In time, as we rode, the huts appeared more frequently, changing from little more than log hovels into rough-planked houses with thatched roofs.

By now the sun stood high and white in the sky, but the ground remained as frozen as ever. While my breath no longer resembled steam in the chill air, I alternated placing my ungloved hands under my tunic to warm them.

Justen rode with his cloak open, without gloves, and without any sign of discomfort. My buttocks were sore, my hands chapped and chill, and my legs threatened to cramp, even with repeated standing in the stirrups to stretch them.

As we traveled down another of the unending gentle hills, the packed red road-clay merged, over a kay or so, into a packed sand-and-pebbles surface frozen into shallow ruts. Gairloch's hooves clicked on the smooth small rocks, and I worried about his catching a stone in a hoof.

The roadside lands bore the winter-stubble of maize and the turned soil of recovered root crops; the farm houses came closer together. In time we descended toward a small river, the first I had seen larger than a stream since I had landed in Freetown. Though the river was surrounded by some low brush, I could see no trees along the stream-bed either to the north or the south.

Where the road flattened near the bottom of the hill, it also straight-ened and ran arrow-like to an ancient stone bridge across the river.

"The bridge marks the edge of Weevett," observed Justen.

"Is that important?" I was bored with the same-looking huts and houses, with the sullen people who looked away from us, and with the rolling gray and brown of hill and valley after hill and valley, sheep after identical and smelly sheep.

"In a way," answered the gray wizard, "since the countess's soldiers do not have the right of summary justice within the towns of Mont-gren."

Summary justice? Again, I nearly winced. Justen kept reminding me of exactly how little I knew, and how many pitfalls Candar pos-sessed.

Even before we crossed the bridge into Weevett, the rank odor of concentrated sheep and wool wafted from the west to greet us. That, combined with another ill-defined rancidity which I did not ask Justen to explain, turned my travel bread breakfast into a leaden mass squarely in the middle of my guts.

Uuurrrppp . . . I winced at the burp, but Justen didn't even smile; he was guiding Rosefoot around a small wagon pulled by a mule. A woman in shapeless herder's gray trudged beside the mule, edging toward the animal as she heard us but not looking up, not even as Rosefoot delicately stepped around her.

Whufffff . . . That from the mule as greetings when we resumed the center of the road just before the bridge. Beginning perhaps half

201

a kay beyond the bridge, cottages clustered together on both sides of the way.

"We're expected at the Weavers' Inn."

"Expected?"

Justen smiled a thin smile and shook his head. "Lerris. Contrary to what you must believe, gray wizards do not roam the landscape and travel aimlessly from point to point. Like everyone else, we have to make a living."

"In Weevett?"

"Just so." He reseated himself in the saddle as Gairloch's hooves struck the granite paving stones of the bridge.

Click, clip . . . click, clip . . .

"May I ask what your commission is here?"

'Oh, so delicately put!" Justen laughed. He actually laughed, if only for a moment. "I don't believe in glamor, just in a good job and money. Some years ago I struck a bargain with the Count of Montgren. He wanted his duchy to be prosperous and famed for *something*, and I wanted a more secure income. I made a proposal, and he nearly threw me out.

202

"Then he thought better of it, but I raised the price. After all, even gray wizards have some dignity. That's why we're here."

"You haven't told me anything," I noted.

"The sheep," Justen added. "The famous sheep and wool of Montgren."

"I know. They're famous. Even some of the weavers in . . . some of the weavers I know . . . praise the wool." I paused. "Are you saying you have something to do with that?"

"Immodestly, yes. That is why we are here."

I shook my head.

"Since you are here, you can help."

I didn't like the sound of that at all, but I owed Justen. "How?"

"Don't worry. It's a menial job, but purely one of order."

I waited.

"Healthy sheep bear healthy lambs and good wool. Each year, I check the ewes and the breeding rams to ensure only the healthy ones are bred," he explained. "That means four visits to Montgren, and it takes several days. In the fall, I check the lambs as well."

It couldn't be that simple, but I knew little enough to question. So I remained silent and let Gairloch follow Rosefoot.

The stone-paved streets of Weevett were narrow, though the cottages were fenced and set far back from the main ways. The town layout was simple. Two main streets—one north-south, one east-west—met at a central square. There were no more than two dozen other streets, half of which ran north-south and half east-west, creating a grid pattern.

On the south side of the town I could see, over the low one-story cottages, what appeared to be warehouses or large workshops.

"Carding houses," said Justen curtly.

"For wool," he added even more curtly.

I shrugged. The gray wizard's mind was clearly somewhere else. So I studied the town itself, noting the plain-planked cottages with their painted and opened shutters, colored-gravel walks, trimmed waist-high hedges, and now-empty flower beds and flower boxes. Compared to Hrisbarg or Howlett, Weevett was indeed an ordered place.

In the center of the square was a stone pedestal bearing the statue of a man on a horse; carved into the stone supporting the statue were the recurring shapes of sheep. Around the pedestal was a winter-browned lawn, except on the north side, right under the pedestal, where rested a small pile of dirty snow. A low stone wall and a raised walk outside the wall separated the green from the pavement.

Around the central square were ranged half-a-dozen well-kept stores—dry goods, a wood-crafter, a produce market, a butcher, a leather-goods shop, a bakery—and the Weavers' Inn, which from the outside appeared nearly as ordered as the Travelers' Rest had been.

Across the square from the inn was a two-story stone building, with a flagstaff from which flew a blue-and-gold banner. On the blue triangular lower section was a golden coronet, while the upper gold section bore a black ram.

Although a good score of people walked to and from the shops and stores on the east and west sides of the square, no one neared the stone building on the north side.

A single wagon waited in front of the leather-goods store.

Justen and Rosefoot headed straight for the equally orderly stable behind the Weavers' Inn; going down a narrow paved alley beside the tan-painted plank siding of the two-story inn.

"Ser wizard . . ." the stableboy greeted him.

Justen nodded, flashed a brief smile, and dismounted.

203

"Are you a wizard, too?" asked the towhead.

"I am what I am." I forced a laugh.

Justen ignored us both, uncharacteristically, and unfastened his saddlebags with quick deft motions.

By the time I helped the young ostler settle both ponies in clean, adjacent stalls in the airy stable, Justen had disappeared. Assuming he had gone to the inn, I followed and found him talking to a man—presumably, the innkeeper.

"This is Lerris, my assistant this time."

The innkeeper nodded politely, the pointed ends of his bushy mustache hardly moving at all. "The room next to yours is his."

That stopped me. No questions, no problems—just mine.

The innkeeper glanced briefly at me as I stood there holding my saddlebags and pack; then turned back to Justen. "I thought you might bring help."

Justen nodded in return, his thoughts clearly elsewhere.

"Would you like some dinner?"

"As soon as we . . ."

"Ah, yes . . . follow me."

Up the clean and well-varnished white-oak stairs we went, and down a wide hallway. We had the two corner rooms. Or rather, I had a nice room with a real bed, dresser, mirror, and wash table, and Justen had a suite, or at least a bedroom and sitting room.

Since the gray wizard wanted to be left alone, I went to my own room, washed up, and then headed downstairs to fill my quite-empty stomach.

The only problem with the inn was that although it was clean, somehow it still smelled faintly of sheep and wool. Did all of Weevett echo the animals?

The innkeeper led me to a corner table, warmed by a low fire and set with actual utensils and glass goblets.

By the time Justen arrived, I was drinking redberry and working my way through cheese and a mutton pie, brought by a pleasant-faced if heavyset girl who resembled the innkeeper too much for coincidence.

Justen said nothing of a conversational nature until after he had sipped a golden wine I did not recognize and munched through a slice of black bread and a hard and pungent white cheese. Between bites he gazed into a space I could not see.

"You'll earn that room tomorrow."

"Is that when we start work?"

He nodded.

I had questions, but the gray wizard wasn't exactly encouraging them and I was still hungry. So I ate, and Justen nibbled at his bread and cheese.

But there was one question that kept nagging me; so I asked. "You said that the magicians built the new town center of Fvren, as if that explained something."

Justen smiled faintly. "That's not properly a question, but I understand the import." He took a sip of the golden wine. "The older wizards of Fairhaven understood that chaos cannot build structures which last—"

"What about the roads?"

"The roads are not quite the same thing. Chaos is quite efficient at removing rock and stone. So long as it does not touch what remains, the roadbed is as solid as the stone which is left. And the few black wizards used order-mastery, after the stonemasons built the retaining walls and drains, but that was before . . ." He shook his head. "Sometimes I wander too much. You asked about building. Stonecutters build better than chaos-masters. The old town center at Fairhaven proves that."

I still didn't have the answer I wanted, but Justen was staring into space, as if I had called him back into the past. So instead, I finished my mutton pie and let him stare.

"Your meal is paid for," the gray wizard said some time later as I finished a redberry pastry. He stood up, pushing back the spoke-armed chair, and nodded. "I'll see you here at dawn."

I nodded with a full mouth, but he was gone before I could swallow.

There wasn't much else to do except finish stuffing myself. Then I rose and walked out into the late afternoon, wrapping my brown cloak around me.

Fewer souls were visible in the square, but that might have been because of the thickening gray clouds and the few wispy flakes of snow that drifted across the stones with the gray winds.

In time, I retreated back to my room and lit the oil lamp.

With a sigh, I recovered *The Basis of Order* and opened it again. It was still boring, or I was tired, or both, and I turned out the lamp and climbed onto the bed for a nap.

When I awoke again it was pitch-dark, with only a single street lamp visible through the window. I ignored the growling in my stomach, and pulled off my clothes and climbed under the coverlet. Falling asleep was still easy.

XXXII

Sheep—I hope never to see another sheep as closely as I saw the sheep of Weevett, nor to smell them. By comparison, rancid butter smells better, at least if it is not *too* spoiled.

Like Justen, I wore a borrowed herder's jacket and trousers and boots, though I had to stuff some raw wool into the toes of the boots.

206

According to the gray wizard, what he was about to do was pure order-magic. "Just because it's ordered doesn't mean it's pleasant," he added. "That's why I'm free to do as I please most of the rest of the time."

I followed him from the rough shed to a pen or corral, where there must have been over a hundred of the black-faced creatures.

Urrrr . . . uppp . . . My stomach protested, although my nose was already numb, and not from the chill of the wind. The sun beamed brightly but not warmly, and the wind whipped a thin coating of snow across the ground, scudding it into piles here and there against fence posts, in frozen ruts, and on the sheltered side of the empty wool-sheds.

Briskly, Justen strode over to the gate where a white-haired, lean, and tanned woman stood. Her hair was thick, nearly as short as mine, and she smiled openly at the wizard. Her gray leathers were clean, and half a step behind her stood a taller man, balding, wearing stained leathers and holding a crook.

"Justen . . ."

"Merella."

Then I noticed the squad of crossbowmen ranged along one side of the shed behind the woman. Glancing in the other direction, I found a few other armed soldiers. My feet carried me after Justen.

"Who's the youngster?"

"My current assistant. This is Countess Merella of Montgren. Lerris, who understands order but not sheep."

The countess's smile became a grin. "He didn't expect me. You never tell them, do you, wizard?"

Justen shrugged. "It works better that way."

"Pleased to meet you, your highness." I inclined my head, although I didn't know what you called a countess.

"It's good to see you, Lerris." Then the smile was gone, replaced by a more businesslike look. "We lost too many because of the duke and the rains. Is there anything . . . ? We separated out the cripples and brought the least-damaged ones."

"We'll do what we can." He turned to me. "The ewes to be bred this year come through the chute here one at a time. We check them to make sure they're as healthy as they look. If you feel something . . ."

"I tell you?" I asked.

Justen nodded, turning to the countess. "Lerris has a well-developed sense of order, and that will let me use my energies, I hope, on the cripples and the problems."

"As you wish—so long as the results stand." The countess's tone was neutral, although her voice was harder than before.

Justen looked at the herder. "Send one through alone first."

. . . *Bheeeaaaa* . . . A black-faced four-legged wooly heap bumbled down the chute—really, just two low fences set three cubits apart—that led from a gate in one corral to a second empty corral.

I tried to feel the sheep, and the action wasn't quite so hard as I had feared, since there was no sense of disorder, and even a faint underlying sense of scheme and order. Looking at Justen, I said. "She seems fine. No disorder, and a faint sense of order . . . health . . ."

He nodded. "Can you strengthen that order just a bit?"

I didn't know how.

"Watch and use your senses."

So I did, and what he did to the sheep was like smoothing the grain of fine wood to bring out its natural flow. That's not quite right, but that's what it felt like.

"Send another one."

With the second, I was able to do what the gray wizard had, with a little help, and by the fourth or fifth ewe I was working alone, with Justen watching. Until a larger ewe, perhaps the twentieth, came skittering down the chute.

Even before the animal got to me my stomach turned, and the beast seemed to glow in a whitish-red fire underneath its wool.

"Justen . . . this one . . ."

Even the gray wizard seemed to pale momentarily, but he just nodded to the head herder. "Pull this one out for the white corral."

"Chaos?" asked the Countess. I had forgotten she still remained, watching the procedure.

Justen nodded as another herder guided the diseased, chaotic animal toward a smaller fenced area.

By then the flow of animals had increased, and I was breathing sheep, tasting wool, and feeling ready to *baaaa* myself.

In some of the ewes, the underlying order-flow was barely there, and those I strengthened as I could.

Black-face . . . *baaaaa* . . . oily wool-taste coating my tongue . . . *baaaa* . . . *splaaattt* . . . "Fine . . ." Black-face . . . "Pull this one . . ." Sheep gas . . . dung . . . oily wool-smells . . . *baaaa* . . .

The parade of animals seemed endless—until the corral was empty.

I looked up, somewhat dazed. The countess had left somewhere in the middle of processing the first corral—when, I could not have said.

"Over here," Justen said.

I thought I saw a few more silver hairs in his head, but that could have been my imagination. I trudged in the direction he pointed, my eyes burning, my stomach turning, growling and empty.

Across the field waited another large corral of sheep.

I glanced upward. The sun had not even reached mid-morning. "Oh . . ."

That was the way the morning went . . . ewe after ewe, with Justen looking grimmer and grimmer with each chaos-disordered ewe set aside.

By noon my eyes were blurring, and there must have been close to a hundred of the chaos-tinged ewes crowded into the white corral.

"Take a rest, Lerris." Justen's voice was firm. "We'll get something to eat before we finish up here, and then ride over to the southern gathering.

"There's more?"

Justen's smile was half-amused, half-grim. "You've just begun. Two days here, and another two days at the gatherings outside Vergren. There you don't get an inn the first night, just a pallet and a tent."

I sagged against the split rails of the corral while Justen approached the white corral, remaining propped there while two herders funneled the ewes to him one by one. This time, he actually touched each one.

When he was finished, about two-thirds had been returned to the herd. The remaining animals milled around the corral.

With slow, measured steps, the gray wizard moved back toward me. The sun glinted on hair at least half silver, though his face seemed no more wrinkled, unlike the times after Frven.

"Why so much chaos?" I asked.

"How can you tell?" he responded, steadying himself on one of the low chute-rails.

"You've been withdrawn for the last two days, looking where only wizards look, and paying little or no attention to anyone. I don't know you, but it seems more than work."

"You're right." He shook his head. "Nature seeks balance, and Recluce went too far this time." He frowned. "I hope," he added under his breath.

At the last words, I frowned. "You hope Recluce went too far?"

"Not what I meant. I hope it is a question of natural balance." He pushed himself away from the chute-rail and began to walk toward the middle shed. "Let's eat. They're setting up a table in one of the sheds."

Dinner was a hot soup, cold sliced mutton and cheese, black bread and redberry preserves, and as much hot cider as I wanted. Unfortunately, to me it all tasted like oily wool. The food steadied me and stopped the protests from my guts. About the time I started to feel human again, we trooped out to start all over with another bunch of ewes.

Then I climbed on Gairloch and rode to the southern gathering grounds, where we worked until we could not see. I could barely finish supper before collapsing.

The next day was the same, and so was the day after, except that first we rode until nearly noon. On each day, the countess appeared for a time, looking nearly as grim as Justen.

The fourth day wasn't quite as bad, although it was after dark when we returned to the Weavers' Inn.

"Just take the robe in your room and follow me."

"What . . ."

209

"We're taking a bath."

And we did, in a small room off the kitchen, with hot water and soap, and for the first time since leaving Recluce I felt clean. We left the borrowed clothes there and wore the robes back to our rooms, where I found clean sheets on the bed, my own clothes cleaned and brushed, my boots shined, and a small purse with five gold pennies.

I thought I'd more than earned it.

By the time we actually dined the room was deserted, the fire low. We were served by the innkeeper himself. The veal was tender, the sauce succulent, and the golden wine like a fine autumn, perhaps the first time I had really enjoyed alcohol. Neither of us felt much like speaking until we had finished the main course and sat looking at a large redberry pastry.

"You did well, Lerris."

"I see how you earn whatever they pay you," I answered, returning the compliment as best I could. "That's hard work."

"There hasn't been that much disorder since near the beginning," mused the gray wizard, stroking his chin thoughtfully.

"You mentioned Recluce. What did you mean?"

"I'd hoped that the Recluce efforts against the duke had rebounded, so to speak, but the signs aren't right. This is all too recent, almost as if . . ."

"As if what?" I took a small bite from the pastry.

He shrugged. "As if . . . well . . . as if you had gone with Antonin."

"How could this happen? Does it take as much work to sow chaos as it took for us to heal it?"

"Less work. That's the problem. Destruction is almost always easier than construction. It's as though Verlya or Gerlis were working together with Antonin and Sephya. Or Sephya has gotten much stronger." He shook his head again. "But that's hard to believe." He sipped the golden wine.

"Chaos-masters don't work together?"

"Cooperation, beyond an apprentice-master or a male-female bond, is almost a contradiction in terms for chaos. Then again, the great ones seldom have to, since there are few to oppose them."

"You oppose them," I ventured.

"Not directly. I'm not order-pure enough for that." He set down the glass. "I'm tired, and tomorrow we start for Jellico."

"Another commission? More sheep?"

"Actually, in Jellico, it's seeds."

"Seeds?"

"Good seeds beget good crops, and Certis grows oilpods, the kind they squeeze for the scented lamp-oil that Hamor prefers . . ."

I yawned. Some aspects of wizardry and order-mastery were still boring. At least, though, the seeds couldn't smell . . . I hoped.

XXXIII

Off to the left was a line of trees that met the road about two kays ahead in what looked to be a grove. Under the pale blue sky, warmed by the winter sun, the frost and whatever snow might have fallen earlier had melted away from the road, and the stubble of the fields and occasional meadows.

211

Now that we had crossed the Montgren Gorge and passed into Certis, the occasional fenced field and extensive sheep meadows had largely given way to entirely fenced fields, now covered with maize stubble or other grain stalks. The huts were larger, and many even boasted woodlots back away from the road. But the landscape and the countryside were boring. After all, how much creativity is there in fences and huts? And how long can you pass them without being lulled into stupor by their similarities?

Justen did not talk that much, and I did not press the gray wizard.

Wheeee . . . uhhh . . . Gairloch tossed his head, prancing for an instant, then slowing down.

Wheeee . . . eeee. Whatever it was, Rosefoot agreed with Gairloch.

I looked at Justen.

"They're thirsty," he said.

"Is that a stream up ahead?"

"I believe so. There is even a pavilion of sorts there, if I recall."

"Pavilion?"

"A roof erected on four timbers, nothing more than a rain shelter."

A rain shelter we didn't need, but it was probably better than stopping by the roadside.

The pavilion was there, but a nearby oak had pulled up its roots, toppled, and broken the ridgepole. Between the fallen green oak and the collapsed pavilion, most of the travelers' area was unusable, although a path worn by other travelers led down a drop of half-a-rod to the stream.

At the top of the incline, I dismounted and led Gairloch toward the water.

Whee . . . eeeee . . . He tossed his head, and I studied the trees that stood back off the water course. I saw nothing. Then I tried to sense chaos. Nothing there either.

"Well . . . here you are . . . drink what you can." I looped the reins over the saddle and got out my water bottle.

Wheeeee . . . eeeeee . . .

"I know it's not a warm stable, but it *is* decent water." Standing upstream from Gairloch, I smelled the water, licked it from my hands, felt it with my mind. Nothing—just good cold water. So I drank some, scooping it up with my hands, while trying not to slip off the brown grass-tuft where I squatted. Then, after wiping my face on my sleeve, I filled the canteen and replaced it in its holder.

Justen—where was he?

I grabbed for the staff, then eased up the incline to the rest area.

The gray wizard was nowhere to be seen, but a man in a soldier's vest and a chain mail shirt appeared from behind the mound of collapsed thatch, a plate skull cap secured with leather thongs. His sword was unsheathed and pointed in my direction.

"Another pilgrim . . ." His voice was raspy, his brown beard scraggly, and his step measured.

I could have outrun him, even to Gairloch, but I didn't know where Justen was and who might be with the soldier, and whether they might have a crossbow, a longbow, or a rifle. So I took an even hold on the staff, arranged my feet, and waited.

"What do you want?" I asked. It seemed like a fair question, even to a maniac with a glint in his eye and a sword in his hand.

"Just your horse and your money."

"That's a bit much."

"Damned pilgrim. You're all alike."

Whssttt!

I let the first stroke pass by.

Whhsttt!

Thunk! Even I was surprised at how unskillful he was, at watching his sword fly onto the hard clay.

I waited to see if he would go for the sword on the ground or the knife at his belt.

His eyes darted from mine to the staff and to the sword and back. Then he sighed. "Quarter?"

I nodded.

Click.

I ducked and turned.

Swish. The blade of the heavier man nipped the edge of my cloak, and I wished I had discarded it as I staggered sideways.

Thunk.

Clank. His foot skidded on something, and he stepped back.

I used the instant to duck out of my cloak, regaining a balanced stance and concentrating on the unshaven and grizzled veteran before me. His eyes were bloodshot, but his hands seemed steady enough.

His blade dipped, then turned.

I did not move, watching eyes and edge simultaneously.

He stepped back and sheathed the sword. "Damned wizards. Begging your pardon, ser, but I didn't know which kind you were."

I tried not to let the confusion show as I looked from the one, who was trying to stand on a very sore leg, and the older man who watched us both.

Both soldiers' leather vests had two irregular light patches on the shoulders, with two small holes within the lighter colored space. Winglike insignia had recently been removed.

Their chain-mail shirts scarcely qualified as armor, except to protect against spent arrows and weak slashes, but their swords had been serviceable enough.

Neither one bore the taint of chaos. Neither did they exactly radiate order. Which left the possibility of unpleasant mercenaries running out on their contracts and turning bandit. I wished Justen were around, but the gray wizard seemed to have vanished.

"Wizard problems?" I asked. "Just wizard problems?" I added.

The older man, mostly gray-haired although he did not look much older than Justen, spat onto the road. The younger looked at the sword lying on the frozen clay.

"You can get it, if it stays in the scabbard." I did not relax my

213

control of the staff until he sheathed the sword. "You still have to explain why I shouldn't do something unpleasant to you."

"Ha! Begging your pardon, young wizard, but you can't." The older soldier spat again and looked toward Gairloch, who had edged backwards, but otherwise made not a sound.

"That's not quite true, friend." I smiled pleasantly. "I cannot do anything destructive, but what if I were to decide that with each unpleasant act you do, your nose would grow a thumb? Or that you would begin to grow again?"

"What . . ." asked the one I had disarmed, looking toward me, then toward his companion.

The older man swallowed. "You're young to do that."

I smiled again. "I don't know if I'd necessarily do it right, but even a mistake wouldn't hurt me, so long as I don't involve chaos."

He blanched. "We're hungry."

I nodded.

"That wizard, he didn't keep the duke from getting killed. Or the rain from getting the crops."

"Why didn't you stay with the new duke? Dukes always need soldiers."

The two looked back and forth.

I wasn't sure I wanted to hear the story, but I shifted my grip on the staff.

Finally, the younger one swallowed again. "Well . . . it wasn't our choice. Grenter—he was the squad leader—sent us out to round up some . . . pilgrims . . ."

I must have raised my eyebrows.

The older man added quickly, "This was under the old duke, you understand."

"They must have heard about us coming. They were all gone from where they were staying."

"Where was that?"

"In Freetown . . . the Travelers' Rest, it was called."

"*Was* called?"

"The wizard burned it. He had a hard time, even with his helper. We didn't see that. Grenter sent us to find them before they left the city." The younger ruffian looked around, then back at me, and swallowed.

A thin cloud drifted across the pale sun and the wind picked up, throwing a few dry leaves onto the roadway.

"We caught up, Herris here and me and Dorret and Symms, with two of their women. Hard blond woman and a looker, black-haired. I wish we hadn't found them. Dorret never knew what happened."

"What *did* happen?" I prompted.

"The blond put a throwing knife through his throat so quick I didn't see it happen. He's down gurgling and clutching at his neck, and Symms jerks out his blade and tries to spit her. Except that the looker has a blade, and she makes him look like a recruit."

The older man, Herris, coughed and spat.

I looked at him.

"Fydor has it right," he acknowledged.

"There were still two of you."

Herris glared at me. "The nasty blond had two knives left and she wanted to use them both. The other woman's a born killer. She never raised a sweat, and she smiled when she killed Symms."

"So you let them go?"

They looked back and forth. Finally, the younger one looked at the ground and said. "I yelled for help, and the second squad came from the other side of the market, not all of them, but there were three."

"Don't tell me that two women butchered them, too?" I let my voice get sarcastic, even though I was enjoying hearing how Wrynn and Krystal had mangled some of the duke's forces.

"Not all of them. One guy, Gorson, got away with just losing his right hand and a shoulder wound. They killed the other two."

"And you two just left them?"

They both looked down.

Finally, Herris spat again. "They were witches. They were from Recluce. No way I'd go against devils like that."

"Where did they go?"

Fydor shrugged, his eyes avoiding mine. "I'd guess they went to Kyphros. The autarch likes good women blades. They didn't take this road, and that leaves the mountain road or the coast."

"Ser wizard, you don't look all that surprised . . ." Herris still didn't look at me.

"I've crossed blades with the dark-haired one."

"Blades?"

"Staff against blade."

Herris stepped back. "I'm real sorry, ser. Real sorry. Wish I'd never met either one of you."

Fydor followed his example and backed away.

Then both of them were walking quickly, almost running, looking over their shoulders as they headed back in the direction of Weevett. I watched them go, my mouth half-open.

"Very impressive, young Lerris." Justen sat astride Rosefoot, next to the toppled oak, watching, as I suspected he had been all along.

That he had left me to fight them alone angered me, even as I was proud that I had managed it. But Justen wouldn't care one way or the other. "How did you do that without the heat waves?"

Justen smiled. "That takes practice. You could do it right now with the distortion lines, but you have to equalize the temperature on both sides of the mirror to avoid what you call heat waves."

"You didn't answer the question."

"I'll explain some of it while we ride. The rest is in your book. Rosefoot had a drink while you were dispatching that pair." Justen did not move the reins, but Rosefoot turned and carried him from the clearing in the wayside grove and back onto the main roadway.

"My book?"

"Lerris, it doesn't take a mind reader to see your thoughts. You're clearly from Recluce. You have the talents to be a first-class ordermaster, and you were surprised—not curious, but surprised—to see my copy of *The Basis of Order*." The gray wizard looked ahead, toward the southwest.

I ignored him and went to get Gairloch, not that I had far to go. He waited just at the top of the incline. I almost fell off him, scrambling into place and trying to catch up with Justen and Rosefoot.

More smoke plumes rose into the pale blue sky, angling toward the northwest. Behind the wind, I could see clouds building again, over the hills in the distance to the southeast. With the warmth of the sun and the southern air might come rain, or worse, sleet.

"How far to Jellico?" I asked as we came abreast of him.

"More than another day."

"How many other towns are there along the way?"

The gray wizard smiled faintly. "A scattering, though few with inns, and fewer still even the size of Weevett or Howlett."

We rode a time further before I asked another question. "How can you hide in plain sight so that I cannot see you or the heat waves?"

"That is the same question." The gray wizard coughed and cleared his throat before continuing. "What is sight?"

I tried not to sigh. I asked a simple question, and, instead of an answer got another question. "Sight is when you see someone or something."

Justen sighed. "What is the physical process of sight? Did not anyone teach you that?"

I looked as puzzled as I felt, not understanding what he had in mind.

"Light comes from the sun, chaotic white light. It strikes an object and reflects from that object. The act of reflection partially orders the light. Those reflected rays enter your eyes. What you see is not the object at all, but the light reflected from that object. That is why you cannot see when there is no light. Now it really is not that simple, but those are the basics. Do you understand what I mean?"

I wasn't *that* dense. "Of course, my eyes see a reflection of reality, not reality itself. That means that when I feel things, that feeling may be truer than sight?"

Justen nodded, without taking his eyes from the road or looking at me. "Remember that some real things cannot be felt, and many chaos-touched objects are not real but can hurt nonetheless. But you are right." He cleared his throat again. "There are many ways not to be seen, but they all involve two ideas. The first is touching someone's thoughts so that they do not know they have seen something. That is the chaos-way because it destroys a link between perception and reality."

"The way of order?" I prompted.

"That is much more complicated . . ."

I nodded at that. Anything involving order was more complicated.

"Light is not straight like an arrow, not exactly, but like a wave upon the ocean. Light can be woven with the mind, although it takes practice, and you weave the light around you so that it never quite touches you. Actually, it is not difficult as an exercise, but using it can be very dangerous unless your nonvisual perceptions are well-developed."

"Nonvisual perceptions?" Just when I got the idea, he added something else.

"What you call feeling out things . . ."

"Oh . . . but why?"

Justen shook his head, muttering something about basic physiology and wave theory.

217

Finally, after we had ridden up a gentle slope that overlooked a park-like setting, unlike the kays and kays of peasant fields, hogs, and huts we had passed, I asked again.

"Lerris, why don't you use your brain? It is meant for thinking, you know."

I waited.

"If you cut yourself off from light, then your eyes don't work either. No more easy answers. You ask rather than work things out, and then you won't remember."

So we rode on, and I ignored the continual growling in my stomach.

XXXIV

218

Jellico? How did it differ from Freetown or Hrisbarg or Howlett or all the other hamlets and towns masquerading as places of importance?

No expert yet at judging people or towns (as I was becoming ever more painfully aware), I did observe that, unlike Hrisbarg or Howlett or Weevett, Jellico had walls. Those walls rose more than thirty cubits in near-perfect condition, and the massive iron fittings of the eastern gates were oiled and clean. The grooves for anchoring those gates and the stones in which they had been chiseled were swept clean.

A full squad of men—twelve or more, in gray leathers—patrolled the gate, inspecting each traveler entering, each occupant or citizen departing.

"Master Wizard, you've traveled our way once again?" The serjeant's voice was firm, respectful, but not subservient, matching the trim gray leathers of his vest and trousers and his well-kept heavy boots.

Of the other soldiers, two were moving bales and baskets in a produce wagon pulled by a single donkey, while a third held the harness. Another was watching as a peddler emptied the contents of his pack onto a battered pine table set by the edge of the gate.

On the wall overhead, barely visible behind the parapet crenelations, a pair of crossbowmen surveyed the stone-paved expanse outside the walls where the inspections occurred.

"Wizards do travel," replied Justen.

"And this young fellow?" asked the Certan serjeant, inclining his head toward me.

"Serving as my apprentice—for now, at least."

"That wouldn't be an apprenticeship of convenience, Master Wizard?"

Justen turned his face directly upon the serjeant, his eyes weary with age, conveying experiences best left unrepeated. That was what I saw.

The serjeant stepped back, then nodded. "Sorry to bother you, gentlemen." His face was pale.

When I lifted the reins, my hand brushed my unseen staff in its lance-cup. Briefly marveling at my newfound ability to cloak small objects by wrapping the light around them, I swished the reins and Gairloch carried me up to the farm wagon.

One soldier had ripped off the wagon seat and was lifting small bags from the narrow space underneath. The blond-bearded young driver trembled in the grasp of the other inspecting soldier.

I glanced back at Justen.

"Hempweed." Flat, unconcerned.

"No!" screamed the man.

One of the guards looked at me and I swished the reins again, letting Gairloch carry me past the granite walls and into Jellico, then slowing to let Justen and Rosefoot draw abreast.

"Will they execute him?" I asked.

Justen eased Rosefoot along a narrow side-street bearing left from the main gate highway. "No."

Even less than fifty rods into Jellico, the viscount's control was evident. No street peddlers, no beggars, no litter, no refuse. While the streets were brick, they were level, even on the side street down which we proceeded, even in the narrower alleyways we passed.

"What will happen to him? That farmer?"

"He's no farmer, just a young idiot hired to drive the wagon. They'll brand his forehead with an 'X'. The guards turn back all branded people. If ever he is found within Jellico again, he will be executed in the main square.

"Just for smuggling?"

219

Justen shook his head slowly. "The inn is just ahead."

"But why?"

"For disobeying the viscount. Except for beer and wine, drugs are forbidden. So is the practice of magic without the viscount's seal of personal approval. So are begging and prostitution, or selling goods without a seller's seal."

I looked at the space, where, with effort, I could see the staff that no one but me or another good magician could see. I shivered.

"We'll stable Rosefoot and Gairloch first."

The Inn at Jellico—scarcely an original name, but Jellico didn't seem a town for originality.

"What sort of magic gets the viscount's seal?"

"As little as possible. Healers, mainly of the orderly kind."

"There are white healers? Chaos-healers? How could they?"

Justen shook his head, and even Rosefoot tossed hers. "Healing takes two forms, Lerris. One is helping restructure and re-order the body, knitting wounds and bones, using order to create natural splints and heals, or strengthening the body's resistance to infections. All that is order-based. That's basically what we did with the sheep. It's more complicated, but pretty much the same process with people. Some infections can be treated by destroying the minute creatures that create the infection. That's chaos-based and can be very chancy if you don't know how to fine-tune your destruction. Read your book. The theory is all there, and I shouldn't be telling you any of this.

"Remember, Lerris, you don't have the viscount's seal. Whatever happens, try to remember that. Being my apprentice wouldn't help. Reading your book would."

At that point I was ready to take my invisible staff and crack the gray wizard. Exactly *when* had I had time to read anything? But what good would arguing have done? Justen would have asked how long I had had the book, and then I'd have to admit I *had* had the time, until recently. Of course, it wasn't until recently that anyone had given me enough knowledge and information for the book to make sense.

In the meantime, as Gairloch picked his way across the brick-paved courtyard of the inn, his hoofs clicking ever so lightly, I wondered why Rosefoot's steps were virtually silent.

"Why would some healers be licensed and not others?"

"Money. A licensed healer pays a percentage to the viscount."

Once in the stable, Justen and I were left to brush our mounts.

220

Why was it that in the larger towns, the ones with walls, the reputation of the mountain ponies was so fierce that no stableboy seemed willing to handle them?

With considerably more practice, Justen was finished long before I was, and suggested that I join him in the inn when I had settled Gairloch and left my staff appropriately concealed.

Whheee . . . eeee . . .

"Yes, I know. There's only hay and no oats, but I'll see in a while, after I figure out how to untangle this mess."

"Does he listen?" asked the black-haired apprentice ostler from two stalls away, where he was grooming a tall chestnut.

"He listens, but doesn't think much of what I say." I didn't bother to gauge his reaction as I returned the brush to the shelf over the stall and slung my gear over my shoulder.

The wind had dropped off, the sun had reappeared, and the courtyard was almost pleasant as I walked the distance to the inn.

No sooner had I walked inside than Justen took my arm and guided me to a corner table in the public room. Most of the tables—all red oak, if battered—were occupied, and the air was stuffy, the warmth augmented by the flames of a large stone fireplace.

The dark panelled walls and low ceiling added to the oppressiveness.

"A gold wine," Justen told the girl.

"Redberry," I added. "What do you have to eat?"

"Mutton pie, mutton chops, mixed stew."

"Try the stew," suggested the gray wizard.

I needn't need much encouragement, not after the days in Montgren. Mutton was fine, but not every day, and not when everything smelled like it.

"Recluce is trying something," said Justen flatly.

"What?" I sipped the redberry, which helped ease a slight hoarseness, a leftover from breathing too much sheep.

"I don't know, but you're part of it."

I just looked at the gray wizard.

"Oh, not consciously. I suspect you've been used. That was an extraordinarily talented group of dangergelders that the black masters dropped on Candar, talented enough to confuse any actions the masters might otherwise have had in mind."

I took another sip and waited.

221

"You alone radiate order wherever you travel, yet it's hard to pin it to one person. That black-haired blade—she has everyone talking, almost enough to make them forget the assassin who preceded her. And the preacher . . ."

"What about the others?"

Justen shrugged. "You heard about the blond with the knives, and you could probably tell me more about the others."

I decided against it. If Tamra, Myrten, and Dorthae hadn't been brought to the attention of the powers-that-were, there was no reason for me to be the one to do it.

"Why do you think it was deliberate?" I asked instead.

"I don't know, but you're really too young to be here. That bothers me." Justen looked into his glass and said nothing more, even after the two bowls of stew arrived.

In the end, I went upstairs early, discovering that my legs were still not quite used to riding.

The single candle in the tiny room Justen had procured, with two narrow beds not much more than pallets, seemed adequate enough for some reading, and I pulled the black-covered book from my pack.

The introduction was as boring as I remembered. I sighed, then began to leaf through the pages, nodding as I saw that the last half of the book actually dealt with specific topics—aligning metals (whatever that meant), detecting material stresses, weather dynamics and cautions, healing processes, order and heat-based machinery, order and energy generation.

At that point, I wasn't quite sure whether to start all over at the beginning, or to kick myself. For nearly half a year, I had been carrying at least some of the answers to my own questions in my pack. Of course, that assumed that what was written down made some sort of sense, and that you could actually apply it. But I neither kicked myself nor started at the beginning. Instead, I started on the section on healing, since I wasn't ready for more boredom.

Not only did the words make sense, but so did the ideas, and I began to understand why what we had done with the countess's sheep had worked and what Justen had alluded to in his remarks about the importance of the body's internal order.

"So you finally decided to see if the book made sense?"

I almost jumped off the pallet when the gray wizard opened the door, realizing how late it must be by the fact that the candle was near to guttering out, and how long I must have been poring over the words on healing by the stiffness in my neck.

"You're that far?"

I shook my head. "Reading about healing . . ." I confessed.

"You couldn't take the introduction, I gather?"

"No . . . I've tried three separate times, and after half a year it's still boring."

Justen yawned and began to take off his tunic. "Go back to it when you can. I didn't, and I'm still paying." He turned his back to me and pulled off his boots. "It's time to get some sleep."

I closed the book and began to pull off my own boots.

After the long days of riding, the concentration on the book, and the comfortable bed, I thought I would drop off to sleep. Lying there, exhausted, it shouldn't have been any trouble at all.

Except . . . things tingled at the back of my mind. Like why Justen's explanation for his work didn't exactly answer all the questions. Then there were Tamra and Krystal. I'd heard about Krystal, yet Tamra should have been the more visible. Somehow, I should have heard something . . . somehow . . . from her, or about her.

I couldn't believe that she had just disappeared, but news didn't exactly speed from one duchy of Candar to another.

Somewhere I finally fell asleep . . . looking into the darkness . . . until I shivered with a deep chill, and tried to turn over. Except I could not move.

White!

A white fog curled around me so tightly that I could neither see nor move. I could not speak—trapped somewhere in nothingness, a nothingness bright enough to burn my thoughts.

You promised . . . The words echoed without sound through my head, but I could not respond, could not see, twisting as I did within my skull. Yet the person feeling the whiteness was not me, for all the familiarity of the feeling.

Was I dreaming? Or had Justen again enslaved me in that white prison? I couldn't even see my arms, or move, or even feel whether my muscles would move. Yet I wasn't in my bed—that I knew.

You promised to show me the way . . . the way . . . the way . . .

In the white fog, that mind-blinding light, were shafts of yellow, red, blue, violet—all spearing me, slashing at one thought, then another.

223

Then a door closed, and the whiteness was gone.

Sweat poured off my forehead as I sat up in the clean darkness.

"You promised . . ." The unspoken words echoed in my thoughts, an edge to them that was familiar. But I had never said anything about promises. I hadn't thought about promises.

Then, I knew why the words were familiar, and my stomach turned. I only hoped that it had been a dream, that Tamra was not trapped in that same kind of whiteness that Justen had shown me. But I wasn't sure. Not at all.

XXXV

Wheeee . . . eee . . .

Gairloch was still protesting when I checked on him after a breakfast of three overpriced and overbaked corn muffins eaten next the two hung-over and scowling cavalry troopers. As usual, Justen was nowhere around, having left with the dawn on some wizardly errand.

My haste in downing the leaden starch may have contributed to the growls from my own guts that nearly drowned out Gairloch's gut-level protests.

"Plain hay just not enough for you, fellow?" I set the saddlebags on the stall barrier, checking to see if my old saddle and the worn blanket remained where I had racked them. They were still there, proof either that the inn was honest or that my gear was worth less than that of other potential victims. My still-shielded staff remained tucked in the stall corner, but I did not actually handle the wood, since the shielding disappeared whenever my hands touched it.

"Better," was all that the gray wizard had said about my concealment efforts, and that admission had seemed grudging enough.

Wheeee . . . eeee . . .

". . . oooo . . ."

Thud.

The soft scream from outside the stable might have gone unnoticed between Gairloch's protests and my conversation except for the sound of that impact.

With little thought, I grabbed my no-longer-invisible staff and burst from the stable, looking around the courtyard. Not only was the courtyard momentarily vacant, but I heard nothing for an instant.

"Now . . ."

The voice came from the alleyway, and, like many another perfect fool, I followed the sound until I came across two well-dressed bravos two rods or so toward the town center, standing in the morning shadows. Both looked up and toward me, the shorter one on the right releasing a woman in ripped clothing, then pushing her toward the brick wall behind him.

The taller one already had his sword out, but he looked at me, and then at my staff . . . and laughed. "You're already dead, boy." He gestured to his companion, the one who had held the woman. "Let's go, Bildal."

Without even looking at me or the huddled heap on the bricked pavement of the alley, the two strolled, almost arrogantly, toward the far end of the alley, the end that opened onto some sort of square where I could see wagons and horses passing.

Around where I stood, looking from the backs of the departing bravos to the huddled and silent figure against the bricks, the back walls and iron-banded rear doors of homes or businesses remained steadfastly closed, the alley deserted.

I shifted my study to the woman, who looked back at me blankly, unmoving, although her black eyes moved from my face to my staff and back. Tears oozed from her eyes, and her lips were tight. A reddish abrasion covered most of her left cheek, as if her face had scraped against the rough brick walls. Her clean, white, and plain blouse had been ripped open across the front, and she hunched her shoulders and crossed her arms as if to cover her breasts, partly revealed by the treatment accorded her and her garments.

Despite the gray streaks in her black hair and the pockmarks on her face, the gaps in her garments showed more of a slender and curved figure than she would have wished as she eased herself into a sitting position without using her hands. Both wrists hung oddly, and the tears continued to seep from her eyes, though her mouth was set firmly against the pain.

225

"Do with me as you will, black devil. Your days are numbered now."

I must have gaped. Here the woman had been beaten, assaulted and nearly raped, and I had saved her from that and possibly worse treatment, and I was a black devil?

"The viscount will catch you."

I shrugged, feigning a calmness I did not feel. Since I might as well be hanged for a wolf as a sheep, I set down the staff and gently let my fingers touch her wrists.

"Ohhhhh . . ."

What exactly I did, that I could not say, except that with what I had learned from working the sheep and with something from what I had read, my mind put enough of the pieces together. My thoughts and senses touched the bones and flows and orders and disorders that wound through and around her system.

"Oh . . ." she repeated more softly, gazing at her straightened wrists.

"They're not fully healed, and I can't tell you when they will be, exactly. Just be careful."

226

At that, or because of the sudden lack of chaos within her system, she fainted, leaving me with yet another problem, and probably the local witch patrol gathering to collect my scalp.

No one was going to be pleased, not the way things were going. Not Justen, not the viscount, not the beaten lady, although she would be younger and more attractive than she had been in years once she healed, and certainly not me.

Even so, I couldn't leave her unattended in the alley. That meant staggering back to the stable with lady and staff, and hoping that no one saw.

"What have you there?" bellowed the old and rotund ostler, appearing from nowhere as I crossed the courtyard.

"A lady of dubious virtue, and in the morning yet!" chortled one of the formerly sour cavalrymen. "Share your prize, young fellow?"

"First . . . have to collect," I explained.

Justen appeared in the stable door, a bemused expression on his face—bemused, until he saw the ripped clothes and the bruised face. "A healer?" he asked.

I shook my head firmly. "Rest . . ."

Justen shook his head. "Bring her in here."

"Not in my stable!"

A quick something passed from the gray wizard to the ostler, who shoved the coin into his belt.

"I have to check on feed." He grinned at me broadly as he headed for the main street.

The cavalryman half-grinned, half-scowled, but made no move to inspect the "merchandise" as I stumbled into the stable.

"What did you do?" hissed Justen.

"Nothing . . . much." I laid the woman on a loose pile of hay, not at all gracefully, trying to talk and not to gasp as I caught my breath. I felt drained, as if I had run a kay or so in heavy sand.

"You idiot. You healed her. How many people saw the staff?"

"Worse . . . than . . . that. Used . . . staff . . . bravos . . . then she cursed me . . . healed her anyway." I began to put the blanket on Gairloch.

Justen turned to the stableboy, standing there open-mouthed.

Without a gesture, the youth collapsed onto the straw.

"What are you doing?"

"Putting him to sleep. You'll get the credit, provided you get out of here soon enough."

"Leaving before the viscount arrives with the local witch patrol?"

The gray wizard stared at me. "How do you plan to get by the city guards?"

"Can they stop what they don't see?"

Justen shook his head, then walked toward his saddlebags. "Keep saddling."

I kept saddling. Gairloch didn't even whinny.

"Here." Justen helped tie a large canvas sack of provisions behind the saddle. Nothing special, just faded and heavy gray canvas, filled almost to overflowing. The contents had to represent a goodly portion of Justen's stocks. Then he concentrated, and the sack appeared to vanish. "Remember to do that. It makes you less of a target." Then he grinned. "I'll get your pack."

I finished cinching the saddle and put the staff in place, then re-membered to weave the light around the staff so that it also appeared to vanish. It wasn't really weaving light, but changing the way the light reflected from the wood and steel, and the steel was the hardest part. A lot of steel, and you couldn't avoid the heat-wave effect—that was clearly the case with the Brotherhood ships.

By the time I had Gairloch ready, Justen slipped back through the stable doorway, carrying my pack and cloak. "You'd better get moving."

"What will you do?"

He smiled sadly. "What apprentice? You're a free wizard who deceived everyone."

"Thank you." I didn't mean for disowning me, but he understood anyway.

"I just hope you've learned something from all this. You're going to have to cross the Easthorns, but you should be able to handle it if you take the south pass. That's the one that the south road from Jellico leads to. Now get on Gairloch and make yourself unseen." He shook his head again. "And don't let anyone touch you. If they have any sense of order, it could unravel the reflective pattern. And please read the introduction to your book *before* you try anything else."

Those were the last words from the gray wizard as I sat on Gairloch and wove reflections around us.

Wheeee . . . eeee. Gairloch didn't like being blind. Neither did I.

"Easy, fellow." I patted his neck.

228   *Wheeee . . . eeee.*

I patted him again.

Sitting astride Gairloch was strange when I could see nothing except a featureless black. Sounds penetrated, but not sight. But we couldn't just sit there. So I nudged Gairloch with my heels and we stepped out blindly into the courtyard, slowly, since I could not sense people or objects unless they were close to us.

Click . . . click . . . Gairloch's hooves sounded like thunder in my ears.

"Stableboy? Where's the stable lad? The chestnut needs a rubdown . . ."

We eased around the rotund porter, hugging the brick wall of the alley until we were in the street, and I turned Gairloch southward, around where the central square seemed to be. The eastern gate was the closest, but instinctively I felt that we had more cover within Jellico, at least until they talked to either the woman or the stableboy.

. . . click . . . click . . .

. . . creeakkkk . . .

". . . hold that wagon . . ."

". . . *told* her that young blade was no good . . ."

". . . watch it!"

"Make way! Make way for the guard!"

Feeling rather than seeing four mounted guards trotting toward the inn I had just left was more than a little unsettling, since my perceptions were not sharp, giving me only a rough outline of bodies and objects.

Under my hands, the reins felt slippery . . . and even with the wind-gusts ruffling my hair and the cold tingling at my ears, the sweat dribbled down my face and my neck like icy trickles from a glacier.

. . . *Wheeee* . . . *eeeee* . . .

I patted Gairloch again to steady him.

". . . way for the guards . . ."

". . . no horse over there . . . don't *care* what you heard . . ."

At the first intersection, with no walls to hug, and storefronts and doors opening on both sides of the road, I eased Gairloch into the middle of the road, continually patting his neck with one hand and straining to sense objects and bodies before they could collide with us.

". . . guard revolt in Freetown .. shameful . . ."

"Did you hear about the autarch?"

". . . in the market's scarcely worth eating . . ."

". . . swore I saw a horse there for a minute . . ."

I wiped my forehead, glad that I was not permanently blind, as we walked *click* . . . *click* . . . *clack* . . . down the stone-paved streets of Jellico toward the south gate.

". . . . way for the guard . . . make way . . ."

". . . after someone . . . second detachment this morning . . ."

Another five men clattered past as I edged Gairloch toward the street edge.

. . . *Whheeeee* . . . *eeee* . . .

Then we took a wrong turn, leading back toward the square.

". . . five pennies for a pound of yams? . . ."

". . . try somewhere else, if you like . . ."

I managed to get Gairloch turned around in the narrow street without brushing into anyone, but began to wonder if I should have stayed visible until I neared the gate. Of course, then someone would have seen us disappear, and that would have been that.

I sighed—too loudly—next to an open window of a house that projected too far into the narrow way.

"Who was that?"

Gairloch and I eased back southward. In careful steps, we finally reached the southern gate.

From what I could tell, there was nothing different occurring from the time when we had entered, even if it happened to be another gate. Close to twelve guards were stationed around the area, but my perceptions did give me a small jolt.

Shielded much the same way I was, on the open ledge above the gate itself, rested a large caldron filled with oil. Under it was a set of burners—not in use at that moment, thankfully—but I wondered what else I had missed. That, and the fact that the good viscount used visual concealment, sent another shiver down my spine.

Slow step by slow step, Gairloch picked his way through the gate area. I kept patting his shoulder.

". . . under that sack?"

". . . open the pack slowly . . ."

". . . blackstaffer loose in the city . . ."

"Where's Jrylen?"

I didn't like the conversation between the figure that seemed to be the guard captain and the messenger who had raced up on foot, nor that Gairloch and I were less than a rod from the pair.

". . . on the wing . . ."

"Get him here now. What does the blackstaffer look like?"

I patted Gairloch again as we eased through the open gate, slow step by slow step, and out onto the stone pavement leading southward.

. . . *click* . . . *click* . . . *click* . . .

"GET HIM UP HERE!" The guard captain's voice echoed out toward us. I shivered, and not from the wind out of the north, though that was chill enough. Crossbows carried a long way.

". . . hold up here, mother. Them's guards having a stew about something . . ."

We edged past the battered and narrow wagon on which two thin figures, radiating the honest disorder that had to have been age, sat and pulled a single mule to a halt.

". . . keep moving, old farts . . ."

They didn't but we did. I had to force myself to keep breathing with each step from Gairloch, to keep patting him and sending reassuring signals to him. Without the pony I would have been wearing crossbow quarrels.

The bitterness of frozen and rotted field stubble swirled past me,

230

and my legs seemed like they would knot into cramps so tight I would fall from the saddle . . . and my throat was tight . . .

When we reached the crossroads a kay from the gate I began to relax, but did not drop the light-reflective shield. While I was convinced we were too far for either an order-master or a chaos-master to detect the shield, if we appeared on an open road in plain sight of the walls, even a kay away, it would only be instants before a troop was dispatched. And although Gairloch was steady, I doubted that he could outrun true cavalry chargers on the road. In the mountains, perhaps, but not on the road.

So, cloaked from sight, I rode the south road quietly, as the surface changed from stone to smooth-packed clay, angling always toward the mountains I could sense vaguely in the distance until I was certain that the walls of Jellico had vanished behind multiple rows of the low rolling hills that seemed to lead toward the mountains.

Even past noon, even with the steady kays we had covered, wagons passed. Horsemen passed, and two post-carriages. I even had to ride around peddlers on foot, and a party of pilgrims, the one-god variety.

First the hills were low and rolling, covered in winter grass or crop stubble, the fields arranged in regular patterns and confined by low stone walls, with occasional hedgerows. Those huts close enough to the road for me to sense were ordered enough, if impoverished and stark.

When we crossed another road, running east-west—or so it appeared to my limited senses—I encountered no more wagons, and but a single horseman, a post-rider, I suspected.

As the hills had become steeper, the cultivated fields gave way to grasslands, separated from the road by a stone wall whose maintenance was haphazard. The smooth-packed clay turned to mud frozen in ruts, and Gairloch's pace slowed even more.

Very shortly thereafter, over the crest of the second hill past the other road, beside a high tangle of brush in a dip in the road, and after listening carefully for what I might not sense, I unwove the shield.

The wind was chill by mid-afternoon, and thick gray-roiling clouds had covered the blue skies of that morning when I had left Jellico. For all that, never had the gray of the sky, the sere brown of the grass by the roadside, the tan-gray of the stone walls at the field edges, never had they seemed so vivid.

I dismounted and studied the brown tangle where the hedgerow

231

overtopped the wall, then glanced to the wonder of the clouds, taking a deep breath of air that seemed fresher just because I could see with my eyes again.

Near the top of the hill, further along the crest and away from the road, grazed a handful of black-faced sheep. Even seeing them was welcome.

I patted Gairloch. "You're one hell of a pony."

He didn't even whinny, just accepted it.

I took a long drink from the water bottle. My throat was dry. Not knowing what action might dissolve our cover, I had done nothing but ride and had held nothing but the reins throughout the long departure.

Thurummm . . . urummmm . . . As if to greet me, along with the thunder, light raindrops began to fall upon my upturned face. At that moment, I didn't care.

XXXVI

By nightfall I cared a lot more. First freezing rain had come down nearly in sheets, gradually turning the rutted road into a surface as treacherous as glass. Like knives, the ice fragments slashed from the sky. The hills were steep enough to make climbing impossible, but not rocky enough to contain caves or outcroppings.

In the end, I figured out what to do. Under a scrubby tree next to a stone wall, I created something like the light-weaving, except that it kept out ice and water.

Easy? Hardly, and with each rumble of thunder I felt more drained, though I forced myself to keep eating and drinking, knowing that I needed the energy to hold together the weather-net that sheltered Gairloch and me in a barren area, with but the marginal shelter of the hedgerow and a short stone wall.

Whheeee . . . eeee . . .

"Easy . . ." I patted him for at least the hundredth time.

After the ice-rain came the snow, thick and wet at first, then cold and fine. Keeping the finer flakes from us took less energy, and by the time it was close to midnight the wind and snow had slackened enough and drifted deep enough against the wall and brushy hedgerow to provide a natural barrier. That let me relax my net and build a fire.

The warmth from the small blaze helped as I continued to weave a shelter and climb into my bedroll. Gairloch's internal order and appearance indicated he was far more accustomed to the hard weather than I, and finally I let go of the weather screen and collapsed into sleep.

Whhheeee . . . uh . . .

The morning was gray, with windy gusts blowing the lighter snow into the once-clear area and over all but the warmest of the fire's ashes.

Yee-ah! Yee-ah! The shrill call of the vulcrow jolted me full awake. Through a half-haze of fine snow-fog and sleep, I lifted my head—and wished I hadn't, as a line of fire split my skull down the middle.

"ooooo . . ." mumbled a strange voice that resembled mine. The pain eased, but did not cease as I let my head rest on the quilted fabric of the bedroll.

Whhhsssssss . . . Even the whisper of the snow echoed like thunder through my skull.

My arms ached more than in the first days with Uncle Sardit, more than after Tamra's drubbing me, more even than after Gilberto's hellish exercises.

". . . ooooo . . ." I wished whoever was moaning would stop, but that didn't happen until I realized I was the one doing the moaning.

Yee-ah! Yee-ah!

Wheeee . . . eeee . . . whufff . . .

Between the damned vulcrow sitting on the hedgerow and Gairloch suggesting that it was either time to eat or get up, I eventually woke up and levered myself into a sitting position, not even high enough to see over the wall and the snow drifted above it.

My cheeks tingled from the cold, and ice crystals fell from the steam of my breath. The fire in my skull not only burned; the bones surrounding my brain felt like a smith's anvil pounded by an unrelenting hammer.

Thinking the water bottle might help, I reached through the powdery snow for it, ignoring the minor arms cramps until I had it . . . and dropped it. Of course the water had frozen solid.

The fire was warm ashes, nothing more, and light snow covered

233

all but the center cinders. How long it took to get the fire started, who could tell? My fingers nearly froze, since I had never replaced the leather gloves I had seared apart in Frven. The branches I had broken and set aside for fuel had frozen together.

Gairloch whuffed and whinnied, and each whuff and whinny cut through my ears like a knife. My legs cramped at each movement, and the wind blew out the fire three times, besides flinging dry bitter flakes into my eyes whenever I really needed to see something.

Order-use magic was out—that is, if I didn't want to finish destroying my body—and it seemed impossible to get enough warmth to get some water and food into my system.

On the other hand, I somehow doubted that much of a search for me was going on, not for a while. So, after much flailing, the fire burned again, and I found a small package of pressed grain which I fed to Gairloch. Except that I held it, half-leaning against him while he ate it.

In time, using the one battered skillet in the sack, I melted some of the snow, taking a few sips myself but letting Gairloch have most of it.

Then I ate—what, I'm not sure, but it didn't matter that much— and crawled back into my bedroll.

The fire was back to ashes when I woke again, and the sky was still covered with the featureless gray clouds. The wind gusted, and my head still ached and burned.

Wheeee . . . eeee

". . . don't like it, either . . ." I mumbled.

The flailing to re-establish the fire was about the same, since I had to stagger through knee-deep snow down the hedgerow to find enough branches and sticks for fuel. But I was getting somewhere.

Sitting by the fire, I ate some more, drank some more, and felt the headache subside a bit more.

Clearly, we weren't traveling anywhere quickly, and there was no point in trying, not when the road wasn't even visible except in the higher and more exposed places where the wind had swept the snow off in order to build waist-high drifts—if not higher—in the depressions.

While I had no schedule to meet, we had not even reached the true base of the Easthorns. Was there any chance of crossing them?

My eyes traveled to the southwest.

Surprisingly, I could see the darkness of conifers on the lower slopes, as if the mountains had received less snow than the hills beneath them.

I shivered and forced myself to eat another few mouthfuls of the travel bread. Then I told my reluctant body that it was time to loosen up. The protests were monumental, enough that I nearly lost what I had just eaten. So I leaned against Gairloch, my eyes damp in frustration.

So damned unfair . . . but fairness sure as hell counted for nothing.

I kept moving, if more slowly, and melted some more water for Gairloch and gave him the rest of the grain cake. Half of Justen's sack was for him, a division of provisions that never would have crossed my mind.

As I struggled to lift the large canvas sack of provisions back onto Gairloch, I wondered how long it would be before I could see things in advance. I mean, there was nothing special about the provisions, just that same faded and heavy gray canvas, still filled almost to overflowing and representing a goodly portion of Justen's stocks. But, in the instants while I was trying to escape Jellico, he had packed with more forethought than I had since I landed in Freetown.

Justen—I already missed the gray wizard. Now all the choices were mine, and it had already become clear just how little I knew about the real world of Candar. At the same time, Justen hadn't been that much better than my father, Talryn, Tamra, or the half-a-dozen others who had more knowledge than I did—and refused to share it. Each of them had given me just enough for me to know there were unanswered questions . . . and said it was up to me to find the answers.

Yee-ah! Yee-ah! The vulcrow was back, probably waiting for us to die, but I had a different idea.

Finally, sometime after midday, under the featureless gray clouds that obscured the time, I swung up on Gairloch and let him take his own pace through the snow. He avoided the wind-swept areas, still icy, and made his way along the side of the road.

Unlike me, he seemed to enjoy the ride.

My guts ached, and while the headache had diminished to a dull pounding, my eyes burned and my hands trembled.

Gairloch walked carefully and I hung on, occasionally sipping from the water bottle I had tucked inside my cloak, now containing half ice and half water.

Despite the gusts and the chill, I sweated and the dampness froze on my forehead, then seemed to freeze-boil away.

By midafternoon, as the sky darkened, the lower slopes of the Easthorns were closer and the snow was only ankle-deep. More important, it had apparently not rained first, and there was little ice on the open spots in the rutted road. Gairloch still preferred walking in the lighter snow than on the frozen clay.

The sweats had left me, as had the headache, replaced by a light-headedness and a feeling of weakness.

I kept looking for somewhere to stop, but the hills had grown increasingly more barren and rocky as we trudged toward the lower slopes of the Easthorns, which now seemed to get no nearer.

Meanwhile it got darker, and I peered through the blowing snow as the wind rose, looking for another hedgerow, another sheltered spot, at least one out of the wind.

Wheee . . . eeee . . .

"That goes for me, too."

Night had not yet overtaken us, and we could have traveled longer, but a darkish shape not far off the road resolved itself into something—an abandoned hut, a waystop. Who could tell? I wasn't sure I cared. I risked trying to feel whether the place was disordered, and immediately recovered the headache I had almost forgotten about. The hut was chaos-free, all four sides, and it had a roof of sorts, made of slate shingles though half were missing, as well as an open hearth beneath a hole in the roof.

With no door and two oblong holes where shuttered windows had been it was drafty indeed, but the remnants of the door and the shutters were enough for a small fire to warm the space occupied by one tired young man and a strong pony.

We ate, and we both slept, and the next morning was merely cold, with stray staffs of sunlight peering through the breaking clouds, and light gusts of chill air.

Best of all, my headache was gone, though my back was sore and my muscles ached. In the warm darkness, it looked as though the Easthorns had moved closer, as though I could reach out and touch the conifer-covered lower slopes of the foothills.

That wasn't exactly right, but we did reach the road-marker noting the road to Fenard by mid-morning, and by then had reached the edge of where the recent snow had fallen. While there was snow under the trees, the occasional tracks on it, and the finger-width distance between its white and the brown of the tree trunks told that the storm that had attacked me had not reached the Easthorns.

I shivered again at that thought, looking back over my shoulder, but saw no one and nothing on the road behind. I did wish that I had possessed the ability to conceal Gairloch's tracks, but surviving the storm and cold had been hard enough.

Not more than another kay past the road-marker we passed a narrow stream that disappeared underground right to the east of where we stood. Warmer than the air, a fog rose from the water, and I let Gairloch drink as he would while I rinsed the canteen and washed my face and hands in the pleasantly chill flow. Before I had finished washing, my friend and companion found some tufts of grass still partly green to nibble.

For the first time since scrambling out of Jellico, I could peer into the supply sack provided by Justen while there was light enough to see. Even so, I almost missed the off-white square tucked between two oatcakes wrapped in oiled paper.

Folded into a square the size of my hand, it bore one word— "Lerris." My head was still swimming and I did not open it, but tucked it instead into my belt pouch and continued to search for another package of travel bread. I found it, and a small pouch of spiced dried apples.

While I ate travel bread and dried apples, Gairloch alternated slurps of water from the not-quite-underground river with bites from the narrow stretch of grass nurtured by the spray from the fast-moving water.

Glancing overhead, I realized that the clouds seemed to be darkening and thickening once again. So I finished as much as my stomach would hold without rebelling and climbed back into the saddle.

Then we started up the narrow road again, winding in and out of ever-steeper hills, and at each turn I looked for a sign of other travelers, or wayfarers' huts, or some shelter, with one eye checking the sky visible in the space between the hills.

237

XXXVII

Surprisingly, after another ten kays or so of trudging, when even the untiring Gairloch was flagging and I had dismounted to struggle alongside him on foot, the road began to descend, not much; or perhaps it only leveled out.

We rested and shuffled on, and rested and shuffled on, and I marveled, when I wasn't puffing and panting, at the contradiction between the lack of any place to stop or even rest, and the clearly maintained rock walls supporting the roadbed and the arched stone bridges. Guard rails? There weren't any. Nor were there road-markers or signs. But there was also no sign of chaos, only solid stonework.

Coming around a wider curve than I had seen so far, the road opened into a small valley, leading through a snow-dusted meadow of browned grass toward a group of three low stone buildings. Plumes of smoke rose from two of the three, the two on the right. I climbed back on Gairloch.

The stone road-marker at the edge of the meadow read "Carsonn." No explanation, just the name. The faintest of mists covered the valley, bearing an odor I could not place, not of brimstone nor of fire. Finally, after weaving a shield around the big provisions sack but not my saddlebags, I shook my head and chucked the reins.

A rail-thin man waited by the central structure, under a peeling sign bearing a line drawing of a cup. "Welcome to the Golden Cup, traveler." His voice was neutral.

The center building was entirely of stone, even to the peaked slate roof, except for the roof beams, doors, and narrow windows—built to withstand storms and a heavy winter. Yet the meadow grass bore a touch of green, and the snows along the road, though it was still early winter, had not yet been that deep.

I glanced behind the innkeeper to catch the crossbow leveled at me from the stone embrasure flanking the closed double doors of weathered white oak. "Not exactly the friendliest of welcomes." I nodded toward the quarrel.

"Not everyone from Certis is friendly, and not all travelers claiming to come from Certis are from Certis."

I ignored the veiled reference. "A room and some hot supper?"

"Three golds for you, a silver for your horse."

"*What?*"

"We have to bring the food either from Jellico or Passera." The innkeeper shrugged. "You can travel on, if you like. Or camp in the meadow for a silver."

In my shape, and in poor Gairloch's, the alternatives weren't exactly wonderful.

"For three golds, I'd hope for a hot bath and the best· of repasts. And more than hay for my horse."

The innkeeper finally smiled . . . faintly. "Hot water we do have. Even real soap."

The stone-walled stable was almost empty, though the stalls were clean. Two mules were at one end, next to a black mare. A tall bay whuffed as I led Gairloch past him and two more empty stalls.

Tired as I was, I brushed Gairloch until his coat regained some shine, letting the innkeeper, who seemed to double as ostler, bring a wooden bucket of grain. He, too, for all his bluster, kept a distance from Gairloch.

In the meantime, I racked the saddle and tucked the provisions and my staff into a corner above the stall where, invisible as they were, no one would likely run into them either.

"Little enough food there for you to travel another four days to Passera, especially for your horse. There's not much forage."

"I might need to buy some grain cakes, then . . ." I suggested.

"Half-silver for two . . ."

I shook my head. Commercial extortion, or so it seemed; but I wasn't thinking all that well and said nothing.

"Supper first," I indicated, "then a bath and bed."

"Whatever you wish, but we take payment in advance." Most innkeepers made a pretense of affability, but not this one.

Supper, taken alone in a smallish dining room with a warm fire and only five tables, was provided by a plumpish woman wearing a stained white apron. It consisted of spiced brandied apples, a thin pepper-laced potato soup, and thick slices of tough mutton with even thicker slices of brown bread. I ate it all, and drank three glasses of redberry.

"Quite a lot for a slender fellow," observed the woman, whom I took to be the innkeeper's wife. The innkeeper himself had vanished.

I shrugged. "It's been a long cold trip."

239

"Mountain weather's been warmer than usual."

"It was warmer than the blizzard on the hills of Certis—ice, thunder, and snow up to my knees."

A puzzled look crossed her face, then passed. "Would you like anything else?"

"Directions to my room, and then the bath."

"The bath room is at the end . . . that way." She pointed in the direction of the stable. "I'll show you your room."

I barely glanced at the room, apparently the smallest of a half-dozen, if the doorways and spacing between them meant anything, and left only cloak and saddlebags there. My coins were in the openly-displayed purse and in the hidden slots in my boots and belt. Then we walked back toward the bath, down the stone-walled corridors. Even the interior walls were of stone, saving the doors themselves.

Hot water they had, flowing from some sort of spring. The stone-walled room had been built around the spring, clearly, and the source of the faint metallic odor in the valley was definitely from the hot springs, of which there had to be more.

Metallic-smelling water or not, bathing in the rock tub chiseled from the stone was wonderful, loosening aches I hadn't even recognized. I didn't leave that healing flow of heat and relaxation, and dry myself with a thick brown towel, until I resembled a prune.

I also took the liberty of washing my undergarments and wringing them out. After all, for three golds I deserved a few extras, and neither the innkeeper nor his wife said a word when I walked back toward my room barefoot and wearing just my trousers, with the rest of my clothes draped over my arm.

The room, with a single narrow window looking out on the back meadow that I could not see in the darkness, contained a bed, a narrow wardrobe, and a candle in a sconce above the bed. The window, two spans of real glass on a pivot frame, was wedged shut.

The bed, narrow as it was, actually had sheets and a worn coverlet. I thought about blowing out the candle. Certainly my eyelids were heavy enough, but the paper corner protruding from the belt pouch recalled the letter or note I hadn't even read.

So I sat on the bed and unfolded the heavy paper. The reversed images of some letters where the two sides had been folded together told me that, despite the careful phrasing, the words had been placed on the heavy linen paper in haste.

Lerris—

In traveling, even a wizard can be trapped while asleep. *Read* the section on wards (alarms) in your book before you sleep in strange covers.

Try also, for your sake, to take the time to read the entire book before you make one too many mistakes. Spend some time doing something simple and thinking. You can't think and learn if you're always on the run.

-J-

Since the gray wizard had been right more than once, I levered myself off the bed and pulled *The Basis of Order* from my pack. Then I slowly thumbed through the end sections until I found "Wards", taking several deep breaths to keep my yawns from overpowering me.

I didn't quite understand the theory, but the mechanics were less difficult than healing that damned woman or even weaving my weather-net. The interesting part of the wards were that they would work without my conscious direction. The bad part was that they didn't do much besides warn.

I thought there might be more, but if so I wasn't in shape to learn it. So I slipped the door wedge and bar in place, put my knife under my pillow, and blew out the candle. My eyes closed before the light died.

I woke with a jolt from a dream of endless mountain trails. The room was dark, black, yet a ring of light from the wards surrounded the door.

. . . *iiiittt* . . . *chhh* . . .

I tried to get the sleep out of my mind, reaching for the knife, then almost laughed.

"Anything I can do for you?" I called.

The sounds stopped but no one answered, although I could feel two bodies on the other side of the rough plank door.

I waited, and they waited.

. . . *iiiitttch* . . .

"I really wouldn't, if I were you," I added casually, wondering what I would do if they attempted to break the door.

The prying noise stopped again, and I tried to think, when all I really wanted to do was sleep.

241

The wedge wouldn't hold up long, not against a determined attack. The whole sneaky effort meant the innkeeper was only after the weak.

I walked across the cold stone floor and let my feelings examine the door and the frame—solid oak set in stone, with the hinges on the outside, swinging into the room.

Then I shook my head. Idiot, idiot . . . the innkeeper didn't want into the room. He was placing a bar through the iron handle on the other side to keep me from going out. The stone walls, the narrow window, all made sense. The innkeeper just didn't like direct violence.

I checked again. The two were gone, now that they were convinced I was safely captured.

Lighting the candle, I stood up and walked to the window. If the wedges came out . . . Finally, I nodded and began to dress, wincing at the chill undergarments. They were still damp, but I could only hope my body heat would take care of that.

Then I went to work on the window as quietly as I could, thanking Uncle Sardit silently the whole time. Not easy, but the exertion warmed me up. The chill and heat had taken their toll on the glues, and with a little help here and there, I managed to slide the whole window into the room.

Out onto the frozen grass went my pack, cloak, and saddlebags. If I had been a pound heavier I wouldn't have made it through the narrow opening.

Getting the window back in place I cheated, using some of the sense-weaving order-strength, but even by my father's lights, using power to fix something wasn't tempting chaos.

Then, I walked slowly, cloaked in darkness, to the stables. Gairloch was fine, munching on some sort of grass.

Setting another round of wards, I recovered my bedroll and curled up on some straw in the stall next to Gairloch.

The first hint of light woke me, not the wards, which I dropped. I saddled Gairloch, listening for the innkeeper and hearing nothing. Then I used an old staff to pry open the storage closet and took six grain cakes, which I stuffed into the provisions sack. I really wanted just to take them just to pay the innkeeper back. Besides, with the provisions from Justen, I wasn't even certain I would need them. But the Easthorns looked cold, and Gairloch had saved my neck already and then some.

In the end, I left four coppers, probably too much, but that was the least my wonderful innate and growing sense of order would let me leave. After all, despite his dubious hospitality, the innkeeper had bought them somewhere, and leaving the coins made me feel better.

After sliding open the stable door, with the reflective cloak around us, Gairloch and I stepped out into the silence of the winter dawn.

. . . *thunk* . . . *thunk* . . . *thunk* . . .

Less than a kay across the meadow, we came to a brook. I dropped the shield, looking for signs of pursuit; but the inn remained dark, without even a plume of smoke from the chimneys. After Gairloch drank, I replaced the cloak of reflected light until we reached the road and the marker that featured an arrow and the name "Passera." The edges of the road contained drifted snow, often up to Gairloch's knees, but the wind kept most of the road clear, almost as if it had been designed that way.

Still, more than once we had to flounder through crusted and drifted snow gathered in the most sheltered elbows of the road.

Not knowing who or what to trust, and how, I avoided the next inn, instead finding a sheltered cleft up a canyon from the road. Getting to the cleft and concealing our tracks was more work, in the end, than fortifying an inn room would have been, but I slept more soundly, even on the narrow, rocky, frozen ground out of the wind. And it didn't cost me three golds or the equivalent duke's ransom, though I did wake up with the tip of my nose nearly frozen.

Climbing the eastern walls of the Easthorns wasn't quite as draining—not quite—as surviving the winterkill storm. While it had taken two days to escape the storm, it took nearly two days more after Carsonn just to get to the top of the southern pass. In that whole time, I passed three other groups heading toward Certis, all of at least four riders, and all heavily armed. They had made my passage possible, in one instance having shoveled through a small snow avalanche across the road.

They never saw me or Gairloch, not when I heard them from a distance and removed us from the road and their sight.

The weather never changed—cold, cloudy, with gusty winds sweeping in and out of the canyons and carrying fine dry snowflakes. What's more, at the top of the southern pass, there wasn't even any view, just a crest in the road that ran between two nearly sheer rock walls. At one instant, I was riding uphill; and the next, downhill.

Not until I reached the top of the foothills overlooking Gallos, another day, and another night spent under an outcrop shivering even within my bedroll, did I find a view.

For nearly three kays the trail down was nothing but an open ledge slanted against a blackish granite.

Halfway down I stopped, able to see anyone approaching in either direction, and guided Gairloch into an alcove back from the road. I climbed up to a flat overlook to look out over Gallos under the first full day of winter sun since leaving Jellico.

Gallos didn't look much different from above than I imagined Certis might have, just mixed and muddy browns, divided by thin gray lines that had to be stone walls or fences, and infrequent gray-brown and wider curving lines that were doubtless roads.

Down toward my right, to the north, where the road broke away from the rocks and entered a line of forested hills that separated the meadows and hedgerows and stubbled fields from the Easthorns, I spotted an interweaving of smoke plumes in a cultivated valley. What I could see of the valley looked small, in any case. Passera, I guessed.

Leaning back against the rock alcove with Gairloch right below and with the afternoon sun warming the black slab behind me, I finally re-read Justen's note.

I still hadn't had time to read the whole book, and on the mountainside wasn't exactly the place to do that in any case. But Justen had been right more than once . . . and that was more than enough reason to think about what I was to do before I descended the rest of the way into Gallos and Passera.

Besides the simple matter of survival, I had two problems—neither insurmountable, but both requiring solutions. First, my supply of coins, not exactly large to begin with, was running short, even despite Justen's provisions. The loss of nearly four golds for a short night's lodging in Carsonn and the graincakes for Gairloch had not helped in that matter; although, balanced against the payment for the sheep-healing, I was somewhat better off than I would have been, and a good hundred fifty kays further toward the Westhorns.

Second, I still didn't have the faintest idea of the problem or cause or whatever-it-was that I was supposed to resolve. This business of blind traveling and quests was getting tiresome, if not plain boring.

Whatever I didn't know, I did know two things. If I kept blundering into towns and problems, sooner or later an unseen crossbow quarrel or rifle shot would leave me in less than ideal shape, if not dead. That assumed that Gallos would allow rifles; some of the Candarian duchies classed firearms as chaos-weapons, rather than undependable heat-energy weapons. But dead would be dead, one way or another.

I'd also realized from the unusual nature of the storm on the hills of Certis, and from the unguarded look of the nasty innkeeper's wife when I had mentioned the unseasonable storm, that the ice and snow had not been entirely natural . . . not at all. It also meant that some-one hadn't exactly been able to locate me, with magic or otherwise.

Gairloch—the pony was another question I had ignored, and kept ignoring. Why did he trust me, and a few ostlers only? Had his pres-ence in Freetown been coincidental? Or a matter of odds?

I looked away from the view of Gallos and down at the not-quite-shaggy golden-brown of his heavy coat. No animal less sturdy would have managed what we had gone through nearly so well.

With another sigh, I reached out with my feelings . . . looking . . .

. . . and came away shaking my head. Gairloch was a mountain pony, but not just a mountain pony. Just as I had strengthened the innate sense of order within the sheep of Montgren, so had someone strengthened that order within Gairloch, to the point that the pony would lash out or shy away from anyone manifesting disorder. That was all, and yet . . .

I shook my head. Someone, something, had thought farther ahead than I cared to speculate. Even with my back against the warm rock, I shivered.

I still wasn't thinking fast enough.

So I sat on the outcropping and tried to think out what I had to do next. I had to learn what was in the book and to apply it. I had to make a living of sorts with enough space and time to read. And I had to avoid getting much notice. That was especially important, partic-ularly if my disappearance from an apparently locked room in Carsonn were relayed to Antonin or whichever chaos-wizard was after me.

I didn't understand *why*, though. I wasn't as dangerous as Justen, and Tamra was certainly as much a threat as I was. I shook my head, wondering where she was and what she was doing.

Avoiding further notice meant avoiding Passera. If it took a whole troop to cross the Easthorns, a single rider would be seen as magician, or bandit, or common thief, and even given my recent outlays, the amount of coins I carried would give full suspicion to one of those assumptions.

All this led to the need to reach Fenard, a town large enough for

245

me to seek a woodcrafter who needed an extra hand without raising too many questions.

I sighed. Every time I thought, the problems got more complex and involved more than just me.

"Come on . . . we've got another piece to travel, and a few more nights on the road."

Click . . . click . . . Gairloch's shoes clicked on the smoothed stones of the highway as it descended down the long slope to Passera, and, eventually, toward Fenard.

XXXVIII

246   The blond woman juggles the knife as she rides, glancing ahead, then back at the rotund trader perched on the gray mare that walks heavily beside the lead pack mule. "No trouble yet."

The trader eyes the black-haired woman—shapely, even in the faded blue tunic and trousers—on the scarred battle-pony, who scans the road ahead.

The older woman, the black-eyed and black-haired one, turns to catch the trader's appraising stare. She touches the blade at her belt, and a faint smile crosses her lips.

The trader sees the smile and the hand on the hilt of the blade and shivers. "See . . . anything?" he stammers.

"Could be . . . there's a line of dust headed our way. Only a single rider, though. No trouble there."

"You fixing to join up with the autarch?" asks the trader, each word tumbling out almost before the last is finished.

"Why?" asks the blonde.

"The word is that Kyphros needs blades; the autarch doesn't care whether they're men or women, just so long as they're good."

"I don't know . . ." The blonde's voice is flat.

"We'll see after we deliver you . . . and collect our pay . . ." laughs the older woman.

Her laugh is not a laugh, and the trader shivers again.

The blond woman rides further ahead, and the dark-haired woman's free hand strays toward the hilt of her blade.

XXXIX

Skirting Passera was easy enough, except for the river bridge that held towers and a guard force. While the towers would hold against brigands, I doubted they would stop even a few score of well-trained and armed men.

They didn't have to. The gate just had to stop us. So Gairloch and I waited nearly till dusk, until I sensed the gate about to open and slipped through going the other direction. They even left the gate open while three of them checked under the bridge from the mountain side.

I didn't wait for them to finish, taking Gairloch step by slow step across the stones, hoping that the gentle click of his hooves would be muffled by the rush of the narrow river below the bridge.

All the practice had given me a fairly good sense of place without seeing, but I still worried that someone could see through the reflective shield. In a way, it was faith, sheer faith, to walk beside an armed guard with a sword ready to use, separated from that violence by the thinnest of light-curtains . . . and I couldn't even sigh.

Beyond the gate, Passera was open enough, though Gairloch and I quickly left it well behind as we continued into the forested hills beyond the town. I dropped the shield as soon as possible after turning into the trees once the road curved out of sight.

From that point on, I would be a journeyman woodworker, with only a horse left because of my unsettled youth and the trouble in Freetown.

With each step toward the plains of Gallos, the hills became more gentle, the trees less frequent, and the air warmer, if a temperature that left the clay of the road a cold gelatin rather than stone-hard ice could be called warm. The rock fences by the road gave way to rock posts and split rails, and these in turn were replaced by all-wooden rail fences that seemed too spindly to contain stock or to hold up against a strong wind.

The infrequent and clear brooks gave way to half-empty or totally empty canals flowing in grids between ever vaster and flatter expanses of stubbled fields.

After Passera, I finally stopped in a crossroads with no name and slept in the stable with Gairloch. It looked cleaner than the battered inn. Even so, the cost was three coppers for me and two for Gairloch. I didn't ask about a room.

For breakfast, I paid another copper for half a loaf—a *small* half-loaf—of brown bread, and a cup of redberry.

From there, another day took me into land so flat and treeless that you almost couldn't tell where the horizon was. In the middle of the treeless expanse flowed the River Gallos, nearly a kay across and less than a rod deep in early winter. Two side-by-side stone spans crossed it, one for traffic in each direction, each one wide enough for the largest of farm wagons. Another night in a stable followed, but the Prosperity Inn in Neblitt offered edible food and a clean straw-pile for no more than the night before.

The right-hand road out of Neblitt and the end of the third day brought me to the low hills leading up to Fenard, and the welcome sight of trees. Bare and leafless trees, not conifers, but trees nonetheless.

It also brought the second guard station.

"Where are you bound, young fellow?"

"Fenard."

"For the guards?"

I looked at the two brawny soldiers and shook my head. "I don't know much about war. I'm just a journeyman woodcrafter."

"Where are your tools?" the narrow-faced one asked.

"That's my problem, ser. I was in Freetown . . . and things changed rather sudden-like . . ." I shrugged.

The two looked at each other. "Any weapons?"

"Just my belt knife. I can hold my own with it."

The guards, veterans each, tried to hold back their grins. So did I. I would have grinned in their place.

"You understand, young fellow, that if you can't support yourself, you have to leave Fenard or join the guards?"

"I would?" I asked, trying to look puzzled.

"You would."

Creaakkkkk . . . A wagon pulled up onto the stones behind me.

"Be on your way, fellow."

I flicked the reins, and Gairloch carried me forward and up the slope. Three hills and a bridge later, and near supper time and twilight, we stopped at the city gate. On the horizon to the north and to the west I could see a glitter of light, presumably the not-too-distant Westhorns.

Unlike Jellico, the wall around Fenard was token, where it existed, and the gate was more of a formality than a real check. A bored and much flabbier guard than the one at the hillside gate looked at me and waved me on.

Once in the streets, I stopped a youngster, round-cheeked and grinning, to ask for directions to the quarter with the most woodworkers.

"Mills, you mean? They're out the mill gate, not in the city."

"No, fine carpenters, crafters."

"The kind that make cabinets and chairs?"

I nodded.

"That's by the mill quarter, straight down the market street there, as far as you can go. A copper, and I'll show you myself, take you right to the Tap Inn, where Masters Perlot and Jirrle drink. They might be there now."

I tossed him the copper. "I can barely afford that, boy."

The barefoot youth just grinned. "Come on. Move that toy pony."

I could have found the Tap Inn with little difficulty, and even one copper was getting to be important. Sometimes you guess wrong, and the youngster probably needed the copper more than I did.

At the crossing of the unnamed street to the mill gate and the market street, also without a name written down anywhere, stood a narrow two-story timber building. Only the hearth and chimney were stone, although the street-level walls were a grayed plaster applied over the old timbers. The roof bowed, and pigeons roosted under the eaves on the end away from the hearth.

A portly and balding man stood, in a leather vest and no jacket, levering a long pole into the street's single oil lamp. As Gairloch skirted a tinker and his pushcart, the man coaxed the lamp into light, even though the sun's red ball had not yet dropped from the twilight sky.

Two middle-aged men, not quite stooped nor erect, wearing dark

249

cloaks, stepped into the narrow doorway on the market street side. As the door opened, a burst of laughter escaped.

". . . scoundrels . . ."

". . . away from . . ."

My guide pointed. "That's the place. The stable's in back."

"What's your name?"

"Erlyn. You can find me near the east gate most afternoons." He turned and was gone, almost at a run.

The Tap Inn was mostly eatery and drinkery, with five empty stalls that barely merited the title of stable, but there was an overhead loft, and another copper gained me the privilege of paying three coppers to sleep there and three more to stable Gairloch. The stablehand was rushed, trying to get back to the inn, where—from his club, heavy arms, large belly, and low voice—his job appeared to be keeping order while stuffing himself from the kitchen.

"No trouble, boy! You understand? Keep that mountain beast under control, and close that stall door."

I nodded and began to brush Gairloch.

Much as I needed to eat, and to listen to the whispered soul of Fenard as unfiltered through loosened tongues, I was in no hurry. I forced myself, after I had found some grain for Gairloch, to amble into the Tap Inn through the same side door I had watched the older men enter.

Holding back, I winced at the din while I let my eyes adjust. Half a dozen men gathered at the sole round table in the room, each cradling a tankard—big earthenware mugs, really.

Four widely-spaced wall oil lamps and a low fire supplied the light. Grease burning off a stove somewhere and green wood burning in the fireplace supplemented the acrid smoke. Add to that the sourness of spilled raw wine and cheap beer, the sweat of working men, and the combined odor defined the Tap Inn. I preferred the stable.

Instead, I eased for a small corner table—vacant, as I discovered, because it wobbled alarmingly on the uneven plank floor.

"Wine or beer?" The serving-girl had unruly black hair, a thin face and body, and a livid slash-scar from the right corner of her mouth to her ear.

"You have redberry?"

"Costs a copper, just like a beer."

"Redberry. Bread and cheese?"

"A copper gets you two slices and a small wedge of yellow. Two, and you get four slices and a wedge of white."

"Two slices and the yellow." I put two coppers on the table, then covered them with my hand.

She nodded and left. "Red stuff and a small bread and cheese."

The six men around the center table were joined by a seventh.

"Rasten! Always the last. Did your new apprentice have to slaughter the horse for glue?"

"Double vine for the man!"

Thunk! Redberry slopped onto my hand, and by the time I looked up the girl was flirting with the stooped Rasten. He didn't seem to mind at all.

The pair, not much older than me, sitting a table away began to talk louder, to be heard over the older center group.

". . . you think about Destrin? That daughter . . ."

". . . she's nice enough . . ."

". . . no future there . . ."

Seeing the serving-girl coming, I had the coppers and my question ready. "Which one is Perlot?"

She jabbed a thumb at the seven, including Rasten the latecomer. "Silver hair, thin guy next to the fellow nearest the door. Want anything else?"

"Not now."

She was headed back to flirt with Rasten.

The bread was neither fresh nor stale, but somewhere in the middle; but the cheese was sharp and cool, better than I expected.

". . . benches for the pits . . . and they wanted black oak, for that price. Can you believe that?"

". . . another wizard loose in the Easthorns . . . walked through a wall . . ."

". . . just an excuse because the fellow skipped and didn't pay, that's all . . ."

The pair nearest me got up and left. No one took their place.

Sitting in the corner on the long bench, I nursed one redberry, then another, listening not only to the older group, but to others scattered throughout the room . . .

". . . apprenticeship? With his daughter? That's a prison . . ."

". . . he'd like those golden chains! Wouldn't you, Sander? Wouldn't you?"

". . . frig out . . ."

". . . say some of the old duke's guard trying to carve out their own place . . ."

". . . Northern Kyphros . . ."

". . . wilderness . . ."

". . . autarch will show them . . ."

". . . how you'd like her bed? . . ."

"Let's have another round."

"Who's paying?"

Between the continuing smoke from the kitchen, the pervasiveness of soured beer and wine, and the acridness of green wood in the hearth, my eyes burned, but I kept listening, waving away the thin serving-girl with the scar down her cheek, nursing my second red-berry, and watching . . .

Perlot pulled back his chair, and I started to stand up, then sat down. Approaching a craft-master in a tavern was an invitation to trouble. So I waited for him to leave before I made my way out to the stable and Gairloch.

Although the air was cleaner and the stable far warmer than the Easthorns had been, my sleep was restless, as if the thunder of that sudden winter storm in Certis still echoed in my head, and I kept hearing the phrase "another wizard in the Easthorns." In time I did sleep, though I woke and washed in the trough before the stablehand arrived.

He didn't know exactly where Perlot's shop was, but pointed generally to the far side of the mill quarter, and I greased him with another copper to leave Gairloch for the day.

"Before sunset, boy!"

I didn't grin, but we both knew that he wouldn't touch Gairloch with even a pitchfork. All being late would cost me was money, and I was losing that fast enough anyway.

Perlot's Crafting. That was what the sign read. Under the sign was a display window with a cabinet and a wooden armchair, both darkened red oak in the Hamorian style. The crafting was better than anything I had seen since leaving Uncle Sardit, and the cabinet might even have gotten a nod from him.

Since the door was ajar, and no customers were standing in the waiting area, I stepped inside.

On the other side of the half-wall, the craft-master was directing two others, a junior apprentice, and either a young journeyman or senior apprentice slightly older than I was. They were discussing the composition of an oil finish.

"You there. I'll be with you shortly."

"Please don't hurry on my account, mastercrafter," I answered, carefully inclining my head. Then I walked to the back side of the display window to inspect the three-drawered cabinet, comparing it more closely to my recollections of Uncle Sardit's work.

"What do you think?" Perlot's voice was even more raspy in the morning.

I turned to face him.

"Well . . . you seem to know something about woodwork. What do you think?"

I swallowed. "The finish is superb, as are the proportions. The grain on the side panel is angled, not much, but enough to detract. Since the joins are hidden, I can't say much about the strength, but the mitering doesn't jam the wood or leave gaps."

"What about the wood?"

"The cabinetry is better than the oak. The design would have been better in black oak, but that might have raised the cost to more than most buyers would pay."

253

Perlot nodded. "You're looking for a job, that's clear, and you know what's expected. That's clear, too. I can't help you." The words rushed together, as if he wanted to be done with them.

"I see." It was my turn to nod. "Do you know any crafter who might be able to use a junior journeyman?"

The mastercrafter rubbed his chin. "Among the good ones . . . no. We all have more relatives than work." Then he laughed. "If you're as good as you talk, you might try old Destrin. He could use the help, but . . ." The man shrugged.

"Where could I find him?"

"He has a place in the jeweler's street, across the market square." The crafter looked over at the youth and the young man, then back at me.

"Is this a hard time for woodcrafting?"

"Not wonderful. Not terrible. I'm no Sardit, but sometimes we come close."

I managed to nod without dropping my jaw.

"You ever seen his work, young fellow?"

"Yes. I once saw a chest he made—black oak."

Perlot pursed his lips. "Why do you need a job?"

"I left home young. I didn't like my apprenticeship. My uncle said I was too unsettled. So I headed for Freetown. Then, what happened there forced me to leave . . . rather suddenly."

"It forced more than a few people to leave." His voice was dry. "Well . . . I wish you well. Try Destrin, but I'd advise you against using my name. That's your choice, of course."

Before I had even reached the door, the crafter was back among the finishes.

Gairloch remained in the stable while I sought out Destrin, heading toward the jewelers' street and following the sketchy directions provided by Perlot.

The structure itself, faced in dark-red brick and sharing common walls on both sides with more recently-painted houses, bore only a small sign above the shop door: *Woodwork*.

The house had two doors—one which covered a stairway up to the second-floor quarters, and an open doorway on the street level leading into the woodshop.

254

The wide shutters on the lone woodshop window were open though a trace askew on their hinges, as if the pins were worn down and had not been replaced in years. The blue paint on the window casement and upon the shutters themselves had faded nearly to gray, where it had not peeled away to reveal a battered and faded red oak beneath. From what I could tell, there was a small attached structure in the back that might have once housed horses. Certainly the other houses in the area had such small stables.

I stepped inside the open doorway and stood at the edge of the workroom.

While the workroom wasn't a disaster, the little signs of chaos were everywhere—the careless racking of the saws, the sawdust in the chalk drawers, and the cloudiness of the oil used with the grindstone.

"Yes?" A dark-haired man—slightly stooped shoulders, thin-faced, and wearing a clean if worn leather apron over dark trousers—glared at me.

"I'm looking for Destrin."

"I'm Destrin." His voice was thin.

"My name is Lerris. I understand you might be interested in having some help."

"Hmmmmmmmm . . ."

'I'd be willing to work on a junior journeyman basis."

"I don't know . . ."

Shaking my head, I let my skepticism show through as I looked over the incipient chaos, saying nothing.

Destrin stood by a half-finished tavern bench, backless. The seat was in place, and he had drilled the holes for the pole legs. At a glance, I could tell it was made from three different kinds of wood—scraps or cast-offs, probably. Not quite a crude piece, but definitely not up to the quality or the array of the tools, nor to the size of the workroom or the house or the merchants' neighborhood.

"Well," he demanded in a thin and testy voice, "can you do this kind of work?"

"Yes." I didn't feel like elaborating.

"How can you show me?"

I glanced around. The bins were empty, except for scraps. "I'll make something, and you can judge for yourself. All it will cost is some scraps and the use of your tools."

"They're good tools. How can I be sure you know how to handle them?" His thin voice degenerated into more of a whine. "Acccuuu . . . ufffff . . . ufff . . ." His hand touched the workbench to steady himself, but his eyes stayed on me.

"Watch me. Or work on your bench while I show you."

"Hhmmmmphmm."

I took that for agreement and began to rummage around. In the end, I found a piece of red oak with some twisted grains at one end that could be turned to an elaborate breadboard, and some smaller plank-ends of white oak that would make a small box, perhaps for needles.

That turned out to be the easy part. None of the small saws or smaller straight planes had been sharpened in years, and the peg plane was clogged with sawdust and chips in a way that indicated it had been forced. So I cleaned it first, then oiled it and sharpened it. I managed to do the same with the other planes, but the small saws were beyond my ability, except to clean them.

Destrin kept looking at me as I cleaned and sharpened the tools, and then as I cleaned off the second bench, re-racking all the odds and ends into the old cabinets that seemed to have a place for everything.

255

Only after I had done that, and I realized it was well after noon, did I lay out the wood pieces for the box.

"Father . . ." A light voice came from the now-open door at the back of the shop, a second staircase to the quarters. "I didn't know anyone was here." The girl was golden-haired, thin like her father, and petite, although definitely feminine in shape and demeanor. Her voice was thin like his, but not whiny, just thin, or tired. Her face was not quite elfin, with a short but straight nose a touch too long to be called cute, and her eyes were a brown-flecked green. She wore a faded blue apron over calf-length brown trousers and an equally faded yellow shirt. Her feet were in sandals.

"I didn't mean to surprise you. My name is Lerris," I told her.

She looked from her father to me and back again.

"I'm trying to persuade your father to take me on as a journeyman."

"Hmmmmphhmmm," noted Destrin. He coughed again.

I wondered if that were his way of avoiding commenting on anything. Again, I said nothing as I finished measuring the wood scraps.

"Would you like to join us for some dinner?" she asked. "It's only soup with some fruit and biscuits."

Destrin glared at his daughter.

"Neither one of you knows me. I appreciate the offer, but, until I finish something of value for Destrin . . ." As I spoke I could see the woodcrafter relax.

"Let me bring you something to drink and some fruit at least."

"I wouldn't object to that, mistress, but I need to keep working."

She looked down, then retreated up the stairs.

As usual, everything took longer than it should. I had to readjust the wood vise, including a minor repair of the fastening on the bottom plate, and the sawing took longer because the blades weren't as sharp as Uncle Sardit's.

In fact, though I only took a few minutes to gulp down the sliced soft apples she set out along with a battered blue clay mug, it was nearly supper time before I finished gluing the last joins together. The whole time, Destrin had "hmmphed" along with the bench, barely finishing his by the time I put the little white oak box into the setting clamps.

It didn't take very long to groove a rectangle on the top and chalk out a simple four-point star, then carve and chisel out the shallow design.

The box was good and workmanlike, not exquisite, but better than much of what I had seen.

"You know woods and tools," Destrin said grudgingly.

"It's nice," observed his daughter.

"Better than nice, Deirdre. Fetch a silver or two in the market." He almost smiled.

I shrugged, not wanting to correct the older man. I didn't know Fenard, but I doubted that the box would fetch more than a half silver. "Are you interested in a journeyman?"

"Can't pay much."

"I don't ask for anything up front. You get half of what I can make and sell. I pay two coppers an eight-day for room, and another two for food, but if I clean out the old stable I can put my pony there."

Destrin's head jerked up at the mention of the pony. "Where are you from, fellow?"

"Up the North Coast. I went to Freetown, but I had to leave. There was no work after the black ones closed down the port."

"You could afford a horse?" asked Deirdre.

"Hardly," I laughed. "He's a shaggy mountain pony, and he doesn't eat too much."

"Another two pennies for the stable."

"Two pennies, but only if I don't make you a half-silver an eight-day."

Destrin reflected, but not for long. "All right. And you sleep here in the shop. There's a small room in the corner."

That was all I wanted, for the moment. I needed some funds, some time to think and to read *The Basis of Order*, and somewhere to stable Gairloch.

"You have supper with us upstairs," added the craft-master. He looked around the shop.

I understood. "After I clean up a little."

He nodded.

Destrin was getting a good deal, but he wasn't likely to ask the questions that the other crafters like Perlot might.

In the end, I didn't eat with them, instead persuading Destrin to let me get Gairloch and work on the stable.

Unlike the shop, the stable had simply been closed. Destrin had clearly never had enough extra wood to use it for storage, and it didn't take long with the old broom I found to make one of the two stalls suitable for Gairloch, at least for the night. Finding time to get him exercise might be a greater problem, but that worry would have to wait.

XL

Destrin had so many problems that it was hard to know where to begin, and that didn't even count Deirdre. Some of them were easy enough to correct, just given a little time and effort, like reorganizing the shop back to its original and functional pattern.

Some took my own funds, because Destrin didn't see any use in them, like having the small saws sharpened by a good tinker. For Destrin there wasn't any use. He knew he couldn't produce small work—not good enough to sell in the market. But I could, and I needed to sell things to avoid spending myself out of the last few golds I had.

Even though Deirdre looked longingly at the little white-oak box I had made to show that I knew woods and woodworking, Destrin agreed that I should sell it on the following eight-day's-end market.

I didn't intend to sell only one box. That meant going to the mills to find woods, preferably scraps.

The first miller, Nurgke, was blunt. "Scraps? Not even for sale, not to you *or* to Destrin. The scraps go to Perlot or Jirrle. They're my best customers, and they need them for their apprentices." He had silver hair and hard brown eyes, arms like tree-trunks, and an open if unsmiling, face.

Nurgke's mill had two big saws, run by waterwheels from a diversion of the Gallos River. In spite of his bluntness, his mill conveyed a sense of order. Even the stones in the millrace were set precisely, and the grease for the waterwheels was set in measured dollops for application by his apprentices.

"Impressive," I told him as I surveyed his operation. "You prize order highly."

"I praise profits, woodman. Order brings profits."

I couldn't argue with that. "Who else might have wood scraps or mill ends for sale?"

Nurgke pulled at his long chin, then frowned. "Well . . . Yuril doesn't have any arrangements, but he does mostly firs, stuff for poles and fences, farm uses, not much in the way of hardwoods. Then there's Teller . . . but he's almost under indenture to the prefect. You might try Brettel. He used to mill for Dorman." He saw my blank look and explained. "Dorman was Destrin's father. Best cabinetmaker in Candar. Some said he was as good as Sardit in Recluce, maybe better." The mill-master shook his head. "Destrin's a good man, been through a lot, but he doesn't have the touch." He looked at me. "Brettel might help you, but don't sell him a song. He never forgets."

With Nurgke's admonition fresh on my mind, I rode Gairloch back around the perimeter road of Fenard, the wide and cleared granite-paved way just inside the fifteen-cubit-high stone walls, until I got to the north gate and the north road leading out to Brettel's mill.

The wind whipped around us, and the light dimmed as the clouds darkened. By the time we reached the mill, light crisp flakes were falling upon the frozen ground, leaving a lacy finish over the fields of stubble behind the wooden rail fences.

I had to wait for Brettel, who was wrestling with the replacement of a saw.

So I studied his mill. Like Nurgke's, his radiated order, but an older and longer-standing sense of presence. His millrace was also perfectly stoned and mortared, but some of the stones had been replaced. The stream dammed for his high pond had to be the one that joined the Gallos River on the east side of Fenard.

The lumber and timber storage warehouse radiated an age greater than the stone walls of Fenard, yet there was no debris and the roof timbers were more recent and carefully varnished.

The warehouse was chill—no fires or hearths with that much lumber around, but I wondered how much timber and how many planks split because of the changes in heat and cold.

"You? Who are you, and what do you want?" Brettel, like a broad and bandy-legged dwarf, stood shorter than to my shoulder, and his voice was a clear tenor. For all the abruptness of his words, the tone was pleasant.

"I'm a new journeyman for Destrin, the woodworker. My name is Lerris."

"Destrin? What are you running from, young fellow?"

I grinned. "I'm not, at least not exactly. I worked for my uncle, but he said I was too unsettled and told me to see the world and to come back when I could settle down." I shrugged. "You can't see much of the world when you run out of coppers. So I agreed to work for Destrin as a journeyman. He supplies tools and lodging and gets a large share of what I produce."

The mill-master looked me over. "No sign of chaos. The worst you could be would be an honest scoundrel, and that's the least of Destrin's problems. What do you want from me? My best-cut timbers without paying a copper?"

I shook my head. "I'm not that ambitious. I prefer smaller pieces for now. Scraps and mill ends, if you can spare any."

Brettel pursed his lips.

"I can pay a little," I offered, not wanting to seem too eager, but not wanting to appear as a beggar, either.

He shook his head with a rueful grin. "I don't know what you are, but you're neither a thief nor of chaos, and anything would help Destrin, I think." Then he fixed his eyes on mine. "But leave his daughter alone. She's my god-daughter, and while his pride won't let me foster her, she'll have an honest man of Fenard for a husband." The last words were like light iron, and I stepped back.

"I didn't know . . ."

He laughed, and the laugh was deeper, not at all like the tenor of his voice. "You wouldn't. I wouldn't say anything, except you're good-looking, probably talented, and will leave her sooner or later. There are plenty of others . . . now, about the scraps . . ."

I waited, trying not to hold my breath.

"Follow me. You can take anything you want from the burn bin, but don't leave a mess. The mill ends are in the other bin. Those we sell. You get out what you want into a pile, then either Arta—he's the skinny fellow with red hair—or I will talk about how many coppers it's worth."

In the end, I gathered one bag full of red and white oak scraps, enough to do three or four small boxes, and enough mill ends for three coppers to do a breadboard or two and a small chair.

Brettel watched as I carefully packed the woods into the old basket I had taken from Destrin's stable.

"Good luck, young fellow. You seem to know woods."

"Thank you. What I do with them is what counts."

He nodded and was gone, and I chucked the reins.

Wheeee . . . eeeee.

"I know. I know. You don't like carrying wood. But if you want to stay dry and get fed, you're going to have to carry wood."

Gairloch carried me out into the wind and the swirling snow that had covered not only the fields, but the perimeter road, with a light white blanket.

Destrin "hhhmmmmpphed" as I brought in the wood and stacked it in the unused bins on what had become my side of the workroom. He had a fire stoked in the side hearth and a ragged sweater on under his apron.

"What's that for, boy?"

"Some boxes, breadboards, and a small chair."

"Do a good chair, and it will sell. Boxes don't do so well these days."

"If they don't sell, I'll make other things in the future."

Deirdre just watched until I began to measure. Then, as if the details bored her, she slipped through the back door and upstairs.

The hardest thing was not to hurry. Even though I knew nothing was going to happen immediately, I felt like every moment counted, that I should be working all the time, and I did work under the lamp some nights.

Destrin was wrong. I finished two boxes, and with the white oak one, took them to the market on eighth-day. Getting in cost me a copper, but I found a spot by the dry fountain, next to a flower seller, and set out the three boxes on a tan cloth I had borrowed from Deirdre.

The snow had half-melted, half blown away, but the wind still whipped in from the north, and less than a score of possible buyers wandered through the square.

"Those are nice, young fellow. Where are they from?" asked the rotund woman with the cut flowers.

"Here. I'm a new journeyman for Destrin, the woodworker."

"You made those? You mean he actually has someone who can make things like old Dorman did?" She leaned down and studied the boxes. "Well . . . they're not as elegant as Dorman's . . . rather plain . . . but they look well-made."

"May I see the one on the end?" interrupted another voice, that of a slender man in gray leathers.

261

I didn't like his narrow face or the cold look in his eyes, but I nodded as I handed him the red-oak box.

The man studied it minutely, looking at the joins, at the grain angles, and the fit of the top. Finally, he handed it back, almost with a disappointed look on his face. "Decent workmanship. Fair style." He nodded curtly and stepped away.

"I guess that means you're all right, fellow."

"Who was that?" I asked. "Some inspector for the local guild?"

"The prefect doesn't allow guilds. He says they just cause graft and corruption."

"So who was he?"

"That's old Jirrle. He and Perlot and Dorman used to fight over who was the better crafter. Now he does the fine cabinets for the gentry, the big merchants, and the prefect."

"Can I see that box in the middle? How much is it?" A woman in a shapeless gray overtunic that failed to conceal her bulk jabbed at the white oak box.

"A silver," I responded.

"It's not worth more than a copper or two . . ."

In the end, I sold the white oak for six coppers, and the two others for five—just enough to leave me nothing after the cost of entering the market, the cost of the wood and paying Destrin's share, and my eight-day's lodging and board. That did leave the wood for the chair paid for, but the lack of profit wasn't the most promising of starts.

XLI

Over the next few eight-days, my cash flow improved, and I stopped going to the market, instead displaying my products on the stage in Destrin's window. With winter full upon Fenard, mostly demonstrated with howling winds, and occasional light snows, being able to sell without either paying the market fee or shivering on the cold stones of the square was a definite improvement.

The first chair brought three silvers, although I ended up having to buy a finish varnish for it and putting a satin sanded gloss on it.

Destrin "hummphhedd" and moaned, but finally gave in when I insisted that his cut came after deducting the expenses for materials, since I was the one buying them. Deirdre still watched occasionally as I worked, and Brettel still let me have the small scraps free. Even the larger mill ends cost but a few coppers.

Gairloch liked every opportunity to leave the confined stall, and that was another problem. Stalls had to be cleaned, something I had forgotten. Cleaning the sawdust and scraps from the shop, with the fragrance of cut wood, was almost a pleasure compared to wielding a shovel and slop bucket. Sometimes I even had to wash parts of the planking—and my hands turned red from the freezing water and coarse soap—but something inside me wouldn't let me not keep either the stall or shop spotless.

As I worked more with the tools, and Dorman had left tools every bit as good as Uncle Sardit's, my hands became nearly an extension of my thoughts, and I could almost feel how the grains and the strengths and lesions in the woods flowed together. Sometimes it wasn't even boring, and I could begin to understand how and why Uncle Sardit looked at wood.

"What are you?" demanded Destrin as I stepped back from the parlor chair I had gotten a commission for. It wasn't perfect, not to Uncle Sardit's standards, but even he would have called it a good piece. I had deepened and widened the seat grooves, knowing who would use it, and the spools and braces were a shade heavier to bear the extra weight, yet the proportions did not show that extra strength. "Acufff . . . cuffff . . ." He reached out a hand to steady himself. His face paled.

I leaned toward him. "Are you all right?"

". . . Be . . . all . . . right . . . just an instant . . ."

He wasn't. Even when he straightened up and stopped coughing, he was pale. For the first time since I had come to Fenard, I reached out with my feelings beyond the woodworking to touch Destrin . . . and nearly recoiled from the impact. The threads of order within his body were faded, dying a fraction of a span at a time. Yet there was no chaos, no tinge of evil, just as though he were far older than he was, as if he were an ancient.

263

Almost without thinking, I lent him some internal order, a touch of strength.

"Who are you?" he repeated, as though his coughing attack had never occurred, but he edged closer to the hearth.

I wiped my forehead. "I'm Lerris."

Destrin shook his head. "A master trained you, Lerris. I'm a poor excuse for a crafter, and I know it, but I can recognize quality and skill. Sometimes you look like Dorman when you touch the wood, or just let the plane graze an edge. You are in a different world. When you look at a piece of wood, you look like you see all the way through it."

I did, but there wasn't any reason to tell Destrin that. So I shrugged, and I was shrugging a lot in Fenard. "Like you, Destrin, I'm trying to make a living."

". . . aocuffff . . . acuuu . . ." He waved me away.

This time, with what I had given him, he recovered quickly.

"Damned chill . . ." he mumbled. Then his eyes met mine, and, as if he recognized what I was, he shook his head. "What will I do when you leave?"

I looked back at the chair. Destrin had raised a real question. "You had this shop before I came," I said firmly, but it was no answer, and we both knew it.

Outside, the wind whistled, shaking the front shutters and rattling the display window.

"Are you ready for supper, papa?" Deirdre stood by the stairs, looking as petite and fragile as always, as if a good breeze would carry her away. Yet there was iron behind that seeming fragility, as I had discovered watching her negotiate with a merchant's wife over some curtains she had provided.

"Good time to stop," agreed the crafter.

While Deirdre served a barley soup, it was a hearty soup, and the biscuits were fresh. Young or fragile-looking, she could cook, and she always had a pleasant, if shy, smile.

That night, with my back against the brick of the wall and my feet up on the pallet that served as couch, bed, and study area, I eased out *The Basis of Order*. The cover was getting battered, perhaps because I had read through the slim volume at least twice.

Reading didn't mean understanding, unfortunately. Some things were easy enough, like the business with the sheep had been. Or like helping strengthen Destrin's body to fight the wasting disease. I could understand what the disease did to Destrin, but there was nothing I could do. Oh, Destrin looked better after my intervention, and I would do what I could, but slowly, slowly, he was dying.

Even the damned introduction to the book didn't help: "Learning without understanding can but increase the frustration of the impatient . . ."

Or how about ". . . All things are not possible, even to the greatest . . ."?

Wonderful, just wonderful.

I closed the book and looked at nothing.

Too many questions kept nagging at me, even as I continued to force my way through the damnable *Basis of Order*. At times, I would sit there under the lamp, later than I should have been up, knowing that my eyes would burn the next day, struggling with the conflicts and the ambiguities.

I couldn't read the book from front to back. That I had given up early. So I read the back sections first, the ones on the mechanics of order, and I tried some of them out, like aligning metals to strengthen them or change their characteristics. Those were easy, at least on nails or scraps, after a little practice.

And, using a pot of water and a candle as a burner, I could figure out how the weather modifications worked . . . sort of. What scared me there were all the qualifications and warnings about large storms changing harvests later in the year and creating droughts elsewhere. But the pot of water and the burner weren't going to change anything except make the air in the shop a little damper, and that didn't hurt the wood at all.

So I sat there, back against the wall, feet up on my pallet, trying to make sense of what I had learned . . . or thought I had learned . . . and realizing that some things were not possible—even for the ordermaster I wasn't.

A glimmer of yellow from the shadows caught my eye.

. . . *whhsttt* . . . A whisper of slipped feet followed.

Deirdre stood back from the curtains to my alcove. How long she had been there, I didn't know, but her dark eyes flickered from me to the book and back.

In my shorts and nothing else, I felt undressed.

265

"You can come in, Deirdre."

She did, but not far, only just inside the curtain that served as the doorway to my alcove. She wore an old maroon woolen robe over a worn white shift, and her shoulder-length hair was tied back.

"Lerris?"

"Yes?" I turned and swung my feet off the bed, setting them on the floor and sitting sideways on the pallet bed.

"Were you once a priest?" Her voice was soft, as it always was. Not timid, just soft.

I did not answer her, and she said nothing, finally sitting on the end of the pallet, the faintest scent of roses reaching me.

"You couldn't sleep."

She shook her head. "I worry about papa."

"So do I."

"I know . . ." She edged herself toward me. "He sees it, too. He won't say anything." She reached out a slender hand and laid it on my forearm. Her fingers were firm and cool against my skin, and I swallowed, fighting against wanting to hold her.

"Lerris . . ." She eased even closer.

I tried not to shiver. It had been too long since I had held a girl, far too long.

"Please . . . stay . . . whatever you want . . ." Even though she had moved almost beside me, deep within she was shivering, and not with desire; yet at the same time she was calmly purposeful.

Taking a deep breath, I removed her hand. "Deirdre . . . I will do what I can for your father." I took another breath. "I want to hold you—really hold you—and more, but that would not be fair to you or to your father." Then I smiled crookedly. "And if you stay that close to me for long, it will be *very* hard for me to behave myself." I wasn't kidding. She smelled warm and wonderful, and she brought home how lonely it had been. But she didn't want me. She wanted me to save her father.

She edged back, just enough to let me know she was grateful, but not enough to make me think she found me that unattractive—or something like that. I wasn't sure.

"Thank you." That was all she said, but she meant it, and that was enough. She sat there for a time. Finally, she asked, "Where are you from?"

"A place far away, so far that I may never be able to return."

She looked at me, and I looked back, and she opened her mouth and then closed it before asking another question. "Why are you here?"

"You'd have to say that it's a pilgrimage of sorts, a time for me to learn, and to decide."

"Have you learned things you didn't know?" She wrapped the robe around herself more tightly, reminding me that the shop was chill, that winter still held Fenard.

The cold didn't bother me as much as it once had, but that was because I had begun to look at my own internal order, I suppose.

"Some days . . ." I admitted. "I never seem to learn what I thought I was going to learn, though."

She nodded at me to continue.

"I left woodworking once, when I was an apprentice, and I wasn't sure I'd ever do it again. It seemed . . . well . . . it was boring. Why would anyone want to care about whether the grains lined up just right, or whether there was too much pressure on the clamps?"

"You seem to like it now . . . some days I stand and watch you, and you don't see me, even when I'm almost beside you. Grandpapa was like that."

I licked my dry lips, catching the scent of her again, and feeling my heart beat faster. "You'd better go."

A faint smile crossed her face as she rose, almost a grin, but touched a little with a sadness I could feel without reaching. "Thank you."

She was gone too soon, and almost too late, and I wondered what harm it would have done to have taken what she had offered. But the words of my father, and Talryn, and the book hammered at me, and I knew I had done what was best. Enjoying Deirdre would have been deceiving her, and, more important, deceiving me. Yet my heart was still beating too fast, and my body ached, and I dreamed of golden-haired girls, and a black-haired woman, and even a redhead, and woke sweating and sore. But I woke knowing what I had to do.

XLII

The squad leader looks over her shoulder. "Tell Gireo to drop back another hundred rods." Her body adjusts automatically as her mount starts down the long slope that will lead to the Demon's Triangle— the mythical intersection between Freetown, Hydlen, and Kyphros.

"A hundred rods?"

"Twice the separation he's got now."

"But we can't reach him if they attack from the rear . . ."

"We can. We're not his good-luck piece. He's a big boy."

"But . . ."

Her hand touches the hilt of the blade. "You replace Gireo." Her soft voice carries across the road, still shrouded in the mist laid down before dawn. Under the cavalry cloak and hood, her long hair is tightly bound up in black cords.

The man shakes his head, but turns his mount back uphill.

In time, the trooper called Gireo urges his gelding up beside the dark-haired woman who has shed the cloak and folded it into a saddlebag. She wears the still-untarnished silver firebird on the collar of the leather officer's vest.

Gireo's eyes burn as he takes in the slender officer. On foot he would look down on the woman by more than a head.

Her eyes seem to look through the fog ahead.

He opens his mouth.

"Quiet." The word barely carries the distance between them, yet it arrives with the impact of a quarrel.

Gireo shuts his mouth, but his teeth grate inside his cheeks.

"Gallian regulars," mutters the squad leader. "Damned ghouls." Her eyes look again into the mists. "Wizard . . . not this far from Gallos."

She unsheathes her blade, nudging her mount into a quick walk. "Get the others to close up . . . quietly."

Gireo drops back, but says nothing to the two troopers in file behind him, as he glances from them to the squad leader. The road flattens out as it nears the valley below, and the damp and packed clay of the roadbed dulls the sounds of the Kyphran squad.

Ahead, a flickering pinpoint of light appears, then disappears, shrouded and unshrouded by the ground fog rolling out of the Little Easthorns.

Gireo looks back toward the squad leader, but she has vanished into the mists. He frowns, but does not unsheathe his blade.

The Kyphran squad rides downhill.

Whhheeee . . . eeeee . . . eeee . . .

. . . eeee . . . eeee . . .

Clink . . . clunkh . . .

The sound of a single set of hoofs thunders toward the Kyphrans.

"Form up!" The single command is snapped out of the fog like an iron lash, and even Gireo turns his mount.

The squad leader lets her charger carry her past the first two files. "Move it!"

Almost reluctantly, the Kyphran troopers urge their mounts forward into a trot.

Nearly a dozen Gallians are in the saddle as the Kyphrans break out of the fog and lumber toward the invaders.

The squad leader has resumed the van, and her blade flashes, though there is little light to reflect from the cold steel.

Whhhsttt . . . hhstttsss . . .

". . . damn . . ."

"Your right, Gireo!"

". . . aiee! . . ."

All the sounds are from the Kyphran side. The Gallians fight silently.

Whhsttt . . .

". . . you!"

". . . chaos . . . bastard . . ."

Whhssttt . . .

In time, the Kyphran squad draws up not far from the abandoned fire that still flickers through the morning fog. One mount and man are missing. Another mount's saddle is empty. A dozen figures wearing the purpled gray of Gallos are sprawled in and around the camp.

The squad leader reins up by the fire. "Gireo, get the weapons and strap them to one of the Gallian mounts."

"Get them yourself."

The squad leader sighs, but the blade is in her hands. "Do you want to die on your horse or on your feet?"

269

Gireo shrugs. "You couldn't win on foot in an honest fight." He swings off the chestnut gelding.

She smiles and dismounts.

He leaps forward even before her foot is clear of the stirrup.

She dives under his blade and emerges from the roll with her own blade before her.

Whhssskk . . .

Clinnkkk . . .

Whhhstttt . . .

His blade slips from his fingers as the blood fountains from his throat, as his knees crumble. "Bitch . . ."

Even before he has finished dying, she has resumed her seat on the charger. "Hyster . . . gather the Gallian weapons."

The thin bearded man looks from the giant on the ground to the slender woman upon the horse. He swallows, then dismounts without a word.

Two other men exchange glances.

". . . see how fast her blade is . . ."

". . . kill you as look at you . . ."

". . . killed seven of the Gallians, though . . ."

She lets the whispers continue for a time, then clears her throat. "Let's go."

XLIII

Since what I had to do would further upset tradition in Fenard, I needed someone with a personal interest, and Brettel was the only one possible.

I kept telling myself that as Gairloch carried me out the north road to the mill-master's operation. Perhaps I had just picked the day because the sun was finally out, and the wind down, and the air so clean and clear that despite its bite on my face, I wanted to sing. I didn't. That would have been inflicting too much on poor Gairloch.

The thoughts of song died as I neared the mill and the gray stone warehouse.

"Lerris, what brings you here? Did you finish that chair?" His silver hair glinted despite the afternoon overcast, and his smile was welcoming.

"You gave me the order two days ago. Good chairs take some time." I grinned right back at him, but I couldn't sustain the expression.

His eyes raked over me. "Come on into the parlor."

"Would that be all right?"

"I'll be there shortly. I need to tell Arta about some cuts. If you want some redberry, Dalta will get it for you."

He was off, his short legs propelling the big torso and broad shoulders toward the mill with a walk that would have been running for most men.

Wiping my forehead, I dismounted and tied Gairloch to the post, loosely. Although he needed no tying, there was no point in advertising either his training or my abilities. I wondered if the people at the Travelers' Rest had ensured that a mountain pony was always there at Felshar's Livery when dangergelders arrived, or whether it had been specially set up for me. Talryn, nursing a guilty conscience?

Although the afternoon was clouded, the dampness and heat, and the lack of any breeze at all, created the feeling of walking through a hot bath in winter clothes. My growing internal order-mastery let me handle cold, but heat was another question.

At the long one-story house beside the lumber warehouse, I lifted the brass knocker and let it fall.

A young woman opened the door.

I smiled in spite of myself. Seeing the eyes as blue as the sky after a rain, hair as bright as spun gold, skin more finely finished than the silk of white oak, and a figure like a temple statue, I could have cared less that she came to less than my shoulder.

"May I help you? The mill-master is in the main building . . ." Her voice was firm, yet smooth as a good finish on black oak.

Gathering myself back together, I nodded. "I'm Lerris, the journeyman for Destrin. Brettel asked me to wait for him in the parlor." I paused. "Are you Dalta?"

"I'm Dalta." She smiled politely, with a natural warmth that prom-

271

ised nothing while cheering the afternoon, and for some reason I
thought of Krystal, though I could not have possibly said why.

"He mentioned redberry."

"I'll take you to the parlor."

She even provided me with a glass—a real glass tumbler—of redberry, and I sat in a chair probably made by Dorman, since it matched
one I had seen in his plan book, and wondered what Brettel's consort
looked like to have produced such a daughter.

Then I wondered about Deirdre, and whether what I was planning
was fair. Recalling Talryn's acidic comments about fairness, I ended
up shaking my head.

"You look like hell, Lerris . . ." Brettel carried another tumbler, but
his steamed. The odor of spiced cider filled the room, mixing with
the smell of burning wood from the hearth.

"That's about the way I feel."

"You look like you want to ask for something out of the ordinary."

I nodded.

"Don't tell me you want to marry Deirdre."

"No. That would be wrong for both of us, but she's part of the
problem."

Brettel sipped, delicately for such a broad man, from the tumbler,
waiting.

"You know Destrin's failing . . ." I began.

"He doesn't look well."

"I can't maintain the business too much longer."

"I can't say I'm surprised." His face darkened.

"Hold it. I'm not walking off soon . . . but I need a favor, and not
for me."

He took another sip as his expression slipped back to neutrality.
"Why are you asking me?"

I decided to blurt it all out. "I need to train an apprentice for
Destrin. He has to understand or feel woods, and he has to be older
than the normal apprentice, and I really want him to be suitable for
Deirdre."

"That's a big order. Who appointed you Destrin's keeper?"

"I guess I did. No one else was helping him. Now that I've made
things profitable. I can't just leave it. But the time will come . . ." I
shrugged again.

"Why can't you stay?"

"For now, I can. The time will come, probably before too long, when . . ."

"You're awfully mysterious, Lerris. Why should I do this?" The man was pressing, but he had been good to me, and I could tell he embodied order.

I looked around the parlor, let my senses expand. No one was within hearing distance. "What do you know about Recluce?"

Brettel just nodded, not even looking surprised. "There's always been something more about you. Are you helping Destrin?"

I knew what he meant. "As I can, but there's nothing anyone could do."

"You'd do this for him?"

"He's a good man. Not a terribly good crafter, but a good man. And he fights each day because he feels he can offer Deirdre nothing."

Brettel scratched his left ear, then took a long pull. "Do you have any ideas where such an unusual apprentice might be found?"

"How about the younger son of one of the woodlot owners or the farms where you log? You might have a feeling . . ."

"I might . . . does he have to be older?"

"No . . . but not too much younger . . . gentle at heart, but stubborn, if that's possible . . ." I closed my mouth, realizing I was revealing far too much.

"You worry about me?"

"A little," I admitted.

"You should." Then he smiled. "But I told you I was Deirdre's godfather, and whether you came from hell itself, something needs to be done. Let me think about it. They are a couple of youngsters that just might do." He chuckled and added, "And their parents would believe we were doing them a favor."

I finished the redberry while Brettel thought.

"I'll get back to you," he told me while ushering me out.

An eight-day later Bostric arrived.

So did a commission for a red-oak chest for Dalta's dowry, with instructions to take my time and do it right . . . as if I ever would have done it any other way for Brettel.

Bostric was gangly, red-haired and freckled, initially as shy as a spooked quail, at least when I was around, and stubborn as a cornered buffalo. But he listened, and he could feel the woods. In his work on

273

L. E. MODESITT, JR.

the woodlot, he'd even used a saw and tried his hand at carving. His figures of people and animals were artistically better than mine.

Destrin just humphed, between coughs and when he had the strength to do so, and Deirdre made larger portions of the ever-present barley soup. Boring it might be, but she smiled more, when she wasn't fussing over her papa, and that was about all I could expect.

I still sometimes dreamed about golden girls, and sometimes about a black-haired woman, and woke up sweating and worse. I wondered why I dreamed of Krystal, but had no answers. All the time, Bostric slept soundly in the pull-out pallet we had built for him in the shop.

XLIV

Brettel's commission gave me another idea. I decided to make two of the chests, keeping the pieces for the second red oak dower chest in the stable when I wasn't working on it. If I didn't do it, no one else would, and Destrin really never looked at what I was working on until it was close to completion.

He was usually wrapped up in his benches and plain tables and fighting out the coughing attacks. When he wasn't, he worried about Bostric or me.

"He's all right, Lerris. He's just not you." If I heard it once, I heard those words a score of times as the winter drew out.

Bostric had more potential than Perlot's Grizzard, of that I was convinced, but he still didn't have the confidence, and only time would build that.

First, I made him work on breadboards, but only a few, mainly to give him confidence. The market for breadboards was limited, and designing and carving breadboards that didn't sell wasn't building confidence. I called them display pieces, and two actually sold, right from the window.

Then I talked to Wryson, who ran the dry goods store off the jeweler's street, and persuaded him to commission a storage chest, a simple piece but lined with cedar, to provide summer storage for woolens.

Doing it took twice as long, because I made Bostric do a lot of things I would have done.

"Why don't you do this, ser? I have to struggle, just getting the lines right."

"So did I," I snapped. "But will I always be here?"

"If you're not here, honored mastercrafter, how will I learn?" He said it in a respectful tone with a straight face. Only his eyes betrayed him.

"I'm not a mastercrafter. I'm just a journeyman woodcrafter."

"I understand, ser."

He gave me that hangdog look, and with his unruly red mop, freckles, and bushy eyebrows, resembled a sheepdog more than an apprentice. Then, maybe the two were similar. Sometimes it was hard to remember how frustrated and bored I had been, and how I would have liked to have said what I felt.

"But, honored journeyman, I still don't see what you want."

I couldn't help grinning. "Sorry . . . you're right. It is hard to learn how to do." I took the calipers once again and showed him what I wanted, then I watched and corrected him when necessary, trying not to laugh.

In the end, on that piece, everything worked out. Wryson was pleased, and placed an order for another chest, but not until early in the fall, when he would be getting his last shipment of finished woolens from Montgren.

Sometimes, it didn't work out so well—like the chair for Wessel. Bostric had trouble with the spooling, and that was my fault. He wasn't ready for it, and I had pushed too hard. We gave his effort, sturdy enough, to the Temple sisters, and I completed the second one myself. The bonus almost paid for the extra wood.

Deirdre turned out a matched cushion that made the piece even more spectacular, and I made a mental note to have her do more work like that in the future. She would be a real partner for Bostric.

After that, I suggested that Bostric try a bench to match the ones Destrin was making for the Horn Inn, perhaps the seediest drinkery in Fenard. At least, the breakage and Destrin's low prices had given him a steady, if poor, income.

Destrin had hummphed at my suggestion, coughed some more, but hadn't openly objected.

In the meantime, to try to upgrade Bostric's finishing skills, I had sketched out a child's table for him, scaling down a simple one from Dorman's incredible plan book. Once I had gone through it several times and explained the reasons for everything, Bostric finally nodded. I could sense the understanding.

The table turned out well, although it sat in the window for more than an eight-day before Wryson, the dry goods merchant, paid two silvers for it and a matching pair of armless chairs. I think that was because the weather had closed in, drifting snow over the roads toward Kyphros, and an expected shipment of Kyphros silverware had been delayed until after the holidays. So he needed a year-end present for his littlest.

I put my share into the hidden strongbox to go with the dower chest, and Bostric bought himself a pair of boots, barely used, but an improvement over his muckers.

Still . . . the table had been an experiment that almost hadn't sold, and that bothered me. We couldn't count on the weather to save us every time.

I rubbed my chin, then looked at the white oak I was working for a corner cabinet. White oak was so clean, but that meant that any mistake was there where no one could miss it, at least no one with a half-trained eye. Strangely, the same was true for black oak, but for the opposite reason. Everyone scrutinized it so closely that inevitably the flaws were discovered.

With a silent sigh, I looked over the boxes and the side table on the display stage and out into the mid-morning . . . gloomy as only a late-winter morning could be in Fenard.

Finally, I added another log to the hearth.

"I'll be back."

Destrin hummphed, hunched himself into his sweater and looked at the square storage box on his bench.

Bostric, behind Destrin, raised his eyebrows at the box, then looked to me. I glared, and he sighed. Destrin wasn't always communicative, but Bostric was going to end up with everything, and the least he could do was accept Destrin's faults.

"Do take care, honored journeyman," Bostric called. His voice was mock-plaintive.

I swallowed another grin and drew my cloak around me as I stepped into the chill on the street, making sure the door was closed behind me. My steps carried me toward the market square.

As I stepped onto the sidewalk beside the avenue, one of the few streets with an actual raised stone sidewalk separate from the road surface, I could sense a tension in the chill and damp air. Without even a hint of a breeze, the odor of wood smoke hung over Fenard, imparting an acrid edge to every breath.

A tinker pushed his cart listlessly toward the square. Behind him waddled a balding and white-haired man carrying a satchel. Neither looked up as I skirted them.

Overhead, the sun was lost behind the featureless gray clouds that appeared unmoving.

Clink . . . clink . . . clink . . . At the sound of the coach on the stones behind me, I stepped toward the bricks of the shop walls. *. . . clink . . .*

A glimmer of golden wood caught my eye, just as the unsmelled odor of chaos gripped at my feelings, as the chaos-master's coach rolled slowly by, drawn by the two oversized white horses I had first seen on the road from Freetown the previous fall. Behind the coach were the same two guards on their matching chestnuts, and the same dead-faced coachman drove.

Outlined in the coach window was the profile of a woman, the veiled woman I had seen at the inn in Howlett. The coach rolled down the avenue before I really cast my senses at the passengers.

Crack! The whiplash was metal, but I nearly cringed on the street from the force of the reaction, and from the immediate dull ache. Retreating behind the defenses Justen had taught me, I forced my steps to remain even as I continued toward the square.

"Geee-haw . . ." The mechanical voice of the driver echoed from the bricks and stones.

I did not rub my forehead, much as I wanted to, wondering at the fleeting impression I had received of three people within the coach. There had only been two, that I knew.

By the time I had passed by the square, with the rusted open market gates patrolled by the prefect's guards, and further toward the palace, I could see that the heavy iron gates of the palace had already closed.

I shook my head slowly, turning back toward Destrin's. Every time

277

I acted without thinking, I exposed myself. Now Antonin would know that there was at least one order-master in Fenard. The contact had been so brief, and his response so automatic and contemptuous, that I hoped he would not recognize me as an outsider or from Recluce.

I hoped, but there wasn't much else I could do, except keep on woodworking and learning . . . and trying to think before I acted. And all of that without letting my boredom push me.

Overhead, the clouds remained gray, but the faintest hint of a breeze touched my cheeks.

XLV

278   *Perlot's Crafting*—that was what the ornately-carved sign read. The chiseled letters, old. temple-style script, were painted black. A pale hard-finish coat that did not carry the gold overtones of most varnishes let the warm red-oak tones shine through.

As the morning mist beaded on my cloak, I tied Gairloch to the post in front of the shop. The winter had dragged out longer than usual, and when spring had come, the rains and the cold had mixed, like in the downpour that flooded the stable because I had neglected to clean the drainage gutters outside Gairloch's stall. Cleaning muck, and hay, and ice chunks, with the rain sheeting across my neck and back—that had been a real joy, and cleaning myself afterwards hadn't been much more fun.

"You must really like cold baths . . ." Bostric had observed with a straight face in his oh-so-respectful tone.

"Next time you can join me." I had told him, but it had only stopped the banter for a while, until I was back working in dry clothes.

Recalling Bostric's teasing, and glad that spring had finally come, I studied the chairs in the window—drawn especially to the sitting-room chair on the right. That design I had never seen, not even in Uncle Sardit's sketchbooks. The curves of the legs were understated, minimal, yet made the chair seem more delicate than it was.

"You!"

I looked up at the gruff voice.

A thin man, not much older than I was, a thin film of sawdust stuck to the sweat on his forehead and wearing a tattered gray shirt under his leather apron, glared at me.

I returned the look evenly. "Yes?"

"Are you—"

"Invite him in, Grizzard," added a raspy voice from within the shop.

Grizzard looked puzzled, and I just stepped around him. Directly inside the shop were three chairs, elegant in the Hamor style, but a trace too heavy in the legs and squared cross-braces. Between them was a low table, the kind whose use I had never figured out except as a place on which clutter collected.

While all the pieces were good, they were clearly high-class rejects, too expensive for the tradesman, and not quite good enough for the gentry. Probably Grizzard's work, rather than Perlot's. Somehow, Perlot never would have let a poor piece get that far.

Reddish coals glittered in the corner hearth, with a warmth I could feel even from the doorway. Perlot stepped around a bench and toward me.

I nodded.

"So we meet again, Lerris, or should I say craft-master Lerris?" Perlot stopped behind the chairs, next to the half-wall that separated the small waiting area from the workshop.

I bowed to the mastercrafter, and I meant it. His work was good, some of it, like the chair in the window, not only as good technically as Uncle Sardit's, but possibly even more inspired. "I was admiring the sitting-room chair. It's possibly the best piece I've seen like that."

The narrow craggy face creased as he frowned, and the craft-master closed his mouth. Then he wiped his hands on the underside of his apron. "Mean that, don't you?"

I nodded again.

"Grizzard, stop standing there like a dolt. You still haven't finished the detailing on the chest."

"Yes, ser." Grizzard scurried around us, the puzzle lines still graven in his forehead.

"Would you sit down?"

"Only for a moment, ser." I eased into the chair toward which Perlot had gestured, and he sat down across from me.

"Like to set things straight, young fellow . . ."

"There's nothing to set straight, mastercrafter. You didn't know me, and you had never seen my work. I could have been a wood-grifter from Freetown or Spidlar—"

Perlot motioned me to silence, and I stopped.

"You're not. I've looked at your work. It's better than any journeyman's here in Fenard, and it's getting better. Some is mastercraft level, like the chair you did for Wessel."

I must have lifted my eyebrows.

Perlot smiled. "He asked me for my opinion. I told him that he stole it from Destrin, and that it was the best single piece in his house, including the dining-room set I did last year."

"You flatter us."

"No. I don't flatter. It's not Destrin, poor soul. It's you. What do you intend to do? Take over Destrin's shop, and his daughter, and put him out to pasture?" The question was idly phrased, but the dark eyes hung on me.

I shook my head slowly. "Sometimes I wish that I could. It would be simpler that way. But that would not be fair nor right. In too many ways, I am still a journeyman, with more than a little left to learn."

Grizzard was trying to listen and concentrate on the detailing, and both efforts were suffering.

This time Perlot nodded. "Bostric won't ever be in your class."

"He will be a good craftsman, given time and training."

"He might be." The mastercrafter smiled. "Don't sell yourself short, young fellow. You've changed a lot in the time since you came. Besides, there's a difference between the quality of your cabinets and the quality of your soul." He laughed. "Poor Destrin. First-class soul, but . . ." Perlot shrugged.

"I don't think you can craft good wood without order in your soul," I added.

"Nor do I, boy. But an orderly soul doesn't guarantee good work. Having an orderly soul and being an order-master are two different propositions." He stood up. "What will you do about that chair in the window?"

"Nothing. It's your design." I grinned. "Now . . . if I can find something as good—and different . . ."

"You mean that, don't you?"

I nodded.

"Give Destrin my best, Lerris. Do what you can while you're here."
He stood up abruptly.

With that dismissal, I also stood, but did take the time for a last
look at the chair before stepping out into the spring warmth.

Gairloch waited patiently, as always.

Wheeee . . . eeee . . .

"I know. You don't get enough exercise, but I try, and one of these
days, we'll take a longer trip. Just be glad that you're not hauling wood
for the mills. You could belong to a carrier and not to a poor and
impoverished woodcrafter."

Gairloch didn't seem impressed. So I patted him on the shoulder
after I mounted. He didn't flatter me, honest beast.

Perlot's comments about Bostric bothered me. While I wished I
could avoid it, before long I would have to talk to Brettel. Destrin
continued to fail, and nothing I could do would help but prolong his
failing.

XLVI

Teeel . . . leeell . . . An unfamiliar bird warbles from beyond the olive
groves.

Sccuuuffff . . . Soft steps cross the graveled courtyard leading to
the cavalry stables.

A single torch flickers in the holder by the stable door, where a
tired youngster wearing the greens of the autarch snores softly.

As the steps pause, a woman with long dark unbound hair looks
down at the youngster. She wears a peasant dress, yet carries a bulging field pack whose straps press into the lithe muscles of her shoulders.

After a sad nod, she eases around the sentry and into the darkness
of the stable, counting the stalls until she reaches the third.

Whufflll . . .

". . . Easy . . . easy . . ."

In the darkness, the dark-haired woman eases the pack off her shoulders and lifts the two soft leather bags, and the heavy powder within each, out of the field pack she has carried from the engineering barracks. Next she checks the empty set of saddlebags before placing one bag of powder in each saddlebag, carefully fastening the clasps. The map she leaves tucked inside the waistband of the skirt.

She walks through the darkness to the end of the stable, where she eases the field pack into a corner. While it will certainly be discovered in a day or two, how and why it was placed there will not matter. Her squad will be leaving to face the Freetown rebels in the morning.

Her steps, even more silently, carry her back out past her mount and past the still-snoring stable guard. In time, she slips into her own room, where she lights a single candle, ignoring the woman on the occupied narrow cot. She rips off the peasant blouse and skirt and immerses herself in the tub of chill water she drew after the evening meal.

"At this time of night, Krystal?" asks a sleepy-eyed blond woman, sitting up and swinging her legs onto the floor.

"Never . . . again . . . no matter *what*."

"What?"

"It doesn't matter." The dark-haired woman jabs a hand toward her own cot. "See those scissors?"

"Yes. Why?"

"Would you get them?"

"You're not . . ."

"I am. Like I said, never again, not even for the best of causes." She has dried herself and is pulling on bleached and faded undergarments.

"You aren't making sense."

"I am. For the first time, I am." Her lips quirk into a genuine smile as the long black tresses fall away.

XLVII

With the flowers in the street boxes in bloom, and a brisk breeze from the north, the walk along the avenue was pleasant enough, even if I felt Bostric was always about to lurch into me. His feet always threatened not to follow his body—or the street ahead.

Destrin was back in the shop muttering over a simple box—just a box for Murran, the wagon-master who carried spices and silver along the north-south road from Fenard through Kyphros and all the way to Horgland on the South Sea. He would probably still be muttering and coughing when we returned.

No single street in Fenard bore a sign, but everyone named them— the avenue, the street of jewelers, the north road. I'd learned the names of many just by listening, but as for the side streets, the alleys, I doubted anyone who hadn't spent a lifetime in Fenard or a great deal of time loitering would ever know all the names.

The names changed. I overheard Deirdre and Bostric talking about when the grocer's lane had been the place of old inns. But the avenue was the avenue, the only really straight and perfectly-maintained street in Fenard. That might have had something to do with the fact that it ran from the prefect's palace past the market square and straight to the south gate.

Because the day was pleasant, and because I wasn't in the mood for doing detail work on the writing desk, not with Destrin in good enough health, temporarily anyway, and because Deirdre was sniffling and sneezing from the early flowers blooming, I had volunteered to wander past the market square to see if the cloth merchants from Horgland had arrived.

Bostric, of course, was happy not to be in the shop, caught between Destrin's complaints and my demands.

"We're actually taking a walk, honored journeyman?"

"Bostric. Enough is enough—unless you want to stay with the honored shop owner and feed the fire."

"While feeding the fire would be a great honor . . ."

"Bostric . . ."

"I'd prefer the walk."

Sometimes, I could see why Brettel had been able to find Bostric so quickly. His humor wasn't exactly subtle, yet I had the feeling there was more depth there, hidden behind the obvious and respectful disrespect.

Clink . . . clink . . .

I nudged the apprentice, and we stepped toward the shop fronts as the single post-rider trotted toward the palace.

"Wonder what news he brings?"

"He doesn't look happy. Perhaps the autarch . . ." He broke off as a soldier in the dark leathers of the prefect neared.

The soldier, shorter and squatter than either of us, his eyes fixed beyond the street, plunged straight at us, as if we did not exist.

I could sense an emptiness there, no aura at all, except for a faint white kernel deep within.

"What—" Bostric looked at me. "What was that?"

I thought I knew, but only shook my head. "He had somewhere to go. He's going to get there without taking a single turn."

No one else on the street—not the man in blue silks and leather with the long sword, nor the peddler woman with the sack, nor the urchin with the missing tooth and red hair—not one even seemed to notice the rigidity of the man's mission as they stepped or scurried aside.

Across the street, between two gray stone houses, there were two boxes of early-blooming red flowers flanking a narrow street, where with an almost furtive look the man in the blue silk shirt and dark-gray leather vest stepped out of sight.

"What street is that?" I asked Bostric.

"What street . . ." he mumbled in return.

"That alley over there, between the flowers. You seem to know all the streets."

"That's no proper street." He was flushing.

"No proper street?" I teased him, a little glad to have him on the defensive.

"Not a proper street . . ." His words were dogged, and he didn't look even in my direction.

"What do you mean?" I glanced toward the red flowers and the narrow alley—whose contents were lost in the shadows.

"All right. I'll show you. You'll see." Turning suddenly and stretching his long legs into nearly a run, he crossed the avenue so sharply I was hard-pressed to keep up with him.

We were both past the flowers before I had much of a chance to look around, or to react to the fragrances, a dozen or more different odors—roses, nightfires, lilies, and others I could not recognize, so many that my senses reeled.

Narrow the way was, not much more than half a rod wide, and short, not more than a dozen houses on each side before curving to the right and ending in a wall that seemed to separate the street from the market square. The polished marble stones were spotless and bore no trace of horses or coaches.

My eyes strayed up to a balcony not much above my head. There stood a woman, how old I could not say, though she was red-haired and older than I, wearing only a thin cotton shift so sheer that I could see every line of her body and even the dark nipples of her breasts.

". . . two young gents . . ."

I swallowed. No wonder Bostric had flushed.

He didn't look at me, but his steps flagged, and he halted. "Here. The street of . . . ladies . . ."

"Street of harlots, young fellow . . . we know what we are."

I didn't see the woman whose hard voice made the statement, since my eyes, in turning from the redhead on the balcony, had fallen across a blond woman wearing nothing but a robe, unbelted enough to show small high breasts quite fully and that she was a blond in all aspects, and that those aspects were all well-formed.

I think I forgot to breathe; my eyes blurred, and in shaking my head I looked down the way where a brunette, wearing only a filmy skirt, was drawing the man in blue silk inside a doorway.

In the open and unglassed window of a house closer than where the brunette had enticed the dandy lounged another semi-clothed woman, this one with impossibly-formed breasts, also uncovered, and with the tiniest of waists.

"Your pleasure here, young fellows . . . two or more, if you wish . . ." That voice came from the left, where my eyes flickered almost despite themselves, alighting on the low balcony opposite the redhead. This one was black-haired, with long flowing tresses that swirled over the creamy skin of her otherwise uncovered breasts and shoulders.

I swallowed again, feeling my trousers suddenly far too tight, as I viewed that hair across the impossibly beckoning breasts of the raven-haired harlot.

Bostric . . . he wasn't as silent as I was . . . his breath so loud that it penetrated my daze . . . partly.

". . . one of the woodcrafters . . . I think . . ."

The identification was so whispery I almost missed it, but the words sent a chill across my neck, enough of a chill that I sent my feelings toward the black-haired wench.

"Ohhh." The heavy and squat woman beneath the illusion radiated not only chaos, but a coiled illness deep within, like an ooze-green serpent. My senses shifted to the redhead above and caught not only her scrawny leanness, but the long knife along one hip, and the vacant smile. What my eyes saw, my senses refuted. My guts twisted, and I had to re-swallow bile and whatever else remained from breakfast.

Underfoot, the polished marble turned into rutted and cracked stone and clay, littered with certain items from the interiors of sheep, as well as other items. The odor of flowers was overlaid with other, less desirable odors.

Bostric stood like a statue until I jabbed him in the ribs and took him by the elbow.

We both stumbled out into the avenue, though he merely looked dazed. If I looked the way I felt, morning fog would have looked more substantial.

"See . . ." Bostric said. "See . . ."

I said nothing, just forced my feet to carry me toward the market square, breathing deeply and trying to get the odor of rotten roses out of my nostrils and my memory. Shaking my head and squinting, and asking myself who had recognized me . . . and why.

I shivered, and reached out again, this time to Bostric, recognizing the slender thread of suggestion planted upon him.

While it would have been the effort of an instant to snap that thread, despite the ugliness of that tie, I could not. So I infused Bostric with some additional order and let him shake himself free.

"Wheee . . . ewww . . ."

"Yes," I added. "Let's see about that cloth."

"Cloth? You can think about cloth after that?"

"It's a great deal safer." I tried to keep my tone wry.

"Safer?" Bostric's eyes flashed in my direction. "Lerris . . . ?"

I knew what he was thinking. "Yes." My voice was tired. "I do like women. Healthy, young, and unmagicked women."

"Unmagicked?"

I ignored his last question as we walked past another half-living guard stationed by the gate to the market square. The coldness surrounding him was hard to ignore, but I did, letting my eyes search for the bright-colored banner that Deirdre had described.

Looking for cloth merchants was easier than speculating on the magic behind the Street of Harlots.

Even past the empty fountain, halfway across the paving stones of the square, past the potters' stalls, past the split-wood baskets from the farms, past the red-and-gold patterned blankets displayed by a twisted little man, there were no colored banners nor cloth merchants.

Bostric shivered as we passed Mathilde, older but still blond, if plump, and bulging out of unwashed brown trousers and a tattered and open cloth coat. The flowers in her pots were already wilting within from the chaos contained in her blood. No evil there, just honest disorder.

For all Bostric's shivers, I would have bedded a dozen Mathildes sooner than any of the ladies on the Street of Harlots. The deeper I looked at Fenard, the less I liked it. But would that have been true in any place where I stayed long enough to really look?

I didn't know.

What I knew for certain was that the cloth merchants hadn't arrived, and that I had no intentions of going anywhere near that narrow street again.

287

XLVIII

Cling.

"Wonder who it is?" mumbled Destrin.

I looked at Bostric. He stood there, plane in hand. I looked at him hard and he jumped, setting down the tool and hastening to the door.

Despite the late spring warmth in the air outside, Destrin had the window closed, a low fire in the hearth, and an old and raveled sweater on under his apron as he worked on yet another tavern bench.

The work was going well enough, but every time I patted myself on the back, it seemed like something like the stable flood occurred. Regular storms I couldn't attribute to disorder or Antonin. Even after my experience an eight-day earlier in the Street of Harlots, I couldn't blame the weather on Antonin, and that was the problem. How could I separate what belonged to Fenard from whatever the chaos-master was weaving?

The other problem was that there wasn't all that much I knew how to do in working with order. Yes, I could provide support for Destrin, reinforce Bostric's basic goodness, and help a few good souls resist the twists of chaos sent forth by whoever was sending them forth. But beyond that? I shook my head slowly.

"You all right, Lerris?" Destrin bent toward me.

"I'm fine." And I was. Winter had departed, and I enjoyed the spring, watching Deirdre, and visiting the market. I just didn't enjoy the heat in the shop.

Wiping my forehead, I studied the grain of the white oak, asking myself again why I had agreed to do a writing desk. Without Dorman's faded plan book, I would have been in even bigger trouble. Even so, it took all of my concentration to visualize the desk, to mentally draw the pieces from where they lay buried in the wood, and try to fit them together.

That sort of mental exercise helped, not only in crafting, but somehow in beginning to understand more of *The Basis of Order*. I had read the slim volume twice, and half of it was still unclear. As was the desk for Dalta, Brettel's daughter, the desk he wanted as a wedding gift. That made the third piece he had commissioned, far more than he needed to do even as a friend of Destrin's. Dalta would have an entirely furnished house before long, and she wasn't even betrothed!

"Here, ser." Bostric handed a flat envelope to Destrin, then returned to smoothing the kitchen table we had roughed out together.

I knew I was forcing the red-haired youth, even more than Sardit had forced me, but how much time I had I didn't know, certainly not enough, however long it might be, to carry him through a full apprenticeship. Already his touch was defter than that of Destrin, and while Deirdre was older than Bostric, a few years was not insurmountable, and he was kind enough at heart.

I repressed a sigh. How had I gotten into this mess?

"Lerris!"

288

I glanced up. Destrin had paled. "Accufff . . . accuu . . ." He grasped for the bench.

Bostric looked to me.

"Just get the line right," I told him as I walked around the end of the bench.

"Look at this." Destrin rasped, thrusting the heavy paper at me.

I glanced over the announcement.

Be it noted that the Prefect must maintain the defenses of the Kingdom of Gallos against the growing threat of invasion by the Autarch of Kyphros, and be it noted that Gallos must combat the unrest in the smaller eastern principalities of Candar caused by the actions of Black Recluce. These demands on the Treasury require an increase in the quarterly levy.

That was the standard language. Underneath, a different hand had penned in darker ink, "Destrin the Woodcrafter, quarterly levy, five golds."

Originally, the tax bill had showed three golds, but the three had been crossed out and the five written above it. The change bore the initial "J." A heavy blue-waxed seal had been affixed at the bottom.

". . . can meet the first one . . . but we won't eat much but barley soup. There is no way I can make the second one, even at year-end. We can't afford the wood for the holiday buyers if I have to pay five golds." Destrin leaned against his bench, his breath coming more quickly.

Looking at the thin man, I could see the distress. His system was wasting away, bit by bit, even with the order-strength I had quietly added to his wasting frame. I didn't know enough to stop the degeneration, only to give him energy and keep it at bay.

"We'll find a way," I assured him, keeping my voice confident, even as I wondered how.

"But . . . how?" The old crafter gulped for air. ". . . Accuuu . . . accc . . . aaccc . . ."

"We'll find a way." I looked back at my workbench and the white oak. "Starting with the desk for Brettel." I wondered, though. Just as the shop was beginning to rise significantly above the expenses, the levy went up. The last levy had only been a gold and five silvers. It had been doubled, and then someone had added another two golds—scarcely coincidental, I felt, but who was I to say?

Who set and collected taxes went beyond my knowledge. I was having enough trouble with woodcrafting and trying to read and learn *The Basis of Order.*

"You need something to drink after that," I added. "Come on. Let's see what Deirdre has."

Destrin looked puzzled, as well he might, for I had not pushed him quite so hard before; but his face had gone beyond pale into a grayish shade, before I added just another trace of order to his struggling heart and practically took all his weight—not that he was that heavy any longer—as I helped him up the stairs.

"I'm . . . all right . . ."

I didn't say anything as he leaned on me and crossed the room to his favorite chair.

Her face calm, Deirdre had set down the cushion she was working on and crossed the large room to meet us. She said nothing, just looked from Destrin, still clutching the tax bill in his clawed hands, to me. Then she went to the shelf and poured a mug of redberry as I eased Destrin into the battered armchair.

As the old crafter sipped the juice, I nodded to Deirdre. "I've got to check Bostric," I explained as I left. That much was true. It had to be. The more I learned about order, the more fearful I was of self-deception, knowing that I practiced it all too often anyway.

The other thing I was going to do was open the windows so Bostric and I didn't die of heat poisoning.

XLIX

"Captain Torrman wants you to take the hill path and hold it against the rebels," announces the messenger, spewing forth the words in one long burst before taking a deep breath.

The squad leader looks at the messenger. "When? Are we expecting the entire army of the Duke of Hydlen to reinforce us?"

A bewildered expression crosses the youngster's face. "That was the order . . ."

The squad leader takes a slow and silent breath, then purses her lips. The wind whips her short black hair away from her face, and the black eyes turn full on the messenger. "We have the message."

The youngster shrivels under the darkness of her gaze, then salutes. "Will that be all, leader?"

"Tell Captain Torrman that we will accomplish his objective."

"What, leader?"

"Tell the captain that we will accomplish his objective." Her soft voice is even colder, and the bells that ring in it are the bells of a funeral dirge. "Provided he guards the southwest road to Gallos," she adds.

"Provided he guards the southwest road to Gallos?" The messenger repeats the words.

"That is correct. He must use the rest of his forces to hold the southwest pass."

The messenger sits astride the pony, his mouth not quite hanging open.

"That will be all," the officer adds. "You may convey my reply to Captain Torrman."

The messenger looks from the cold-eyed woman to the troopers behind her. One fingers a knife, and the messenger looks back to the officer.

"That will be all," she repeats.

The messenger swallows and lifts the reins, then nudges the pony back downhill.

The squad leader looks down at the valley to the north, then at the folded square of the map she needed and paid too much for, for all that many others would have said she paid little indeed of true value. She takes one breath, then another. Despite the cold bath of the night before last, she feels unclean, as if she had not bathed in weeks. Her hand touches the hilt of her blade. Her head lifts, and she studies the hills to the east.

The trooper beside the squad leader swallows as he watches his superior study the map. He edges his mount sideways toward another woman, a blond woman with a pair of knives at her belt, the only other woman trooper in the squad.

"She's not going to follow the captain's orders . . ." he whispers.

"Look down there," returns the blond, gesturing at the roiling dust rising from the road at the far end of the small valley they survey. The packed figures of the soldiers are not visible, but both know they are there. "Would you?"

"Torrman's killed leaders for less . . ."

"All right . . ." The woman wearing the leather officer's vest looks at the two whispering subordinates, then urges her mount to the east, not toward the hill path below, but along the ridge line.

"That's not where Torrman ordered us . . ."

The squad leader ignores the not-quite-whispered statement drifting up from the third file as another trooper grabs the protester by the tunic.

". . . remember Gireo, you idiot . . ."

The swallowed gulp almost brings a smile to the blond woman's face, but the squad leader's eyes remain fixed on the space between the hills.

". . . don't like this . . ."

". . . just shut up . . ."

". . . Torrman's a mean bastard . . . gut the whole squad . . ."

". . . she's right. Take the hill path, and you won't have any guts left for Torrman . . ."

". . . still don't like it . . ."

". . . got any better ideas?"

Even with all the mutterings, the squad follows the black-haired officer as she picks her way toward the combination dam/levee that holds the irrigation water for the year's crops. The heavy-set man, the one who had gulped, looks from the hill road below to the dust cloud heralding the advance of the Freetown rebels.

The officer's eyes flicker from the dust-cloud at the northeastern end of the narrow valley to the trail before her and to one of the aqueducts that carry the water beyond the valley and toward the dry steppes of Southern Kyphros. One hand touches the thin oilcloth-wrapped bundle behind her saddle, then strays toward the second and heavier set of saddlebags.

The dust cloud has moved perhaps a third of the way across the valley, another two kays, when the squad leader dismounts under the iron-bound gates of the dam. The cold iron reinforces every joint and every red-oak timber, bracing the iron-hinged floodgates closed.

Above her and to the south rise the stone walls that contain the four aqueduct channels. An iron wheel rises above each tunnel, but each wheel is locked in place with an iron bar and a double lock. The locks are each the size of a farmer's fist.

The squad leader shakes her head as she studies the floodgates and the iron-bound timbers that hold them closed.

". . . what . . ."

". . . shhh . . . knows what she's doing . . ."

Finally she retrieves an iron bar perhaps two-thirds the length of her arm from the oilcloth-wrapped bundle behind her saddle, then a short, rough-toothed bow saw. She carries both with her as she again approaches the water gates.

"The olive groves may suffer," she says to no one, "but if the autarch could do it, so can we." After scanning the timbers, she begins to pry the iron edging away from one.

Puzzled expressions cross several faces, but her squad remains mounted, waiting.

As she pries the edging away from the wood and exposes the red beneath, she halts.

"Kassein."

The heavy-set man dismounts, handing the reins to the blond woman. "Yes, sher?"

"Take this saw. Cut through this timber as far as you can—until the saw begins to bind."

"Bind?"

"The wood will try to grab it." She walks to another timber, and begins to pry.

The blond trooper hands the reins of two horses to a third man, dismounts, and walks up to the leader. "I can do this better."

The squad leader nods and hands the pry bar to her. "I'm going up on top. I'll leave the second saw. Weaken as many as you can." Five quick steps carry her back to her mount. "Darso, you stay here and help with the sawing. Altra and Ferl will stand guard, just in case. Take turns with the saw."

"I'm not . . ."

"I know. You're cavalry, not a carpenter. But if you don't saw, you'll be dead cavalry. You can tie the horses to that root there."

Back in the saddle, she nods at the remaining five troopers, and all six begin to pick their way along the slanting trail to the north, round and toward the top of the dam.

. . . *creeakkkk* . . .

. . . skkkraawwww . . . skrawaaawwww . . .

When she dismounts at the top of the dam and glances out toward the west, the dust cloud has almost reached the middle of the valley. "Damn . . ." The saddlebags come off the horse, and she forces herself not to show how heavy the bags are as she sets them down carefully, well back from the lake. She then loosens one set of buckles, easing the wax-impregnated and oiled leather bag containing the heavy powder out of the stiffer leather of one saddlebag. The other saddlebag remains closed. With a deep breath, she lifts the waxy leather container and walks out onto the flat stone bulwark that holds the iron hinges of the floodgates, finally setting her burden down with exaggerated care.

Creaaakkkkkk . . .

The dark-haired woman studies the gates, trying to determine whether they have begun to bulge or separate. "How many have you got done?" She leans over the stone wall.

"Five completed, maybe another five to go."

The officer looks at the water, lapping less than a cubit below the overflow spillway, then at the gates. Then she bends over the wall again. "Finish up the ones you're on, and mount up. Follow us up here."

"Those beams are solid . . ."

"I know. I know." The woman with the still-untarnished silver firebird on the collar of her green leather vest straightens up and looks at the leather bag resting on the stone by her feet.

With a deep breath, she bends.

"One should be enough . . ." She studies the dust cloud, and the ant-like horses that lead the more than a thousand renegade soldiers thrown out by the new duke.

Clickedy . . . click . . .

Below, the five troopers scramble onto their mounts and guide the horses along the narrow path the rest of the squad had taken earlier.

As the blond woman leads the remainder of the squad upward and toward the top of the dam, the squad leader returns to her mount and extracts a thin coil of waxed rope from her normal saddlebags. She carries the rope back to the dam, where she studies the dark-green water behind the main floodgates.

In quick sure strokes, she cuts four equal lengths from the coil. Two she sets aside. One remaining section she inserts through a plug in the coated leather before tamping wax around the edges. The second section she ties to the neck of the bag. Trying not to hurry, she slowly lowers the bag into the water, paying the rope—around which the fuse is threaded—out slowly, until the bag rests four cubits down. She ignores the puzzled looks from the mounted troops in the defile to the north of the dam.

At last she ties the connecting rope to the nearest iron wheel, and threads the second rope through the wheel as well. After retrieving the coil and the other two sections of rope and setting them on a boulder beside where the blond woman now holds the reins to her mount, she stops.

"All of you—back up and around that corner."

Not waiting to see if her orders are obeyed, she moves almost at a run to the dam, where she studies the valley. Should she wait? The effect would be greater. But what if . . . ? She shakes her head and eases the striker from her belt.

Scrtcccc . . . click . . . . . . hhssstttt . . . A long spark leaps from the striker to the loosely-threaded rope fuse, followed by a tongue of flame licking its way toward the water and the bag of powder suspended in the heavy green below.

".. . devils . . . she carried *that* all the way from Kyphrien?"

"One white wizard . . . all that it would take to blow us all to hell . . ."

".. . demons protect their own . . ."

She sprints off the dike as fast as she can, throwing herself into the saddle. For the first time ever that her squad has seen, her booted heels spur her mount.

Once behind the rocky ledge with the rest of the squad, she reins in and waits . . . and waits.

"Hell!"

She turns the horse, starting to edge back toward the dam.

CRUUMMPPP . . . The blue-green water surges up perhaps three cubits above the floodgates.

"Is that all? . . ."

Creeeaakakkkkk . . . snnaaapppp . . . SWUUUUUSHHHHHHHHHH-HHHHH . . .

As the gates buckle open, the spring's accumulated runoff gushes forth down the narrow gorge, gaining speed as it drops the nearly one kay toward the narrow valley floor.

295

". . . gods have mercy . . ."

. . . wheee . . . eeehuunnn . . .

". . . easy . . . easy there . . ."

". . . now . . . you see why you never cross her . . ."

The black-eyed woman, whose eyes are now darker than the black of her irises, nudges the horse forward to the stone wall, where she can watch the wall of water sweeping down on the unprepared rebels.

At least one Kyphran banner flutters on the high ground where the southwest road offers the only escape from the lake that the grassy valley has become.

The olive groves will suffer, but the Autarch needs trained troops more than olives.

•

•

•

L

The drawing was simple enough—a wooden armchair, with the five spokes supporting a simple contoured back. Dorman's tools, old as some of them were, were more than adequate for the job, and in adapting an old Hamorian design in the faded book, I thought Bostric and I could deliver the armchairs for less than Jirrle. The dining set would have meant bidding against Perlot.

"We can do it," I said quietly.

The glint of gold from the back of the shop told me that Deirdre was watching from the darkness pooled at the bottom of the stairs that led up to the family living quarters. I almost sighed. She was certainly pretty enough, and willing, but . . . somehow . . . that would have been poor repayment for Destrin. I think both Deirdre and I knew what could not be, not that either of us was totally happy about it.

"For eight golds or less?" asked the crafter. He still had on the ratty sweater, and the rear window was open but a trace.

I wiped my forehead before answering. "With what I have in the stable, plus the logs—say four golds. Five or six days' work over two weeks. We bid ten."

"If you can do it, then I'll mark the bid," Destrin said slowly. His color remained grayish, despite all I had done.

I didn't like doing work for someone like a sub-prefect, especially in Gallos, but steady as the income from the benches was, and despite Brettel's commissions and the work from Wessel and Wryson, there wouldn't be enough coin to meet the quarterly tax levies. That left only a few choices, like indenturing Deirdre to one of the local gentry, or a work indenture for Destrin himself—not a personal indenture, but that of all his output to the prefect or a local merchant. Destrin couldn't meet the terms of an indenture, and the default would leave Deirdre penniless. As for indenturing Deirdre—I shivered at that.

Since the bids were publicly opened, Jirrle couldn't use whatever influence he might have to change the award.

· Even if we were successful, that only bought Destrin and Bostric time, perhaps a year. Unless the levy were reduced, the shop would have to close. But in a year, a great deal could happen.

As for me, a lot of questions about the prefect still remained unanswered. How could a ruler who opposed local corruption so fiercely be so close to Antonin and his lady Sephya, who appeared to be nearly as adept as the white wizard himself?

297

"You sure we can do this?" Bostric asked yet again. Sawdust stuck to his forehead, glued in place by his sweat. For once, there was no mock-respect, no banter, and that told me that even he was worried.

I sighed. Doing the work was getting to be the least of my problems.

"Would anyone like some cold redberry?" interrupted Deirdre. "Allys had a little ice left over."

I nodded, wiping my forehead again.

"I'll take mine without ice," Destrin whined.

"Ice, please," Bostric added. "I need to cool off even more now."

Both Deirdre and I ignored his added comment. Destrin hadn't heard it.

Deirdre served me first, and I drained nearly all of it in one gulp, trying to cool off from too much warmth in the shop. Destrin was always cold, and while I could take the cold, adapting to too much heat was far harder.

Finally, I wiped my forehead again. "I'm taking a walk."

Neither Destrin nor Bostric said a word.

"Will you be back by midday for dinner?" asked Deirdre from the stairs, where she had stopped.

"Probably. I just need some fresh air and to think a while."

She nodded and was gone, her feet barely whispering up the steps.

After leaving the leather apron in my alcove and pulling one of my two plain shirts, I stepped out onto the street.

Left or right? To the left lay the square. I turned right, taking a deep breath of the cooler outside air, avoiding a puddle that still remained from the rain the night before. The evening showers hadn't been as bad as the ice and rain storm several days earlier, but for the past eight-day late spring fogs had clouded the streets in the early morning right after dawn. Just as winter had been late in leaving, so too spring had lingered.

Click . . . click . . . My boots rang on the stones as I ambled down the street of jewelers and around the corner into the wider street where the healers practiced.

Not all my time was spent in the shop, nor in cleaning the stable, nor riding Gairloch, nor in obtaining the woods from Brettel for our work. Besides my slow night-studies of order, and my cautious attempts at applying them in small and hidden ways—like creating stronger glues by working with the internal order of the broths—I also wandered through the streets of Fenard, just somehow trying to understand why it felt the way it did.

According to the book, feelings preceded understanding. I hoped the understanding didn't lag too much, because I was definitely having worried feelings, particularly after having seen Antonin and Sephya entering the prefect's palace.

Even recalling her gave me a chill, more so than seeing Antonin, or feeling him brushing me aside . . . or walking down the healers' lane.

Each healer had a different sign.

Rentfrew—Disease Casting. That one was in white letters upon a red background, over a doorway that radiated, to my senses, a dull white-red.

I forced my feet not to cross to the other side of the pavement.

Clickedy . . . clack . . . clickedy . . . A black horse pulled an equally-black carriage away from an awning-covered doorway further up the street, heading away from me.

Healing. The letters were etched into white oak and painted green.

No aura surrounded that doorway. Either simple physical medicine with herbs and the like, or a pretender—or both.

Another doorway bore only the sign of a snake twisted around a staff. Why, I had no idea.

A woman wearing a heavy cloak and a broad-brimmed dark-leather hat with a black veil glided from a doorway almost in front of me and back down the slanting pavement toward the street of jewelers. The odor of roses upon roses told me more of what she was even than the sickness buried within her—that disorder that had so wrenched my guts when first I had sensed it in such profusion when Bostric had led me into the street of harlots. Since then I had noted it within a woman peddling combs in the square, and even in a lady attached to one minister.

Supposedly, a high chaos-master could remove the disease, but the price was reputed to be more than most women would pay.

I shook my head and kept walking.

"Love philtres . . . love philtres . . ." hissed a voice from the shadows, understandably enough, since street peddling outside the square was forbidden. The woman's face was thin, scarred on both cheeks, and pock-marked. The disorder within was worse, and I hastened my steps.

Tenterra—Nature's Healer. A guttered-out lamp, painted bright red, swung idly in the breeze beneath the sign. The doorway was banded in cold iron and barred—a tacit announcement that chaos was barred from Tenterra's. So, of course, was order; but who would know?

". . . love philtres . . ." The words hissed up my spine even after I passed three more closed doorways and reached the black awning. The door underneath was black oak, banded in black iron, and bore no name nor any sign.

I could feel nothing, either of chaos or order, and passed back onto the far end of the jewelers' street where it curved around and led back toward the avenue. Even when you started in one direction in Fenard, you could end up going somewhere else.

Did I want to pass by the palace gardens? I shrugged. Even my simple shirt felt clinging and warm as the sun struggled to break through the low clouds that had been fog at dawn.

Two guards, one by each side of the gate, each bearing a halberd in addition to a short sword, watched as I walked toward them. If I looked to my right, I could see the green leaves of spring just barely

blurring the outlines of the oak and maple branches extending above
the stones of the wall. On the other side of the avenue were the grand
town homes of the ministers.

"You! What are you doing here?" The nearer guard lowered the
halberd slightly, as if in threat.

"Just taking a morning walk."

"Not for the likes of you," he growled.

As I drew nearer, slowing and stopping, I could feel the incredible
sense of chaos that enveloped him. Yet beneath that disorder was a
kernel of something else, as if the disorder had been dropped upon
him, and he had been too weak to resist, but too strong to surrender
totally.

Without thinking, I reached out and strengthened his basic honesty
and order, letting it push away the chaos as I stood there. "You're
right. I'll be going." As I left him standing there, I could sense the
honest confusion as he tried to recover himself.

Click . . . click . . . The sound of my heels on the polished stones
of the street before the ministers' houses echoed loudly in my ears.

300

". . . who was that?" whispered the second guard.

Clink . . . clink . . . The sound of horses and mounted men rebounded from behind me, and I stepped as close to the side of the
street as I could, looking back over my shoulder. A troop of fresh
cavalry rode in my direction. Standing aside in the shadows that had
begun to appear as the sun burned off the last of the morning fog, I
watched.

The standard-bearer, younger than me, borne by a chestnut, passed
by with an impassive face and a reek of chaos, a reeking disorder only
compounded by the armed men who followed.

Clink . . . clickedy, click, click . . . clink . . .

As I leaned back against the brick wall of an unknown house, I
slowly gathered my near-shredded senses back into myself, marveling
at the array of chaos-energy expended on the troop. Marveling—and
suppressing the urge to retch.

Antonin and Sephya—it had to have been their work.

Why I didn't know, but Antonin's hands were on it as surely as
though he had signed the city the way Uncle Sardit signed a chest
with his maker's mark.

With the horses safely past, I eased my steps back toward Destrin's. Had I been unwise in helping the guard struggle against un-

wanted chaos? Probably. Would I have done it again? Had there really been a choice?

I tried not to shrug as the sun ducked behind another cloud and the shadows faded into gray again.

LI

Patterns—there are patterns everywhere. That was what the book said, and what everyone had tried to point out to me. Just by creating ice crystals too small to see, some of the Masters of Recluce had started a change in climate that prostrated the Duchy of Freetown.

People create patterns, too, and by becoming Destrin's journeyman, my presence was changing the patterns in Fenard. How much the order I had added changed things . . . who could tell?

Before I rode Gairloch out to the mill to check the available black oak for the sub-prefect's chairs, I made sure to cross the market square, stopping to buy a biscuit, nodding to the few people I recognized or thought I recognized, and listening, always listening.

The high clouds were hazy and gray, yet the day was humid, almost steamy, and sweat dripped from my forehead. The late and short spring was turning to summer.

The market looked the same as always, a scattering of small stalls, carts, and merchandise strewn across the open expanse of granite, all of it able to be moved at day's end when the sweepers pushed through their brooms and refuse carts and the open space returned to a cavernous granite-walled emptiness.

The prefect was bright, or his advisers were. Half a silver a day was what it cost to use the market if you had a stall, a penny if you could carry your wares on your back. For that you got guards posted at each street departing the plaza and guards who patrolled in leather vests with clubs. You also got some guards who looked like merchants and hangers-on. If you couldn't fit your goods in a single stall, you had to find a permanent store or sell to someone who had one.

A fair trade, all in all. Sellers got a place relatively free from theft and graft. The prefect got revenue and information, particularly since his open market was one of the few in Eastern Candar exempt from major corruption. Reputedly the autarch's markets were better, but the prefect's border posts supposedly confiscated anything coming from the south without the prefect's authorization.

I hesitated as I neared the fountain.

". . . did you see the golden coach?"

". . . came through the west gate, as if it had come from below the Westhorns . . ."

The second speaker was Mathilde, the plump blond flower lady whose flowers seldom lasted more than two days. People with chaos in their blood should never handle living things, yet they seem to enjoy plants and pets and delight in gossip. She bulged out of a long tunic and stretched the seams of her faded purple trousers. Unwashed and gnarled toes protruded from her battered sandals.

"Probably some retainer of the prefect's," I offered gratuitously.

"It couldn't have been. There were two armed guards and a blood-red banner on the coach staff. The prefect doesn't allow mounted armed guards inside the city gates, saving his own."

"Maybe they forgot . . ."

"Young fellow, are you trying to provoke me?"

I grinned at the flower seller. "Just trying to be charitable to the poor guards that had to chase their boss across the countryside."

"Poor guards, my trousers! That coach was worth a fortune, and the geldings that carried those guards were a matched pair. And I saw a veiled woman in that coach, the kind they sell in Hamor only to the wealthiest of landowners. Not only that, but the coach was of wood and leather, without a scrap of iron . . ."

I shrugged. "Some chaos-wizard, then, on his way to help the new Duke of Freetown. That's where everyone is headed to make their fortune. He just stopped to pay his respects to the prefect."

"Wrong again!" cackled Mathilde. "The coach is stabled at the prefect's palace."

"Why does the prefect need a chaos-wizard?" asked the peddler, as she unpacked and placed her crooked pots on the ledge by the dry fountain that had not worked since before I came to Fenard.

"The rumor is Kyphrien . . ." hissed Mathilde.

Kyphrien? I almost stopped then and there. Instead I looked at a

302

particularly crooked pot, so ugly I could never have been tempted to buy it. "Kyphrien? The autarch?"

"Why not?" asked Mathilde. "The prefect and the autarch aren't friends."

I nodded and put down the pot, well-aware that the ragged man edging up to look at the other pots on the lower step of the fountain was some sort of spy for the prefect, and a chaos-tainted one at that. "Do you think the autarch is planning something?"

Mathilde saw the ragged man in the tattered brown leathers that were a shade too clean and shrugged. "Who knows what rulers plan? I just sell flowers, like you work wood."

Looking at the flowers mock-regretfully, I grinned falsely. "I'd buy some, but I'd better get to the mill."

"You still supporting that broken-down crafter? Why don't you open your own shop?"

"I'd have little without him. Someday . . ."

"Oh . . . it's the golden-haired daughter . . . you want it all, you schemer . . ." She leered at me, and the pot peddler looked at us both as if we were crazy, while the ragged spy looked at no one.

Listening again, I stepped down from the fountain and headed toward Fair Road.

". . . never see better-cured leather west of Recluce . . ."

". . . only half a silver for this, scabbard and all . . ."

"Fresh yams! Fresh yams!"

Wiping my dripping forehead with the back of my short-sleeved working tunic, I saw another man in ragged leathers, not following me, but watching the arms merchant and noting the blades.

". . . the finest in worked steel . . . flexible enough . . . sharp enough to cut a spider's web . . ."

". . . finest Hamorian cotton . . . cool to wear . . . the finest in cotton . . ."

"Winter-saved apples, order-spelled and ready to eat . . ."

I shook my head at the fruit vendor's outrageous claim. Winter-saved apples they might be, and even kept in the coolest of root cellars, but order-spelling fruit took more effort than any order-master in his right mind would ever want to do—unless you were talking about killing off the vermin, and cool water and care did almost as well.

". . . a half-copper for a tale of adventure! A song of joy . . ."

303

A thin woman in rags lingered around the minstrel's corner. Her muscles were too heavy and her skin too smooth for her to be the beggar she played.

I did not shake my head this time, but I wondered what the autarch wanted to know, and why Kyphrien was important.

At the iron gates to the market square, gates which were rusted open, I suspected, three guards watched the road and the passers-by. Two in leathers, with their clubs and blades—and one posing as a stonemason's helper. The mason was restoring a damaged arch leading into a leather shop.

The shops on that unnamed street I never frequented, not with my limited funds and disinterest in pure luxury.

My feet carried me automatically toward the turn leading back to the alley behind Destrin's and the stable. Gairloch needed the exercise, and Brettel's mill was far enough to make it better for both of us if I rode.

Another reason for Destrin's problems—the shop he had taken over from his father had catered to the personal needs of merchants and their ladies, supplying a level of crafting Destrin could not match. Destrin's rough benches and chairs belonged in the trade quarter, but he refused to move from the once-proud house and shop.

Again, I thought about the bid on the chairs for the sub-prefect, wondering if it had been a good idea, even though I could see no other alternative.

Gairloch could tell I was worried, and he danced around a lot as I saddled him.

"Settle down!" I finally snapped. And he did.

I kept thinking about the bid on the chairs.

Compared to the work that would be involved in completing the sub-prefect's chairs, getting the bid for them had not been all that hard. Destrin had signed the paper, and I put it in the envelope. Then we all had gathered on the steps of the sub-prefect's house the next morning.

"For a bid of ten golds, the commission on the five matched chairs is let to Destrin the woodworker."

"What?" Jirrle had been on his feet, his face purpling. But a younger man, with similar features, hauled him back down.

"Bids were also received from Jirrle, the woodcrafter, and from Rasten. If the chairs are defective, the bidder will pay a default fee of one gold and the second bidder will be awarded the commission."

304

I had winced at that, not that I expected the quality to be inadequate, but was that phrase merely a way to get out of the contract? I shook my head, not knowing what exactly I would do if that were the case.

Although Brettel's mill was nearly a kay farther down than anyone else's, he offered better prices, at least to me. He also knew what was happening. Few of the other crafters talked to me, for I was only a journeyman working for an excuse for a woodcrafter.

"Lerris! What now? Some seconds on green oak? Perhaps some red oak limbs?"

"Actually, I was looking for something else . . . green oak twigs for baskets!"

Brettel shook his white and silver thatch. "That bad, now?"

I raised my shoulders. "Black oak."

"So . . . the rumor was true. You did underbid Jirrle and Rasten on that chair set. Jirrle was livid. He said that Destrin couldn't make one straight spoke, let alone enough for a single chair. I agreed." Then the mill-master grinned. "I didn't tell him that his journeyman was probably going to do it all."

"Me? A broken-down excuse for a woodworker?"

"Is that what he called you?"

"Not to my face . . ."

Brettel's face dropped the joviality. "Black oak's expensive, Lerris."

"I know. We can cover it, and what choice is there?"

"Didn't the tavern benches help? Those were better than anything Hefton ever turned out."

"They helped, but the quarterly assessment is coming due."

"Deirdre?"

"Unless we can deliver on the benches . . ."

Brettel shook his head. "Old Dorman feared this, but what else could he do?"

I shrugged. "I owe him something."

"What if the prefect finds out you're a craft-master?"

"Brettel. I'm scarcely a master. I never even technically finished my journeyman training . . ."

Brettel's eyebrows raised, and I realized my mistake.

". . . but there's no requirement in Fenard for guild certification . . ."

". . . so that's why you chose Destrin . . ."

"I had a problem with the mastercrafter . . ."

The mill-master nodded to himself, as if I had cleared up a minor mystery. "What do you need?"

"Black oak. I'd like to look at the logs."

Brettel frowned again, but I couldn't help it. I needed to see the wood before it was shaped. We couldn't afford any wastage.

He turned and headed toward the racks at the back of the brick stacking-warehouse.

I followed, glancing around and noting again how orderly Brettel kept his milled timbers and planks.

"Here you are. Graded in size down. The ones with the two red grease slashes are a gold per log, the single reds are five silvers, the blues are two silvers, and the yellows are one silver."

I'd figured it out already, how to use the heartwood for the spokes and braces and the wood around the heart for the backing and seat plates. Now all I had to do was find four logs that met the measurements.

"How much more if I ask for the cuts?"

Brettel shrugged. "Nothing, if you stay and they're normal straight runs through the saw."

I began checking the blue logs, sensing them as well as looking, but only two were right, and that meant I needed two reds.

After a time, I pointed. "These two, and this one."

"I'll give you the bigger one there for five silvers."

I stared again, all too aware of my double sight as I studied the log Brettel had fingered. On the outside it looked generous, but the heartwood was not old and hard and dense, even brittle, but soft and spongy. When you bought black oak, you were paying a premium for the heartwood, so dense it rarely decayed, and so tough that the best in edged steel was barely good enough to cut and shape it.

"That's not quite right," I told Brettel.

"It's fine," the mill-master insisted.

I shrugged. "It's not what Destrin needs. Either this one—" I pointed to the smaller log to the right "—or that one."

Brettel raised his shoulders, obviously thinking I was crazy, turning down the larger prime log for the smaller ones. "Then it's still five silvers each for the two single reds."

"That's what I'll need."

Brettel didn't quite shake his head as he greased the stump end of the four trunks with Destrin's mark, a large "D" with a half-circle over the top of the letter. "Who's paying?"

"I'll take care of it." I had the coins in my belt. While Brettel was honest, he wasn't about to cut black oak on my word. I scrambled around to come up with the coins.

He checked them with the cold iron, just out of habit. "You want to do the cuts now?"

"If you can."

"Things are slow today. With that wizard at the palace, people aren't working. They're all afraid to do anything." He trundled a work cart to the log pile, then unstrapped the log clamps.

"They were talking about some coach in the market . . ."

"Antonin's, I'd bet. He's often here to meet with Gollard."

"Gollard?"

"The prefect."

"Does that have to do with Kyphros?" I wondered how I could help Brettel with the heavy log.

"Gollard . . . wanted . . . the sulfur springs back . . . in the Little Easthorns." In between words, with the aid of a steel bar and the clamps, singlehandedly the mill-master had levered the first log onto the cart.

"Can I help?"

"Just . . . get . . . in the way."

"Sounds like he wanted to make more gunpowder." Why, I couldn't see, since anyone with the slightest hint of chaos-ability could set the devil's brew off from a distance.

"Who . . . knows . . ." Brettel was working on the third log. "The autarch's cavalry . . . carved up . . . Gollard's . . . elite troop. With raw recruits. Some wench . . . killed . . . his son-in-law." Brettel stopped and grinned. "Not a few people cheered that."

I shook my head. After all my time in Fenard, I still didn't know why the prefect and the autarch were at each other's throats. "Why?" I asked.

"Why what?" Brettel handled the last small log as if it were a toothpick. I doubted that I could have even moved it.

"Why are they fighting? The autarch and the prefect, I mean?"

Brettel strapped the logs onto the cart before answering. "Rumor has it that her mother was a wizard's daughter—"

My mouth nearly dropped. I had assumed the autarch was a man.

"—And that the mother used her wiles to split off what used to be Gallos south of the Little Easthorns. Then the mother conquered old Analeria after the prince died. The daughter took over a few years ago and added parts of the Westhorns that Hydlen claimed, but never really ruled. Gollard figured, in his best guess, that the daughter wasn't a wizard. So he tried to retake Kyphros.

"He almost made it. Broke her army and the cavalry, but the peasants rose and burned their fields and opened the dikes. The cavalry couldn't maneuver in the mud, and some mistakes were made. No one was clear how, but instead of a victory, Gollard lost half his army and most of his officers.

"The autarch started recruiting women, the best she could find." Brettel shrugged. "Now Gollard's troops usually lose, but the autarch never enters his territory."

By now, we were approaching the saw; the belts leading from the waterwheel were motionless.

"What cuts?"

Taking the grease pencil, I outlined what I had in mind with each of the logs.

"Should have thought of that myself." Brettel pursed his lips. "Need to set this up. I can make these and deliver the planks and those square sections late this afternoon."

"That would be fine." I took the hint, and walked back to where I had tied Gairloch while Brettel began to set up the saw.

Wheee . . . eeee . . .

"All right." I patted him on the shoulder and pushed his nose away from my pockets, which were empty.

Kyphros versus Gallos—order versus chaos? Or was it that simple? Woman versus man? The more I found out, the less I knew, and I suspected I was far from the first man to realize that.

"Come on." I mounted my shaggy beast and flicked the reins. "Come on."

Whheee . . . eeeee . . .

"All right," I said again.

So we halted by the bottom of the millrace for him to get a drink of the cold water, and I even stopped by the granary and bought a small sack of feed for Gairloch.

LII

After getting the bid for the sub-prefect's chairs, and after getting exactly the lumber I wanted from Brettel with a bit extra thrown in for no extra cost, we still had to actually craft the chairs.

Besides worrying about the actual work, I worried about a lot of other things. I worried that Destrin would get sicker and die. I worried that Bostric would slip with the plane, or that I would get careless.

I worried that Jirrle would somehow find a way to attack me. I worried that Antonin would find out exactly who and where I was and attack. Even though I ate, I felt harried and thinner.

"You look tired," Deirdre told me.

Since I felt tired, I probably looked that way as well.

Every night I set wards on the shop, but I wasn't sure what good they would do, and I kept my staff close to my bed.

I used my senses to keep studying the wood each step of the way, checking to make sure that no hidden cracks or stresses would erupt to mar the wood or the finish. When I found two, both Bostric and Destrin thought I was crazy for refusing to use sections of what appeared to be perfectly good wood.

"It's good wood, Lerris."

"Not good enough. It's flawed."

"How? Where?"

"It just is." How could I explain without letting them know I was a beginning order-master?

"If the honored craft-master who claims he is only a journeyman says so, it must be so."

What bothered me most about Bostric's flip comment was that he and Destrin both looked at each other, nodded, and didn't say anything more.

I groused and I growled, and even Deirdre stepped away from me at dinner and supper.

Not only did I do the smooth finish myself, I even worked with the varnishes until I had what not only looked right, but felt right all the way through. Then I spent time steeping the chairs in order, reinforcing their strength with order and more order, until chaos itself might have had a hard time sitting in them.

We got all five chairs done. And done well.

Brettel lent us his cart and Gairloch even pulled it, with more than a few protests, to the same front steps of the sub-prefect's steps.

I hadn't planned on the welcoming committee. Not only was a scowling Jirrle there, but Perlot stood at the back, as did other crafters I did not know.

The sub-prefect was not there, but a thin man in a uniform, some sort of functionary, was.

First they had us line up the chairs side by side on the granite paving-blocks. In the morning light, the officer stared and scowled. He looked under the chairs. He studied the joins, the finish. He compared each chair with every other chair. He ran his fingers over every exposed surface.

Bostric, standing beside me, began to sweat, even though the day was overcast and the heat of the late summer day had not yet arrived.

I pursed my lips, knowing that the inspection was far from normal.

The one reassurance was Perlot's presence. With each inspection, with each frown by the officer and each accompanying scowl by Jirrle, Perlot's faint smile became more pronounced.

Finally, the officer turned to me. "The chairs seem acceptable." He pulled out a long paper and a servant proffered a pen. "Put your mark at the bottom."

I read the paper, but all it said was that the sub-prefect had accepted five chairs for the sum of ten golds. So I signed on behalf of Destrin, copying his mark as well for good measure.

The officer's eyebrows raised, but he said nothing.

Jirrle edged forward to look at the chairs, finally shaking his head and looking at me. For a long time, it seemed, his eyes rested upon me. I just waited for the coins, which arrived in a leather pouch.

Although I could tell they were good, I checked each against the steel of my dagger, since no tradesman would have done otherwise. The officer nodded, as if to himself, and seemed reassured.

Jirrle looked back at the chairs, then at me, before walking back toward the avenue.

The other crafter I did not know also stepped up to the chairs. Unlike Jirrle, he stepped up to me. "Good work." He nodded pleasantly, and his whole manner inside and out was honest, even if there were traces of chagrin beneath.

As the officer's servants began to carry the chairs inside, the officer sniffed down his nose. "That is all, tradespeople."

I inclined my head. "Thank you."

He ignored me and turned.

"Damned fine work there," rasped another voice. Perlot stood by the cart traces.

Whheeee . . . eeee . . . Gairloch wanted out of the traces—the sooner the better. Bostric looked at the pony nervously, then back to me.

"Thank you."

"No. I mean it. Sedennial was trying to find a reason not to accept them, and he couldn't."

I'd thought the same, but the chairs were good. They should have been. I'd sweated enough over them.

"You underbid them—more than just a little, given the quality." The craft-master's voice was wry.

"Master Jirrle seemed upset . . ." I observed in a neutral voice, checking the cart harness.

"He was, but he'll get over it. Good day, Lerris."

Perlot smiled briefly, and stepped out into the lane with his quick short steps, looking pleased with the world as he left us with a restless mountain pony and an empty cart. Most important, we had ten golds, five of which could go toward the quarterly levies.

"What do we do now?" asked Bostric, wiping his forehead.

"We get out of here before they tell us to, and we find some more work to do. Hopefully, something that you can do more of."

Bostric swallowed. "I can't do things that good."

"Not yet. That doesn't mean you can't learn." I led Gairloch around to get the cart facing toward the avenue, then climbed onto the hard board seat. "Come on."

Bostric scrambled up next to me, and we headed out to return him to the shop and the cart to Brettel.

LIII

A face in the window caught my eye. What was Perlot doing at the shop? Destrin was upstairs resting, and technically it wasn't my place to meet with another craft-master.

Setting down the plane, I crossed the room, sniffing at the smell of barley soup drifting down the stairs. We had eaten earlier, but Destrin had not, and Deirdre was probably feeding her father a late noon meal.

Bostric looked up.

"Keep at it," I told him. "And think about where the grains will meet."

"It's just a tavern bench. But I heed the words of wisdom."

I just looked at him until he began to check the lines of the grain.

Perlot had stepped inside the shop doorway, and stood waiting. He wore his working leathers, but he had pulled on a rough shirt and a vest.

"I apologize, craft-master. Destrin is not available at the moment." I inclined my head.

"No apologies needed, Lerris. Several of us are gathering at the Tap Inn after the day ends. I was hoping you could join us. Your apprentice would be welcome to sit with Grizzard and the others."

I kept my mouth in place. The invitation was serious, and, in effect, an announcement that the other crafters had accepted me. Had that been Brettel's doing? "I thank you, and would be honored."

Perlot smiled faintly. "I think we're the ones who are honored. Destrin is fortunate to have found you. Until tonight." He nodded and was gone.

Only after he had gone did I sigh. Perlot himself had crossed the town and the square to invite me. Maybe, just maybe, my plans might have a chance of working out.

Bostric glanced up from the bench as I walked back, his bushy red eyebrows lifted.

"We've been asked to join the other crafters for a drink after work."

Bostric just nodded, as if it were the most natural thing in the world. For him, perhaps, it was. I had encouraged him to spend his free time with the other apprentices, knowing that, if my hopes were fulfilled, he would need the contacts in the years to come.

Picking up the plane, I studied the internal framework of the chest for a long time, knowing that something was not quite right. How long it took, I didn't know, but I finally ended up planing and readjusting one of the drawer supports for the second drawer. From there it got easier, as I entered the flow of the wood and the design. Part of the problem was that the design was an adaptation of one of Dorman's plans, and even partly original pieces were much tougher.

"Lerris . . . ?"

I shook my head, realizing more time had passed than I realized. "Yes?"

"Hadmit has closed," Bostric noted tactfully.

The jeweler stayed open later than anyone else. I began racking the tools, noting that Bostric had already been quietly putting away Destrin's tools.

Before long, I had told Deirdre that we were leaving; and we had washed up and were striding across the square. The only thing that bothered me was that I knew I'd have to clean Gairloch's stall when I returned, as well as get up early in the morning to ride him.

Clink . . . clink . . .

We had to hug the edge of the mill street on the other side of the square as a troop of the prefect's cavalry rode in toward their barracks. Three of the horses at the end were riderless, and a dark splotch stained the leather of the last empty saddle.

The stink of sweat and blood hung over the riders like fog, not obscuring the taint of chaos that also clung to them and to the sabers they bore. To my senses, the blades shimmered like dull-red embers.

Clink, clink . . . clink . . .

"Make way . . . make way . . ."

. . . clink . . . clink . . .

Neither prisoners nor bodies trailed the empty horses.

Looking at Bostric once the cavalry passed, I shook my head. "Bad news."

He nodded, and we kept walking.

The Tap Inn had not changed. Even without a fire in the front hearth, the main room was smoky, as acrid as before.

"Lerris!" Perlot had been waiting, and I hurried over, leaving Bostric to his own devices.

313

"Sorry. We worked a shade late, and then we had to wait for the prefect's troops."

Perlot gestured around the table. "This is Jirrle, his son Deryl, Rasten, and Ferralt. Usually, Hertol is here." He put a hand on my shoulder. "This is Lerris, who has decided to follow Dorman's tradition and give me a run for my money, or would if he hadn't decided to make children's furniture better than regular pieces."

They all chuckled at that, and Perlot pulled out a chair. "What will you have, Lerris?"

I had to grin sheepishly. "Just redberry, mast—"

"Just Perlot, Lerris. Just Perlot."

"What's this about troops?" asked Deryl.

I shrugged. "Don't know, but about a score of cavalry rode back in. They lost, it looked like. Empty saddles, and no prisoners, and they looked tired. Some of the horses . . ." I shook my head.

"Hell . . ." muttered the man at the far side of the round table. "He's out squabbling with the autarch again."

The same thin girl with the scar across her face appeared next to Perlot. Her face was still thin, but a bulge below her apron indicated she had been more than merely flirting with someone. "What else, masters?"

"Redberry for Lerris, here, and I'll have another beer." The craft-master handed her his heavy empty mug.

". . . the autarch's already proved, after the way they dispatched those rebels from Freetown . . ."

"I take it that the prefect should avoid trouble with Kyphros?" I asked politely.

Jirrle cleared his throat. "Gallos has a proud history, and the autarch should honor that history and the natural geography . . ."

"What he means," added the balding Ferralt with a grin, "is that the prefect wants old Gallos back, as well as some other territory . . ."

"Ferralt!" snapped the older man. "I said what I meant."

"He's on the prefect's advisory council . . ." whispered Perlot.

"Are all the autarch's soldier's women?" I asked.

"Hell no," added Deryl, setting his mug on the table with a thump. "Just the best ones."

Thunk! Thunk!

"Here's the red stuff and the beer. Two, please."

I handed two coppers to the woman. Perlot looked surprised, but did not protest.

"Women soldiers are uncivilized," added Rasten.

"What he means," explained Ferralt, "is that they only fight when they know they can win."

"Like that one Torrman was complaining about?"

"The black-haired one the autarch promoted over his cousin?"

I swallowed a deep pull of the redberry. "Could someone explain?"

Rasten glared at Ferralt, who grinned. Finally, Ferralt shrugged. "Torrman is married to my sister. His cousin is also Torrman, except he took service with the autarch because the former prefect—that's a long story. Anyway, the younger Torrman was in line to be sub-commander, except a new squad captain pulled some stunt with water and wiped out the Freetown rebels without a single casualty.

"The autarch promoted her instead. Torrman challenged her to a duel, and the bitch made him look silly. So he played dirty and threw something in her eyes. That didn't stop her. Instead she took off his sword hand—blind, he swears. The autarch gave him a pension—and a warning."

"You believe that?" I asked. I did, but I wanted to know whether Ferralt had something else in mind.

"It's true," interrupted Jirrle. "The bitch is from Recluce. The autarch, damnable bitch as well, doesn't care. She only cares if her troops are the best."

A momentary silence dropped over the table.

"Lerris, what brought you here?" asked Perlot, almost desperately.

"Recluce, I'd have to say." I took a sip from the mug, trying to figure out how to tell the truth without being deceptive myself. "As I told Perlot here,"—I gestured to the crafter—"after leaving my apprenticeship, I was trying to make my way in Freetown, when the old duke ran afoul of Recluce. The rains came and turned the meadows to swamps. The clouds never left, and then the duke was dead, and wizards were running all over the place." I winced inside at the slight exaggeration. "So I took what I had and got a pony and left."

"Why did you come so far, and where were you from?" asked Jirrle.

I shrugged. "As I told Destrin, I'm technically only an apprentice. I don't have any guild certification. Hrisbarg was too small to support another crafter, and," I raised my eyebrows, "have you seen Howlett and Montgren?"

That brought a chuckle from everyone but Jirrle, and I continued before he could ask me again where I was from. "As for Jellico, you can't walk the streets without a permit and a seal. So what could a poor apprentice woodworker do? What would you have done?" I addressed the question to Deryl.

"I guess I would have come to Fenard, just like you did. How did you get across the Easthorns?"

"It wasn't easy. It was cold, because I couldn't afford to stay in the inns there." And I couldn't, but not for reasons of cost. Still, the misrepresentation hurt. "The heavy snows hadn't fallen, but I had to wait until a caravan cleared one snowfall from the road. I was afraid poor Gairloch would be skin and bones by the time we got to Passera."

"How did you get into Jellico?" asked Rasten.

"Anything else around here?" asked the serving girl.

"Nothing for me," said Perlot.

"Nor me," I added.

"Another mug."

"Me too."

"Not here."

"I was lucky, ran into a healer, and traveled with him for a while, but he had business in Jellico."

Jirrle frowned, even as he sipped from the heavy brown mug.

"Where did you get that design for the chair you did for Wryson?" asked Perlot quickly.

"I looked through Dorman's plan book, then just made some changes to make it more suitable for Wryson."

"He's a diplomat," chuckled Ferralt. "Ingenious way of bracing it. Do you mind if I try that?"

"Not at all. You might find a better way, though. I did that in more of a hurry than I would have liked." Or than Uncle Sardit would have advised, either.

"Why the child's table?" That was Rasten.

"That started out as a project for Bostric. He's turned out to have a real feel for the woods, and I wanted to give him something that . . . well . . ." I finally shrugged, hoping they would understand.

Even Jirrle nodded slowly, although the frown never left his face.

"Maybe we ought to do more work like that," began Deryl. "Some of the gentry pay well for garb for the little ones. Why not furniture? I once heard about the miniature palace in Hamor."

Thunk! Thunk! Thunk! Thunk! The girl dropped the heavy mugs on the table like mallets, one after the other.

I glanced over at the table where the apprentices sat. They looked more relaxed, which reassured me. Bostric seemed positively loquacious.

". . . then . . . he talks about grains, grains, and more grains, about feeling the wood, like you could see right through it . . . but it's scary sometimes, because I get the feeling he can . . ."

"Hell . . . all of them can . . . why they're craft-masters . . ."

"One each, gents," snapped the serving-girl, her tone crisper and shorter than the first time I'd been at the Tap Inn.

"What other projects do you have lined up?" asked Jirrle slowly.

"Not a lot. We're still scrambling. There's a corner chest, and a dower piece, and another couple of benches for the Horn Inn . . ."

"There will be more," added Perlot, "with all the praise you're getting from Wessel."

"We do the best we can . . ."

As the door opened, I turned to look, and realized it was pitch-dark out.

"What about . . ." began Ferralt as he looked at Deryl.

"I'm going to have to leave." I eased out of my chair. "Destrin's not feeling that well, and I never fed the pony . . ."

"Won't you stay a little longer . . . ?" grumbled Jirrle.

I could tell his words were false, yet he wanted me to stay.

"I wish I could."

"Perhaps we could hear more the next time," added Perlot.

I just nodded. In no way did I want to tell more than I had already. On the way out, I stopped by Bostric's group. "You can stay a while." But I didn't wait for an acknowledgement.

". . . doesn't seem that scary . . ."

". . . not all that old . . ."

As I stepped out into the night, I tried not to sigh. Sooner or later, and probably sooner, the speculation would push me into giving away too much. The afternoon clouds had cleared, and the stars glittered, with the new moon just a crescent above the western horizon.

Further down the market street, the lanterns from the Horn Inn flickered with the breeze that brought the scent of cut hay from the fields to the north of Fenard.

Jirrle—the man bothered me, had bothered me from the first time he had inspected my boxes in the open market.

Even as early in the night as it was, the streets had cleared, the good and solid citizens for the most part having headed home. In Fenard, work started with the dawn. I suppressed a yawn, remembering that I had put off cleaning out Gairloch's stall.

I rubbed the end of my nose after the acrid odor of burned grease left a lingering itch, then picked up my steps as I passed the first cross-street toward the square from the Tap Inn.

Halfway toward the next cross-street, I stopped, almost paralyzed by the feel of disorder ahead. After turning, I took several quick paces back and into the shadows, wishing I had my staff with me.

Click . . . clink . . . The sounds were faint, almost inaudible.

A cloak of reflection slipped around me, and I hoped I was doing the right thing, that the danger ahead was merely that of armed assassins, and not a chaos-master.

Two men appeared, slipping toward where I had been. While I could only sense them, not see them, one was older, slighter, tinged with the white-red fire of chaos. The other was just a hired blade, faintly disordered, but not chaos-evil.

They searched each side of the street, moving toward me. In turn, I moved from the shadows into the main street, where they would only look, while they might concentrate and poke into the corners and alcoves.

Click . . .

The second sound came from behind me, from the direction of the Tap Inn.

I forced myself to breathe easily, standing flat against a bricked wall between shops with their night shutters down, feeling exposed and open, and relying only on a reflective shield. The knife in my belt felt inadequate, especially against the drawn blades of the pair that walked toward me.

From the inn came a second armed pair, searching and moving toward me.

I almost held my breath as the bulkier assassin walked right by me, holding a blade at the ready. As soon as they were more than a few paces past, I took one quiet step, then another, edging toward the square and toward Destrin's.

". . . disappeared . . ."

". . . left the inn. I saw him."

"He's not here."

". . . in one of the houses?"

I let them argue, stepping quietly toward Destrin's, not dropping the cloak until I was safely inside the stable.

Whheee . . . eeeee . . . eee . . .

"Yes, I know. Your stall is filthy. I didn't ride you today, and you're out of food."

The food came first, and I brushed Gairloch for a while, both to reassure him and to think. Then came the shovel and the pail. No one had told me about the mess horses make, or the enormous effort it took to keep one stall clean.

Late indeed it was by the time I got back to the shop, and Bostric was pulling out his bed.

"How did it go?" I asked, washing my hands again in the basin I had refilled.

"Fine. They say you won't stay here, that you are a wandering type. Is that true?" Bostric had had more than a beer. Otherwise, he would not have dared to ask the question, not without his more overly-respectful tone.

I shrugged. "Probably. Go to sleep."

He did, and I thought about the armed men. Clearly, Jirrle had known something about it, but whether he had just known or actually put them after me was another question. The fact that all their swords had felt the same told me that they were the prefect's men.

I was running out of time, but so far, no one apparently wanted to move directly. That forebearance wouldn't last, and I would still have to watch for the assassins.

LIV

I did not sleep well that evening, even after setting and checking the wards. I tossed on the narrow pallet, sweating as I pondered what I knew. The "J" on the tax levy had to have been Jirrle. Jirrle was some sort of advisor to the prefect, and Jirrle did not particularly care for me.

319

Then, to make me even more uneasy, in the night skies, thunder raged. Not the thunder of honest clouds striving among themselves, nor the man-made thunder of gunpowder blasting. Not even the illusory thunder of the wind created by chaos-masters bent on enhancing the fears of an already too-ignorant population. Thunder such as this had I heard only once before, on the plains of Certis, when the ice storms and the blizzard had done their worst to destroy me.

So I tossed and sweated, and, on the other side of my curtain, Bostric snored—loudly, and without any sense of rhythm.

In the end, I did sleep, and without dreams that I remembered, which was probably for the best, since I woke with a start just before dawn. I was soaked in sweat, though the night had been cool for summer, even for a long summer that was drawing to a close.

After using the facilities off the alley, little more than an outhouse that drained into a covered sewer, and washing in cool water drawn from the covered tank in the back, I felt closer to human. Some fruit and a biscuit from the tray Deirdre brought down helped more.

We could have eaten upstairs, but in the mornings I never bothered, since I liked to get started early, especially in the warm weather.

"Why . . . oh, why am I apprenticed to a master who loves mornings . . . ?" Bostric looked worse than I felt, but the words were merely a ritual he intoned every morning. He splashed his way through a sketchy wash, then wolfed down what I had left on the tray.

"They're all talking about you . . ." he mumbled.

"Oh . . . ?" I was checking the chest against the sketches and the plan book.

"Jirrle thinks you're from Recluce . . ."

I swallowed a cold lump in my guts, saying nothing.

". . . Deryl thinks you want Deirdre and the shop, and Grizzard doesn't see anything remarkable in you and wonders why anyone is making such a fuss."

Shrugging, I took a last sip of the redberry and set the mug aside.

"Jirrle also told Deryl that the chairs for the sub-prefect were going to cause trouble . . . but he wouldn't say why."

Trouble? Chairs causing trouble? Then I shivered, recalling the reaction of my own staff to chaos. Once again, in pushing too hard, I hadn't thought through the consequences. And the chairs had been black oak.

"Are you all right?"

320

I shook my head. "I'm . . . fine. I just realized I had forgotten something." Although I knew I needed to talk to Brettel and I had finished the dower chest for Dalta, I had held off on delivering it, perhaps because we had received so much from Brettel. I didn't want to impose so soon again on the mill-master, whether he was Deirdre's godfather or not. In addition, Bostric was not quite ready. But now I would have to watch every corner for the Duke's assassins . . .

Despite what I had seen, except for Jirrle, nothing pointed toward me, yet I felt some greater force was rushing from beyond my perceptions straight for me. Or was I just imagining things, believing I could sense what I could not understand? The world of order and thoughts just made life more confusing, not less.

Already, summer was coming to a close. The grasses were browning, and the hand of the long hot summer pressed down upon Fenard like an open stove. With the heat, the varnishes gave off more fumes, even in the late mornings.

Although I tried to do the finish work while Destrin took the rests that grew fractionally longer each day, sometimes he persisted in tinkering with his benches, even as he coughed his lungs out.

"Acc . . . accc . . . cuufff . . ." No longer did he pale when he coughed—he was pallid all the time.

"Let Bostric finish those joins," I suggested.

"I just came down. Are you trying to push me out again, Lerris? I'm the shop-master. It's my business, and no outlander will tell me how to run it." He glared at me, even as he had to support himself on the bench. "Acc . . . accc . . . acuuufff . . ."

"I'm not trying to push you anywhere. Bostric is your apprentice, and he's here to help you. If I can help him learn, fine. But how can he help if you insist on doing everything?" I pressed a touch more order upon his system, but only a touch. He was so fragile that anything more would have done more damage than the coughing.

"Papa . . ." added Deirdre. When she talked to her father, her voice was firm, gentle, no matter what the pain she held inside.

"All of you . . . you all want to put me away . . ." Even as he protested, Destrin let Deirdre lead him up the stairs.

I laid down the plane and motioned to Bostric as soon as Destrin was out of sight. We looked over the bench Destrin had been resting against, rather than working upon.

"Can you clean this up and finish it?" I asked.

321

Bostric studied the seat plate. "How would you suggest I fix this?" He pointed to the beginning of an off-center hole, probably angled when Destrin started coughing.

"You've got one or two choices—fill it and reset. Or cut the size and redo the spokes. Make it more ornamental . . ."

Bostric licked his lips nervously.

"Go ahead. Destrin can't finish it." I didn't know how accurately I spoke.

Whhssttt . . .

Deirdre stood at the stairs. "Lerris . . . ?" Her voice was almost matter-of-fact. That she stood there at all told she needed something. Resourceful in all things, from running the accounts to developing her own cushioning business to running the shop and household food budget, she had asked nothing—except once. Yet behind the quiet facade, I had begun to understand, lay a strong will.

"I'll be right there." Catching Bostric's attention, I said, "Destrin and I need to discuss something. If a customer should show, just ring the bell, and I'll be right down." Then I followed Deirdre up the stairs. If she hadn't been so upset, I almost would have smiled at Bostric's hidden appraisal of Deirdre.

"Papa . . . he's moaning, and he doesn't know who I am . . ." The seaming work she did was neatly laid on her table by the rear window. She probably earned more from the sewing than Destrin did from his infrequent benches, and saved more than that from her handling of his accounts.

Bostric would do better than he knew, and I only hoped I had the time to help him be more than she knew.

Destrin lay upon the wide bed, eyes closed, breathing raggedly and quickly, a bluish tinge to his fingers and a grayish look to his face. His eyes opened. "Kyren . . . where's . . . girl . . ."

"I'm here, papa." Her thin voice was low.

"Kyren . . . so . . . cold . . ."

As I reached into that frail and wasted body, the burning, the pressure seared me, and I had to grasp the bedpost, even as my senses touched the knotted heart, easing a cramp here, letting the blood flow and strengthening what I could, the parts that had yet enough firmness to strengthen. It took a long time, gently as I had to work, and I didn't remember sitting down.

"Lerris . . . Lerris . . ." A cool cloth touched my forehead.

My head was not splitting, but a dull ache and a great tiredness encouraged me not to move.

"Something to drink? Redberry?" I asked hoarsely.

Deirdre brought me a cup. A few sips and I felt almost normal, if light-headed. I eased myself out of the chair and tiptoed over to the bed. Destrin's color was no longer grayish, only pale, and he slept. I nodded, but wondered how much longer I could hold him together, and whether I should, recalling the pain I had felt in touching him. My eyes blurred for a moment.

"Lerris?"

I had forgotten Deirdre was standing beside me.

"You saved him . . . again." Her voice was neutral.

"Yes." I shook my head. "I don't know, Deirdre. I don't know. He hurt so much."

She looked at me, questioningly, for the first time with tears flowing from both eyes.

"I stopped the hurt, but for how long?"

"Poor . . . poor papa . . ."

"Don't let him get up. Tell him he has a chill."

"How long?"

I knew what she meant.

"If he rests, if he is quiet, perhaps half a year, but that's just a guess. He could have died today, but he doesn't want to."

"Poor papa . . ."

That afternoon, I paid Wryson two coppers for the loan of his wagon and followed it, and the red-oak dower chest, out to Brettel's house. In case it was to be a surprise, I had covered it with a blanket.

On the way across the avenue and toward the north road, we pulled up for a cavalry troop returning. A single prisoner, blindfolded, hands tied behind her back, wearing green leathers, swayed on the last horse. A dark splotch stained her short-cut blond hair. The prefect's troops had left her an empty scabbard, perhaps because, disoriented and wounded, she still radiated order.

The last four horses bore only empty saddles, and the reek of disorder, of chaos, was faint, as if expended in whatever battle they had fought.

". . . make way . . . make way . . ."

. . . *clink* . . . *clink* . . .

"Make way . . . make way . . ."

Sensing primarily tiredness and pain, nothing resembling new-cast chaos, despite my awareness extension, I waited until the troop had passed. Still, I was on edge until the wagon pulled inside the big stone warehouse. The woman in green bothered me. She could have been Wrynn or Krystal. She wasn't, but she could have been.

"Lerris, you're earlier than I expected. I told you to take your time." He still grinned.

"Do you want to see it?" I glanced around.

"Dalta's at the market square."

Using both arms, I moved the chest, still covered, from the wagon.

"Here." Sperlin—Wryson's driver—got a copper I couldn't afford. "Just go straight back."

"Thank you, ser."

Not until the wagon rumbled down the ramp and back onto the north road did I turn back to Brettel.

"You're thinner, Lerris, hunted-looking."

"We passed a cavalry troop .. lots of empty saddles."

Brettel just shook his head. "Why? The autarch isn't bothering him."

I didn't know the answer, either, except there were more soldiers in Gallos.

"Do you want to see the chest?" I changed the subject back to the reason I had come.

"Of course, of course."

After lifting the blanket gently, I waited, watching his face.

He looked for a long time. Finally, he turned to me. "I can't afford that. That's a piece worthy of Dorman or Sardit—their best."

While it wasn't that good, the chest was exquisite, and equal to the lesser but good pieces my uncle had done. But comparisons weren't fair. I could see into the wood, and they couldn't.

So we stood there for a time, and Brettel kept gazing at the chest. "She won't appreciate it."

"She will. Later, at least."

At last, he looked at me.

"Why are you here? Now?"

"To ask that you allow Bostric to marry Deirdre."

"Why now?"

"Because Destrin is dying, and I have to leave before it's too late, and before anything becomes too public. I only hope I haven't waited too long."

"There's a problem, Lerris."

"I can see a number." My voice was wry, even to my own ears.

"While Bostric has taken over the bench work and the simple chests, and his work is better than Destrin's was, you're still the craft-master . . ."

"I'm no craft-master." I felt I had to protest, but my guts turned at the thought that I actually might be approaching that level.

"No . . . not if you compare yourself to Perlot and Sardit. And Dalta's chest there even gives that the lie. If you consider Rasten or Deryl or Hertol or Ferralt, already they can't compare. Not at all."

"Look," I said. "Deirdre's a good seamstress, almost good enough to carry the household on her own. It won't be easy for them, but she has a dowry—"

"She does?" the mill-master asked.

"I made her a chest like Dalta's, not quite as good, and she has a small dowry of five golds, not much . . ."

"Lerris . . ." He shook his head.

"I know . . . it's not really enough, but—"

"Lerris. What are you? You're a stranger, who has lived here little   325
more than a year, who has held death at bay, who has redeemed my god-daughter's hope and future, and restored her father's honor, and provided a dowry. Would that my own sons would go so far."

I was embarrassed at the tears rolling down his cheeks. So I said nothing. After all, if I hadn't done what I could, who would have?

"We need a wedding soon, while Destrin can still appreciate it."

"Have you asked him?"

I shrugged. "No. I was afraid to upset him."

"Let me come back with you. Better now than later. Ask him again while I am there."

Brettel washed the sawdust off his face and uncovered forearms, changed from his leather apron into a linen shirt, and mounted a black mare—all in the time it took me to drink a glass of redberry.

We rode back together. Thankfully, we saw no more of the prefect's troops.

LV

Destrin sat in the armchair, his color face gray-hued under the pallor, but without the deadly blue of the morning.

"I brought an old friend," I said, but didn't get any further in my explanation.

"Godpapa!" Deirdre didn't quite shriek as she saw the mill-master. "It's been so long."

"Here to pay your respects to the deceased, Brettel?" Destrin's voice was waspish.

"No. I'm here to discuss my god-daughter's future."

"You can't foster her. I told you that—"

I touched Destrin's shoulder and tried to calm him, both physically and by infusing him with a touch of order. "That's not what he means . . ."

Destrin leaned back in the chair, but his color was even a shade more gray.

Deirdre looked from me to Brettel and back again, raising her eyebrows.

"May I sit down?" Brettel didn't wait for an answer, instead lifting one of the straight chairs from the table and setting in on the worn wooden planks directly across from Destrin. "Lerris, get a chair."

So I did, and I got one for Deirdre, and waited for her to sit down. It was her life we were talking about. She looked from her father to Brettel to me once again, then licked her lips.

"What's this about my Deirdre?" Destrin's voice remained sharp.

Brettel looked to me.

I swallowed. "I think that she should consider a marriage proposal . . ." I began.

"A master hand with wood you are, Lerris. But would you do right by her?"

"No. I wouldn't. That's why I'm not asking. My asking for her hand could lead to her death."

Even Brettel swallowed.

Destrin, surprisingly, didn't. He did look at me, long. "You're honest, boy. I won't say much, but could you answer a question for me?"

I shrugged. "If I can . . ."

"I'll try to be indirect. Was your woodcrafter master the only one Dorman respected?"

I had expected something along those lines. Destrin was a poor crafter, but perceptive nonetheless. "If I understand those involved, I think so."

Destrin sighed. "Had to be. So . . . you're proposing for Bostric?"

"Oh . . . !" Deirdre covered her mouth, but I heard the dismay, and it ripped right through my chest, like one of the prefect's chaos-swords might have.

"I don't have any better ideas. I can add some to her dowry, and I have crafted a red-oak dowry chest for her . . . Before long, I need to leave, or you all could be in danger. Between Bostric's family and Brettel . . . in the future . . . I would hope that would provide . . ." My words trailed off. I hated making the case for Bostric, and there were lumps in my chest and in my guts. My eyes were blurred.

Yet deep inside, I knew I was not right for Deirdre, but that did not make my task any easier.

"*Snnnffff.*" Deirdre was blowing her nose.

"Hell of . . ." Destrin shook his head. "You like her, don't you?"

"Yes. That's what makes it harder."

"You'd outlive her?"

I knew what he was driving at, knew why he was asking.

"Yes, if I survive the next few years. Probably by a lot."

Brettel nodded, then added, "Why are you asking this?"

"Because I care, and because it's the only way I can try to protect her, to allow her as much of her own life as possible."

Both older men looked at each other.

"We'd like to talk for a moment, Lerris . . . Deirdre . . ." Destrin's voice was calm, almost relaxed.

Deirdre stood up as I did. "Papa, Godpapa . . ." Her voice firmed. "I need to talk to Lerris for a moment—alone. Please excuse us." She looked at me with a smile, extending her arm almost like one of the ladies from the street.

Propped up as he was in his chair, Destrin looked from Deirdre to me and back again. His brow mirrored puzzlement, and Brettel just touched his shoulder and nodded.

I looked at Deirdre, somehow very regal in that moment, even in her faded blue trousers and blouse and old white apron. She seemed

327

somehow relieved, yet, beneath the relief, I could sense the tension, like a coiled spring, or worse. So I took her arm, and we walked toward the far end of the main room. I stopped, but Deirdre eased me on into her small room with the narrow bed, scarcely larger than the space I occupied in the shop below, save she had a window overlooking the alley and the stable. Her arm released mine.

Click.

"What . . ."

Her finger touched my lips to stop my words, and I could tell she was trembling.

"Lerris . . . ?" Her voice was uneven.

"Yes?"

"I know you're some kind of wizard . . . but . . ." She took a deep breath. ". . . would you ever hurt me?"

"Of course not," I protested, wondering where the conversation was going, and why she had closed the door. That faint scent of woman and roses reminded me of a night too long before and best forgotten.

"Not ever?"

"No. Why?"

Crack!

My head rang, and my eyes blurred from the force of her open hand, and when I could see, I could see the tears streaming from her eyes. "Why . . . ?" I shook my head.

She just stood there sobbing. "Don't you understand?"

Whatever it was, I certainly didn't understand it, but all I could think to do was reach for her hands. She let me take them, and we stood there for a time as she sniffled out the sobs.

Finally, she swallowed. "I'm . . . not . . . not a brood pony . . . I'll . . . do anything . . . for papa . . . and for you . . . but you . . . could have . . . asked . . . You . . . could . . . . have . . . asked . . ."

I was the one swallowing then, and finding it hard to see. Good old stupid Lerris, working like hell to save the girl, and not even asking her. But, even as I kept swallowing . . . I realized the tension within Deirdre was gone . . .

"Sorry. I just wanted to do what—"

"Lerris?"

"Yes?" My voice was level, since I didn't know what to expect.

"There's one other thing."

The one other thing was two arms around my neck and warm lips

328

on mine and a very feminine body pressed close against me. Very close against me, and pulling me down onto her and the bed.

We lay there for a long time, only holding and kissing. Then, slowly, before I lost total control, I let go of her and rolled away.

She sat up on the narrow bed. "That's what you're going to miss." She smiled sadly. "And what I'm going to miss."

I just stood there.

"Thank you . . . for me, for papa . . . for caring . . . and for being you . . ."

By then I couldn't see anything, but neither could she. So we ended up hanging on to each other again, and I cried as much as she did.

Thankfully, neither Destrin nor Brettel interrupted, and, in time, we pulled ourselves apart.

There wasn't anything else to say, not then. After we wiped our faces, she opened the door.

". . . just fine . . . Destrin . . . too damned honorable . . ."

". . . so you say . . ."

". . . you know it as well as I do . . ."

Deirdre grinned for the first time, even with the sadness beneath. "You *are* too honorable . . ."

I didn't have any choice any longer, not if I wanted to survive. I still had to explain it to Bostric, although I thought it was less likely that he would either haul off and hit me or kiss me. So I left the three to discuss details and went down to the shop.

Bostric was working on the tavern bench, and doing so quite effectively, having shortened the piece to cut out Destrin's mis-drilling.

I pulled out the two stools and set them by my workbench. "We need to talk."

Bostric could read when to tease and when not to. He took one look at the side of my face, which was probably still red, nodded, and set down the shaper.

"Sit down," I said as I pointed to the empty stool.

"Is there a problem?" For once, he looked worried.

"Yes. But it's more mine than yours. Brettel says that your family has not arranged any future alliances—a marriage or anything like that. Is that true?"

"That's true." His voice was cautious. "I'm the fourth son, and my brothers are healthy. The land is too small for me to inherit anything."

"What do you think about woodworking?"

"I told you. I'll never be in your class."

"Do you like it?"

The redhead nodded. "I like the woods, and living in Fenard is better than the farm."

"What do you think about Deirdre?"

This time his mouth did hang open. "You . . . can't . . . she likes . . ." He shook his head.

"I take it that you find her acceptable." I kept my voice dry.

This time he grinned.

"I have to leave before long. You know I'm not from Fenard. Brettel and I did not want to promise you anything until we saw—"

"—Whether I could be a woodcrafter?"

I nodded.

"But?"

"Deirdre can almost take care of herself, but without a husband in Fenard, she cannot hold the property. Destrin can't last much longer, and I couldn't even marry her out of convenience." I swallowed. Leaving Deirdre was going to be harder than I realized.

"You like her. A lot."

"Yes," I admitted. "But that doesn't matter." And when my mind and heart were only sad, not rebelling at the statement, I knew that what I said was true.

Bostric shook his head. "I don't understand you. You're the finest crafter in Fenard since Dorman, and you will walk away from fortune and a beauty who loves you?"

"I don't have any choice, Bostric. Please don't ask." I cleared my throat. I was still having trouble seeing. "I take it that your family won't object. Oh, and she does have a small dowry."

"No. They'll be so happy for me, just joyous that clumsy Bostric actually found a beauty with property—"

"Stop it!" I put an arm on his shoulder. "One of us needs to be happy, and you and Deirdre can be happy together."

"Yes, oh wizardly craft-master."

I punched him on the arm, but not too hard. "And I'll . . . do something creatively wizardly if you ever do anything to make her unhappy . . ."

He paled. "I think you would."

I shook my head. "Just love her." What else could I ask? If he did that, most everything else would follow, especially with Brettel's help.

"I know it won't be easy—not with Brettel looking over your shoulder."

He looked at me strangely before shaking his head.

Then, for a time, I sat down in my corner alcove.

LVI

Despite my resolve and Destrin's agreement, nothing could be arranged as quickly as I had hoped. There were banns to be posted, agreements to be formalized, and parties to be attended—parties held by Bostric's parents, by Brettel and his family. While I went, I stayed as much in the background as possible, hoping that all the festivities would eclipse me. Everywhere I went, I watched, looking like a wolf for the hunters. But I never found them, and with each failure, my guts tightened, as I wondered whether the next instant would find me in the sights of a crossbow. Yet until Deirdre was taken care of, I did not want to leave. But my staying was stupid, and I wrestled myself night after night.

As the fall waned, the sun dropped from the zenith, the rains occasionally fell, and the grasses greened again, Destrin lay stiller and stiller upon his bed, not even arguing with Deirdre, sometimes unable even to eat.

Deirdre was quiet, though she still sometimes favored me with a smile, and I smiled back, and both smiles hurt, and I knew I should leave.

In the end, once again, I had no choice, not if I wanted to live with myself. Each day, more soldiers rode out to the slaughter, faces blank, and they were younger and younger. Each day, more girls and women wept and damned the autarch. Only the conflict kept the assassins from me, I suspected.

Antonin's strategy was working, working all too well, fueled by the prefect's anger against the autarch. What could the autarch do? Let the bloodthirsty chaos-ruled Gallian soldiers kill her people and troops?

Still, I could not afford to take on Antonin himself. Remembering the power he had displayed in sweeping me aside earlier in the year, I wasn't ready for that. But I didn't think I had to, not yet.

I pushed Bostric unmercifully, mindful of Brettel's concerns, not daring nor wanting to leave Fenard yet, not until I could be assured that Deirdre and Bostric would be all right, yet worrying that my continuing presence might endanger them all.

At the same time, I was all too aware that, despite my efforts to learn the knowledge contained in *The Basis of Order,* all too many sections of the book I had merely learned by rote, without really understanding what lay behind and beneath them.

There was no one to ask, especially about the more cryptic phrases—the ones that *seemed* so simple, like the one that read, "and no man can truly master the staff of order until he casts it aside." Or the one about "love no one until you can love yourself, for love of another is merely empty flattery and self-deception for one who cannot accept himself without pretense." The second one sounded right enough, but how honestly could a man love himself without pandering to his own wishes to see himself as he wished?

Then there was the one that went: "Order and chaos must balance, but as on a see-saw. The power of chaos is for great destruction in a confined area, for order by nature must be diffused over vaster realms. If you would battle chaos, or establish order, you must limit the area and the time in which it must be balanced." While that one really seemed simple, I didn't have the faintest idea of how to limit chaos.

Knowing I could not limit chaos did not keep me from walking the streets more often. I finally had let Deirdre sew me a set of clothes suited to holidays and relaxation—still of dark brown, but the fabric was a close-woven cotton. When she refused to let me pay more than the fabric cost, I put the difference in the hidden strongbox that would be her dowry.

"Now you look the craft-master," Bostric had said, and I wished he had been joking.

I had just shaken my head.

The first real chill dropped on Fenard early, even before the early melon harvest, although it did not frost. I ambled through the market at mid-day, hoping to pick up some fresh melon for Destrin, the honey-sweet kind that eased the dryness in his thin throat.

White clouds, tinged with gray, floated above the western horizon, as if coming from the Westhorns, but the breeze was light, and the warmth almost summery. I wiped my forehead more than once as I looked for some of the light green melons.

Ahead was Mathilde, the flower lady, who kept casting her eyes at the long wall, as if trying not to. That was where the prefect displayed the results of his justice—the heads of those who displeased him. Usually, the heads were those of common thieves, or a deserter from the prefect's guards, or a murderer.

I looked up there. This time, there were two heads. I could feel the chill in my guts and the bile in my throat as I saw the woman's head, seeing the short blond hair—Wrynn? Then I looked again and saw the dark splotch on the short-cut blond hair and the difference in the shape of the face—recognizing the captive I had seen being brought back by the prefect's soldiers. But it easily could have been Wrynn, and who knew where she was?

Whispers went around the square, and the whispers weren't for the Kyphran soldier, but for the other head—that of an older man, who had clearly been blinded and tortured first.

"... why ..."

"... devil chairs ... someone said ..."

"... killed the whole household ... the prefect did ..."

"... why the sub-prefect? ... don't understand ..."

I did not run, but stood there, stone-still behind Mathilde. The example of the sub-prefect left my guts churning. Because the man had displayed something of order in his house, or because ordered chairs had burned someone of chaos—*that* had been his fate?

The golden coach was gone, with Antonin in it, and now I was out of time and out of excuses. No guards had yet moved against Destrin or the shop, and none moved the streets while I stood in the square, but that could change.

My head and then my feet turned toward the avenue. I walked to the shadows by the palace and cast a cloak around myself, letting my feelings sense whether a guard troop might be moving into the city.

First, there were the two guards by the main gates. While scaling the wall looked easier, I had no idea what wards Antonin or any other wizard might have placed there. Wards couldn't be used on the main entrances, or they would be warning someone every instant, especially during the day, since there were bound to be soldiers and ministers and horses in and out of the palace all the time.

333

I just stood there beneath the wall, far enough away so that my breathing would not be heard, and sat down in the shade and waited.

Clink . . . clinkedy . . . clink . . .

The first horse passed by, heading for the barracks, carrying another chaos-ruled killer.

I kept waiting, my heart still beating too fast.

. . . clickedy . . . click . . . clickedy . . . click . . .

The delivery wagon never reached the palace gates, but turned at the sub-prefect's vacant house.

. . . click . . . click . . .

Another soldier, this one walking tiredly toward the barracks.

I took a deep breath, trying to relax. The relaxation lasted until the next sound of hooves.

Clickedy . . . click . . . clickedy . . . click . . .

"Hold it."

Unseen, I eased toward the rider and his horse, another one of the chestnuts.

"I'm Captain Karflis with a message for the Military Council."

"Yeah, he's Karflis. He shows up the day before the council meets."

Click . . . My foot caught on a curb my senses hadn't distinguished.

"What's that?"

I froze, knowing they couldn't see me.

"Relax. It's broad daylight. There's no one in sight."

Creakkkkk . . .

As the iron gates swung open, I followed the good captain on foot, and not too close to the rear of his horse, but close enough that any sound I might make would be covered by the louder impact of the chestnut's hooves on the stone of the courtyard inside the gate.

I stopped as he dismounted, sensing almost a fountain of chaos somewhere off to my left. The captain, however, turned right, and I decided to go with him. Following the captain into the palace was almost as easy, since he walked with a heavy tread and his boots echoed on the marble floors.

From the courtyard, where he left the horse with a military ostler, or whatever they were called, he passed another pair of guards in the main hall. Then he bypassed the grand staircase and walked through a small archway to the side, leading to a narrow corridor that opened into another hallway at the back of the palace. After a left turn, he walked through a red oak doorway with an elaborate stained-glass mural inset over the open door. My senses did not distinguish the scene all that well, except there was a lot of lead around the glass panes.

"Captain Karflis. You are expected. The marshall is inside." Another pair of guards flanked the closed door to the right of the desk where the other officer—I assumed that from the gold on his shoulders—was sitting.

This time, I barely made it inside without getting the door shut on me, and I actually brushed the captain, recoiling from the swirling chaos locked within him as I did so.

He brushed at his coat. "Spiders . . . or something . . ."

"How goes it, Karflis?" The marshall was thin, that I could tell, and his voice was flat and cold.

"The autarch refuses to attack until our men cross into her territory. She has a new weapon that flings crossbow bolts in greater numbers beyond the range of our wizards to detect them."

"How effective is it?"

As Karflis continued to stand facing the marshall and to report, I studied the room, from the high and arched ceiling to the cold, if large, hearth, from the table with four chairs around it to the large desk behind which the Marshall sat.

". . . not much more effective than crossbows . . . really . . ."

"You have heard of her strike here?"

Karflis bowed from the waist. "Ser?"

"Devil-forged chairs, spells upon once-loyal soldiers . . ."

Both men were filled with that tight and coiled loop of chaos, but in the captain's case, the order beneath, that core of honest blackness, still refused to submit, and I gauged the strength of the chaos, then reached for the captain with my senses, making a change here and there. Nothing that would be obvious for a while.

The marshall bore no trace of order, only a white-red coil of disorder and evil. Since I could not destroy, not if I understood the implications for myself, I just gave him some well-needed rest, and he fell asleep on his desk. Within instants, he was snoring.

I would have liked to hear more, but what he said would have made no difference, and attacking the palace, in my own way, would force Antonin and the prefect to look within the palace, rather than in Fenard—at least for a while.

Karflis looked around in confusion. "Hersil!"

335

Click!

"He just fell asleep as I was talking."

The two guards had crowded inside the room, their swords drawn on the captain, and the officer who had been outside followed, barely a step behind.

Like the marshall, the two guards were lost to order, and I put them to sleep as well. While it was only temporary, a little confusion would not hurt.

The other officer gaped as his guards sagged into sleep. "Wizardry! There's a wizard around here! Call Tallia—"

Putting him to sleep took longer, because I was already tired.

I sat down on the thick plush carpet whose color I could not determine from my sense of place alone, and thought. What I was doing wasn't going to work.

Out of five men, four were beyond redemption. While I could easily have removed the chaos from their souls, that chaos was so much of their being that they would have died, or been mindless idiots. And besides, destruction was destruction, at least according to the book.

I shook my head.

Karflis stood there, also shaking his head, confusion over his own mental state warring with confusion over the collapse of the marshall and the three others.

A thought occurred to me, and I let my feelings reach for the sleeping young officer, trying to see if I could determine the source of that chaos. Only a hint, but it pointed, if pointing was the right word, to something else, that something I had sensed in entering the palace.

I got up, as silently as I could, and walked over one guard's sleeping figure and through the now-open door and back into the outer office, leaving one still-puzzled captain behind.

Back down the marbled corridors, past three or four sets of guards until I could sense that deadly fountain of chaos—a tumbling stream of white. My hands were trembling . . . so I sat down again in a corner, where anyone passing would not trip over me, wondering what in hell I was doing wandering the corridors of the prefect's palace.

After a time, and with a silent sigh, I stood, feeling like a mouse in a house full of cats, or dragons, assuming such beasts existed some-

336

where. Slow step by slow step, I neared the chaos pool. Except it was just a fountain in the courtyard, a simple fountain to the eyes. The courtyard was paved in granite and the walls just simple stone walls. The fountain was a jet of warm water coming from a man-sized stone vase.

The courtyard was not even guarded, but then again, it didn't need to be.

Even for me, it was like walking against the ice storm on the plains of Certis, of battling the heart of a thunderstorm, or worse.

A fountain of warm water, that seemed all, but the warmth came from deep below, fueled by some sort of chaos, and twisted by something beyond, like a mighty lock of something insubstantial.

With my thoughts I could trace the twisted patterns, but that did no good, because they weren't patterns. They were chaos. Each time I tried to follow a line of force, it seemed to dissolve.

Then, I remembered a passage from the book, the one about bringing order from chaos—about creating a mirror of order. The reflection of chaos as order would either order it or destroy it—if the mirror of order were stronger than chaos. If not . . .

337

I didn't want to think about the consequences. So I summoned up my own strength and began to create a sort of mirror around the fountain, a pattern like what I could sense, but ordered. I struggled to reflect the odd twists, turning them into a deeper harmony, substituting order for chaos, in equal shape and force, and it was strangely like working out the pattern of a chest or a writing-desk.

My eyes blurred, though I could see nothing.

My legs trembled, and I sat on the granite stones.

My arms felt like water, and I let them drop.

My head was throbbing, and splitting, and I let it, but I struggled, fighting to reflect that fearful pattern, realizing that I might well end in that white prison demonstrated by Justen if I did not succeed.

My eyes twitched against closed lids.

My breath panted as though I had run uphill for kays.

And I held the mirror pattern against the fountain.

Clunk.

The blurriness was gone from the blackness before my unseeing eyes, and my legs remained weak, but did not tremble. My head ached—but both patterns were gone.

Only the splash of water remained.

"... help ..."

"... Tallian ..."

I began to walk toward the other courtyard and the gates, understanding that there would indeed be hell to pay, and before too long, either.

"... wizardry!"

"Tallian says to check around the fountain!"

Two guards ran past me toward the fountain courtyard I had left, one of them nearly hitting me as I dodged against the wall.

In all the rushing, I just waited until the gates opened. Then I walked to the market square area and reappeared out of the shadows, not that anyone was watching, with the half-dozen horsemen speeding from the palace.

I did not quite run to Destrin's, belatedly realizing what could well happen. But I did burst in the door.

"Bostric."

"What . . . ?" One look at me and his face was probably as pale as mine felt.

"How fast can you and Deirdre get to Brettel's?"

The most-recent journeyman in Fenard gulped.

"Never mind. Just get Deirdre down here. All hell is about to break loose."

"But . . ."

"Do it." I gathered my staff and pack, the book, and the small strongbox with Deirdre's dowry, before hurrying out to the stable to saddle Gairloch. He didn't even whinny.

When I got back into the shop, Bostric and Deirdre each carried a small sack.

Deirdre looked at me. "Papa . . . he won't leave . . ."

I dashed upstairs.

Destrin sat in his armchair. His eyes were clear.

"We need to leave, Destrin."

"No." He shook his head. "You're right, Lerris—wizard, or whatever you are—but I'm not strong enough to keep up with you young people. You can care for my Deirdre. I can't, and I'll slow you down. And I'm almost dead anyway . . . would have died seasons ago without you."

"We can take you."

"I'll fight you, young wizard." He smiled a yellow-toothed grin.

I could tell he would. "Good-bye, then, Destrin. I won't be back."

"I know. Take care for my Deirdre."

There wasn't much else to say. I reached down and hugged the cranky old man, but my steps were heavy down the stairs.

"You . . . couldn't . . ."

I looked at Deirdre. "He'll fight to stay in his house. Trying to take him would kill him."

She nodded, but the corners of her eyes were wet. Then she ran upstairs again.

I pursed my lips, wondering how soon the soldiers would reach us.

"What are we doing, Lerris?"

"Going to Brettel's."

It seemed like forever before Deirdre came down, and her eyes looked back up the stairs. "He . . . said . . . he'd scream and yell . . . if I didn't go . . ."

Destrin would be cranky to his last breath.

Then I felt like hitting my head with my hand. I tiptoed back up the stairs. With Destrin it was easier than with the guards. Almost before I could react, he was asleep.

He weighed little enough, even for me.

Deirdre's eyes widened as I carried him down.

"He's just asleep."

I put Deirdre on Gairloch, just so she could hold the sleeping Destrin, and we started out, my feelings extended as far as I could.

I didn't like what I was about to do, but, again, there wasn't any choice.

"Bostric? Deirdre?"

They looked at me. "I'll be right with you, but you may not be able to see me. If the guards see me, they might . . . get upset . . ." I finished lamely. What I said might be true, but I didn't know. They might be more than upset to see me, but with Antonin off fighting the autarch, I wasn't sure if anyone had actually traced back how the chairs had come to the sub-prefect, or if anyone really cared.

I just couldn't chance it.

"If you say so, wizardly one," quipped Bostric.

Deirdre looked at me. "Whatever you say."

Bostric frowned, but I'd be gone before long, and he would have her all to himself, the lucky bastard.

So we set out toward the north gate. Even carrying the staff that I

339

had used so little over the past year, all I could sense was a vague confusion in the direction of the palace, even after we reached the gate.

The guards scarcely gave them a second look, although I did weave a light cloak around the sacks and packs.

When we reached Brettel's I reappeared. It was still mid-afternoon, with the dusty dryness that comes when the crops are nearly all in and the grass has browned. In the unseasonable heat, I felt like I had been up for two days straight.

"You were here."

"I said I would be."

"Lerris?"

I turned to the approaching mill-master, feeling my legs tremble, and sat down abruptly before I fell, still holding the staff.

"You're hurt!" Deirdre exclaimed.

"Just tired." I glanced up at Brettel, who looked like an angry giant from my viewpoint on the ground.

"I should have known." His eyes were focused on the black staff.

"All hell is breaking loose," I added. Not only was I exhausted, but my speech was getting repetitious.

"What did you do?" The mill-master looked less than amused.

"Me? I just created a little order."

Brettel snorted. "Get Destrin into the guest wing, the bed in the small room." He was talking to Dalta, the blond vision.

Enough energy returned to my legs that I could stand.

". . . Bostric will stay in the mill quarters with Arta, and Deirdre will sleep somewhere in the main house . . ." He turned to me. "What about you?"

I shook my head. "I need some food and rest, but staying here is too dangerous to you. Even being seen here isn't good."

"No one here will speak."

"No one saw me come here," I affirmed, leaning on my staff.

He looked both worried and relieved.

I waited until the others began to follow Dalta. Then I handed him what had been in the strongbox. "That's Deirdre's."

He didn't insult me by insisting it was mine or any such nonsense, just accepted it gravely. "Thank you."

"Thank you. I regret having to leave so soon, but . . ."

"Now—" he began.

"Do you really want to know?" I asked. My voice was hoarse and tired.

He nodded.

"Antonin set up a fountain of chaos in the palace. They must have bathed the soldiers in it or something. That's why . . ." I shook my head. I couldn't explain exactly why the fountain had turned them into mindless creatures ready to follow any order, but I knew it had. That was why the officers stayed away. They had to think. Besides, they were already corrupted.

Brettel frowned. "You seem to think Antonin is evil, Lerris."

Was a goat stubborn? "Yes."

"Does that make the autarch good? How do you know she isn't worse."

I nearly shivered right there, in the heat and all. Given the history of Candar, the legacy of Frven and the White City, it was a good question. And I didn't know the answer. Finally, I shrugged. "If that's the case, neither one is going to be very happy with me."

Brettel smiled wryly. "I'm glad you feel that way, but I'm also glad you refused Deirdre. You're either going to be very powerful or very dead before long."

The sadness in his eyes told me which he thought it would be.

I slept the rest of the afternoon, although I had never been able to sleep in the light except when I was sick. But then, I'd never melded chaos and order before.

Deirdre woke me. She did it with a kiss on the cheek—a gentle one—then sat down at the foot of the bed—Brettel's bed. Who his wife had been, I had never learned, except she had to have been beautiful and special.

"Will you come back?"

"Not unless you treat me like Brettel."

"That will be hard."

We both knew that.

"Would anything else be fair to Bostric? Or you?"

She kissed me again, lightly, as she stood up. "Supper is ready."

By the time I washed, everyone was gathered around the big table—Dalta, Deirdre, Bostric, and Brettel. Destrin, they said, was still resting, but seemed fine, if pale.

The stew was good, the berry biscuits better, and the conversation nonexistent. It was time to go.

Deirdre, Bostric, and Dalta stood on the porch, waiting, as I walked to the stable with Brettel. Inside were two newish saddlebags, stuffed, in addition to my own older saddlebags and bedroll.

"You didn't have—"

"Lerris." The tone was firm. "You didn't have to do what you did. All I ask is that you do your best to keep the innocents from getting hurt too badly."

"I'll do what I can." I knew exactly what he meant. Whether what he wanted was within my power was another question entirely.

I saddled Gairloch, then put the staff into the holder, and added the saddle bags.

"Do you know where you're going?"

"Kyphrien first, to answer your question."

"And then?"

"That depends on the answer. Probably into the Westhorns to find something I've avoided."

Brettel pursed his lips. "Good luck."

He walked me part way to the road. Even though she never left the porch, I could tell Deirdre was crying, and my own breath was ragged. For some reason, as I turned Gairloch onto the north road in the twilight and drew my reflective cloak around me, I thought of Justen, the gray wizard, wondering how many good-byes he had said over the years, and how many times he had returned to find only change and death waiting.

LVII

In addition to making my way to Kyphrien, that maligned capital of Kyphros, I had one other little chore to attend to, one I wasn't exactly thrilled about as Gairloch and I plodded back around the north road again.

This time I chose the east gate, not because east was where we were going, but because the guards there were the sloppiest. Nothing ever came from the east.

The main trade roads ran north and south, and south was the road to Kyphros, which is where I was headed and where the prefect's troops all rode or marched. The east road, as I well knew, only straggled across broad farmlands from the Easthorns, and few traders or anyone else traveled that route.

Sloppy or not, I stopped well beyond the guards, listening behind my cloak of light, and checking the ramparts above the gate. There were no bowmen on duty. The sun had dropped behind the city, and the shadows were long.

". . . Rephren should be here . . ."

". . . bastard's late . . ."

Creaakkkk . . .

"Another damned farm wagon."

"It's your turn . . ."

". . . lazy frigger . . ."

As they turned to the farm wagon, I dropped the reflective cloak and let Gairloch walk toward the guards.

Click . . . click . . . click . . .

"Where he'd come from?"

The stouter guard turned to me. "Where to, fellow?"

I gestured vaguely. "The mountains." With mountains in three directions, it was an honest answer, especially since it was true.

"What's that?" He pointed at the staff, which I had purposely left unconcealed.

"That's my staff." I edged Gairloch practically on top of the poor man, forcing him to back up.

"I don't know . . . wasn't there something . . . ?" he frowned, looking at the other guard, who was pawing half-heartedly through empty sacks piled around a few open sacks of potatoes in the wagon bed. A grizzled farmer, clearly waiting to head home with what he had not sold, watched silently from the wagon's bench seat as the younger guard checked the produce.

"I'm sure there was, officer," I said politely, "but since I'm leaving it can't matter that much." I flicked the reins and guided Gairloch around him.

"Wait . . . you!"

At that point I drew the cloak around us, and spurred Gairloch down the stone ramp.

"Wizard! That fellow was a wizard!"

". . . huhh . . . what fellow . . ."

I left them to sort it out.

Cling! Clang! Cling! Clang!

By the time the alarm chimes rang, I had eased up on Gairloch and began to let him walk until we reached a narrowed lane, which would, in time, wind its way back around Fenard to meet up with the south road toward Kyphros.

Before long Antonin or Sephya, or both of them, would be back. They could not have missed the change in the city's order-chaos balance. Even now I could feel it, and I suspected a great many illusions were wearing thin, perhaps even those cloaking the street of harlots. Then again, understanding how even I liked to deceive myself about women, perhaps not.

Gairloch walked on, his steps shorter, as they always were when he walked blind, until we were shrouded by trees and shadow, and I dropped the cloak. Night would be as good a cloak for a time.

Wheeee . . . eeee

I patted his shoulder. "I know. You don't like the darkness. Neither do I."

It was well past full night, and moonless, before we turned onto the south highway. The section we traveled was empty, but the dust bore the traces of horses—another cavalry troop, I thought, headed toward Kyphros.

I did not see any trace of coach tracks, nor sense any lingering odor of chaos, but I kept my ears open for the drumming of hooves as Gairloch bore me southward, past farm cottages faintly lighted by single candles or lamps, past darker clumps of sheep behind railed fences, past the occasional howling dog.

Some sort of insects whirred and chirped and buzzed. And I rode steadily onward into the night.

In time, we came to another river, spanned by a stone bridge, a bridge well-mortared and solid, the sort of bridge that would resist any chaos-master's efforts.

A thought occurred to me, and I grinned. The bridge was solid, and over running water, which might help.

So while Gairloch drank, I studied the bridge, finally drawing from the calmness around me a greater sense of order, and of purpose, and infusing it into the stones. Lying there on the long fall grass, I thought long and hard, trying to recall more from the book, knowing there was more I wanted to do.

But I waited, letting my mind drift through what I had learned until the knowledge returned to me.

Then I tuned the bridge to the order underlying the superficial chaos of the river, and to the order of the deep stones underneath.

I almost whistled as I remounted Gairloch, except I was tired again. Using order was work. The hard white cheese that Brettel had packed helped restore me, as did the water from the canteen I had filled at the river.

That bridge was going to cause Antonin, or at least the Prefect's chaos-washed troops, some trouble.

By the time the crescent moon had appeared, both Gairloch and I were tired, and took refuge in a copse of trees—a woodlot, really—not too far from the road. I did set wards before I collapsed on the bedroll.

Again, I dreamed of a black-haired woman, but the details eluded me, and that bothered me. Were my dreams pushing me toward Krystal because she was from Recluce, or for better reasons?

A bright gray sky woke me, sunlight diffused through high thin clouds. That, and the extraordinarily cheerful sound of some bird I did not know and wanted to strangle.

After stowing my bedroll and saddling Gairloch, I rode until we crossed another stream, where we had breakfast. By now we were in the flattest of the low rolling hills between Fenard and the Little Easthorns, that not-quite-mountain range that ran nearly three hundred kays north and south to connect the Westhorns with the proper Easthorns.

In her generally boring lectures on geography, Magistra Trehonna had noted in passing that the Little Easthorns were contrary to normal geology and might well represent a very early attempt at geological chaos-mastery. If so, the perpetrator probably had not survived the attempt, one way or another.

I doubted the theory, especially considering the effort it took me to accomplish generally minor tasks like neutralizing chaos fountains and order-trapping bridges.

Theory or not, we had another day or two of travel and more than a few bridges to cross before we reached Kyphros . . . and I had more than a few questions I needed to ask myself. More important, I needed answers for myself, and I was the only one who would find them. That was all too clear.

LVIII

After two days of riding through the boring rolling hills of Southern Gallos, two days of avoiding towns, and two days of dried fruit, travel bread, and hard cheese, and stream water, I was ready to leave Gallos.

Only twice had we had to leave the road to avoid the hard-riding troops of the prefect. In both cases, the cavalry detachments were headed toward Kyphros, not back to Fenard. On one other occasion, we caught up with three wagons filled with supplies and had to sneak around them.

Except for that time I rode openly, without shields, feeling that the locals wouldn't care who rode by, and that using order might call more wizardly attention to me than necessary.

Late on that second day we came to the first bridge over the Southbrook, a structure half-timber, half-stone, which required three spans to cross the slow-flowing water. But it was past mid-morning the next day before we reached the second bridge—a single stone span.

With that second bridge over the Southbrook came the reminders of war.

The odor of smoke drifted toward me first, faint, like the left-over burnt wood smell in an uncleaned fireplace that has stood unused over the summer. Acrid, like charred leather, like the hides left from burning diseased animals. Pervasive, like the unseasonable clouds and fog that had clung to Freetown.

Wheee . . . eeeee . . . Gairloch tossed his head.

"I know. If it smells that bad to me, it's worse for you."

His steps clattered on the paving-stones of the bridge, echoing into the morning. The echoes rebounding from the stone walls of the bridge were the only sounds. Even the insects were hushed, and not a single birdcall warbled or whistled through the air.

I shivered.

Beyond the bridge, the road began to wind and climb toward the not-so-distant hills beneath the Little Easthorns. Everything was relative, I supposed. Without having seen the Easthorns, I would have found the dark slopes on the horizon impressive. Now they just appeared as another barrier.

The hills belonged to the autarch, which meant that we were nearing the border between Gallos and Kyphros.

With the wind from the south came more of that lingering acrid-sweet odor of ash and charred hide. Gairloch *whuffed* again as he carried me southward over the stone bridge and onto the packed-clay highway heading uphill. The browning grasses beyond the road edge were damp, and not with dew. Gairloch's hooves left clear imprints in the dark-red clay of the road. Whatever rain had fallen the night before had not carried much beyond the Southbrook or the hills of the Little Easthorns.

The sky was a crystal blue and cloudless, promising one of those late fall days that reminded me more of summer than the approaching winter.

Yee-ahh! Yeee-ah! The distant call of the vulcrows echoed through the stillness of the morning. Ahead and slightly to my right, over the crests of perhaps three hills, circled two of the black birds.

My hand edged toward my staff, which I had not bothered to conceal. The sun was a white-yellow point in the sky, somehow not really connected to the damp road clay, the circling scavengers, or to me.

Gairloch was thirsty, and I pulled up on the reins and guided him back off the road and down toward the shore of the placid river, stopping on a sandy stretch not much wider than Gairloch's length. From a half-submerged log, a small turtle glared at us, then scuttled off his perch.

Ploppp . . . Only a faint rippled pattern even marked that the turtle had been there.

I dismounted, looping the reins over the saddle, and let Gairloch do his own drinking.

Yee-ah! Yee-ah!

My eyes returned to the vulcrows circling in the distance, but the calls had come from closer birds. Closing my eyes to what I could see with my eyes, I cast out for the vulcrows and the source of their interest.

With my still-sharpening sense of place, I could sense Gairloch placidly chewing left-over green grass by the river bank, and almost could I feel the color of the grass. Then . . . it could have been my imagination.

Beyond Gairloch, beyond the near hills . . . someone . . . something . . . was out there. I tried to project my senses beyond Gairloch, beyond the river, more toward the hills ahead, in the direction of the vulcrows' calls.

. . . darkness, and shiny brass, and blued steel . . .

The prefect's soldiers. Waiting ahead.

Turning my attention behind me, back into Gallos, I searched . . . and found more darkness, more brass and blued steel, riding up from behind me on the road that would lead them and me onward into Kyphros and into more death on both sides. Wonderful! I had the prefect's troops in front of me and behind me.

I opened my eyes and looked back across the bridge toward the rolling brown plains that I knew remained behind me, behind the hill, then eastward at the light dusting of snow on the very tips of the uncovered rock of the Little Easthorns. Further to the west, to my right, just barely visible, a hint of gray clouds had begun to billow, as if to represent the chaos of the wizard who resided in the rocks of the unseen Westhorns that lay beneath or beyond those distant clouds.

The Westhorns, and Antonin, would have to wait, at least for a while, until I had seen enough of Kyphros and the autarch to ensure the answers to Brettel's questions and my own doubts.

While it was just past mid-morning, the menace that awaited me lay some distance ahead, and like Gairloch, I was thirsty. Hungry or not, I also needed to eat.

The river water was cold, cold enough both in drinking and in washing the grime from my face to encourage my appetite, and to open some trail bread and dried fruit from two packages near the top of the saddlebags provided by Brettel. Being able to perceive what was inside closed sacks had some advantages in the dark and when you didn't want to open sealed provisions. I grinned, thinking how I had wondered how Justen always knew where things were.

Still munching on the bread, I wondered about the soldiers ahead, and about the vulcrows, the ones I had not seen, only felt, over the next hill, and those circling further away.

The breeze from the south increased, and with it came the odor of ashes and charred hides. I had to concentrate to finish the slice of the second dried apple. After filling my canteen and taking another long swallow of cold river water, I reclaimed Gairloch from his browsing.

"Come on. It's time to figure out what's ahead."

Whufffff . . .

Gairloch's steps became more skittery as we neared the top of the hill beyond the bridge.

Yeee-ahh, yeee-ahh, yeee-ahh . . .

Just before the crest of the hill at the right edge of the road was a square limestone marker, no more than knee-high. Only two words—"Kyphros" set above "Gallos," with a line separating the two. But someone had tried to scratch a skull next to the "Kyphros."

Casting my senses ahead of me, I could feel nothing living . . . except for the vulcrows perched in a barren low tree just beyond the hilltop.

Whuffff . . .

We passed the marker and continued over the crest, the odor of ash even more pronounced in the light breeze.

". . . *uuugggghhhh* . . ."

My guts nearly wrenched out of my body, and I swallowed hard to keep the just-eaten bread and fruit within me.

Except for the two vulcrows perched on the leafless trunk of a white oak, nothing lived.

Except for the road, which only bore a white dusting, thick white ash covered the entire hillside nearly a kay in every direction, so white that it first looked like a blanket of snow. Only a few blasted tree trunks, all white oaks, poked through the calf-deep ash.

Yeee-ahh . . .

The pair of vulcrows flapped into the late morning sky, heading south toward those circling the higher hills.

Wheeeeeeee . . .

I didn't blame Gairloch as he pulled up short of the ash.

"Easy . . . easy . . ."

There was nothing there. My staff was cool to the touch, and nothing lived. Nothing.

But I knew that the white ash represented the remains of men, women, horses, grasses, trees, birds, insects, and even fall flowers.

My guts twisted again.

Wheeeee . . . *eeeee* . . .

"Easy . . . easy . . . we have to go on."

More than ever I had to go on, deeper into the war zone that was Northern Kyphros, deeper into the destruction that seemed so unnecessary to me, and so critical to Antonin and the white wizards.

". . . come on . . ." I patted his neck and flicked the reins.

Skitterish step by skitterish step, Gairloch carried me straight down the ash-dusted road.

At the bottom of the hill the ash ended, almost as though a line had been drawn, and the fall grasses and the scrub brush resumed. The road clay was again damp, and I wondered if the rain had been created to damp the ash into place.

I shook my head. Who knew why the chaos-wizards did all that they did?

Yee-ah . . .

The echoing cry of the vulcrow reminded me there was more of the same—or worse—yet to come.

At one time, the hills had been farmed. The stone pillars of fences remained, as did a few rotting split rails. Every so often, we passed a chimney emerging from a thicket of bushes or even standing alone and rising out of a hummock of grasses.

The hills were not wild again, nor were they tame, but somewhere in between. Abandoned apple trees still ran in orchard rows with gaps showing those that had died and not been replaced. Taller blocks of mixed oaks and conifers outlined old woodlots, while scrub oak and redberry meadows indicated once-cleared fields.

With each hill, we neared the circling vulcrows, and an underlying sense of white menace.

Yeee-ah, yee-ah . . .

To the west, the clouds kept building. My stomach continued to churn.

Finally, I put a shield around me. Not one that would just keep me from being seen. Like me, any chaos-wizard could have seen through a visual reflective shield. This shield would keep someone from throwing energies at me. Light is energy, and if I could keep light from touching me, I ought have been able to keep from being turned into white ash. The only problem was that I still couldn't see with my eyes because the shield kept light and energy from touching me.

I wondered why I didn't cool off, but my body did generate heat. That brought up another question—like why my body heat didn't fry me inside my shell—but I let my thoughts work on the shield . . . and the shield let energy escape.

Could I build a shield that worked both ways—letting no energy enter or escape? Probably, but for what reason?

Wheeee . . . eeee

Yeee-ah . . .

By now it was early afternoon, and we had nearly reached the top of a particularly long hill. From what I could tell, the vulcrows were circling over the next hill.

I cast out my senses.

The fight was over, for the soldiers were methodically moving on foot, their horses tethered or picketed.

A point of white resided there as well, a living point of white, a chaos-wizard.

There was no point in trying to avoid the soldiers, not with more than a score of them plus a wizard who could track me. But I didn't like it. I had no desire to be any sort of hero. I just had less desire to be run down until I was too exhausted to fight. Besides, the soldiers couldn't fight what they couldn't see.

The wizard was another question.

Still . . . I looked behind me, as far as my senses would carry me. I wished I hadn't.

Wheeee . . . Gairloch tossed his head, as if in warning.

351

More than twoscore cavalry had passed over the Southbrook bridge and now trotted onward, less than two long hills behind. Behind them . . . much further behind, I could sense a rolling wave of chaos; and I couldn't tell for sure, but would have been willing to bet that it centered on a white-gold coach and Antonin.. Where he had been when I disrupted the prefect's chaos-fountain, I didn't know, but he was definitely on my trail.

All of this had developed because I'd wanted to do something to repay Destrin for his support and to ensure a future for Deirdre. But given the results, and Justen's warnings, and Antonin's meddling in the war between Gallos and Kyphros . . . it wasn't as though I had much choice. Someone thought there was a real wizard loose, and all my actions had pointed to me—and I scarcely knew what I was doing.

So they wanted me, whatever the cost. All too predictable.

I glanced back over my shoulder.

Wheeee . . . uhhhh . . . wheeee.

Gairloch's protest jerked my head back toward the crest of the hill before us.

Right-handed, I chucked the reins. "Come on, old fellow. We can't exactly turn back."

Whheee.

"No, we can't. The prefect might let you haul baggage carts, but I'd end up at the festivities in his central square. The central attraction, you might say." I extended my left hand toward the staff, still safe and waiting in the saddle holder. "Oooo . . ." The subjective heat flashed to my fingers even before they reached the black lorken of my staff.

Something was definitely waiting over the crest of the trail, where those soldiers and their attendant wizard waited.

I shrugged. What choice did I have? A few worn-out soldiers and a less capable wizard ahead, or fresh troops and Antonin behind?

The choice was clear enough. I just didn't like either alternative.

I wiped my forehead, even though I knew neither the sun's heat nor glare had reached through my shield.

Wheeee . . . eee . . .

"I know. There are evil types behind us and worse in front of us. But you're going to have to give up the idea of hauling baggage for the prefect."

352

Again, I tried to sense what lay over the hillcrest before me, whatever it was that Gairloch disliked. All I could feel was a sense of heat, of the fire that was the chaos trademark.

Wheeee . . .

"I know." I chucked the reins again. Then I grabbed for my staff.

Tra . . . tra, tra, tra. The faint sounds of a horn echoed from behind me. Just wonderful. On a beautiful, sunlit fall day in Candar, I was sitting in the middle of a road between Gallos and Kyphros. A wonderful day for a picnic or even a ride. Too bad there were blood-thirsty Gallians behind me and in front of me, and a wizard with each troop.

Wheee . . .

"I know. It wasn't exactly my idea, either."

So we crossed the hillcrest and started down.

Clink . . .

Downslope, more than a score of armed troopers were mechanically looting what had to be bodies. The mechanical nature of the movements told me that the victors—this time—had been the prefect's troops.

"Harmin! Form up your squad! Wizard says there's an armed man coming."

In spite of myself, I grinned. Me, an armed man? With a small knife and a staff that was only defensive?

"Deres, Nershal, move it!"

Five mounted figures drew together and began walking uphill.

Clink . . . clinkedy . . . clink . . .

"How far?"

"Right at the hilltop!"

"There's no one there!"

Nerve-wracking as it was, I guided Gairloch onto the side of the road, into the grasses, gambling that the scrunched sounds of damp grass would be less obvious than hoofprints suddenly appearing on the clay road.

The nearest rider passed less than two arm-lengths from us as the five men headed up the road.

"Check the road for hoofprints!"

Somebody was thinking—unfortunately.

We kept moving toward the troop. The wizard, a blob of white mounted on a horse that was probably also white, waited in the shade of a tall pine downhill from the man who shouted the orders.

Wheeee . . . eeee . . .

"What was that?"

"Quiet," I whispered into Gairloch's ear, patting his neck. "Quiet . . ."

We had to get closer to the white wizard, but not seem as though that were my purpose. So I kept Gairloch headed downhill, paralleling the road.

"He's past you! You idiots! Turn around! Look for hoofprints! Marks in the grass!"

By then we were nearly abreast of the heavy-set officer who bellowed. Beside him were two other mounted men, plus two prisoners on horseback—at least they were blindfolded and had their hands tied behind them. And I was powerless to do anything to save them—not with my own order powers, at least.

Still . . . I found myself turning Gairloch across the road, straight toward the officer.

"He's headed toward you." The flat voice carried uphill from the shaded wizard.

"He's headed this way!" The officer yanked his sword out, as did the pair beside him.

Hsssss . . .

353

"Aeiiii . . . damned . . .

Hsss . . .

Clang . . .

"Harmin!"

Wheeee . . . eeeee . . .

Almost easy, it was. Just a quick blow with the staff to the wrists of all three men—who still couldn't see me. So chaos-filled were they that the mere touch of the staff was agony. And I encouraged their horses to run—after knocking the reins of the two captives' horses from the hands of the third man.

Then I jammed the staff back into the holder and used my knife to slash at the bonds of the prisoners. That took too long. Trying to cut through rope from pony-back isn't easy.

Whhhhsttt!

A bolt of pure chaos-fire licked around me, and I expanded the shield around the two.

"Hold still!" I hissed.

"Mmmmmppphhhh . . ."

Gagged, of course, and probably telling me to get on with it.

"Harmin! Get the bastard!"

Whhhssssttt . . . Another sheet of flame cascaded off my shields.

I cut the woman's wrist a bit, but finally severed the heavy cord, and pressed the knife into her hand. "You'll have to free your friend!" I snapped, reaching up and yanking off the blindfold. "Don't scream. You can't see me!"

". . . not a silly bitch like . . ." she muttered as she used her other hand to rip off the blindfold and the gag.

Gairloch wheeled away from the two captives. While I would have liked to run like hell, unless I kept the wizard busy there was nothing to keep him from frying the captives.

So we charged, as much as a mountain pony and an idiot wood-crafter with a little ability with order-magic and a good staff could charge.

Whhhssssttt . . .

The heat and force nearly collapsed my shields in on me, somehow drawn to the staff before me.

Thumpedy . . . thump . . . Gairloch's hooves actually drummed on the meadow turf, and I grabbed for my staff again, hoping my trembling knees could hold me in place on the suddenly very unsteady Gairloch.

"They're escaping!"

"Who's escaping?"

Whhhsttttt!

The staff deflected the fire, but that was all it would do, gathering some and letting the rest sheet off, almost as if I were fighting with it, rather than with the other wizard.

Whhhssttttt!

"You see that?"

"Forget the wizards! Get the captives!"

"Where are they?"

Whhhsttttt!

Gairloch and I half-tumbled, half-thundered downhill toward the wizard on his white horse.

Whhhsttttt!

"Just keep going . . ."

I got the staff ready.

EEEiiiii! . . .

The white horse turned.

WHHHHSSSSTTTTTTTTT!

"Aeeeeeiiii . . ."

"Ouuuffff . . ."

Staff and firebolt had met at the white wizard's fingertips.

For a long instant, I sat there, momentarily near-deaf with the hissing still crackling in my ears . . . shaking my head . . . before realizing that the white horse had reared, and that a dead man lay on the turf, still dressed in white. Even as I watched, his face turned to ashes and bones, and then the bones began to disintegrate . . .

"There he is! Another wizard! A black one!"

My shields had gone with the clash, leaving me in full sight of too damned many Gallian soldiers.

"Jernan! The captives!"

Shaking, head splitting, guts turning, I nudged Gairloch past the heap of ashes that had been a white wizard, and back toward the road.

"Use your bows!" bellowed the heavy-set officer. "Your bows, idiots!"

Somehow I gathered enough of a light shield around us, just enough to cloak us for a while as we both staggered away.

"He's gone!"

"Guess where he is!"

355

I don't know what they did—except that if they shot at us, they missed. I did know that I was now in big trouble. Antonin wasn't about to overlook the killing of another white wizard, however accidental it might have been.

And the autarch's troops, assuming the captives made it back safely, wouldn't be thrilled about a black wizard running around loose, either. While I wasn't a black wizard, that was bound to be the way I would be described.

My head ached. My buttocks ached. My eyes burned. My ears kept chiming in discordant minor keys, and there was a taste of bile in my throat. I'd played hero, and rescued two whole captives—maybe—and alerted every white wizard in Candar.

Whheeee . . . eeee . . .

"Yeah . . . I know . . ."

Somehow we tottered along through the afternoon, at least long enough that the simmering disorder that represented Antonin and the mess I had made disappeared behind us.

In the meantime, the clouds from the west rolled in.

356

Thurrrummmm . . .

The hills became more than hills and less than the Easthorns, and the road stopped rising and falling and turned into a near-steady grade.

Long before sunset, I turned Gairloch up a deserted arroyo that had tufts of grass and a clean, if narrow stream. There was an overhang sheltered from both the road and overhead observation.

Then I unsaddled Gairloch, stacked the saddlebags, unpacked the bedroll, and collapsed. I did manage some silent wards, and a type of shield I'd read about but never tried. It didn't make us invisible, just reduced the level of order that escaped from around us, something not very useful in hiding from bandits, but very useful in hiding from Antonin. The problem was that you couldn't do both at once. At least I couldn't, and Antonin was the bigger problem in the dark.

Wheeee . . . eeeee . . .

Slurrrrpppppp . . .

A wet tongue woke me into near-darkness.

Thurrummmm . . .

Despite the thunder, no rain had fallen.

The ringing in my ears was gone, but not the shakiness in my hands, or the splitting headache that felt like thunder between my ears.

After crawling down to the brook, dunking my head and drinking, the shakiness subsided to an occasional tremble, and I realized my crawl had covered my trousers with mud. I also realized that Gairloch was hungry.

"Good horse . . . good pony . . ." I patted his neck, but he nipped at me just enough to indicate words weren't what he wanted. Two grain cakes took care of his problem. He was a pig, but he'd saved my neck too many times to count. So I munched on travel bread, ignored my headache for a time longer, and brushed my four-footed savior.

Then I had some fruit and more bread and went back to sleep.

In the morning, I washed the mud off my trousers and laid them in the sun to dry. We both ate again before I washed myself up and even shaved. I was in no hurry. Antonin clearly hadn't followed me, since I was still alive, and there was no point in heading into more trouble immediately. There was also no point in malingering.

So, slightly after mid-morning, I resaddled Gairloch, packed up the gear, and headed back to the road.

In one thing, I had been wrong. Coach tracks marked the cracking clay of the road.

I shivered, but there was nothing else I could do.

LIX

In a way, following the coach tracks was a relief. At least, I knew that Antonin was not tracking me directly. But then, I wasn't sure that he even knew that I—Lerris—existed. The other thought, even more disturbing, was that he didn't really care, that nothing I had done mattered. Even worse was the thought that perhaps my actions actually benefitted the white wizard.

I frowned at the thought. Antonin had only seen my face once, in a crowded inn, and he had never heard my name. There would have been nothing to connect me to the ordered woodwork or even to the disasters I had created in Fenard. So all that he probably knew was that someone was working order in Gallos and Kyphros—someone strong enough or lucky enough to destroy a white wizard .

That destruction I still did not understand fully, except how close I had come to being destroyed myself. Nor did I understand why Antonin had not immediately set out after me. I could only shake my head and press on.

Gairloch dutifully carried me onward until we were clearly into the tree-covered rocks of the Little Easthorns, steep hills I would once have considered mountains. But then, the way I viewed a number of things had changed.

Around mid-day, when I was looking for another stream or at least a shaded place, we came down another incline into a small dry valley. Gairloch skittered slightly. Underfoot the surface seemed flatter, and I looked around. On the right was a thick grove of scrub juniper bushes. On the left was a large and whitish boulder. I reined Gairloch to a halt.

Whheeee . . . eeee . . .

My spine tingled as I studied the rock that looked no different than any other rock along the dusty road. I glanced toward the scrubby off-green of the junipers, felt the same way. Something . . .

I closed my eyes and concentrated on sensing what was really there.

Or, as it turned out, what was not there. Neither the juniper nor the boulder was really there—just the semblance of each. Behind the semblance was the flat white surface of another wizards' road—one that flew as straight as an arrow down a narrow valley that appeared to stretch east from the Westhorns all the way to the Easthorns.

How many of the damned roads had the old chaos-masters built? Was that how they had held together their evil empire? How had the illusion lasted so long?

Then I felt stupid as I thought it out. The road was old, but not the illusion. Antonin and his coach—they used the road. No wonder he seemed to be everywhere.

Then I began to look at the coach tracks. There weren't any. Something had smoothed them over. None ran down into the valley, and none ran out. But they had led to the crest of the hill behind me.

So the chaos-master didn't want his secret roads noticed. I smiled briefly and flicked the reins. "Let's go."

Before riding on, I noted where the road ran for future reference. The road wasn't evil—just its uses.

We spent another night in the Little Easthorns, up another narrow canyon with a stream that did not merit the name, and even less grass. Gairloch had almost finished off the last of the grain cakes, and I began to worry whether I would have the coins necessary for food once we reached the more inhabited sections of Kyphros.

I washed out one set of underclothes and laid them on the rocks, wringing them dry, wondering as I looked at the overhead clouds of gray whether I should have done so.

After sunset, the thunder rumbled like coach wheels down a canyon road, like Antonin riding forth and sowing destruction across the Vale of Krecia. I thought that was the name of the place where I had met the white wizard, and if it weren't . . . well . . . one name was as good as another. The flashes of the lightning hid behind the clouds in the northern half of the sky, back-lighting those dark sky-mountains.

For all the thunder in the heavens, the air remained warm enough that the light breeze was welcome. I ended up tossing off the cloak and lying on the bedroll barefoot, sleeping in just shirt and trousers.

The rain promised by the thunder did not arrive, and, in time, the clouds overhead vanished and the stars shone like tiny lamps in the sky, clearer than I had seen them since I had landed in Freetown, and nearly as clear as on a midwinter night in Recluce.

Dawn crashed down on me like a tide of light, or so it seemed, with the red ball of sun bursting from a dark sky within instants.

With no reason to tarry, Gairloch and I headed onward and downward. Being on the southern side of the Little Easthorns made a difference in one respect. Kyphros was warmer, a lot warmer, and drier. Even with just a shirt and no tunic, I was sweating—and it was well into fall.

What the place would be like in the summer, I wasn't sure I wanted to find out.

Each step Gairloch took on the hilly road toward Kyphrien raised a reddish dust. Orchards seemed to prevail on the hillsides—orchards and grapes. The trees were of two kinds—gnarled olive trees with small pale green leaves, and some sort of fruit with which I was unfamiliar. There might have been several related types or different varieties of the same type. Whatever they were, the greenish fruits all grew on low spreading trees with dark-green leaves that might have been shiny except for the autumn dust. Some of the green fruits seemed to have an orange color mixed with the green, but since none of the trees were that close to the road, I really couldn't tell.

Unlike the stone and red-oak houses of the more northern principalities, the houses of Kyphros were white; but it wasn't the white of chaos, just a soft off-white painted over timber and stone and plaster. The roofs were mostly of red tile.

Wheeee . . . eeee . . .

"It's hot, and you're thirsty. So am I."

We kept riding, but only until the next cross road, which consisted of half-a-dozen houses and a small building with a shaded porch. By then it was near midday.

I wiped my forehead as I dismounted in front of the building.

"Could you tell me where I might get some water for my horse?" I asked a tanned youngster with shaggy black hair, a boy who might have reached to my waist.

"We have some. You will have to lead your . . . horse . . . around the back." He pointed around the left side of the building. "Barrabra! A traveler!" Then he was gone.

I scratched my head, itchy from the sweat and heat and dust, before taking the reins and trudging toward the corner.

I stopped suddenly. Around the white-plastered corner of the building were several men armed with swords, waiting, and the fear they would have denied boiled from them. I didn't want to fight, and I didn't want to run. So I stood there, reins in hand, wondering what I would do next.

Finally, I reached back and took my staff. That was all I had. I'd never gotten my knife back from the Kyphran soldier in all the confusion with the white wizard.

I spoke loudly. "If I really meant you harm, don't you think I would have fried you where you stood?"

Two of them dropped the swords and ran. One shook his head. The biggest charged around the corner waving the blade in a way that showed he had no idea of how to use it.

Thunk.

Clang. The sword banged against the wall and dropped into the dirt.

"Just leave it there," I said tiredly. "All I wanted was some water."

"But . . . you're a wizard . . ." He was dark-haired, well-muscled, and wore faded white trousers and a sleeveless shirt. On his feet were sandals, not boots.

"Says who? You made enough noise to warn an army."

"What are you?" He looked past me to the other man creeping up behind me.

I half-turned in order to watch them both.

The man who had come from the front did wear boots, the same pale-green uniform, including the green leather vest, that I had seen on the prefect's captives, and the way he carried the sword was more professional.

"Who are you?" asked the soldier.

"Me? I'm a woodworker at heart, who happened to displease the prefect of Gallos."

"Likely story."

He was right, unfortunately. In his position, I wouldn't have believed me either. I shrugged. "All right. I'm from Recluce, and I created a little too much order in Fenard, partly through woodworking, and now I seem to have every white wizard in Candar after me."

"That's not much better." He waited, however, probably for rein- 361
forcements.

So I wove a shield and disappeared. Then I knocked his sword from his hand while he was gaping.

While he was meditating on that, I reappeared, presented the sword back to him with my free hand. "It happens to be true, and I'm getting a little tired of playing games."

He paled slightly. "What do you want?" He sheathed the weapon.

"I'm trying to see if someone I once knew . . ." I raised the staff.

For the first time, he actually looked at the staff, realized that it was black. So help me, the man turned even whiter than the wall. He swallowed. "Why . . . ?"

"I need to know."

"Is she a black-haired blade that can destroy any man?"

I hadn't thought of Krystal in quite that way. "One of them was black-haired and a master with almost any kind of blade. Black-eyed, pale-skinned—

"Hell . . ."

I turned on the other man, who had edged toward his sword, still lying not that far from my feet. "Just hold it right there."

Footsteps thudded on the ground.

"Do I have to disappear again?" I asked the young soldier.

He shook his head. "No. No, ser. We're supposed to bring anyone from Recluce in to see the sub-commander. Those are the standing orders. I should have remembered. The sub-commander was—"

"The sub-commander?"

"She's in charge of training. She does many other things, and she's also the autarch's champion. Perhaps all that is not so wondrous to a magician like you, but she is famed and fabled . . ."

It didn't surprise me—not after recalling the shy lady who had dismembered the apples so quickly, or the woman who had been pressing Gilberto by the time she left Recluce.

"He's going to Kyphrien to meet the sub-commander. I will be the one to carry out the standing orders and to convey him there, for has he not found our waystation? The waystation of Pendril and Shervan . . ."

The others stood back, and that was how I met Shervan.

"You water your horse, and Barrabra will fix you something to eat. Then Pendril and you and I will saddle up, and we will depart for Kyphros," Shervan announced after ushering off the half-dozen armed and able-bodied citizens of the little crossroads.

"That's not a problem?"

Shervan shook his head. "I must only apologize that we did not recognize you. It has been so long . . ."

"So long?"

"We used to receive the pilgrims from Recluce, but seldom do we see them any more."

I nodded, knowing why—Antonin.

Whuuuffff . . . interrupted Gairloch, as if to ask about the water I had promised.

"Ser?" called a strong feminine voice from the covered portico. The shade kept me from seeing more than an ample figure.

"That's Barrabra," explained Shervan.

"I need to water my horse . . ."

"That's a horse?" asked Barrabra, still shrouded by the portico.

I smiled. "He's enough of a horse to have carried me through the Easthorns and the Little Easthorns."

Shervan looked toward the portico with a look I could not quite decipher, but would have said embodied the concept of "I told you so."

I took the reins and led Gairloch around the building to the watering trough. Shervan followed, still talking.

Unlike some towns I had seen since leaving Recluce—places like Hrisbarg, Freetown, Howlett, and Weevett, to name a few—the rear of the whitewashed stone or brick buildings was as clean as the front, and similarly shaded by the protruding tile roof. The housing design confirmed my feelings that in the summertime Kyphros was hot indeed.

". . . and the Gallians, they just keep coming. We never fight unless we have the advantage, and we must kill three of them for every one of us they get. Having the hills and the mountains there helps, but just two eight-days ago some of them got as far as Sintamar." Shervan grinned. "They didn't get back."

I watched as Gairloch drank from the trough, carved roughly from limestone, glancing back toward the north and the clouds that were again building over the Little Easthorns. They didn't look natural, but who was I to say? "Those clouds—"

". . . and the only other one was the knife-thrower . . . such a—"

363

"What knife-thrower?"

"You were asking about the clouds, ser?"

"Later. What were you saying about the knife-thrower?"

"I have never seen such a knife-thrower. Never. No, ser, the clouds, we did not used to have clouds such as those . . ."

"What about the knife-thrower?" I interrupted.

". . . not since the days of the Great White Wizards, they say. You were asking about the knife-thrower. Yes—that was the best. The cowardly Gallians—that was before they became the mad dogs they are now—they ran from the black horse, anywhere to escape the knives and the sword. Such a pair they were! Never had we seen such a pair!"

I was getting ready to strangle the cheerful Shervan, especially since Gairloch had finished drinking.

Whheeee . . . eeee . . .

I fished out the remaining grain cake from the right-hand saddlebag provided by Brettel.

"How—how did you do that?"

"Do what?"

"That food for your horse. You made it appear out of thin air.

Never have I seen that. Not even the Great White Wizard could do that, I would bet."

I sighed. I'd totally ignored the shield around the second set of saddlebags, that minor bit of order-control that left them out of sight. Now Shervan would be telling the world about my marvelous food creation. "No . . . no. I didn't make it. There's a hidden sack there. That's all."

"Hidden sacks! What will they think of next?"

"When will we leave for Kyphrien?" I asked desperately.

"Pendril has to get his horse, and you need to eat, and we need to put your horse with his hidden sacks in a shady place to rest while we eat. Then we will go."

I didn't quite roll my eyes. "Let's eat, and you can tell me about the marvelous pair and the knife-thrower."

"Shervan! Stop flapping your tongue and let the poor wizard have something to eat. The rest of us would like to talk to him, too." Barrabra stood on the raised step that led from a narrow archway in the back of the structure. Her figure was as ample as I had guessed, but her hair, unlike Shervan's short and coarse black strands, was nearly white-blond and shoulder-length, swept away from her broad face with green combs set above each ear.

"Yes. Yes. You see why Barrabra is the one who runs the store. She keeps her mind upon what is important."

"Shervan!"

The young man shrugged at me and smiled.

I shrugged back. "About my horse?"

"Ah, yes. This way."

The side of the structure that we had not yet been to was the stable, empty except for a single palomino. Inside the heavy walls and through the wide circular archway, the air was cool and still.

"You may use any of the stalls, but Pabblo does not like all horses . . ."

I took the hint and put Gairloch in the stall farthest from Pabblo. I did not unsaddle him, nor did I close the stall. If I had to leave quickly, I certainly wanted to be able to do so.

"It's about time," observed Barrabra as Shervan led me into a long dim room dominated by a long polished red-oak table. On each side was an equally long and backless red-oak bench. At each place was a large and empty bowl with an equally-proportioned spoon.

At the table sat another youth older than the boy who had greeted me, a girl with golden hair like Barrabra's but barely coming into womanhood, and just showing curves under her maroon shirt; and two men even younger than Shervan, but wearing the same uniforms.

A woman easily three times my age sat in the middle of the side of the table opposite the door where I had entered. Her gray hair was worn in combs like Barrabra's. Like Barrabra, she also wore three-quarter-length trousers with wide legs, and a loose shirt with sleeves that ended above the elbow. While the younger woman's garments were a dark-green, the ancient's were a pale yellow.

Click . . . click . . . My boots clattered on the tile floor.

"He doesn't sound like a wizard," complained the old woman.

"Grandmere!"

"He doesn't."

"I saw him pull a cake for his horse out of thin air!" announced Shervan.

"You're calling that pony a horse?"

"He's cute," added the boy who had first greeted me. "I wish I could have a little horse like that."

"It's time to eat. It's past time to eat. So sit down. No, not there! You give the wizard the chair."

Shervan bowed and gestured to the chair at the head of the table. I supposed I should have refused and offered it back to him, but the confusion of the conversation was disorienting.

I sat. The place on my right was empty, and the blond girl was seated on my left.

The room was suddenly silent. I swallowed, and it seemed like an eternity before I realized, silently thanking Magistra Trehonna as I did, that Kyphros belonged to the one-god believers. I swallowed again as everyone looked at me.

"In all times . . ." I began slowly, and as I began I could see the tension on the other faces ease. "In all times, there has been disorder. It is the job of right-thinking people to bring order from chaos . . . may we have the will to bring that order. May we have the strength to resist evil and do good."

I bowed my head, since I had no way to end the prayer, not that I could voice.

"Peace under God . . ." added Shervan.

"Very nice . . . it was strange, but nice . . ." said one of the other soldiers.

"He sounds like a wizard," added the old woman who had just said that I didn't sound like one.

"Where's the food?"

"I'm getting it, I'm getting it!"

An aroma of spices and meats entered the long room even before Barrabra arrived with the tray, bearing a huge casserole which she set in front of the older woman before heading back to the kitchen. One saving grace was that I wouldn't need the knife that I didn't have. I fingered the empty sheath, wondering if I had really wanted to carry the knife at all. But that was silly. At least, I thought it was silly, but I still wondered.

"Spiced lamb chili, my favorite! You remembered."

The second tray held two enormous freshly-baked loaves of bread, and that was followed by a pitcher of something and a tray of battered mugs.

With that, Barrabra plopped herself onto the end of the bench next to me and looked at me, face to face. Her breath was like cloves, strong, but not unpleasant. "Do you have a woman, wizard?"

I swallowed.

"I don't think so, Barrabra."

"Well, do you or don't you?"

"Pass the chili!"

"Just take a chunk of bread, and send the loaf to the wizard."

"My name is Lerris, and I'm—" I was going to say that I wasn't a wizard, but the words stuck in my throat. That scared me, the thought that I was even partly maybe a wizard.

"He says his name is Lerris."

"That's better than calling him wizard. He's too young to be called wizard, even if he is one."

"I want the chili!"

I looked frantically at Shervan, but he just grinned and plunged his spoon into the bowl of chili, whatever that was. In his other hand, he held a large chunk of bread.

"About your woman? Is she young? I'll bet she's thin and harsh-tongued. She probably would starve you to keep her looks, just like a northern woman." As she talked Barrabra ladled her bowl full of the spicy mixture from the casserole and began to fill my bowl.

"Here! You need some teekla." Those words came from the other side, from the blond girl who looked like a younger and thinner version of Barrabra.

My eyes darted from one to the other. At that point, the bread tray was thrust under my nose, and I broke off a large chunk.

"Barrabra, he can't have a woman. I'll bet he didn't even have a sister. Did you?"

"No," I admitted, taking a spoonful of the spicy mixture and swallowing it.

"*Ooooffff* . . ." I swallowed again and grabbed for the mug. Hot? Spicy? Neither was an adequate description of the chili. It didn't burn; it seared my throat all the way down.

"Not the teekla, silly. You eat the bread. That's the way you do it," advised the girl, her tone patient and condescending simultaneously.

Since the teekla, with its unknown fruity taste, hadn't eased the fire in my throat and stomach, I chewed off a large corner of the chunk of bread, swallowing as evenly and quickly as I could.

With the back of my hand, I wiped the sudden tears from my eyes, but the burning had in fact diminished.

". . . the post-rider said the madmen lost one of their wizards . . ."

". . . Haylen's cousin said a wizard freed him . . ."

"Ha! He didn't want to admit he got careless! That's all."

"Some more chili, please."

"When are you going to take me to Kyphrien, Shervan? You promised . . ."

Amid the friendly chaos, I took another spoonful of the chili, the stew, whatever it was—a much smaller spoonful, accompanied by a much larger mouthful of the heavy bread. The combination seemed to work. Only my forehead broke out in sweat this time.

"You never answered about your woman, wiz— . . . I mean, Lerris."

I took a small sip from the mug. "Right now . . . I don't have one. It's not wise—"

"I told you, Barrabra! He doesn't look like he knows women."

In that, certainly, the girl was right.

"Hush, Cirla." Barrabra held her hand up. "Not wise? Is it wise to be tempted by every pretty face?"

"I have a lot—" I struggled with both her question and another spoonful of chili.

367

She shook her head. "You men. You think that women are fragile, that only men can do the great deeds."

"I never said that . . ."

"It is not what you said, but what you thought. Would you rather live in Kyphros under the autarch or under a madman like the Prefect of Gallos? Great deeds . . . phewwww . . . dreaming of great deeds only leads to great evils, and too many men dream of great deeds. Give me a solid man any day, one who loves an orchard."

I thought about woodworking, but decided against arguing my case. She would have found something else to throw against men. Instead, I struggled with the chili and listened.

". . . their soldiers are younger each season . . ."

"And so are ours. We're all bleeding to death . . ."

"Pass the bread."

". . . we'll stop in Meltosia. Even from there, it's a good day's ride."

Barrabra stopped talking and kept exchanging glances with the girl Cirla. I ignored both, trying to pick up on what Shervan and the other two soldiers were discussing, but there were too many interruptions. So I ate, slowly and carefully, wondering exactly how badly my stomach and guts would torture me in the days ahead.

The mid-day meal ended as suddenly as it began.

"Enough!" announced Barrabra. "You all would sit here all afternoon if you could. The wizard must go to Kyphrien, and Saltos and Gerarra—" she pointed at the other two soldiers—"must take the watch station from my Nicklos and Carmen."

"So soon?" pleaded the youngster.

"So late. Shush! Clear off the table. Out to the kitchen."

I retreated to the stable with Shervan. "Your sister?"

"How did you guess?"

"A look, and the mention of her Nicklos."

Shervan began to saddle Pabblo. I rummaged around and found what looked to be a short stack of grain cakes.

"If I could purchase some of these . . ."

"No . . . no . . . they are yours. We have fresh grain and grasses."

"I can't just take them."

Shervan shrugged. "Then . . . someday, sometime, make us a gift. Make it for Barrabra."

I thought I understood. "I will." Another obligation, but what other choice was there? Gairloch needed travel food as much as I did. Maybe more in the dry Kyphran climate.

368

Clinkedy . . . clink . . .

"Pendril is here."

The other trooper was heavier than Shervan, older, with a flowing black mustache. "Come on, Shervan. You want to get to Meltosia before Parlaan's closes? He's riding that pony? Ah well, wizards will be wizards . . ." Pendril shook his head.

Shervan winked at me.

I didn't shrug, but I felt like it. Instead, I flicked the reins, and Gairloch carried me out into the full afternoon sun.

The road out from Tellura and toward Kyphrien was the same as the road that had led me into the little crossroads town—hot, dusty, and up one rolling hill and down the next.

Shervan rode his palomino Pabblo, and the other trooper—Pendril, who had not been at the noon meal—rode a black-and-white spotted gelding. Both horses reminded me exactly how small Gairloch was.

"He moves quickly for a pony," said Pendril.

"And the wizard rides well for a wizard, too."

"Are you sure he's a wizard?"

"Am I sure? Let me tell you . . ."

In the first five kays we traveled, Shervan must have told how I disarmed him and how I had made a grain cake appear from thin air in at least three different ways.

By then, the sun had touched the clouds in the west, and the unseasonable heat began to dissipate. I wiped my forehead and began to enjoy the ride, noting that the hills were flatter, not quite so barren, and that some fields held goats—but only in the fenced fields.

"Ah . . . yes . . . the autarch. Any unfenced goat is considered a game animal that anyone may kill or capture—unless it is branded. But if it is branded, the owner must pay two coppers to ransom it back."

I frowned, but I didn't need to. Shervan kept explaining.

"The goat, you see, it will eat anything, and if it eats everything, then the desert will come. We need the goats, but we need the trees, especially the olives and the lemons and oranges." He shrugged. "We also have a lot of good goat dinners."

"I haven't seen any buffalo."

"Kyphros is too hot for them, except under the Westhorns," explained Pendril. His voice was lower and slower than Shervan's. "Few of us would live near the wizard mountains, especially now."

"The wizard mountains?"

"That is where the clouds that bring lightning and fire come from, where the white wizards live, and where too many people have disappeared. To go to Sarronnyn, it is better to go south first, to use the southern passes, or to go north of even Gallos. Going north is not possible any more, either . . ."

"My father said that Sarronnyn was bright, with grassy hillsides, not as cold as Gallos, and not as hot as Kyphros, and the women were always friendly, and they liked strangers. That's what he said." Shervan looked ahead at the dusty and hilly road, then continued without a break. "My father, he used to drive a road wagon for Wistar, but that was when the middle road was open to all, and it took only four days to Sarronnyn, not an eight-day and more like now. That road wagon, it took four horses to pull it, and it glistened like red gold. I remember when he put me up on the seat and let me hold the reins."

Shervan looked back behind us. No one was there. I had already checked. Although we had overtaken a small wagon loaded with covered baskets and had passed a post-rider headed back in the direction of Tellura, the road was lightly used.

370 "I see no one. Do you think we will see one of the Finest?" asked Shervan.

"Here? So far from the hills?"

"But the wizard should see some of the Finest."

Suspecting I had seen a few of the Finest as captives in Fenard, I let the two talk as the horses carried us down the road and further into Kyphros.

Meltosia was nearly a repeat of Tellura, except that, instead of just five or six buildings, it had nearly a dozen, one of which was a long house that took in travelers. Mama Parlaan's house could not have been called an inn, not even in comparison to the Snug Inn in Howlett. But the rooms were cool and the pallets on the hard wooden bedframes clean. The evening meal was another spicy casserole—goat, I gathered, but I didn't ask.

Breakfast was hard rolls not much after dawn, and Shervan woke as talkative as he went to sleep.

"A wonderful morning to be alive. Look at the pink above the hills, and the dew like pearls upon the yucca. A good day for a long ride, and it will be a long ride to Kyphrien, but a sunny one. Don't you think so, Pendril?"

Pendril earned my gratitude by grunting.

The mid-day meal was in a barracks of road soldiers in a place whose name I never learned, distinguished mainly by the fact that the small post controlled the bridge over the first river I had seen in Kyphros—a snaking tongue of water no more than fifteen cubits wide and less than a cubit deep.

"But when the spring floods come, then the waters sweep everything before them and the land is underwater for kay upon kay."

I hadn't asked, but Shervan answered the questions I might have posed, and all too many even I wouldn't have considered.

That was how we reached Kyphros.

LX

"This is as far as we go," Shervan had told me as he and Pendril had escorted me to the low walls around the guard complex.

"Why?"

"Our job is just to get you here. We're outliers, and we're not allowed within the walls. That is, unless we are mustered in for training or for special duties, and that does happen." He shrugged, almost dropping his reins, "As for us, we keep the waystation for stray wizards and let Barrabra tell us what to do. What else can we do?" He smiled apologetically.

I smiled at his expressive face. Since I knew but half the story, I couldn't say whether the restriction made all that much sense, but who was I to quibble? "So what am I supposed to do?"

"You stable your pony in the main stables. You just ride right through the gates on the left. Then you go to the building with the green flag and ask to see the sub-commander. They will mumble and mutter, but you just tell them everything and insist on your right to see the sub-commander. Just insist on it. I'm sure you'll find some way to convince them."

Both men laughed at that.

Their confidence was touching, if misplaced. And I couldn't deny

that it had been a relief to ride the last day without having to weave
shields or worry about being denounced as a wizard or keep hiding
from everyone.

So I rode up to the gate, where the guard looked me over, then
back at the pair of outlier soldiers. "What did you drop on me?"

"Orders! He's supposed to see the sub-commander." Shervan didn't
exactly keep a straight face. Pendril looked in the other direction.

"One of those?" The gate guard shook his head, then looked at
me. "The stable is on the left. Once you get your . . . horse . . .
settled, go straight across the yard to the main building. Don't go
anywhere else, or someone's like to draw before they ask questions."

The stable was right where it was supposed to be, a solid red brick
with a slate roof and a slight but not overpowering odor of horse
manure.

"Official business?" asked the ostler, practically running me down
even before I had both feet on the ground.

I nodded.

"Sign here." He handed me a flat square of parchment and pointed
to a line under the words "stable permit." He stepped back. "If you
can't sign, use your mark. Get an officer or a serjeant to chop this.
Otherwise it's a copper a day. If you lose the permit, it's two coppers
a day." He looked at me and at Gairloch. "Mountain pony?"

"Yes."

"If you want to stable him, you can have the last stall on the right."

Since it wasn't really a request, I led Gairloch to the last stall and
unsaddled him. I did shield the saddlebags, just as a matter of habit.
But I brought my staff with me.

The ostler looked at it with respect. "Seeing the sub-commander?"

"That's what I understand."

"Good luck! Tough lady. Go to the red archway, over there, under
the green flag."

With that I walked less than a hundred cubits, where I found another guard, standing beside the doors under the red-painted archway.
Then I looked at the young redheaded guard. "I need you to take a
message to the sub-commander."

"The Sub-Commander of the Guard—a message from a . . . what
are you?"

"A woodworker, among other things." And I was, more of a woodworker than an order-master, when you got right down to it.

"A message from a woodworker?" The youth in the worked leather and brass vest shook his head in disbelief. "She wouldn't even bother to look at you, fellow."

The wooden beam framing the open door, the beam against which he leaned, scarcely looked able to support him, let alone the archway, what with the cracks and the age of the dusty structure. At the moment, I was tempted to dip into chaos and age him and the structure further, but . . . trusting in Justen and the book, I only sighed. "A wager, perhaps?"

"Ha! What would you have to wager, except your hide?"

"Say a couple of silvers that you can't touch me with that fancy sword—my old staff against your new sword."

I placed my hand on the staff.

He didn't even seem to notice its appearance, so surprised was he with my suggestion. "That's dangerous, fellow. I might take you up on it. It's a crime to strike a member of the autarch's guard."

"Is it a crime to strike your weapon?"

"No." He looked puzzled.

"Well, that might make it harder. Say a gold and you carry my message to the sub-commander."

"And when I win?"

"You have at least some of my blood and a gold penny."

"How do I know you're honest?"

I sighed. "Because the penalty for being dishonest would likely be my head."

"You don't sound like a woodworker . . ."

The youngster was sharp, almost brilliant.

"I never said that's all I was."

His small eyes looked me over, and I could see the scheming beginning.

"I wouldn't, if I were you. The sub-commander already knows where I'm from, and there's not one of you that could best her blade." The words didn't come out quite right, but he didn't seem to notice.

"How would you know?"

I managed to keep my face impassive. Sometimes, I actually can.

Then he swallowed. It took him a moment, but, like I said, the young man was almost brilliant, at least for a Candarian. "You put your staff against her blade?"

"That was some time ago. Doubtless she has improved."

Improved or not, he suddenly realized how close he had come to disaster.

"I could just take your name . . . and leave the decision to her . . ."

I inclined my head to him. "That might be best. My name is Lerris." Of course, that was all that I had ever wanted, but nothing anywhere was straightforward, and for whatever reason, I really hadn't wanted to demand to see Krystal. Call it stiff-necked pride . . . whatever. I still had some.

Still shaking his head, the redheaded young trooper yelled into the barracks. "Bidek! Get on up here."

As soon as another young buck, this one heavier, sloppier, and darker, as well as more disapproving, appeared, the nameless young guard marched across the open courtyard—one of the few in Candar that was actually paved with level and solid stones—and disappeared into a granite three-storied building.

While I waited, I made a few more mental measurements of the area around the doorway, mainly to test the age of the wood, since I had an idea for my defense that would not violate the rules of order, since it was strictly creative.

Using it wasn't necessary, since three guards marched from the wing of the structure into which the young guard had disappeared. He followed behind them a moment later. All four stopped short of me.

The center guard, wearing clean green leather and a blade that radiated effectiveness, looked at the staff and nodded. "The subcommander bids you welcome, order-master. Would you be so kind . . . you are most welcome . . ."

He definitely wasn't used to inviting guests into the guard's domain. I smiled pleasantly. "I appreciate your courtesy and would hope you would be so kind as to lead the way."

". . . order-master . . . oh, shit . . ." Both the nameless young guard and Bidek looked as white as the face of chaos as I saluted them with the staff and followed the three troopers into the granite building and up three wide flights of stairs. The door was bound in solid iron, and the knocker would have waked the dead.

The dark-haired lady opened it herself, and her eyes did not even flicker as she silently stepped back and let us enter. Krystal's quarters were almost lavish for a professional soldier's base, with two large rooms, a conference room with a large rectangular table and heavy wooden armchairs which opened into a covered and railed third floor balcony, and a bedroom/study, although I only glimpsed her more personal quarters as I stood in the conference room.

A large and sturdy oak beam stood behind the door from the main hallway to her quarters.

"The order-master, commander."

"Thank you, Statcha. You may leave us." Krystal wore green leather trousers, tighter than in Recluce, with a short jacket over a green leather tunic. The jacket was ornamental, not designed for battle, and bore gold braid across the left shoulder and matching four-pointed silver stars on the narrow lapels.

I could feel Statcha's eyebrows rising.

Krystal laughed, although she had not yet even turned her eyes to me, and her laugh was more musical and more relaxed than I had heard it. "You know I have nothing physical to fear from one man. And an army could not save me from a chaos-master or an order-master put against me."

All three men backed away, as if they had been lashed, yet her words had been gentle. As she talked, I let my feelings reach out to her blade—surprisingly, that same blade I had bought for her on a day that seemed almost part of another life—and found . . . that the unordered steel had assumed a rough order. As had Krystal. I shied away from reading her feelings, knowing I was afraid to find out how she felt.

Clunk.

"Lerris." Those black eyes turned on me, damping the fire of instinctive command that I had suspected, but never seen. "You look older, wiser."

"I doubt that I'm much of either."

She smiled. "That alone says you're both. It's good to see you, although I didn't doubt I would sometime."

I raised my eyebrows.

"You don't belong in Recluce, and sooner or later . . ." She shrugged, then looked squarely at me. "Why did you come?"

"I needed to find out about the autarch."

"Then why did you ask for me?"

I admired the directness. She was still gentle, but the gentleness had been reinforced with steel.

"Because . . ." I took a deep breath, then shook my head. "I don't know. It seemed the right thing to do, and I'm glad I did it. But I can't tell you why." My pulse seemed to race, as though I were somehow lying to myself, and that bothered me.

"You don't like not being able to answer my question."

I grinned, sort of. "You're right. I don't."

Her eyes brushed past me, then centered back on my face. "Stories about you are circulating all across Candar—except no one knows who you are. When I heard about the blackstaffer who dared the deadlands, it had to be you. When I heard about the gray wizard's apprentice who healed a slut in Jellico and disappeared in plain view . . ."

My stomach twisted a little. If Krystal knew . . .

"Were you the one who destroyed the white wizard near the Vale of Krecia?"

"That was an accident," I admitted.

The sub-commander shook her head. "Still the same combination of confidence and modesty."

"Modest?"

She ignored my protest, looking at the doorway, then back at the desk in the bedroom/study. "Will you stay?"

"No. Not for long, not if I'm to help you before it's too late. To undo what I may have done." At that moment, I wanted to stay, to watch her smile and hear the musical tone of her voice, but the order within me refused to lie to her or to me. "I'm not yet the order-master you called me, and I may never be. I haven't finished what I must."

She shook her head, and I realized that the long black hair was gone, that her hair, rather than being bound up with silver or gold cords, was scarcely longer than mine. "I would like you to stay for dinner."

The words were not a request, simply a direct preference, but Krystal no longer had to ask for anything.

I thought. Leaving tonight wouldn't solve anything, and Antonin did not know who or where I was—yet. Certainly he would within days, but I had to sleep somewhere, and a good night's sleep with the autarch's guards, even in a dusty barracks, would beat another night holed up in a canyon or a thicket. "Yes."

"Let's sit on the balcony for a moment. I need to be at a meeting with the autarch before too long. After that, we can really talk." She walked toward the shaded balcony, where she took a padded chair, and gestured to the one across the small table from her. "I'd offer you something, but I'll have to leave before it comes. I'd rather hear from you—what you are doing, and why you wanted to see the autarch."

"I'm here to warn you, assuming you haven't heard. The prefect has decided to throw in with Antonin. I made the mistake of taking on one of his . . . I'd guess I'd call him an ally, if the chaos-masters have allies. That was the white wizard I ran into."

"Antonin?" Her face reflected puzzlement.

"The most powerful of the chaos-masters. He did something to Tamra and seems able to defy the Masters of Recluce—at least for now." I paused.

"Have you seen Tamra?"

My guts twisted again. "I haven't seen her face, but I've seen traces of her. She's tied up somehow with Antonin, I think against her will."

"Against her will? I can't believe that. Are you sure?"

What could I say to her? The silence drew out, and I looked out onto the paved yard, noting the afternoon shadows cast by the building in which we sat enshrouded the stables and the front gate. Outside of the footsteps and a few voices, the yard was quiet, orderly.

Krystal waited, with the same grace I recalled, but with that added strength, almost like a cat that could spring from total relaxation into an attack.

Finally, I tried to explain. "Chaos is . . . different. You can't use chaos even for the best of reasons without risking being trapped by it. People told me that, but I wasn't sure. They were right, and I was lucky to meet a friendly gray wizard before finding too much trouble." I forced a laugh. "By then soldiers in only two principalities were looking for my head."

"How did you escape from Freetown?"

"I bought a horse and rode out."

Krystal chuckled. "It wasn't that easy, knowing you."

"It wasn't." I didn't elaborate. "What about you? I understand they burned the inn where we stayed."

"I claimed to be from the north and took on the local blades. That included a few of the old duke's bravos. Then I waited in the hiring hall until the new duke took over and agreed to terms with Recluce. That got me a contract with the first road-merchant to visit. When he reached Jellico, we had enough to buy nags for the trip over the southern passes to Kyphrien. I hired on with a freelance arms-master who trains bullyboys for the merchants, learned what I could. He sug-

377

gested the autarch, who likes having women soldiers. Kasee liked me, and I started with a western road patrol. There were a lot of casualties. When the Duke of Freetown's defectors tried to carve out that abortive duchy . . ." She frowned.

"You were the one? I've heard stories about you for nearly half a year." I'd guessed she had been the road commander who had opened the reservoir gates on the supply train, effectively ending the siege of the border fort taken by the defectors. I'd meant to ask about Wrynn and about the incident with the Duke's troops.

Krystal actually flushed, although the paleness of her skin had been replaced with a faint golden tan. "What about this Antonin?"

"He's the one who's turning the prefect's troops into chaos-tinged maniacs. That's why they never surrender, always fight to the death."

She pursed her lips, nodding slowly. "We'd thought it was something of the sort. There are no order-masters in Candar, not that we can find." She looked up. "I can't stay now. I really don't have time to get you settled. Would you mind waiting here for me? You could wash up, and there's some fruit over there."

378   Again, her request was not a request.

"How long?" I saw her face stiffen. "I didn't mean that. I just worry about Gairloch—my horse . . . and I'm not exactly presentable."

"Oh . . . I'll be back well before dinner."

I shrugged. She was the sub-commander, gracious as she had been. "I'll be happy to wait." Surprisingly, I was. I needed time to think. About a lot of things.

"You're certain?" She stood.

So did I. "As certain as I am about anything these days."

Then she leaned forward and gave me a friendly kiss. "I'm glad you came. Relax if you can."

The kiss was just friendly, but as she turned and left she smiled, and I wondered.

Besides wondering, I washed my hands and face, trying not to use all the water or make too much of a mess. Although curious, I did not look at any of the papers on the desk in her bedroom.

Instead, I sat down on the long couch, except that I was tired, and I was not sitting and thinking for long.

Click!

"I see you waited." Krystal's voice was cheerfully brisk, but I had trouble appreciating it, since I was trying to wake up from the afternoon nap I hadn't expected to take, realizing that it was nearly twilight.

"Long . . . meeting . . ." I yawned between words and struggled to my feet.

"There are too many long meetings these days. Will you be all right for dinner?"

"I just have to wake up. I sat down and . . . then you were back here."

Her lips quirked, and I could see a few gray hairs among the black as she stepped nearer. "Lerris . . ." Then, she shook her head. "Later. I need to change, and you need to get into something—"

"A little less travel-worn?"

"Do you have something?"

"It's plain, but I left my bags in the stable."

"I'll send—"

This time I shook my head. "They won't find them."

"I see. You have learned a few things." Her tone was light.

"So have you, lady, I expect."

"Herreld is waiting outside. Have him escort you there and back. We'll worry about a bed for you later. You can change here for dinner, if that's all right."

The word "dinner" disoriented me, after more than a year of hearing dinner as the noon meal, but I recovered and nodded. "No. Whatever's easiest."

Krystal was already heading for the door, and I followed, and just kept going, straight for the stable to recover my pack and better clothes, such as they were.

LXI

"This doorway." Krystal inclined her head toward a carved entrance flanked by two green-clad guards. She wore her sword. She probably slept with it.

Only the guards' eyes moved, checking me out, but I had left the staff in Krystal's quarters. I decided to wear the empty knife sheath, since in some principalities, failure to wear a knife carried certain implications. I didn't remember if Kyphros were one, but if it weren't, no one would care one way or the other. If my pack and staff weren't safe in Krystal's quarters, they weren't safe anywhere in Kyphrien.

"This is a small dinner. The autarch wanted to hear of your adventures." She guided me into the room.

A state dining room it was not. The imperial-style black-oak table was covered with a green linen cloth bordered in gold. The utensils were silver, and the plates were of a china nearly as fine as my mother's best. The "informal" dining room was not much bigger than my parents' dining room, nor much larger than the dining area of the waystation where I had eaten lamb chili two days earlier.

A good dozen wall lamps provided a brightness not often seen at an evening meal in Candar. I supposed the autarch could afford the extra lamp-oil.

We stopped almost after entering the room, and well short of the six people who stood talking by the bay window on the other side of the table, a window that overlooked Kyphrien and the scattered lights of the lamps and torches of the city.

"Krystal." The woman in the green silk jumpsuit with black hair shot with gray spoke.

Krystal inclined her head. "Honor."

"Would you introduce your friend?"

"This is Lerris." Krystal named the six. "Her Honor the Autarch; Guard Commander Ferrel; Public Works Minister Zeiber; Liessa, sister to Her Honor; Finance Minister Murreas; and Father Dorna."

"Honor," I murmured to the autarch. "I am honored to meet all of you." In a way, I was.

"Krystal said you were young," observed the younger woman who looked like the autarch, except her black hair was without the graying streaks. "I wouldn't have guessed from her description." The comment was made with a smile.

The Public Works Minister, thin and white-haired, only nodded, as did the Finance Minister, a heavy-set woman with square-cut short white hair who wore an ornate green tunic over equally ornate trousers.

"Peace," was the only word from Father Dorna, a functionary in

380

the religion of the one-god believers from his aura and garb of black, who radiated neither order nor disorder.

Krystal still wore green, a plain green silk blouse with no frills and a high neck, the same green leather vest, and matching green trousers—cotton, I thought. She wore no jewelry, no rings, and she looked professional, like the Autarch's champion. She walked the same way, her eyes never quite at rest.

The only one dressed more plainly than Krystal was me. My best clothes were the dark-brown cotton tunic and trousers made by Deirdre. Good as they were, certainly not of the quality of those worn by Krystal or the autarch.

"We should be seated." The autarch simply pulled out the chair at the head of the table, then pointed at the chair to her right. "Lerris, if you would."

Krystal took the seat across from me, and Father Dorna sat on my right. At the end of the table was Liessa, the only woman wearing a dress.

I attempted to seat the autarch, but she avoided the question by seating herself before my hand more than touched the back of her chair.

"No ceremony here. My name is Kasee."

I just nodded, not certain exactly what to say, as mixed greenery was placed on the plate in front of me.

"Krystal says you know something of the reasons behind the apparently senseless attacks by the Gallians."

"Some few things," I said, "and some few thoughts as to why." Since the autarch began to question me before taking a bite of the greenery on her plate, I decided that, informal dinner or not, the main course was information, and the chef was a young man named Lerris.

I looked at Krystal. While I thought I saw a momentary twinkle in her eye, her expression was polite and impassive.

"Does the name Antonin mean anything?"

". . . devil . . ." That came from my right, from the priest.

"He is reputed to be a white wizard who lives in the Westhorns," responded the autarch. I didn't think of her as Kasee then, no matter what she had said.

"He is a white wizard. He has allied himself with the prefect, or spends so much time in Fenard that he might as well be allied."

"What does he supply, exactly, to this alliance?" asked Ferrel, the white-haired Guard Commander, whose words were as precise as her plain green tunic. She and Krystal were the sole diners visibly armed.

"Chaos . . ."

"In what form, if you will? What does he gain from it?"

I took a deep breath. "I don't have all the answers . . . but . . ." I continued before the Guard Commander asked yet another question, "he opened a chaos-fountain in the guard quarters in Fenard. The fountain had the effect of submerging reason, since reason is a function of order. The fountain made the soldiers more obedient to commands issued with a—I guess you'd say—chaos-link. I mean, they're more likely to fight and kill blindly."

I could feel Krystal's concern behind her impassive face.

"How did you discover this?"

After forcing myself to take a sip from the crystal goblet and discovering it contained redberry, I answered. "I felt it from where I worked in Fenard. So I—well, it's really not that simple. You see, if Krystal hasn't told you, I left Recluce as a dangergelder. My charge was to reach the Westhorns and to make a decision as to whether I would serve order or chaos blindly. I had a . . . few problems . . . along the way . . ."

No one commented. So I kept going. "When I got to Fenard, I needed time to think . . . and money. That was why I took up wood-crafting again while I tried to work things out. The chaos in and around Fenard kept increasing, not so much that it was that noticeable at first. Antonin—his coach began appearing at the palace more and more. More and more cavalry troops were raised and sent against Kyphros. The quarterly tax levies were raised, doubled in fact." I stopped and took another sip from the goblet, then used the fork on the greenery. Everyone else was eating. I could as well.

"Could you explain the form of the chaos this . . . Antonin . . . used?" asked Ferrel.

"I don't know that I could name it, but it feels white with an ugly red core." I sipped the redberry again. "And it chills me right through."

"You can feel it?" the priest demanded.

"Any order-master could. That's how strong he is."

The servant I barely saw began removing the empty salad plates. Mine was still mostly full. I took another bite.

"Why is this any more dangerous than any other weapon—or the fires that the white wizards throw against our troops?" The Guard Commander was persistent.

"Because it will destroy you from within," I snapped, angry at her apparent denseness.

"Ser . . ." Her voice hardened.

"Ferrel." The autarch's voice was ice. Even I shut my mouth. She looked at me. "I suspect I know what you mean, order-master, but would you explain your last statement."

I swallowed, wondering if I could really put what I felt in words. "All right. Please excuse me if I'm not clear. You have to understand that much of this is new to me, and that very few masters this side of Recluce have been permitted to learn it . . ."

"Permitted?"

I ignored the question from the Finance Minister, figuring that only the Autarch counted. "The strength of chaos is that destruction can be focused. Order cannot be concentrated in the same way. Likewise, order is a passive defense, in that chaos cannot destroy absolute order. Absolute order precludes chaos, but only by restricting its presence from where there is already order."

". . . gobbledygook . . ."

I ignored that also, trying to find the words. "What Antonin is doing is creating a greater potential for chaos in both countries. By sending out Gallian troops to their deaths, he increases anger in Gallos, both at the prefect and at Kyphros. He increases anger and disorder in Kyphros. By increasing disorder, he makes more people susceptible to chaos and less willing to abide by the rules of order, more willing to become part of the killing. I don't know the complete link, but as the disorder increases, so do his powers." My stomach twisted as I began to realize what part I had unwittingly played in Antonin's game.

"I see." The autarch's voice was cold. "If you are correct, we cannot win. If we defend ourselves, we increase the disorder, and if we do not, we perish, and our suffering and deaths will thus increase the disorder."

I wished she had not put it that way.

"Why has not mighty Recluce opposed this great white wizard?" asked Liessa, her voice cutting.

Krystal looked at me. "Do you know?"

I thanked her with my eyes for the direct question. "I do not know for certain the answer to that question. I do know that Recluce seldom

383

meddles with nations other than the coastal trading powers." Even that evasion turned my guts again.

I was reprieved, momentarily, from more twisting by the arrival of the main course—skewered and highly-spiced lamb.

"You are saying that this wizard has no real military aims at all, then?"

"His aims are power for himself, and the white wizards who follow him. He would destroy both your countries, I think, to increase those powers."

"All of this is very theoretical and philosophical," interjected the Public Works Minister. "Could you tell us what, specifically, you have done against this danger? If you have done anything besides observe, that is."

Instead of snapping at him, I chewed and swallowed the lamb cube in my mouth. If I were paying this highly for my meal, I deserved to eat some of it. The only problem was that no one else talked while I ate, and the silence was leaden. I ended up opening my mouth again after several more bites. "I have done what I could. I destroyed the chaos-fountain, and, although I did not mean to, also created the events that led to the death of a score or more of the prefect's more chaos-ridden troops, including the sub-prefect."

"You did not mean to stop chaos?" demanded the priest in a high voice.

I sighed. Explaining the intricacies was getting more and more dangerous, and I knew none of the people except Krystal. While not a one manifested chaos or disorder, they could easily order my death for less fantastic reasons.

"You sound almost exasperated, young order-master," observed the autarch. "Perhaps you could explain your feelings first."

Shrugging, I turned to her. She was the judge, anyway. "You have to understand that I am not from Kyphros, nor from Gallos. A crafter in Gallos took me in, and enabled me to learn more of both order and woodworking. The disorder threatened his family. I employed order to strengthen honestly his business and his health. I also, being what I am, could not but help embody some order in the chairs and cabinets and tables I produced." I turned to Krystal. "Would you recall what occurs when a black staff strikes chaos?"

She did not quite frown, but paused. "Doesn't the staff burn someone possessed of disorder?"

I nodded, then I grinned, looking around the table. "My first mistake was to craft some black-oak chairs for the sub-prefect. My second error was to make them as perfect as I could and to infuse them with order to strengthen them."

They all looked puzzled.

"What do you think happened when the chaos-tainted advisors of the prefect sat in those chairs?"

"Ha!"

"Ohhhhh . . ."

I nodded. "That meant I had to leave Gallos, but I could not leave the crafter unprotected. After all, the chairs would be traced in time to his shop. So I entered the palace in an attempt to do something—what, I was not sure. That didn't work out because I found that attempting to force order on anyone unwilling to receive it is difficult at best. I did neutralize the chaos-fountain and turned it back into mere decoration. Then I left Fenard and came to Kyphros."

"Did you have anything to do with the death of the white wizard?" That question came from Ferrel. She sounded vaguely amused. Why, I couldn't imagine.

"That was a lucky accident." I tried to stuff another lamb cube into my mouth before answering another question.

"Accident?"

"Well . . ." I mumbled, before gulping the piece of lamb. The meat burned and scraped all the way down my throat. "All I wanted to do was to let the two Kyphran captives free. But the wizard kept throwing white fire at me . . . and his fire and my staff collided too close to him."

"How did that happen?" Ferrel was almost smiling, I could have sworn.

"I charged him . . ."

"Do you have a warhorse, order-master? A charger?"

"No. Just a pony."

Someone sniggered.

Ferrel glared at Liessa, who paled. That surprised me. Then she turned to the Autarch, who looked amused, rather than surprised, and added, "It sounds fantastic, but it happened that way. Except for one detail. No one saw our friend here. Is this yours?" She held up my belt knife.

I nodded.

385

"The unseen wizard who defeated the white wizard cut the bonds of my lieutenant, left the knife in her hands, and told her to cut the other captive free. She did not see the charge, but she did hear the white wizard screaming about an unseen armed man. She also saw the fire bolts striking against something until one exploded right in front of the wizard. Our friend here—or someone dressed exactly like him and riding a pony exactly like his—appeared for just an instant."

She handed me the knife, which I quickly replaced in the empty sheath.

"You didn't tell me all of that," Krystal added dryly.

I think I flushed. "It seemed pretty dumb. I never meant to take on a full white wizard. It just happened."

"What are you intending to do next?"

"I don't know. I just don't know." Except I did. So, of course, I had to tell them, or suffer indigestion. "I don't have much choice. I have to go find Antonin."

"The Great White Wizard?"

"Yes."

386   Ferrel looked at the autarch, and the autarch looked at Krystal. After that, they let me finish my dinner. I mean, what else was there to say? They did talk, finally, among themselves.

"Has he always been this modest?" Ferrel smiled as she asked Krystal.

"He was never boastful, but he seems more quiet."

"I still don't understand about Recluce." The voice of the Finance Minister was sharp.

"Perhaps the sub-commander or the order-master could answer your question," suggested the autarch. "Krystal? We ought to let our guest have a few moments' peace."

A wry look flashed across Krystal's face before she spoke. "Recluce is governed by the Brotherhood. They are black order-masters. Recluce has always let chaos rule in any area outside Recluce unless the Brotherhood feels that chaos threatens or hurts Recluce. Anyone they think might ever create disorder must either leave or undergo a trial by exile to prove their commitment to the absolute order of Recluce."

"Everyone? Surely the children of the powerful . . ." questioned Murreas, the heavy-set Finance Minister.

Krystal and I exchanged glances, an exchange noted by Kasee, although she said nothing.

"No," responded Krystal after a brief hesitation. "They are true believers. I know of a case where the son of one of the highest of the Brotherhood was exiled years earlier than any other child would have been, perhaps to prove that no one is above the law."

Liessa looked at me from the other end of the table and nodded nearly imperceptibly.

Hell, all of Kyphros would know my history before I ever got out of Kyphrien, the way things were going, and there wasn't much I could do about it.

After the dinner came small cups of a hot mulled cider, along with a nut-filled pastry soaked in honey. It took my best behavior not to use my fingers to wipe up the last of the honey from the plate. I didn't want to disgrace Krystal, but I'd had few sweets since leaving home, and hadn't realized how much I had missed them.

". . . will you be staying long?"

I'd missed the first part of Minister Zeiber's question, but the intent was clear.

"No."

"And what are your plans?"

I shrugged. "To do what has to be done."

387

"This is rather ambitious. Also, rather vague."

"It is vague," I agreed cheerfully, with a growing awareness of the man's underlying venality.

Krystal's face was impassive, but I could sense the humor beneath the facade.

"I am afraid tomorrow will come early," announced Kasee the Autarch. She rose from her chair. "Krystal, thank you for sharing the order-master with us. And you, Lerris—we appreciate your candor and your willingness to enlighten us." The ruler nodded toward the Guard Commander.

"Thank you, order-master," added Ferrel, "especially for your rescue attempt and the 'accidental' charge. You saved a good score by taking out that wizard. I enjoyed returning your knife, and I won't disabuse the guard by revealing the 'accidental' nature of your success."

"I appreciate your kindness, and your retrieving my knife."

Ferrel nodded and followed the autarch out. We were right behind, but, outside the dining room, in the wide red-oak paneled hallway, the Autarch and Ferrel headed right. I followed Krystal to the left, down the dimly-lit halls, feet echoing in the hushed corridors.

In time, we reached Krystal's quarters, where the faithful Herreld waited. He had the door opened even before we had finished turning the last corner.

"That will be all, Herreld."

He looked at me and back at Krystal.

"If I need anything, I'll ring the order desk." Her smile was pleasant, but formal. "Good night."

"Good night, commander."

Thunk!

Krystal dropped the heavy bar in place with the ease of long practice.

"He wasn't too pleased to see me come in."

Krystal didn't answer the question, instead unbelted her sword and carried it into her bedroom.

Thud . . . thud . . . The "thuds" came from the heavy boots, not the sword.

She returned barefoot, still wearing the blouse, vest, and trousers she had on at dinner. "Let's sit on the balcony for a little while."

Outside, a cool breeze caressed my face. Krystal took the right-hand chair and seated herself in the darkness. I sat and looked over the railing. There seemed to be more lamps in the guard yard below than in what else I could see of Kyphrien. Even the area below seemed dimly-lit for the guard force of a capital city.

"People go to bed early."

"The price of candles and lamp-oil has doubled since mid-summer."

"Oh . . . the war?"

Krystal snorted. "Oil comes mainly from Spidlar or Certis, and the prefect won't let the merchants cross Gallos to reach us. He also has an agreement with the Viscount of Certis. Between the two of them and the merchants' greed . . ."

"Food?"

"We eat a lot of goats, cheese, and olives these days. And beans. We mustn't forget the beans."

"You sound tired."

"I *am* tired, Lerris. We all are. Me, Ferrel, Liessa, and especially Kasee. She's aged ten years in the past year. Dealing with Murreas alone is no banquet, but we need her as much as the Finest." She leaned back on the balcony chair in the darkness, her voice low.

"Obtaining the best troops money can buy?" That had to be the strategy. While Kyphrans like Shervan and Pendril were fine people, they didn't make the disciplined force necessary to pick off Antonin's madmen one at a time.

"It's getting harder and harder, and we're paying three times what the new Duke of Freetown offers. Right now the Finest are two score short."

I didn't know what to say. Instead, I reached over and squeezed her leg, just above the knee, trying to send a little order and strength her way.

"Thank you. Sometimes . . ."

I wished she had finished the sentence. There wasn't enough light to see her face, and my order-senses didn't read facial expressions well. Only a faint wistful longing surrounded her.

"You wish what?" I finally asked.

"That some things had been different. That I were younger. Or . . ."

Again, she left the sentence unfinished, and I didn't ask.

"Sometimes, I do too," I found myself answering.

"You need to find some answers inside yourself first, I think."

She was right. Until I dealt with Antonin, or he dealt with me, there would be no answers. I sighed.

389

"Hell, isn't it?" Her voice was dry.

I had to chuckle. I wasn't quite up to laughing, but her tone was so wry I couldn't help it. It was hell. Sitting on that cool balcony in pitch dark overlooking a city whose streets I had never walked, I talked to Krystal, the sub-commander, the autarch's champion. I looked at a doorway that had once been open, a door through which I had not dared to walk.

Why? I couldn't say. Would that door be open to me again? I didn't know that either.

"I wonder if Kyphros needs another good woodcrafter . . ." I mused instead of confronting myself.

"There aren't many good woodcrafters anywhere. There aren't many masters at anything anywhere, though."

Again, that lingering silence fell, and I heard a single set of footsteps on the stones below. In time, they died out.

"Do you like being a master of the blade?"

"Sometimes. When it's used for good."

"And the other times?"

I could feel her shrug, though she did not move from the chair.

"You try to do as little damage as possible. You can't support the best of rulers without some injustice. Wrynn never understood that."

"What happened to her?"

"Nothing. Not that I know of. She didn't stay with the Finest long. She headed toward Sarronnyn through the southern passes, looking for a place where the people were strong and fair-minded."

"Poor Wrynn." I felt sorry for her. Wherever she went, she wouldn't find what she was looking for, just like I hadn't been able to find the clear answers I so desperately wanted.

"She won't find them," Krystal confirmed, almost reading my thoughts.

"Did you find what you were looking for?" I asked, not quite idly.

"Part of it. I'm doing what I'm good at, and it has some value."

I didn't ask about the rest. One look around the dinner table would have been enough to answer that. Instead, I looked out at Kyphrien, noting that the candles, lamps, and torches were fewer now, as more and more citizens went to bed, stopped carousing, or whatever.

The breeze had picked up, bringing the first hint of chill since I had crossed the Little Easthorns. The faint smell of smoke came with the breeze, the smoke from torches and ill-adjusted oil lamps. Unlike Recluce, Kyphros and indeed, all of Candar, did not use coal-gas lamps.

Krystal's chair creaked. "Lerris?"

"Yes."

"I need some sleep." She stood up and stifled a yawn.

It wasn't a question, and it wasn't an invitation.

"Oh . . . sorry. I'll get my things."

"You can stay here. If you feel comfortable about it." Then she added, and I could hear the smile in her words, "That's just for sleeping."

Lonely as I felt, and much as I would have liked to hold her, and be held, she was right. Not that I liked it, but she was right. I had too many unanswered questions I had not even faced.

"Besides," she added with a short laugh, "it will add to my image."

"What? Having a poor woodworker stay overnight? That will improve your image?"

"Come on inside. You were never a poor woodworker."

"I was a terrible apprentice." I followed her in, letting her close the door. A single lamp burned in the main room.

"That was then." She gestured. "You want the bedroom or the couch? It's long enough and firm enough."

I opted for the couch, ignoring the possible play on words. The quarters were hers, after all.

"Good night." She did close her door, if gently.

Despite my unanswered questions, the couch was comfortable, and I slept more soundly than I had since leaving Fenard. I did not dream, nor wake with cold chills, nor hear the sound of coach wheels in the sky.

I did wonder, before drifting off, what had happened to the lady who had once wanted me.

LXII

I woke up early, in the chill winter grayness before true dawn with the blanket actually around my shoulders, looking at the ceiling and wondering. I had been drawn to Tamra and later to Krystal—but for different reasons, very different reasons.

Krystal was my friend, yet my dreams of her were far more than friendly. And Tamra was a spoiled bitch, yet I still dreamed of her, though less frequently of late. What had changed? Or had anything? Or did I dream of Krystal because she seemed more attainable? Or . . .

"You're a confused mess, Lerris . . ." I muttered under my breath. Acknowledging it didn't solve my confusion, but it might lead to more useful thought on the subject—assuming I had time to think about it.

As silently as I could, I sat up, glancing through the single window. A few thin wisps of smoke already rose into the cloudy sky outside. Krystal's door was shut, but she was awake or just waking up.

I stretched, knowing that going out and achieving the impossible by defeating Antonin still wouldn't resolve the questions whose answers I had sought. Was I going after Antonin in search of a glorious defeat in order to avoid admitting that there were no clear answers, or that they weren't what I wanted?

I shivered. That might be part of my problem, but it wasn't all of it. After all, Justen had mucked around the edge for centuries, probably watching white wizards like Antonin burn themselves out one after the other. That was fine, if you were after a long life, but more than two centuries after the fall of Frven, Candar was still a conflicted mass of warring duchies.

I stood up, letting the blanket fall, and gazed out at the eastern horizon, a faint red pink that subsided back into gray as I watched. Just in shorts, I wasn't even cool, not once I was awake.

Click.

Krystal stood behind me, but I didn't turn immediately.

"Good morning."

"Good morning." I left the study of Kyphrien and turned toward my hostess.

"Woodworking must be good for muscular development." She wore a once-green scuffed leather tunic over a faded shirt with green leather trousers and battered boots. Some of the tiredness was gone from her eyes.

"You're ready to go," I observed. "Some sort of hard work."

She grimaced. "Training."

Another set of pieces clicked into place in my thoughts. "You're trying to buy time while—"

She nodded. "It's not working. The losses are too high."

I understood immediately. With Antonin's chaos-support, the prefect didn't need extraordinarily well-trained soldiers. The autarch did, and after a time the numbers who could be bought shrank, and only so many had the inclination and talent, and even fewer could be trained at any one time.

Krystal presented a wry smile that held little amusement. "We do what we can." She looked at me again, and I felt embarrassed. "Much as I like the view, you need to get dressed. We eat together with the guard in the morning."

I put on my traveling clothes, including the knife that Ferrel had returned at dinner, as quickly as I could. Krystal was doing something at her desk when I peered in, staff and pack in hand, ready to go.

"Records, papers, and accounts," she explained as she pushed back the chair.

THE MAGIC OF RECLUCE

"Surely you don't have to do the accounts for the guard?"

"Chaos, no! But what tactics you can use depend on your equipment and your supplies. Not even the Finest can fight without horses or food." She kept talking as she belted on the sword and pulled on the short jacket with the braid that served as her emblem of office. "Certain tactics cause a higher death rate for horses, and mounted troops need reserve mounts. While we have a grain levy, there's a tradeoff between increasing the levy and taxing something else to buy the grain . . ." She shook her head. "I'm just beginning to understand a few of the complexities. Sometimes, fighting is the easiest part."

I nodded, thinking as we walked out the door and past the near-permanent sentry guarding her quarters. I ignored his hostile look, reflecting on what she had said. Certainly, money was important to something like woodworking, but I really hadn't thought about it as the basis for fighting and warfare.

In that light, what Antonin was doing made even more sense—unfortunately.

"You're quiet," observed Krystal, not slowing her steps one whit as she took the wide stairs down toward the ground level of the building.

"Thinking . . . Almost every day I learn something new, and it seldom answers the old questions. Just adds to the unanswered questions." My guts twisted slightly at my overstatement, and I added another few words. "That's the way it seems, but I guess that's because the answers you find seem simple compared to the new questions."

In turn, Krystal was silent.

The low-ceilinged guard mess hall contained space for more than a dozen-score guards at the long tables. Not quite half the seats were filled as we entered. Only a handful of heads turned, mostly of younger men, as Krystal marched up to the serving table.

She took a single slice of thick bread, a scoop of some sort of preserves, a slice of hard white cheese, a boiled egg, and a steaming cup of a tea so bitter that I could smell it without even nearing the huge teapot.

The cheese and egg were beyond me. I had two slices of the warm bread with the dark preserves, a battered apple, and tea.

Krystal sat at a table in the middle of the room, alone except for me. As I sat down on the worn red-oak bench next to her, I caught sight of Ferrel leaving the mess, also wearing battered leathers.

"You'll pardon me," Krystal said, with her mouth full. "I'd like to eat before business begins."

I frowned. Business?

"Any guard can approach me now, ask questions, or make suggestions. They may not be quite as forward with you here, but there will be some." She continued to munch slowly on the bread she had spread thinly with the preserves.

Me, I had slathered my bread with the sweet preserves, enjoying each bite after my days of travel. Belatedly, I realized I did not remember much of what I had eaten the night before. I had eaten, that I recalled; but besides the salad and the lamb, I didn't recall what had been on the plates.

"Commander?" ventured a hard-faced woman wearing a single thin gold stripe on the shoulder of her vest. "You sent for me?"

I almost choked, wondering when Krystal had sent for the woman, wondering if she ever slept.

"Yes, leader Yelena. Would you be interested in an escort mission?"

The sub-officer's eyes flicked from Krystal to me. "I'd like to know more."

"Where are you going, Lerris?"

I had to swallow several bites of apple and swig the too-hot tea. I didn't know exactly. What I wanted was to find the wizard's road that ran down the Little Easthorns without retracing my route from Gallos.

"I'd like to see a map," I began, "but, in general, along the old road to Sarronnyn, the one that no one uses now."

"The chaos-road?" suggested Yelena, her voice flat.

I shrugged. "I don't know what it's called. But that's where he is, beyond the point where the hidden wizards' roads connect."

Both Krystal and Yelena turned to me. "Explain," demanded the sub-commander, her voice as hard and authoritative as I had ever heard it.

"There are hidden wizards' roads throughout Candar. Sometimes the current roads are built right over the old roads built by the white wizards, but many of the old roads are hidden. There's one that runs, I think, the length of the Little Easthorns. It crosses the road from Gallos to Tellura somewhere after the top of the pass."

"Why didn't you mention this before?"

I was more than a little puzzled at her coldness. "First, you never asked. Second . . . oh, shit . . . I see what you mean . . ."

Now it was Yelena's turn to look puzzled. I thought Krystal had softened slightly.

"Logistics?" I asked. "Troop travel?"

Krystal nodded.

"I don't think it will help, but, if you get me a map, I'll show you where it goes." Another thought struck me. "But unless you have another order-master, it won't help. Where it crosses, the road is cloaked with illusions. Antonin hasn't shared the roads with anyone, but I think he uses them to let everyone think he is everywhere."

"He's been successful in that," snapped the sub-officer. "I'll get a set of maps."

Once she was out of earshot, before anyone else neared, I looked at Krystal. "I'm not a military strategist, and I don't appreciate being accused, even silently, of incompetence. I admit it. I don't know your business. Don't expect me to." I tried to soften my tone. "I know you're against the wall. I can see it. I'd never withhold information or help, not knowingly. But I'm still having trouble learning my own business, let alone trying to understand yours."

Krystal pursed her lips, then met my glance. "I'm sorry." Her tone was still flat.

"Krystal . . . the first time I could have told you about the road was last night. Could you have done anything about it any earlier? Besides, I didn't even know there were any wizards' roads in Kyphros until I found that one, and I came straight to Kyphrien."

The stiffness finally receded. "I am sorry. It's just . . ."

"It's that bad?" I asked.

"Yes. It's that bad. Maybe worse. Look around."

I did. For a long time. Then I swallowed. Fully a third of the guard were bandaged or otherwise disabled or incapacitated. Most of the sub-officers and officers were women, and most of the men were scarcely older than I was.

I should have seen it. No matter how good she was with a blade, no matter how smart and mature, a woman would not have ended up as the number-two officer in a kingdom's military force in little more than a year unless the losses were horrendous or the talent pool small. I suspected both.

"I'm sorry. I'll do what I can." I meant that not just for Krystal or for me, but because of what the people around us represented—the struggle against an old chaotic rule and an attempt at . . . I didn't exactly know how or why, but what I saw accorded with my idea of what order should be, not necessarily what Talryn or Recluce thought of as order.

"Thank you."

"Commander, why were the road-patrol rotations changed yesterday?" asked a young man with a scraggly yellow mustache.

"That's because . . ."

"Commander, will there be additional mounts . . ."

"Commander, how do we get the duty rotation . . ."

"Commander . . ."

I edged away, letting Krystal deal with the guards who approached, marveling at her patience and understanding.

Yelena walked in carrying a long leather tube. I gestured to her, and commandeered a near-empty table.

"Do you have one that shows the border beyond the Southbrook?"

After sifting through the parchments, she laid an older map on the table, smoothing it out. Some of the mountains were named, and the road line matched what I remembered, but the pattern of the peaks was not complete.

396

I measured roughly, thought, and measured.

Finally, I noted an area. "In this area, and it runs due east and west . . ." I tried to describe the thin valley that she should be able to see beyond the illusions, and what the road looked like, and how the long-gone wizards of Frven had planed off the sides of mountains to build their roads. But they had used order as well, somehow. Chaos to destroy the mountains and to create the hidden road valleys, and order to reinforce the stonework and the bridges.

"Can you pass that on to someone else?" asked Krystal.

I hadn't realized she had stood behind us.

"I think so," responded Yelena. "You still want me to escort the order-master?"

"If you would find that acceptable."

Yelena nodded. "How many, and when do we leave?"

"Two plus yourself." Krystal looked to me for the second answer.

"Shortly. The sooner we leave, the sooner . . ." I didn't know what would be sooner, or even what exactly I might discover, but all of us were running out of time.

"Where are we headed?" asked Yelena.

Explaining that took a bit longer, and more struggle with the maps, but there was an old road that *looked* like it went where I wanted and, if the maps were correct, joined with the old main central pass road that led to Sarronnyn. That was the road that no one took any longer because they never seemed to arrive on the other side of the Westhorns.

Finally, I looked up. "That's the best I can do."

"Yelena?"

"It will be interesting, commander."

Interesting—that was one way of putting it.

"Well . . . I guess I'll get Gairloch."

"What . . . do you have a mount?"

"Oh . . . Gairloch is in the stables by the gate."

"We will meet you there." Yelena inclined her head to Krystal. "Honor, commander."

"Honor, leader."

I followed Krystal from the mess into the main guard yard, where we stopped in an open space.

"Make sure you're doing this for yourself, Lerris."

I shook my head. "Nothing's that simple."

"I guess not." She smiled with her mouth, not her eyes. "Then, try to do it mostly for your reasons."

"I'll do what I must, and we'll sort out the reasons later. All right?"

She nodded. "Fair enough. I won't say to take care. But . . . do come back to sort out those reasons."

I wet my lips, feeling the cool wind chill them as I did. With all that I felt, there was little to say. "Until later."

"Until later."

I looked down, then back into her black eyes, seeing the tiredness again.

She raised her hand in a gesture that was part benediction, part salute, and I inclined my head to her, then turned while I could. I did not look back, but kept my eyes fixed on the building that was the stable.

Yelena and two others waited, already mounted, as I walked up with my staff and pack.

"Where's your pass?" demanded the ostler.

"Oh, hell . . ." I had never bothered to get anyone to sign the damned parchment square. "Just a moment."

"Leader Yelena?"

"Yes, order-master?"

"I forgot to have the sub-commander autograph this pass."

"Autograph?"

I kept from shaking my head at the brown-haired sub-officer with the long nose and square chin. "A pass to release my horse."

"Pheww on a pass! Get your horse." She rode into the stable in front of me.

". . . on official business for the Sub-Commander. None of this crap about passes!"

The ostler was backing into a corner as Yelena threatened to ride him down.

I ignored them both and quickly saddled Gairloch, recovering my saddlebags in the process.

The ostler swallowed as I rode out. "Good . . . day . . . order-master . . ."

"Good day." My tone was not totally cheerful. I hadn't wanted to pay for the stable, since my stock of coinage was scarcely deep, and having to ask for Yelena's assistance bothered me.

398   "That's a horse?" asked the sub-officer.

"No, this is Gairloch. You don't think I could really ride one of those monsters you use, do you?" I grinned at the dour officer.

"Glad you recognize it, order-master." I almost fell off Gairloch when she smiled back.

The other two looked at each other and kept their mouths closed as we rode out through the gates into Kyphrien.

Even in the gray drizzle that had begun to fall, the city was light— whitewashed walls, red tile roofs, and limestone- or marble-paved streets. People talked, like a city of hundreds of Shervans.

". . . best breads in Kyphros, by exclusive patronage of the autarch . . ."

". . . and you could have crossed the river barefoot, he drank so much. Never have I seen an animal drink so much, and beyond that . . ."

"Your fortune, not even a copper! Who will grudge a mere copper for knowing all that will befall you."

"Hezira, I said, there's to be none of that. No, none of that, Hezira—that's what I told her, but, of course, she didn't listen. Why would she listen, with her high house and her silk gowns? . . ."

I eased Gairloch closer to Yelena. "Is it always this noisy?"

"No." She shook her head. "It's usually noisier. This is early. It gets louder later."

"Look at the pony! See the pony, Berrna! He must be a northern pony. He's so shaggy . . ."

Outside of the Autarch's walled residence—not really a castle or even a palace—and the associated guard area, Kyphrien was an open and unwalled city, where the houses and businesses scattered further and further apart as we headed north and west toward the Westhorns I could not see. There never was a point at which I could have said Kyphrien ended and the countryside began, but we were on another gently rolling road even before mid-morning.

The drizzle had damped the dust, but not yet turned it into mud. Gairloch matched the pace set by the brown gelding carrying Yelena without seeming to strain, and we traveled through the morning without talking, which was fine with me, especially after the hubbub that had been Kyphrien.

Yet I liked the country, found it friendly, even if it were not as lush as Gallos or even Recluce. The spareness of the colder and rolling hills, which steepened within kays to the northwest of Kyphrien, appealed to me. I even noted several locations that would have been ideal for setting up my own woodworking—with streams high enough for a water supply, not far from the road, and with ample and varied timber within carting distance.

I shook my head—planning to be a workworker, still? Uncle Sardit would surely have laughed. How well he had wrought he did not know. Or maybe he did, and I was the one who didn't know.

Thoughts of working wood would have to wait. If I could deal somehow with Antonin . . . if . . .

I cast my thoughts back over my last encounter—the one with the white wizard—recalling how I had fought with the staff to control my defenses and my energies. What had that meant?

There had been something in the book . . . something . . . . I could not recall it, but made a mental note to look it up.

Mid-day found us halting beside a stream that bordered the road, but we did not actually cross it.

"That's not really a bridle," noted the young man who had followed behind me. "How do you control him in a pinch?"

"I never thought about it." I pulled out some hard white cheese and offered him a piece.

399

Wheeee . . . eeee . . .

Yelena was watering her horse, and, deciding that Gairloch was thirsty as well, I looped the reins over the saddle and thwacked him on the flank, watching as he ambled into the water ankle-deep.

The soldier had taken the cheese, but he looked away suddenly as Gairloch left me.

The other trooper, a woman probably my own age, with short sandy hair and green eyes, surprisingly dark skin, and a ragged scar running across most of her right cheek, stepped closer.

"Cheese?" I offered.

"Thank you." Her voice was simultaneously grave and cheerful. "Are you . . . the . . . order-master? . . ."

I grinned. Why not? "I'm Lerris. Yes, I'm the one from Recluce who knew the sub-commander. She's my friend."

Her eyebrows rose, and I could imagine the stories already circulating through the guard.

"In addition to being a blademaster," I added, "she is also a lady. And my friend."

"I didn't mean . . ."

I waved her apology off. "Rumors are rumors. I care for the lady a lot, but that's all until we have done what has to be done. Then we'll see."

"Are all the men from Recluce like you?"

". . . Aaaccccuuu . . ." I almost choked on the cheese. ". . . No. Probably none of them are as dense as I am."

"The order-master is joking, Freyda," interrupted Yelena. Her voice was cold, but her eyes were smiling. "You'd better water your horse. We're not stopping that long. You, too, Weldein."

When the two were out of earshot, the sub-officer looked at me. "You're more dangerous than you look." But she was almost smiling.

I shrugged. "I can't not tell the truth, and that makes it difficult."

"You can't?"

"Not without paying for it somehow."

She was the one to shake her head. "I'm glad I'm just a leader."

As I reclaimed Gairloch and fed him some corners of a grain cake, I thought about what she said. I had to agree with her. The more I learned and the more I could do, the more complex it got.

LXIII

Kyphros was bigger than I thought. The way the Westhorns angled westward as they marched south meant that we had to ride two days to reach the foothills that almost matched the Little Easthorns in size.

I had guessed that at some point the road, since it was an older road, would cross the wizards' road for which I searched. I didn't know that, but it seemed right.

The first night we actually stayed in a small inn in a town—Upper River. Why it was called Upper River, no one knew, and Yelena's maps showed neither Lower River, or even a stream called Upper River. The inn was clean. That was about all. Dinner was overcooked goat steaks smothered in a strong cheese. The beds sagged, and I shared a room with Weldein, who by then was scared stiff of me, although I had said nothing, and who snored loudly.

The second night we stopped in a place called Quessa. Lodging was in one of the soldiers' way stations there, but staffed only by a couple. I could guess where the soldiers were. The dinner meal was another spicy casserole, followed by a huge fruitcream pie—much better fare than at the inn at Upper River.

Quessa itself was fair-sized for the relatively isolated area in which it stood, with more than a score of houses and stores serving the surrounding farms and orchards. The people were still what I thought of as Kyphran stock, with dark skin, darker hair, and broad smiles. They also talked and talked.

I retreated to the large guest room, the one that Tella and Bardon insisted I must have, and closed the door. The lamp by the double-wide bed was bright enough to read by, and I had some reading to do.

It didn't take long, and all that I found was what I had remembered, a single paragraph, not even a long one. The key words were simple: "Order cannot be concentrated in and of itself, not even within the staff of order, and no man can truly master the staff of order until he casts it aside."

Except the words were wrong, somehow. No matter where my staff was, it still gathered order and repulsed chaos. For a long time,

I looked through the pages of the book, but nothing else shed light on that paragraph.

After I replaced the black-covered and well-thumbed pages in my pack, I stared into emptiness. The pieces were there—that I knew. How they fit, I didn't. The white wizard had died when my staff had touched his fingertips, or at least when it had gotten close. The staff had been nearly as close to other sources of chaos without that violent a reaction, and if a simple staff could destroy a chaos-wizard someone would have gone against Antonin long before. Unless there were reasons to maintain chaos . . .

I didn't like that thought at all.

So I tried to sort out my feelings about Deirdre, Krystal, and Tamra, but the thought of sorting out those three was enough to exhaust me on the spot, and I blew out the lamp and slept, sort of, until the gray of dawn crept through the window.

The next day brought more talking over breakfast. The trip carried us into wilder countryside, with the end of the orchards and fenced fields. The clouds had dissipated, but the chill remained, and we rode in a bright chill toward the unseen Westhorns. By mid-morning, the road straggled through underbrush that had begun to reclaim the less time-trampled edges of the road, and the lands beyond the road that had once been grazing lands were dotted with mature trees and scattered brush, including thickets upon thickets of wild redberries.

A sense of unease lay over the road, growing as we climbed each of the ever-steepening hills.

Yelena's face grew tighter with each hill, and the bigger horses strained and began to puff. On a particularly high hillcrest where the road was wider, perhaps because the hummock of stones and fallen timbers looming in the brush back from the north side of the road might have been an inn or road house in times past, I motioned for the sub-officer to stop.

For the first time, looking to the west, I could see the white-tipped dark bulk of the Westhorns. Even from where we had halted, still a good thirty kays from the foothills beneath those massive slopes, I could also see that they were indeed impressive, and that at least another day of riding lay before me.

"We're getting close, I think. I can feel chaos ahead."

Yelena squinted against the cold bright sunlight. "We're still quite a ways from the Westhorns."

"I can make it from here. You're needed against Gallos."

Yelena shook her head. "Order-master, what would happen if I had to tell the sub-commander that we left you this far short of the Westhorns?"

I sighed. She was right. "All right. Let's go. But if there's too much chaos ahead, I want to be able to send you back."

"Why?"

"Because I might have trouble protecting you." I laughed harshly. "I might have trouble protecting myself."

The chaos I sensed seemed to recede as we rode westward. Either that, or it was stronger and more distant than I had thought.

By nightfall, we still seemed scarcely closer to the base of the Westhorns, although we could see some of the nearer peaks, their ice-covered spires glinting rosy in the sunset.

We camped in another long-deserted farm, sheltered by a single standing stone wall. I set wards, but nothing woke me, and the fourth morning of the trip dawned as gray as the morning when we had left Kyphrien.

I wondered how many more had died on the hills of Northern Kyphros while I rode on my fool's errand toward the Westhorns. Then, again, what else could I do? No warrior, I could but try to bring order where I might.

In a way, that was similar to woodworking, except in crafting I built upon the natural order, whereas in order-mastery—I thought—I tried to strengthen natural order to repulse an unnatural disorder.

"Cheese?" I offered some to Weldein, absent-mindedly.

He took it, equally abstracted, as he looked from the hillside, where we had camped not far from a small brook, toward the mountains. Then he looked at the white cheese, as if wondering how he got it.

"Eat it. It's good cheese. A mill-master gave it to me."

"Why?"asked Freyda.

"Because I helped his goddaughter."

"Was she pretty?" Weldein inquired. His tone was polite.

"Very. Unfortunately," I added.

The two exchanged glances, and, for some reason Weldein blushed.

"She didn't like you?" That was Yelena.

"She did like me."

"If she was pretty . . ." Weldein sounded confused.

I really didn't want to explain, but I sighed and went on. "I found her attractive. She was capable and bright. That just made it worse."

"So you left her for duty?" Yelena asked. "How noble . . ."

"No." My voice was cold, but I couldn't help it. "I left because I had a job to do, and because I realized there was someone else still in my heart, and because . . ." I broke off. What I would have said would have sounded unforgivably pompous. So I shut up. It was probably true, but it was arrogant.

This time all three exchanged knowing glances, and things were even worse.

"What about the goddaughter?"

"I found her a good-looking and talented husband who loved her, and provided a dowry, and we both cried like hell."

That shut them up, but I felt petty about it as we packed the horses for the coming day's ride. Finally, I stepped over to Yelena. "I'm sorry. I didn't mean . . ."

She smiled, as softly as I had seen her smile, and touched my arm briefly. "Don't be. It's good to see that great order-masters are human, that they love, and make mistakes."

I shook my head. "I'm not a great order-master."

Yelena swung onto her brown gelding. "Then there are none."

I pondered that as I climbed onto Gairloch. Perhaps that was the problem, that there simply were no great order-masters to combat the great chaos-masters like Antonin. Then I frowned. A simple solution, too simple. And simple and easy answers were almost always wrong.

By mid-morning, the feeling of impending chaos was stronger, much stronger, and not receding.

The road had not been used in some time, except for a single rider whose prints appeared now and again in the sheltered spots in the clay. How long since the prints had been made, I could not tell. Nor could Yelena.

"We have not had a great rain since summer." She pursed her lips.

I could feel the energy ahead, perhaps as near as over the next hill-crest.

Overhead, heavy gray clouds rolled.

Thurummmm . . .

No rain fell as we rode up the especially-steep hill.

"Stop," I said, feeling the chaos pressure. "There's something ahead."

"Armed men?"

"No." I sent my perceptions forward, but could only detect a small hump in the road, somehow tied down with chaos. Nothing else. "I think it's all right for now."

The hump was a body, or what was left of it.

Yelena rode almost up to the figure, then dismounted, standing back from face-down remains. "Outlier's belt."

"Careful . . . there's chaos there."

The sub-officer nodded. "I know. We've seen this before." She drew her sword and touched the body. A bright blue spark flashed against the steel. She glanced at me. "That's another trick of the white wizards."

Even from where Gairloch and I had stopped, the heat from the spark momentarily warmed the chill noontime air..

She used the sword to lever the body over onto its back. The Kyphran soldier's face was a charred and shattered mass—the target of a fireball thrown by Antonin or Sephya or some other chaos wizard.

I could guess what happened. The outlier had been lured or charmed this far out and then destroyed.

"Chaos fed on him. Too bad we can't feed on chaos. We'd never go hungry any more." She motioned to Weldein. "Let's take care of this. Not much time, but there are stones there."

In the end, all of us created a cairn by the side of the deserted road.

As we remounted, Yelena's remark got me thinking. In a way, chaos fed on chaos. The stronger Antonin became, the more he could destroy, which increased the amount of chaos in Candar. In the whole world, really. If the old masters were right, increased chaos had to be balanced *somewhere* with increased order.

I swallowed hard. If what I thought was true was in fact true, Talryn and the Brotherhood had a lot to answer for, one hell of a lot.

That didn't resolve my particular problem. While I was getting stronger, Justen had been right. It was a slow process. Antonin could literally tear holes in mountains and buildings and infect whole cavalry troops with chaos. It would be years, if ever, before I could confront Antonin directly—and that wouldn't help Krystal or the autarch, or the people of either Gallos or Kyphros.

Justen's method was clear. He kept reinforcing low-level order everywhere around Antonin, from healing in Jellico to sheep-ranching in Montgren. That order limited the indirect spillover of chaos and protected most of the innocents. Just as clear was the fact that Antonin was willing to let all of that low-level order build up, because it allowed him to increase his powers. Which, in turn, let Justen exercise his powers . . .

I rubbed my temples with my fingertips. Was the whole thing an exercise in circles? Was any wizard, white or black, really being honest about it? Was this the reason why no one had answered the questions behind my questions?

"What now, order-master?"

I understood. Now she had the reason to be dismissed—and Krystal needed them in the Northeast more than I needed them here.

"This is as far as you go, sub-officer. This is where chaos starts."

"Are you sure?"

I nodded, wanting to ensure that all of them carried the same message back. "I can't protect you and search for the white wizard, not without endangering us all. I thank you for the escort, for the company, and for your understanding."

"Thank you, ser."

"Thank you . . ."

Yelena held back a moment when the other two turned their mounts. "We'd like to see you again, ser." Then, the hardness returned to her face, as the discipline reasserted itself.

I watched the three until they were out of sight, checking to make sure no chaos waited for them, but I could detect none—not in that direction.

Toward the Westhorns—that was another question. Supposedly, the old road should cross the wizard's road before too long. Supposedly . . . but things never quite turned out as they were supposed to. And when they did, I was finding that I wished they hadn't.

A cold wind blew from nowhere, almost more in my mind than across that high slope where I began the last, solitary part of my quest—if quest were what it was. Why was I traveling a near-abandoned road toward a wizard who had swatted me aside like a fly the last time we had met? What did I think that I could possibly accomplish when Talryn or Justen had been able to do nothing?

Then again, had they really tried? Who was telling the truth? Or was anyone?

I shivered, but Gairloch lifted his head, as if to say we should get on with it.

LXIV

Another five kays beyond the hill where I had helped bury the un-named and unknown Kyphran outlier and where I had separated from my escort, barely into the edge of the foothills, the old road crossed the wizards' road.

I didn't even have to look for illusions. I did cast my perceptions around and found traces of older chaos, indicating that, at one time, some magic had been cast to cloak the road. That had been seasons, if not years, earlier. I shivered. That Antonin saw no reason to hide his road was chilling in itself.

The unnatural valley ran straight east and west, and the trace of coach wheels ran straight and true down the center of the road. Hoof-prints, recent ones, flanked the wheel traces.

I took a deep breath. Suddenly, I had to ask myself what I was doing in the middle of a wilderness looking for a chaos-master. I didn't have an answer.

Instead, still damning myself for a fool, I turned Gairloch onto that clay-covered and white-paved road and threw my senses ahead of me. Then, remembering what I had done earlier, I used the shield that reduced the ability of a chaos-master to discern the order I repre-sented. That shield left us fully visible, but the greater danger was from white magicians, not from ordinary or even chaos-touched sol-diers.

In the distance, actually into the Westhorns themselves, there was another lurking mass of chaos energy, but nothing nearby. Nothing— not wild pigs, not goats, and definitely not people. About what one would expect around an isolated wizards' road. For now, that was fine with me.

Even on Gairloch, as opposed to a coach, riding on the even sur-face was considerably speedier than on the old road from Kyphrien. Despite what I recalled from my conversations with Justen, I found it hard to believe that the wizards' road could have lasted so long. Then again, only the road and the heavy stone bridges had really endured, and Justen had said that the construction had been done by honest stonemasons reinforced with black order-masters, before . . . something had happened.

Once again, I hadn't quite gotten the whole story.

By twilight, we had traveled nearly into the lower reaches of the Westhorns themselves, and those lower mountains loomed so high into the western sky that we had ridden the entire late afternoon in shadow. Their distant pinnacles glittered with reflected light, a cruel white that made the peaks a fitting home for chaos.

Not that I had wanted to ride poor Gairloch as long as I had, but it was twilight before there was a canyon away from the road that both had water, and was passable enough for us to get well clear of the wizards' way itself.

We struggled up a rock and grass slope, around a bend, and behind another boulder before I felt we were removed enough from casual scrutiny.

Whheeee . . . eeee . . . Gairloch was nuzzling at the saddlebags even before I had them off. His nose was wet—and cold from the brook water that felt like liquid ice.

"Don't drink any more," I snapped. A lot of really cold water wouldn't do him much good.

I even touched him and let my feelings run through his system. He either hadn't drunk that much or could handle it. Still, I worried; but then, I was worrying about everything.

He took the grain cake as soon as it appeared, almost including my fingers in the first greedy bite.

"Gairloch!"

He didn't pay much attention, but I hadn't really expected that he would.

After dried fruit, travel bread, and the last of the white cheese, I laid out the bedroll under an overhang. The sky was clear, the stars sparkling like faraway lanterns in the blackness; a chill wind whistled down the canyon. I slept inside the bedroll.

The stream gurgled, and I slept—in a way. I dreamed that I was refereeing a fencing match between Krystal and a white knight, except that the white knight was Antonin, and he kept throwing fireballs at me, and laughing. Every time he threw a fireball, Krystal looked at me and stopped fencing, and he would slash her on her blade arm, until her arm was dripping red. The dream seemed to last all night, and I woke in cold sweats, although the dawn was filled with ice. Frost covered the grass, and a thin layer of rime ice covered even the fast-moving waters of the brook.

The season wasn't quite winter, and in the low Westhorns it was colder than the coldest of days in Recluce, or most days in Kyphrien, I suspected.

Wheeee . . . Gairloch's breath was a white cloud.

"I'm getting up."

When I started moving, I was warm enough, though.

After giving Gairloch a little grain and letting him graze on the sparse grass, I did my own munching on the remaining dried apples from Brettel. My supplies were low, probably less than an eight-day of trail food, but one way or another, I wouldn't need more than that.

The apples weren't enough, and I opened the wax on the last package of cheese, a brick yellow cheese harder and less tasty than the white. The trail bread helped, but I limited what I ate and re-packed the rest.

Then—carefully—I reached out with my senses to the wizards' road. It was as deserted as the night before, with no sign of use.

Long before the sun cleared the hills behind us, Gairloch and I were riding deeper into the Westhorns, deeper along the narrow and artificial valley.

409

In time, having seen nothing unusual, and having sensed nothing beyond the traces of chaos on the road, we began to near the mass of chaos-energies I had first sensed the afternoon before, somewhere on the other side of an even narrower gap in the huge rock wall that, except for the path of the wizards' road, seemed to block any westward passage.

Wheeee. Gairloch tossed his head, as if in warning.

Ahead, the pass opened wide in the morning sun, the sun that warmed my back, grassy slopes rising gently, then ending abruptly on both sides against the rock and crags that distinguished the Westhorns from the lesser mountains of Candar. The pass was avoided by almost everyone—that much was clear from the gravel and clay that held only the traces of Antonin's passage. A few low thornberries and scrub ash bushes grew alongside the road, with its unvarying width of more than fifteen cubits.

In casting my perceptions ahead, I could sense nothing. Nothing. Not even rock, or trees.

"Hellfire . . ." I muttered, realizing what that meant.

Antonin couldn't distort what I saw, but he could prevent my sensing anything at all, except for the feel of chaos itself. That meant there was something to sense.

Just for the hell of it, I would have liked to create a good solid thunderstorm, but with chaos ahead, using the energy wasn't a good idea. Besides, while I still resented Justen's comments about frivolity becoming chaos, I had listened. And I couldn't think of an orderly reason for the rain. Had there been an artificially-caused drought, use of my talents to create rain might enhance order. Maybe.

Wheeee . . . uhhhh . . . wheeee . . .

Gairloch's protest jerked my head back toward the road that slowly rose before us for perhaps another kay. Studying the few trees, scraggly conifers and pines growing at helter-skelter intervals from out of the knee-high mountain grass, I could see nothing lurking around or behind them. Nor was anything visible on the upslope before us.

Right-handed, I flicked the reins. "Come on. We really don't have anywhere else to go, old fellow."

Whheee.

"No, we don't." I extended my left hand toward the staff, still safe and waiting in the saddle holder. "Oooo . . ." The subjective heat flashed to my fingers even before they reached the black lorken of my staff.

Something was definitely waiting over the crest of the road.

I wiped my forehead, suddenly sweating in the cold glare of the winter sun.

Wheeee . . . eee . . .

"I know. There are evil types in front of us."

Again, I tried to sense what lay over the hill-crest before me, whatever it was that Gairloch disliked. All I could feel was a sense of heat, of the fire that was Antonin's trademark.

· I glanced at the hillside to the left and right of the road. Did I really have to keep to it?

A quick survey answered that question. All those short and gently-sloping meadows ended in piles of jumbled rock at the base of rocky slopes that would have taxed a mountain sheep.

I looked again, realizing belatedly what had happened, shaking my head as I did. Once the pass had been a standard narrow gap—or just a solid wall of rock. Then, someone, something, a long time ago, perhaps as far back as when Candar had been united under the wizards of Fairhaven, had blasted through. Not only had they built the wizards' road, but they had rearranged the entire geography.

Maybe, just maybe, Magistra Trehonna had been right. I definitely didn't like that thought.

With the help of the weather and time, the sheer facings had crumbled, leaving what seemed a narrow natural ravine running into the Westhorns. But any crumbled rock had been periodically removed from the road surface. Under Gairloch's hooves was the same white road surface—the same wizard stone—that paved the streets of Frven.

Not that any of that exactly helped as Gairloch and I proceeded toward the crest of the pass, toward that narrow gap in the sheer stone wall that towered hundreds of cubits upward.

Wheeee . . .

On the edge of the hard surface lay a brownish square, the tattered remains of a pack or something, and, in the higher grass behind . . . fragments of white. I swallowed.

Wheeeee . . . eeeee . . . Gairloch's steps skittered.

"I know." I chucked the reins again and looked up.

Ahead, arrayed a half-kay ahead, blocking the entrance to the narrow pass, was a troop. A white-clad, white-faced wizard troop of warriors . . . soldiers . . . at least they all had weapons that glinted in the near-noon sun.

I wiped my forehead again with the back of my sleeve.

In front of the silent, ghost-white apparitions rode a knight on—what else—a white horse. The horse, over four cubits at the shoulder, stood there in the sunlight. Neither the horse's metal breastplate nor the knight's unburnished plate armor reflected the sunlight. Knights had never enjoyed much success, except in service of chaos, because that much plate was a wonderful place in which to concentrate fire. Of course, this knight had probably served chaos far longer than he had ever wanted to.

A damned knight. In more ways than one, I knew. Behind him waited a pack of armed figures, not exactly men. Unhappily, each of those figures carried a sword which glinted and looked razor-sharp.

The knight's helmet visor was down, and he carried a lance pointed in my direction. The lance looked to be a solid pole with a glistening white tip—chaos-tipped, if you will.

All of the predictability of Antonin's tactics did not make them less effective.

The white horse lifted one hoof, then another, carrying the silent knight toward me at an even pace, no spring in his steps, and no wavering. The knight said nothing.

Wheeee . . .

"Easy . . ."

The white-haired, white-faced, white-clothed figures began to walk also, their armor creaking like unoiled doors, without rhythm, without order, their swords almost flapping to an unseen and unheard breeze.

Wheee . . . Gairloch kept moving, if slowly.

"I know. It wasn't exactly my idea, either."

Further ahead in the grass to the right of the road were some more white fragments. I glanced from the ghosts to the bones and the tattered leathers. My eyes scanned the rest of the high grass, glimpsing a few other remnants of other travelers.

The bones were real. So not all of the figures could be illusions; but were they *all* real? My senses didn't say, because the blankness that enclosed the pass ahead foiled that. Still . . . I grinned, half-scared, half-elated, and flicked the reins, then dropped them on the saddle, grabbing the staff with both hands as Gairloch trotted toward the knight and I bounced along with him.

The knight's lance came up slowly, almost as if drawn toward the staff, the white tip glinting in the light, red behind the white of chaos.

Whhhhsttt . . . A line of fire flew toward me, spattering off my staff.

Thumpedy, thump . . . Gairloch carried me toward the lance.

Whhhhsssttt . . . The second fire-line curyed toward us, again spraying around me.

Thunk . . . thunk . . . I knocked the slow-moving lance aside, then struck the rear flank of the white horse.

Hssssttt . . .

Holding the staff in my left hand, I grabbed the reins and yanked Gairloch to a halt. Like a snuffed candle, the other white apparitions had vanished, leaving only the knight and horse—which, as I watched, sagged into a heap on the road, dwindling in size until only a pile of copper armor remained; that, and a long wooden lance with a still-sharpened tip.

The dead zone remained, and I could sense nothing, except with my eyes. Nor could I hear anything, no bird calls, no whistle of the wind, not the slightest of insect chirps or whines.

"Come on . . . let's get moving."

Gairloch didn't object as we rode into the narrow space. My eyes flicked from one smooth wall to the other, from the smooth stone in front of me to the cliff edges above, to the sky over that. All it would take would be one large falling rock—there was nowhere to go.

Then, again, if Antonin blocked the road, he would only have to unblock it, and who but an idiot would challenge the ghost horde?

I looked back and shivered. Slowly, a mist was building around the copper armor.

"Let's keep moving."

A lot of energy had been used to set up that defense, and all I had done was to bypass it; not even contain it, just get through it.

Once the high rock walls dropped away on each side, so did my inability to sense what I might not see. Gairloch had carried me nearly a kay further into the Westhorns.

Again, I glanced back, but the knight was out of sight. So was the white horde. But they were waiting, mindlessly, for the next travelers.

The beauty of the defense was that what happened didn't matter. Some people died. Some escaped, but the deaths and the tales of those who did escape added to Antonin's strength and people's desire to keep as far away from the haunted road as possible. With war between Gallos and Kyphros, who was about to send enough talent and force to clean up an unused wizards' road?

Yeee—ahh . . .

The vulcrow's ugly call reminded me to stop woolgathering and start concentrating again.

I did. That was a mistake, because I asked myself what I was doing on the road in the first place, or the second place, for that matter. Antonin had brushed me aside like nothing. And if my dreams were to be trusted, he had even trapped Tamra, who had been far warier and more capable than I. So what was I doing riding toward his stronghold?

"What am I doing?" I repeated out loud.

Wheeee . . . *uhhh* . . . That was Gairloch's only reply, but he kept putting one foot in front of the other, as if he had no choice.

Maybe that was the answer, the only answer. With all the deaths, and all the sacrifices, maybe I really didn't have much choice either. I didn't like that thought, either, since it made my stomach tighten up, and that meant I did have a choice.

Some choice—cut and run like all the other black masters had for

413

so long; or, probably, get incinerated by the greatest white wizard in generations. That was a choice of being a live hypocrite like Talryn or a dead hero like that poor Kyphran outlier.

"Wonderful choices . . ." I muttered under my breath.

Yeee—ahh . . . answered the near-by vulcrow.

I glanced up.

In the cloudless winter blue sky north of where I rode, two other vulcrows swept in slow wide circles.

Once again, the road stretched ahead down a narrow valley, straight for at least another two kays before it began a gentle turn toward the right, northward.

The mountain grass beside the road was all brown, but I saw no more horses as Gairloch carried me toward the wide curve and I followed the grooved coach traces back toward Antonin.

Mid-morning came and passed. I rode silently along the slowly-rising road, a road so dry that only a few stunted bushes and patches of mountain grass grew. A road so silent that the occasional screech of the single vulcrow that followed us, and the sound of Gairloch's hooves, were the only sounds echoing between those rocky walls.

The pair of vulcrows remained circling behind us and to the north, but the one continued to follow us. I knew why, but doing anything about it would have been stupid. The less capable Antonin thought I was, the better.

Before noon, I stopped at the first water, a brook barely a cubit wide. Gairloch appreciated the water, cold as it was. I did also, and fed him some grain cake, not much, and let him browse on the scattered roadside grass. I appreciated the yellow cheese and travel bread, though they were sustenance and not much more. Eating beat starving. I threw a morsel toward the vulcrow that perched on the rocks on the far side of the road.

For a time, the bread lay on the grass untouched. Then, with a rush, the scavenger swooped down and bore it back to its rock perch.

After saluting the black-feathered creature, I continued slicing and eating cheese. I'd never been the type to tear it right off the block.

The silence continued, and I wanted to talk, even to the vulcrow. Instead, I packed away my remaining travel food, filled the water bottle, and climbed back on Gairloch.

The rock walls flanking the road seemed to get whiter and deader, and the silence increased. Not even insects chirped, and the only living things were a vulcrow, a pony, and a damned idiot. In the high distance, the cold reflection of the high Westhorns glittered.

I kept riding.

Until I found the gates.

At first glance, the valley continued as it had for all too many kays, long, narrow, straight, and dry, the clay-covered white pavement stretching out before me. On the north side, there was a dip in the high rocky walls, and the grassy stretch that led to the near-sheer rock was nearly flat.

I blinked and looked again, sensing the illusion. Behind the apparent grass and rock lay another narrow passage. Unlike the road, the rock walls of this entrance were not timeworn and smooth, but sharp and clear, and the imprint of chaos was far more recent.

As Gairloch stood there, reined to a halt, I studied the reality behind the image, wondering if anything created by chaos could be said to represent reality.

The passage through solid rock was not that long, perhaps fifty cubits, and the rockface through which it had been cut was far shorter than most of the valley walls, less than thirty cubits above the road at the highest. Still, to destroy that mass of rock was impressive.

Midway into the passage were two heavy white-oak gates, their hinge brackets mortared into the rock itself. Both gates were closed.

Blocking the illusion from Gairloch, I nudged him forward. To any bystander, we would have appeared to walk into solid rock.

No chaos-forces touched the gates themselves, save for a thin link across them. A heavy but simple latch kept them closed. While I could have rerouted that thin link and opened the gates without breaking it, I did not. After all, what simple blackstaffer would have known that?

As I opened the latch, a spark flew, but nothing else happened.

Gairloch and I rode through, and I dismounted and reclosed the gates. Simple courtesy.

Once through the passage, the road ran between two treeless and rocky hills, then sloped down to a rock-strewn plain stretching for half a kay toward a towering and shimmering white cliff that held swirling chaos-energies, and glowed even under the noon sun. Beneath the cliff was a castle, composed of a stone house and a wall. The white stone house, barely visible to me even from the top of the hill, must have stood at least a full three stories high, with a white tile

415

roof. Around the house ran a wall of white granite, merging with the cliff at each end.

I shivered. I really wasn't sure I wanted to be there. In fact, I knew I didn't, but I'd backed myself into my own particular corner. How could I not try to stop Antonin after all I had said and seen? How I could possibly succeed was another question.

After another shiver, I looked down at the castle.

No doubt about it—the structure was impressive, but it was small, smaller than I would have thought for a chaos-master of Antonin's standing, and simple. No towers, just a sheer wall jutting out from the flat cliff rising behind it, pierced by a single visible gate. A narrow ravine, too deep to see the bottom from the entrance road where I sat upon Gairloch, and too raw to have been naturally caused, separated the castle and its walls from the more recently created wizards' road that I had followed from the original wizards' way.

Beside the newer road that led from the sharp-cleft rock passage and the castle gates ran a narrow brook, and a few patches of grass sprouted here and there. I dismounted, not wanting to bring Gairloch into that castle. Again, I could not explain why. I did not unsaddle him, but left him free to browse in the shaded area by the brook.

Then I took the staff and began the walk along the sunlit road between the two hills and down toward the castle.

Once I was halfway down the hill, I could see a simple railed and wooden span crossed the ravine, a span scarcely more than a rod in length. It was not a drawbridge, but a plain wooden structure, probably of heavy pine that could be easily fired with chaos-energies.

The castle itself could have been taken within a few days by a competent army—provided the castle's master were not a chaos-master, and provided that any army could have been coaxed into the Westhorns to begin with.

I shivered. The whole place was even more forbidding than Frven, more desolate than the patch of desert created between Gallos and Kyphros by Antonin's reckless use of chaos supposedly on behalf of the prefect, but clearly for Antonin's own benefit.

Not a single banner flew from the white castle. Not a single plume of smoke drifted from the eight chimneys, yet the heavy white-oak gate was open and the road ran straight from the gap in the hills to the ravine and the bridge to the castle.

Like a perfect painting, the castle sat framed by the high cliff and the ravine.

I shivered again, wondering why I was even trying. Then I thought of the nameless outlier, with her blasted face, and the beheaded blond soldier on the prefect's wall, the fountain of chaos, and, more important, the smugness of the Brotherhood, building isolated order, using Antonin as he used Justen.

There was one other factor—I had been used, just as Justen had. It was the only thing that made sense. By fighting the prefect, my attempts at order had led to greater disorder and greater conflict between Gallos and Kyphros. No wonder I had been unmolested until I left. I had done exactly what Antonin wanted. I almost retched right there on that dry and barren road, wondering at the same time why I had to have been so damned slow and stupid.

Instead, I straightened my steps and marched onward toward the ravine and the bridge across it, guessing that the longer before I had to raise a shield, the better. I did let my perceptions sense the area around me, to alert me if Antonin should begin to mass forces against me.

417

I had thought about ringing the castle with a balance barrier, but traveling the ravine and climbing the hill would have been difficult without using order-mastery to bridge some of the gaps, and that use of order would have spelled out my presence like fireworks in the night sky. Not to mention my abilities. And even had I been able to create that large a barrier, it would have failed my purpose.

I needed to get to Antonin face-to-face, and I suspected that he would let me, if only to get an explanation of how I had eluded him thus far. That was a gamble, but not a big one. Besides, I really didn't have much choice.

So step by step I walked downhill, further from Gairloch with each stride, closer to the hidden fires that shimmered behind each stone of the white castle, closer to the fears that threatened to paralyze my spine.

L X V

Not one soul—not even a demon—looked from the empty parapets as my feet scuffed the white stone of the road that arrowed straight for the white-oak bridge and the open gate beyond.

With each step a puff of white dust rose, then fell, in the noonday stillness. Not a breath of air carried down that narrow valley, and the winter day felt like a bone-dry summer afternoon. The ice- and snow-tipped peaks of the Westhorns glittered like glass on their heights to my left, as indifferent as to what might happen as they had been to the rise and fall of Frven or the honest and deadly strategy of Recluce.

Thud. My first step on the wooden span reverberated like muted thunder from the narrow ravine below, all red rocks, needle-pointed and razor-edged. At least there weren't any bones, not that I could see.

Tharooom . . . thud . . . tharooom . . . Walking the white fir was walking across a massive drum. Antonin's coach must have vied with the real thunder when it rumbled across his bridge. . . . *Tharummmm . . .*

Creaaakkkkk . . . The heavy wooden gate, set on massive bronze hinges, eased open even more widely as I watched.

No one appeared. No thing appeared, either, but I could feel the creatures of chaos beyond that open gate—red-sparked and dead-white beings that made the lingering demons of Frven seem merely plaintive.

My fingers were slippery on my staff, and I wanted to wipe the sweat off my forehead. Not all of that dampness was from the heat.

Tharuum . . . thump, thuuuud . . . The drum echoes of the bridge told me that my steps were not exactly even, or ordered. I repressed a laugh, but why I thought it was funny I couldn't say.

Creakkkkk . . . The solid oak gate opened wide to the courtyard beyond the wall, and to the main floor windows, all casements, and all open to let in air and light. No figures appeared anywhere, even as my feet again touched the solid white stone beyond the bridge and outside the gate. Again, I could feel the unseen chaos-energies swirling around the courtyard.

I swallowed and stepped up to the gate.

"Hello the castle." The stone swallowed my words, rather than echoing them.

No answer.

I looked around the gate, let my feelings sweep the courtyard, but the space was vacant. Not cloaked, the way the white knight had been, but vacant. I took one step up to the gate, and another around it. My feet carried me past the gate, and I looked back. The heavy oak structure remained on its hinges—open.

The white-paved courtyard, less than thirty cubits square, was empty and bare, except for a mounting block designed for a carriage, and a carved design above the doorway of the carriage-entrance. The open windows were hinged open slightly beyond the roof line.

Like the castle gate, the doorway above the carriage steps beckoned. Both of its unadorned, gold-varnished double doors stood ajar. A glint of bronze told me that they, too, were set with bronze hinges.

Even with my feelings extended, I could sense nothing living nearby, just the swirling chaos-energies, a deeper underlying chaos, and a greater and a lesser concentration of living white fire on the floor above. That fire had to be Antonin—and some other white wizard.

Thrap! Thrap! I banged the heavy brass knocker far harder than necessary, and the sound echoed into the corridors beyond the doors.

This time I waited. One did not enter the domain of chaos totally uninvited. Standing there—staff in hand, shifting my weight from one foot to the other—I wiped the sweat off my forehead with the back of my sleeve, still marveling at the unseasonable heat, and wondering if the castle were an extension of chaos, or of the demons' hell itself.

I swallowed, then began to examine the stone around me, and the wood of the doors outside which I waited.

Uncle Sardit would have frowned. Even Bostric would have frowned. The mitering on the panel edges was rough, with gaps big enough to slip a knife through. The spaces between the frame and the stone were even wider, as if hurriedly installed, or by poor crafters indeed. The golden varnish had been slopped on, in some places actually showing where raised globs had dried, without even a sanding or a second coat.

Although I did not know stonework, the same careless finishing was evident there as well, with blocks joined and held in place by mortar of differing thicknesses, rather than having the mortar as a sealant for solid and well-fitted stones.

Thrap! I knocked again.

Click . . . click . . . click . . . The steps were slow, like water dripping from a leaky shower. Had I even seen a shower since Recluce?

. . . click . . .

A thin footman not much taller than my shoulder stood and opened the left door fully, stepping back as he did so. His hair and skin were white, as were his jacket, boots, and trousers. The whites of his eyes were reddish-tinted. Only his pupils were black.

"The master bids you welcome." Hoarse and mechanical, his voice sounded as though I were the first person to whom he had spoken since he died. Then again, maybe he only looked dead. Although he might be alive, he bore no energy save chaos, and without it he would have ceased to be. That in itself was another paradox—pointing out that even chaos-masters had to use *some* order.

"I would like to see him."

Without another word, the white footman turned and started down the wide white marble hallway and toward a set of circular stairs.

Click. Behind us, the doors closed.

I grasped the staff, knowing its comfort was short-lived, and followed the footman to the grand staircase.

Once more I was disappointed in the workmanship, especially to see such a well-proportioned and superior design flawed in execution, with columns more than fractionally off-center and stone joints with thumb-width gaps instead of hair-thin lines. Everywhere lingered the hint of a white haze, a dust not quite dust that did not exactly settle on the unevenly-polished marble floors.

Another lack bothered me, but not until I was halfway up the circular staircase did I observe the lack of wall decorations—no paintings, no wall hangings, not even any carpeting.

The whole castle reeked of being unfinished, clearly finished as it was. The lack of order? I wondered, but kept pace with the silent footman.

At the top of the staircase, he turned left for several steps before stopping at a closed doorway that seemed to lead back toward the front of the castle.

Creakkkk . . .

Oak doors should not creak, not well-made doors, but those of the white wizard did. I shook my head, then followed the footman inside.

As I entered, I glanced up at the vaulted ceiling, supported by white oak timbers set twice as close together as would be needed for a normal structure. A faint smile tugged at my lips.

Like the rest of the castle, the great room was white—white marble floors, whitened granite walls, and white-oak framing and doors. The

420

inside wall—the one containing the poorly-fitted double doors through which I had been conducted—was of white-oak paneling, and not the best, either. Even without looking closely, I could see the small lines showing that the mitering and joins were often not flush.

My nose tickled, perhaps from the white dust that my boots had raised as I walked into the room. At the north end of the room towered a whitened granite chimney, fronted by a white marble hearth. A small pile of ashes lay on the stones, but there were no andirons, grates, or screens, and the ashes were cold.

The inside wall, the one of white oak, bore no pictures, no decorations save the paneling itself, although a half-dozen wall brackets bore unlit white-brass lanterns. Identical lanterns were affixed between the casements of the long floor-to-ceiling windows that punctuated the outside wall. Each window, composed of perhaps twenty diamond-shaped leaded panes with an amber tint, opened on pivot bars hidden in the top and bottom of the white-oak frames. Even with all the windows open to the air, the amber tint of the glass cast a golden glow on the room. Despite the open windows, the air bore a hint of ash.

At the south end of the room was the only furniture—a modest circular white-oak table about four cubits across, surrounded by five matching chairs with golden cushions. Against the wall were two serving tables of white oak. The left one bore a tray of covered dishes.

At the table sat two figures.

The silent white footman marched until we were almost at the table, bowed, then departed, leaving me standing there, staff in hand. With his reddened eyes, his gaunt and pallid face, his lank white hair, and his jerky gait, he looked like a marionette—the white wizard's puppet.

Antonin and the dark-haired woman—Sephya—looked up from the table, the ever-present white oak under a golden varnish. Steam rose from their plates.

"Would you care to join us?" His voice was pleasant, as if I were an old acquaintance making a social call.

I smiled politely, just as I had been taught to do, but my stomach twisted at even that deception.

"Not if phrased quite that way, most accomplished of white wizards." I bowed. Bowing didn't bother me. He was accomplished—no questions about that.

"The young fellow has respect, Sephya. You must permit him that." Antonin took a bite from his plate after he spoke.

"He has manners, my lord. Those are not quite the same as respect." Her voice was deferential, not subservient . . . and vaguely familiar.

I turned toward the woman, studying her directly. Apparently-dark hair, but not even shoulder-length, eyes whose color seemed to shift between gray and blue, and a pale complexion. Beneath that . . . I swallowed, and forced my thoughts elsewhere.

One problem at a time.

"He is also perceptive." She took a sip from the glass goblet. "A shade dangerous. He might even have been a worthy adversary, were he not so impetuous."

I swallowed again, realizing that she was delicately trying to get me angry, in such a way that I wouldn't realize exactly what she was doing. "You do me too much honor, my lady."

"She is known for that," added the white wizard. His voice bore an edge. "You haven't exactly explained why you marched down my roads and up to my doorstep. Or a few other minor inconveniences, either." He arched one eyebrow—the right one—and I had to admire that little trick.

422

I shrugged. What could I explain? That I had decided to destroy him? I decided to say nothing.

His eyes seemed to grow whiter as he watched me, but I looked beyond him, trying to measure the chaos that centered, as much as chaos could center anywhere, within and around the room.

"You've provided an interesting puzzle, blackstaffer. You could be rather helpful in some ways." The white wizard smiled and lifted his arm. A small fireball appeared between the thumb and forefinger of his right hand. "Perhaps you would like to learn the workings of fire? Bringing greater knowledge to mankind?"

My skin itched, and the room felt darker, though the sky outside was as blue as ever and the golden light still filled the room.

"To all people?" I forced a laugh, which was hard, because my throat was as dry as a desert.

"You came to me. You are seeking answers, after all." The fireball vanished as he lowered his hand, pushed back the chair, and stood.

I did not smile, but took a deep breath. Antonin was not quite as tall as I was, and his arms were still the knobby arms of a merchant. I stepped back and looked toward the wall of windows, wondering absently if Gairloch were still waiting patiently beyond the two rocky hills that flanked Antonin's private road. "I did," I finally admitted.

"For what? The answers that frightened Recluce refuses to share? Or the power that belongs to all true seekers of knowledge?" His voice had softened, mellowed, filled with the sound of reasonableness.

"Recluce has no fear of you, or of me." As I said the words, the chill I felt from their truth, from my stomach *not* turning, almost had me shivering.

"Indeed? Then it must be true, if you say so. Yet you hesitate in joining us in the search for the answers that Recluce hides from all the world?"

"I'm not sure that a wizard's seeking answers entitles him to receive them, any more than a ruler's starting a war entitles him to victory." My words were a stupid response, tumbling out almost thoughtlessly.

Antonin frowned. He had moved a step or so closer as we had spoken.

"He seems somewhat reluctant to pledge his service to you." Sephya's laugh was hard, and the sound tore at my chest. "Or even to carry out his own quest for answers."

I nodded toward her, trying not to take my eyes from the white wizard.

"Do you wish to enter the white fellowship?"

"Hardly." I laughed, except the sound resembled choking because my heart was pounding and my mouth dry.

"He is brave, Sephya," the white wizard announced. "Brave, but not terribly bright."

I agreed with his assessment—completely.

"So . . ." Antonin raised his arms. "Let me show you some answers."

Whssstttt . . .

A cascade of fire streamed from Antonin toward me.

Instinctively, my staff blocked the torrent of flames that cascaded around me, blazed blackly.

Antonin smiled. "A good staff there. But a staff cannot answer your questions."

WWWWWWHHHHHSSSTTTTTTTT!

Fire flowed everywhere, and my ears whistled and rang from the blaze that surrounded me.

"A very good staff." He raised his arms once more.

The theatricality of the gesture irked me. He scarcely needed to raise his arms. Chaos and order are molded by the mind, not the hands.

423

WWWWWWWWWHHHHHHHHHHHHHHHHHSSSSSSSSSSSTTTTTT-TTT!

The force of the fire nearly knocked me off my feet, driving me back away from the table, leaving me tottering above the stone flooring.

"Are you sure about your decision?" Antonin asked, his voice once more reasonable, as if he had not just attempted to incinerate me. His hands remained poised. "Knowledge belongs to those who seek it, not those who deny it or flee it."

At that point, I acted on faith, not quite sure why I did what I did. Straightening up and taking my staff in both hands, I brought it down across my knee. It bent, but did not break, and a sharp pain ran up my leg.

"That's hardly the way," said Antonin mildly. "Just set it down." He pointed to the stone tiles by my feet. Fire surrounded him, an unseen white blistering flame, and cold red hatred, even as he stepped toward me yet another pace.

Casting the staff aside wouldn't be enough—that would just divide what order I possessed. But I had not been able to break it and my leg throbbed from my failed attempt. The lorken was tough. And it was finely crafted—Uncle Sardit's best. Yet I knew that the best of tools could be a crutch, even if a finely-crafted crutch.

"Just set it down. The staff hinders your search for answers." Antonin's voice was friendly, persuasive.

I gripped the lorken more firmly. Mind over matter? Was that the answer? Whatever it might be, that seemed the only hope.

BREAK—that was what I willed as the hard black wood came down across my knee again. BREAK . . . BREAK . . . BREAK!

Crackkkkk . . .

That black lorken that had turned swords, resisted stone, and stopped iron bars—that iron-bound and indestructible staff—cracked as easily as though it had been a softwood stake. Coolness—a black coolness that quenched the burning with which Antonin's flames tried to bathe me—flowed from the broken ends of the wood, settling in and around me.

Without a word, I cast both pieces of iron-bound black wood at his feet.

Even Antonin's mouth dropped open momentarily, before he danced back from the cold iron on the black wood.

As he gaped and dodged, I stepped forward, drawing a reflective

shield around us, except this one was inside out, directing outside
energies away from us.

His mouth continued to sag as I turned toward him.

"You . . ."

WWWHHHHHHsssss . . .

His fire trickled away against the black coolness I held around me,
and his hands dropped to his waist.

He tried to raise one hand, again, but that shiny dark hair had
begun to silver, even in the instants since the reflective shield had
isolated us.

Whhhhsssttt!

Another blast of fire slashed at me from Sephya, spraying away
from the shield I had thrown around Antonin, and me.

Click.

Antonin had a short bronze sword in his hand, although wrinkles
were appearing on his face. Behind Antonin, Sephya drew a thin blade.
She edged toward us.

I dropped down and dived for the floor, grabbing one half of my
broken staff and flinging it at Sephya.

Clunk!

"Ohhh . . . shit . . ." The staff fragment dropped inside my own
shield's edge, bouncing on the white marble, stopped cold by the
tiniest residual order it bore.

Give me your energy . . . give it to me . . . Antonin's thoughts clawed
at me, demanding the sense of self I had wrapped in the blackness I
held.

Now . . . give . . . give . . .

Like a vise, his thoughts encircled me, within the circled shield I held.

I am Lerris . . . I am me . . . me . . . Just as Justen had taught, I
hung on to myself.

Whhssttt . . . Antonin's fire was barely more than the fireball in
his fingertips earlier, but it burned at my face, and I squinted.

Sephya advanced slowly, as if unsure exactly what to do.

Thwick!

Antonin sliced at me with the short sword. I rolled away, getting my
feet under me, concentrating on keeping the shield around us both.

Give! Give! . . . Like a white hammer, that demand pounded at me.

I circled away, concentrating on being Lerris, holding that barrier
tight around us.

425

The chaos-master's hair had turned totally white, and began to fall like snow.

Hsssttttt! I reeled backwards, a searing pain across my shoulders, feeling like I had been slashed from behind.

Clank!

"Oooo . . . Sephya exclaimed. The blade she had held lay on the floor, white-hot from trying to pass the shield I held.

Thwick.

I skipped sideways, losing part of my tunic to the copper blade as Antonin used my lapse of attention to strike.

GIVE . . . give . . .

Thwickkk!

I dodged again.

Twickk!

. . . and again . . .

". . . think . . . smart . . ." mumbled Antonin. "You'll never go home now . . . you know too much . . ." His words slurred, and his hands were shaking, and the short sword dropped as if it were too heavy to hold.

Give . . . The last thought was nearly plaintive.

Whhhsssttttt!

Still another of Sephya's firebolts flared against the shield.

Clunk . . .

Antonin lurched toward me again, after dropping the now-too-heavy sword.

I dodged, but not quickly enough, as his fingers ripped at my forearm. Each fingertip felt like a brand across my arm, and I forced order at those chaos-dripping burn wounds, shoving Antonin back at the same time.

". . . damned . . ."

I gulped as I looked at the white wizard. The hand that had clutched at me—burning three white scars that still smoldered—that hand shriveled into ashes. And the black imprint of my hand on his shoulder burned through the white robes. As I gaped, the white-clad figure staggered, shriveling and collapsing onto the marble into a crumpled heap.

Whhhhsssttttt!

"Noooooooooooooooo!

Sephya's scream echoed through the great room.

Since she had been unable to penetrate the shield I ignored her, ignored the searing in my arm, and concentrated on keeping the shield intact until the heap that had been the white wizard was truly dead.

Thhuuurruuummmmm . . . A low roll of thunder rumbled on and on, as if it radiated from where I stood, rolling outward like ripples from a boulder cast into a pool.

. . . thuuurrrummmmmmmmmm . . .

CRACK! A blade of lightning flashed outside from a cloudless sky, and I flinched, but clutched my thoughts tight around the shield.

. . . thhhurruummmm . . . The growling in and under the skies, and the lingering echo of the single lightning bolt, rolled and kept rolling outward and away from the castle, until the thunder and the lightning were mere echoes far out across the Westhorns.

Not merely physical, those sounds had carried far beyond my hearing, and I shivered.

With a deep breath I dropped the shield and turned toward Sephya. She had squared her shoulders.

Whhhhstttt!

The heat seared around me, but I deflected it, letting the white flame sheet around me. I took a single step toward her.

Wwhhhsssttttt!

Another step carried me through and past her firebolt.

Whhhsssttt!

Moving as though through glue or old varnish, I managed another long step.

She backed up almost to the hearth.

Whhsttt!

A knife—another one of the bronze blades—appeared in her hand. "Touch me and you lose her!"

I stopped.

She lifted the knife and reversed it.

I threw all the order I had left in me at the knife, trying to order the copper and tin, bend it away from chaos.

"Ohhhhhhhh . . ."

The muscles in her arms stood out as she tried to bring the knife toward her body. I staggered toward her, pouring all the order-feelings I could toward her.

"Ugffff . . ."

Clank . . .

Her legs bent, then buckled as she collapsed against a chair and bounced onto the floor.

I half-walked, half-dragged myself across the white marble squares, toward the doll-like figure sprawled between the white-oak table and the hearth.

After kneeling on one knee, I turned her face up. The slash across her fair neck was more burn than cut, ugly as it looked, although the blood didn't help appearances much.

I left it alone, afraid that any more order-meddling was dangerous, at least until I gathered my own thoughts and strength back.

A quick look toward the white wizard showed me but a heap of white ashes. Even as I watched, the white ash turned to dust, and the dust vanished into the white haze that still filled the castle. Only the white robes and matching white boots remained upon the white tiles of the floor.

I looked back at the unconscious Sephya, noting the slight build, the reddish tinge of hair beginning to replace the black.

My stomach twisted, even as I gathered my last energies to break another mental lock—this time, the one Antonin had provided for the woman who had tried to keep eternal youth by letting Antonin's promises ensnare another near-innocent from Recluce.

I had guessed but not known what had been done to her, not as Sephya, but as another soul trapped in Antonin's web. In a way both Sephya and Tamra had been trapped. Yet Sephya had agreed, knowing that Tamra would in time wither away under Sephya's personality as reinforced by Antonin. The white wizard had not lied, exactly; rather, he let Tamra think she was about to learn how to control the powers she had always been denied. Tamra would not have known that Sephya would control her body.

Thanks to Talryn and Recluce, Tamra had never learned, just as I had not learned, that she already possessed that power all along. Except Tamra had refused to accept her power, insisting that someone else declare her worthy; while I had kept asking for the reasons, instead of acting, and the reasons had nearly become an excuse for not acting.

I took a deep breath, knowing what had to be done before I lost my nerve as I feared my father had.

"Lerris, you can't do that!"

I ignored the caution from somewhere far away, too far away for me to worry about as I looked into the closed eyes of the slim, red-headed figure. Tears were streaming down my face, but they, too, were distant from what had to be done. If I had listened . . . but that was another question, and we all choose our own demon-inhabited hells.

One deep breath, and I plunged, deep into the darkness, away from the swirls of my own thoughts, away from the crumpled clothes that were all which remained of the white wizard upon the floor of his about-to-crumble fortress and palace.

Call the depths of the mind white darkness, the chaos that preceded chaos. Call them what you will, but they are chaos, a chaos so formless that it cannot bear description.

First, to find within that chaos the patterns that were, that had been. What those patterns really were, I did not try to discover, for that would have been yet another rape. Instead, as I discovered, touched, each gossamer thread, I restored it, not reading it, or the joys, tears, anger or boredom it held, but replacing it as it had been before Antonin had changed Tamra's temple to Sephya's harlotry. Even so, the hidden feelings plucked at my own fears, my own worth. Had I the right? Who appointed me custodian? To decide who should live and who should die?

I did what I had to do.

How long that took . . . that was how long it took . . . as long as destroying Frven took my father, for it had to have been him and Justen, the brothers—one building a nation to ensure chaos would never rule again, the other trying to minister to the damned and their descendants in hell. As long as crossing the deadlands . . . as long as my refusing to understand the eternal penance that had ensnared my father . . . and Justen, the damned gray wizard, perhaps the only true gray wizard.

One thread of memory, then another, and for all that I did not look as each was replaced, with each thread grew the sadness. With each thread grew the river of tears that should have flowed from the West-horns to the Easthorns and emptied into the Great North Bay or into the Gulf of Candar.

With the return of each original thread, a false thread floated free, moaning as another part of Sephya died, somehow clutching to remain as I plucked it away from the underlying sadness and the hard-plated gentleness of the redhead I had never really known or seen.

With each thread, I severed my ties to Recluce, for I was destroying a soul to save another.

The last threads I replaced by feel, for even the eyes of my mind were filled with tears.

Then I stepped back into the amber light of that damned white palace. That was all I could do before my knees buckled and my own private darkness buried me.

Yeee—aaaahhh . . .

Yee—ahh . . .

It would have been nice to be wakened by a beautiful lady, or even a friendly one, but it didn't happen that way.

Yeee-aaahh . . .

My mouth was dry, dust dry, and an invisible smith was using my head for an anvil.

Yee-ah . . . yee-ah . . .

My forearm burned and ached simultaneously.

Yeee-ahh . . .

My knee throbbed, and sent shivers of pain to my already beaten skull.

Yeee-ahhh . . .

On the roof above the open window, a vulcrow complained that he couldn't get to the raw meat that was me.

After lurching into a sitting position on the rough marble floor, I slowly looked toward the pile of white garments and the white boots that had been Antonin. The white shoes were gone, and the remnants were still remnants.

Then I looked toward the woman who had been both Sephya and Tamra. She had curled into a ball next to the white-oak table that was already beginning to sag. In the diffused light, her hair was the red I remembered.

A cool wind blew through the open windows, and the weaker late-afternoon light and the shadows outside told me I had been lying on the stone too long. My sore body agreed.

. . . uuummmmmmmmm . . . uuummmmm . . .

The sound of strained stone transformed my too-leisurely observations into motion—*slow* motion.

First I gathered myself together, standing carefully.

Then, after walking to Tamra, I stretched out a hand, gingerly, and touched the bare skin of her forearm. Nothing. Nothing but the lingering odor of chaos, and an overwhelming sense of pain and loss.

Slowly, gently, I pried her limb-by-limb out of her ball and onto her feet. Like a puppet she allowed me to, her eyes open but blank, almost like a china doll. Such a physical coercion wasn't a great idea, I could tell, but I could not carry her. With Antonin's castle sounding near collapse around us, my options were limited.

Together we tottered step-by-step out of the great hall, down the circular staircase, and out the sagging double doors.

Creeeakk . . . scrunch . . . creaakkk . . .

The heavy fir bridge creaked and sagged, but held long enough for us to cross. My heart was thumping loudly enough to hear, and my mouth was so dry I could not close it by the time we stepped back onto the road on the other side of the ravine.

Yee-ah . . .

I ignored the damned vulcrow and concentrated on putting one foot in front of the other, taking a deep breath after every other step. My steps got shorter when we reached the slope up between the hills.

Tamra walked more easily, copying my pace, unthinkingly.

The shadowed spot by the brook where I had left Gairloch was no longer shadowed, but Gairloch was there, looking up from the water.

431

Wheeee . . . eeeee . . .

"Yes, I know. I took too long," I mumbled as I struggled to open the water bottle. The liquid helped, enough for me to realize that it would have been a lot easier to drink from the brook.

The brook water was colder, and Tamra followed my example, after I told her to drink.

Then I got out my meager store of food, mostly travel bread and the yellow cheese I didn't like all that much. I sat on a small boulder by the brook to open the packages. My stomach didn't seem to mind the taste of either, and some of the shakiness left my legs.

I offered a piece of bread to Tamra. She took it, looking at it blankly.

"Go ahead. You can eat it."

She did, mechanically, those eyes still china-doll blank.

It was going to be a long trip back to Kyphrien, a long trip indeed. Slowly, I chewed enough of the bread and drank enough of the water that my head cleared and some of my strength returned—enough for me to touch that scar on Tamra's neck and begin the healing process. She didn't need any external scars. The ones inside would be great enough.

Tamra didn't protest when I boosted her onto Gairloch.

Wheee . . . eeee . . . He objected, skittering aside, nearly pulling the reins from my hand.

"Easy there," I mumbled.

Wheeeee . . . eeeeee . . .

"I know . . . but help me out . . ."

Long wasn't the word for the ride back toward Kyphrien. Until close to sunset, when I finally found another brook and a semi-enclosed spot off the wizard's road, Tamra and I had alternated riding Gairloch, except that he got nasty if I didn't stay close by. She just looked blankly into space, whether riding or walking.

After we dismounted and struggled off the road, we ate—more travel bread and the bitter yellow cheese, plus some very dried sourpears that I had to wash down. Tamra didn't even pucker her lips when she ate them.

As the light died, I put up double wards, which took most of my limited strength—wards against Tamra, and wards against any other outside intrusion.

Neither was necessary. When I woke the next morning, Tamra was looking blankly into space, sitting on my bedroll. So tired I had been that my cloak had been enough for me.

432 "Are you all right?" I asked. She wasn't, of course, but I had to ask. She said nothing, china-blue eyes taking in whatever she faced, but seeing nothing.

She would eat if told, as well as do anything else, including rather necessary functions. That part was hard for me.

The second day was better, but only physically. Tamra remained silent, puppet-like. I could sense no active chaos around or within her, and somewhere deep inside was a coil of tight-sprung order that I dared not touch, though I could not say exactly why. I hoped Justen, the healer as well as gray wizard, could help. In some things, gall was no substitute for experience.

So we rode on, and on, past the narrow gap once guarded by the ghost knight. I saw only the greened copper of a lance tip lying on the left side of the wizards' road, but not even dust or ashes of the knight. The bones and ragged fabrics from packs and clothes remained.

The second night, in the hills outside the Westhorns themselves, was worse. I woke more than I slept, and I swore Tamra just lay on the bedroll staring at the dark clouds overhead, clouds that never rained, never thundered, just shut out the stars.

Before mid-morning on the third day, after we had reached the old road to Kyphrien, a familiar figure appeared on the road, moving quickly toward the Westhorns. Two familiar figures—one on a charger, one on a shaggy pony, accompanied by an armed squad of the Finest. I didn't recognize any of the other riders. They had two riderless horses, just in case.

"Yelena . . . Justen . . ." My voice was rusty, flat. I wasn't exactly thrilled to see Justen, as if somehow seeing him meant I had failed somewhere.

"Congratulations, Master of Order-Masters." He inclined his head as if he meant it.

Yelena did not meet my eyes, instead looking at Tamra. The sub-officer's hand remained close to her well-ordered iron blade, and her lips were tight. "What did . . . what happened? Is she captive . . . or what?"

I looked at Justen, without words. Finally, I spoke. "White prison. I did what I could, but her soul is twisted into the tightest order-knot within . . ."

He looked back at me, levelly. "Did you hear me?"

"I did. I did it anyway."

He shook his head. "She cannot live with those memories."

"I know that!" I snapped. "Why do you think I restored her old memories? She may not remember anything."

"How did you do that?" His words were carefully spaced.

"I just did it. It's like weaving light or energy, except it hurt more, and I didn't get all the pain, just the memories. The pain's separate."

"Order-masters?" began Yelena.

I understood. "Yes. We can talk as we ride, and Tamra needs better care than I can provide."

Justen looked away from me, not even meeting my eyes. Instead, he rode next to Tamra, talking to her in a low voice. Even when we stopped for a midday break, he barely looked in my direction.

No one else looked in my direction, either, not when they thought I was watching, except when we stopped. Then they would offer, most politely, some fresh travel bread or white cheese or fruit. The yellow cheese supplied by Brettel had served me well, but its limited and bitter taste left much to be desired, and that was a charitable way of putting it. So I appreciated the white cheese and dried apples.

Once back on our mounts, though, everyone kept a comfortable distance from Gairloch and me, as if I were contaminated or something. Hell, they even talked to Justen, and he was a gray wizard. Not even Justen seemed comfortable near me. So I rode quietly, drawing into myself.

433

How was I any different from Antonin? I had used every power I knew and some I had only guessed at. Was I going to be another gray wizard? Or worse?

LXVI

Once again, I watched the sun rise and the morning unfold from a balcony in Kyphrien. I stood alone in the early morning. This time the winter sun was chill. The cold refreshed me as the brisk wind whipped up from the city, bringing the odor of fresh-baked bread, as well as the odor of goats. Somehow the goats didn't bother me so much any more, but that might have been the result of an eight-day's worth of meals centering on roasted, stewed, brazed, and baked goat presented with equally diverse spices and side dishes by the autarch's chef.

At least the breakfast rolls I had brought up from the mess—staying in the guard mess for any length of time created a profound and drawn-out silence as every single guard seemed to look at me—contained no goat meat.

My balcony was the one next to Krystal's, with an iron grillwork doorway between the two. Though there was no lock, I had not opened the door since I had yet to see Krystal.

The sub-commander had not been in Kyphrien when we had returned, but, instead, had used the disruption I had created to destroy the remainder of the prefect's border force. Without the backing of chaos, the young Gallian troops were no match for the Finest, or even for the better local outliers. I hoped that the talkative Shervan had managed to weather the action, though I wasn't certain I was ready for conversation with him any time soon.

Whether I was really ready for another conversation, the one with Krystal, was another question. Like me, she wasn't the same person who had left Recluce. Like me, she had forged herself in her own fires into a different kind of steel. I had no doubts that, even with a black staff in my hand, her blade would have proven superior. Then,

434

again, no one was a match for Krystal there, except perhaps Ferrel, and I wondered about that.

Justen had taken Tamra under his wing, as I had hoped, and she had begun to respond. I had only seen them from a distance, but the gray wizard had himself another apprentice. It might do them both good.

Thrap!

I wanted to ignore the knock on the door, but did not, instead walking back inside to the iron-bound red-oak door. The order arrayed on the other side could only have been one person. I lifted the latch.

Justen stood there. "May I come in?"

"Be my guest." I stepped back, aware that the gray wizard had the slightest hint of wariness about him. All the bowing and scraping was already getting to me, and it had barely been an eight-day since I had stumbled from the ruins of Antonin's castle. You would have thought that I had done something great—like leveling a few mountains, or even crafting the most beautiful chest ever seen in Kyphros.

Bravado, luck, and applying whatever skill I had—that was what I had done, not quite like the effort to do a chest or table perfectly, though they were far more alike than I would have guessed when I had first apprenticed to Uncle Sardit.

The other thing I had done, almost unconsciously, was to be honest with myself. Not that I really had much choice otherwise, but that was the other difference between Antonin and me. It had taken a while, most of the ride back to Kyphrien, to figure out the answer to my question. How was I different from Antonin? Even Justen had been different from the white wizard. Could I have ever imagined Antonin working with smelly sheep? And that was the real sin—the real evil—of the white wizards. Pride. The conceit that they would impose their will on the world. Without even mentioning it, Justen had made his point with the smelly sheep of Montgren. And I hadn't even realized that I had learned.

"May I come in?" he repeated.

"Oh, sorry. You reminded me of something." I moved aside.

Justen stepped inside. I gestured toward the balcony.

Click.

I shut the door. We walked in silence outside into the chill, since I didn't feel like being closed in. The granite of the guard buildings was also getting to me.

435

"So why does everyone have to skitter out of my way? Uncle Justen?" I added.

He nodded. "Was it that obvious?"

"Probably, but I didn't see it until I went after Antonin. I'm still angry as hell at Talryn and Recluce. And my father." And I was. The idea of being sent out as his penance, so to speak, grated on me. While I could understand—now—why the answers I had sought were not possible, Recluce had no excuse for the excessive secrecy.

"Talryn's probably quaking in his sandals." Justen's voice was not quite tongue-in-cheek.

"I doubt that. He's probably happy to be rid of me." Strangely, although I was angry, I wasn't *that* angry, and I was less concerned about Recluce than about Kyphros and Gallos.

"Could I ask how you—" Justen's tone was deferential.

"Luck, bravado, stupidity—the usual ingredients of so-called heroism."

"Lerris."

I shrugged. "Chaos-order balance. Simple enough."

436

Justen looked bewildered for the first time.

"Chaos is concentrated anarchy, if you will. Order is diffused by nature. They have to balance. Recluce has gotten stronger by letting Candar create more chaos, in effect letting . . ." I was the one to shake my head. "You know that. You're the one who pointed it out to me." I stopped as Justen shook his head slowly. "I swear you did. But after making Antonin stronger, helping him create more chaos, I didn't have any choice."

The gray wizard looked even more . . . *appalled*. That might have been the best word.

I tried to explain what he already must have known. "Order, except in special circumstances, can't be concentrated. I'm not talking about reinforcing already-ordered people—or sheep—or chairs, but pure order. Chaos can. In effect, because order and chaos must balance, the higher the diffuse order in an area, the greater the potential for chaos. So my efforts to increase order in Gallos just allowed Antonin to create more chaos." Another thought struck me. "I suppose that meant an overall decrease in order-chaos energies somewhere else, but I haven't worked that out. Anyway, once I figured the balance and my contribution, I didn't have much choice. I was as guilty as Antonin for the destruction."

My guts protested. "Not as guilty," I corrected myself, "but I helped."

Justen shook his head, and I ignored the gesture, just wanting to finish answering the question.

"Anyway, all I did to Antonin was throw a reversed shield around us, to reflect energy away from as small a circle as I could hold. He maintained himself by drawing from the chaos-forces around. With the shield up, he couldn't draw, at least so long as I could keep him from taking my order-energies." I shrugged. "Without that energy, he just died."

Justen nodded. "How many people could build a screen like that?"

"Probably any good order-master . . . I didn't think about it."

He nodded again. "How many blackstaffers could and would break their only defense in front of a white wizard?"

"That was stupid, I guess. I didn't know if it would work, but holding onto it wouldn't have protected me for very much longer, and the staff kept getting in the way. Besides, that's what the book said."

"You're right. But . . . no one else, not since before Frven, has stood face-to-face with the highest of chaos-masters and triumphed." Justen gestured out at the town. "You wonder why everyone bows and scrapes and won't look at you? That's why. You wonder why Talryn is quaking in his sandals? Every chaos-master and order-master in the Western Hemisphere heard Antonin fall—"

"That's fine, except I'm not an ancient order-master. I'm even ready for Tamra's bitching. At least that's real. I'm ready to go back to crafting. That's real, too."

Justen smiled. "Who said you couldn't?"

"Right! Good old Lerris is so smart . . . so why didn't I at least pick up some of Antonin's ill-gotten loot before I dashed out? I might have three gold pennies left in my pouch. That's not enough even for tools."

"I suspect that the reward the autarch is about to confer—"

"Another ceremony?" I groaned. Having half the city lined up at the gate and waving banners—very quietly—had been bad enough. Even Yelena had looked in my direction and grinned.

"Your burden to bear. That's another price for heroism."

None of that answered my questions, but then, no one else would probably ever answer them.

"How's Tamra?" I changed the subject.

"Ask her yourself. I'll send her up here shortly." He smiled. "She will bitch at you. She told me she would."

I let him go. He wasn't about to answer the real questions, not the ones I wasn't about to ask, and that still hadn't changed. So I waited.

And waited.

And waited, remembering in time that Tamra had never been punctual for anyone.

Click. She didn't like knocking, either.

Those blue china-doll eyes, cold as ice, took me in as Tamra stepped—clothed in dark-gray once more, wearing a bright-blue scarf—onto the chill and sunlit balcony. Her red hair glinted in the light as she edged up to the railing; then she turned to look at me. She was wearing it longer, with matching black combs sweeping it away from her face.

"Good morning, Lerris."

"Good morning, Tamra."

I walked over to the edge. I was careful out of habit not to stand too close—either to the railing, or to Tamra—and looked out on Kyphrien.

As the silence continued, I said nothing, for it was not my turn to speak.

A puffy white cloud edged toward the sun, casting a brief shadow across the narrow walled balcony where we contained a corner of Recluce, a corner that needed to be expanded beyond the black walls of the Brotherhood, beyond the black walls of Nylan and the narrow confines of the High Temple.

"I should thank you." Her voice was as flat as I had ever heard it.

"Don't. The one who deserves thanks is Justen."

Her hand came to her mouth, but she still did not look in my direction.

"If Justen hadn't given me just enough hints and forced me to answer my own questions, neither of us would be here." My guts twisted slightly.

"You believe that? Or is it just more poor little Lerris?"

Good old Tamra! I actually grinned. "More poor little Lerris, of course. But remember that I *did* have something to do with rescuing you."

"Do you really expect me to fall at your feet and be eternally grateful? To mirror your great shining light?"

I kept grinning. She sounded like the Tamra I recalled. "Well . . . eternal gratitude would be nice . . ."

"You're still impossible."

"Only sometimes. The rest of the time, I look for perfection."

She didn't answer for a long time. Finally, she said, "I meant what I said about not falling at your feet."

"I know that. You want to get out your staff and thrash me soundly again."

"I can't do that—you broke your staff." Then her voice dropped. "We'd fight too much, and if we didn't, I'd hate you, and if we did, you'd hate me."

She was right, but that was one of the answers I had figured out already, one of the few. There were hills south of Kyphrien, not all that far away, with water and trees, even some of the right kinds of trees. "You're right. I realized you were right, back when we talked on the ship. I just wasn't bright enough to understand. Now it may be too late."

"What will you do?" She ignored my unspoken real question.

"I have an idea. But I don't know if the sub-commander of Kyphros would be interested in a mere woodworker who occasionally dabbles in order."

For once, Tamra looked surprised, almost foolish.

"Or having him build a house on a hill not too far from her place of business."

Her mouth opened a shade wider.

"Or having a redhead whom I regard as a sister come to visit occasionally."

For a time, but only for a time, she was speechless.

"You're . . . still . . . impossible. You honestly *think* . . ."

"No. But I can hope."

I left her there when I saw green leathers on the adjoining balcony—green leathers, black hair, and black eyes.

The Sub-Commander unlatched the doorway, and I walked onto her balcony.

"You were successful, I hear." The music was still there, linked within the order she had found.

"So were you, I understand."

She looked over my shoulder. "How is Tamra?"

"Bitchy as ever, thanks to Justen."

"Give him hell, Krystal!" called Tamra before leaving my balcony.

"She does seem recovered." Krystal's lips turned up at the corners for a moment. We still stood there looking each other over at arm's length, or more.

"Recovered enough," I answered, wondering why I was dancing around all the things I wanted to say. "Enough."

439

In the end, I stepped forward and took her hands.

And, like Tamra would have hoped, she took them back, walking to the railing and turning to look out on the city. "You may think you have your answers, but did you ask me?"

My stomach turned. Why was I always doing the same thing, assuming I knew what was best for the women I cared for? "No. I apologize, Highest Sub-Commander, for possibly thinking that the affections of a woodworker who dabbles in order could possibly be of interest to you." I swallowed, looked down, wondering how soon I could get the hell out of Kyphrien—except I needed whatever reward the autarch might offer.

Krystal shook her head sadly. "You're still doing it."

"Doing what?"

"You won't ask anything of anyone. You may want answers, but you never ask for help. There's a difference."

I shrugged. There wasn't much to say. I looked at her short and graying dark hair, although I knew enough to keep her young, just as my father had my mother; at the broader shoulders that carried half the weight of Kyphros on them, and shook my head.

Krystal looked vaguely amused. "Just a moment. I've worn this damned sword straight for the past five days." She unbuckled the belt and laid both sword and belt on the table.

"Damned sword?" I asked. "Not any longer. It's ordered."

"Stop assuming things." She stepped around the table.

"What?"

"Like whether I would be or wouldn't be this or that. I am. I always have been."

"Been what?"

It was another stupid question, but it finally didn't matter. This time, her hands didn't stop at my fingertips, nor mine at hers. We couldn't say anything more. Even the gusts of the full winter wind didn't bother us. Then again, we didn't stay on the balcony long, and she had already barred the door.

Someone knocked, of course, but that was later. Much later.

Afterword

The Magic of Recluce is now twenty years old . . . and still in print, along with the fifteen volumes (so far) that have followed. At the time I wrote it, I was still somewhere between a struggling and a midlist science fiction author, and because I'd never written a fantasy, I didn't even tell my editor. After I wrote it, I just sent it off. Fortunately, David Hartwell and Tom Doherty liked it enough to publish it. Eventually, publishers in other countries also liked it and published it, and new readers liked it well enough that it's been in print continuously since its first publication.

From the beginning, I was more interested in writing a fantasy that combined what I'd call human realism with a logical magic construct, and one that definitely wasn't a Tolkienesque clone. This interest was amplified greatly as a result of, shall we say, an "intriguing" panel discussion on economics and politics in fantasy and science fiction at the very first F&SF convention I'd ever attended. Also, part of that desire was founded on my own reading experiences, because as someone trained in economics who even spent time as an industrial pneumatics market researcher and economist, I'd always had difficulty in suspending my disbelief when other writers depicted thousands upon thousands of armed knights on horseback—on each side, no less. I'd also had trouble with the idea of quests across hostile lands with few weapons and no visible means of support. Then there were the problems with the unspeakably evil wizards and rulers who were also all too often not incredibly bright, but that might have been because of my stint as a Congressional legislative director and then a staff director, where I encountered all ranges of political animals—and all of them were far brighter than the vast majority of fantasy villains, even those whose ethical standards would not have agreed with mine . . . but that brought up another problem. Even of those with whom I disagreed politically, all felt that they were the ones who were doing the "right thing," and that's why virtually all the characters in the world of Recluce believe in what they do . . . and have what they believe are logical reasons for their actions.

From a practical point of view, perhaps the biggest difference between the world of Recluce and my other fantasy worlds and many, many other fantasies (but certainly not all), is that I approached magic use in the way that all humans and human societies have approached anything with "potential"—like tool-users. Human beings are, above all, tool-users. We attempt to find a use for almost anything, and the greater the usefulness, the greater the value. For this reason, I never had much use for the "undependable" magic featured in many fantasies, especially in the years prior to 1990, but still all-too-prevalent today, I fear. Human beings avoid undependable tools, especially if that undependability could kill us. Computers that crash now and again on their own are acceptable—if they're not the ones running power stations—but cars that crash themselves without human error are not. For that reason, I couldn't see widespread use of magic in any society unless magic use was relatively dependable and predictable.

In the world of Recluce, magic is a tool. Admittedly, it is used in somewhat different fashions in different cultures and in different time periods, and readers get to see how those uses change and evolve—and occasionally devolve—over the almost two thousand years that the books cover. As with all tools, using the order-and-chaos-based magic of Recluce requires not only innate ability, but education, understanding, and training. It also exacts its costs on the user, and the greater the unrestrained use, especially by a less-well-trained individual, generally the shorter the lifespan of such users. There are ways around such limits, but the work-arounds still exact costs, if in different ways. No matter how you juggle magic use, there are costs that will be paid.

Another concept behind the use of order-and-chaos magic is analogous to the law of conservation of energy and matter in our universe. Order and chaos tend to balance in the world of Recluce. Concentration of one or the other tends to result in a corresponding increase in the other somewhere in the world, sooner or later, and this can and has had rather devastating consequences at times in the world's history.

At the same time, technology and magic are not inherently antithetical, although each has impacts on the other. Because chaos can set off gunpowder and explosives, unless they are heavily shielded, the use of artillery in ground warfare is highly limited, as is the use of small arms—until the development of metal cartridges.

Two other aspects of the Saga of Recluce tend to befuddle readers used to "standard" endless series fantasies. The first is that there are no more than two books about any one set of major characters, although there are times when major characters in one book are minor characters or historical legends in another. Essentially, each book can stand alone, although it is better to read the first book about a given set of characters before the second one.

Then there's the fact that I didn't write the saga in chronological order. In fact, chronologically speaking, *The Magic of Recluce* is the second to the last book in the series and always will be, for reasons that become clear in the second book about Lerris—*The Death of Chaos*, which was actually the fifth book published because I wanted to write about other times and places in Recluce before getting back to poor Lerris.

Finally, just for the record, the current (because I just might write more in the world of Recluce) "chronological" order of the Recluce books is:

Magi'i of Cyador
Scion of Cyador
Fall of Angels
The Chaos Balance
Arms-Commander
The Towers of the Sunset
The White Order
The Magic Engineer
Colors of Chaos
Natural Ordermage
Mage-Guard of Hamor
The Order War
Wellspring of Chaos
Ordermaster
The Magic of Recluce
The Death of Chaos

L. E. Modesitt, Jr.   443
Cedar City, 2010

About the Author

Although he is the author of more than fifty-five novels—primarily science fiction and fantasy—L. E. Modesitt, Jr., has also been a delivery boy; a lifeguard; an unpaid radio disc jockey; a U.S. Navy pilot; a market research analyst; a real estate agent; director of research for a political campaign; legislative assistant and staff director for U.S. Congressmen; Director of Legislation and Congressional Relations for the U.S. Environmental Protection Agency; a consultant on environmental, regulatory, and communications issues; a college lecturer and writer in residence; and unpaid treasurer of a civic music arts association.

Shortly after his tours as a Navy amphibious officer and then as a pilot, he returned to Denver as a market research analyst and economist, which experiences generated the idea for his first published story, "The Great American Economy," printed in *Analog* in 1973. He then pursued a career in another kind of fiction by becoming the legislative assistant for Congressman Bill Armstrong in Washington, D.C., and later staff director for Congressman Ken Kramer. During his years in Washington, he attempted to regain some hold on reality by writing increasingly more science fiction. Not totally by coincidence, his first novel was published while he was serving as the head of Legislation and Congressional Relations at the U.S. EPA during the Reagan-Burford controversies. These experiences led to the writing of *The Green Progression*, a book almost totally factual and yet termed more fantastic than any of his fantasy novels.

Along the way, Mr. Modesitt has weathered eight children; a fondness for three-piece suits which has deteriorated into a love of vests; numerous canines, the majority of them rescues; and two refugee felines, one of whom has never forgotten that the Egyptians once worshipped cats. Finally, in 1989, to escape nearly twenty years of occupational captivity in Washington, D.C., he moved to New Hampshire. There he married a lyric soprano, and in 1993 he and his wife, Carol, moved to Cedar City, Utah, where she directs the voice and opera program at Southern Utah University and he continues to create and manage chaos, largely, but not entirely, of the fictional variety.